LADY MAYBE

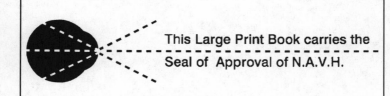

This Large Print Book carries the
Seal of Approval of N.A.V.H.

LADY MAYBE

JULIE KLASSEN

THORNDIKE PRESS

A part of Gale, Cengage Learning

GALE
CENGAGE Learning·

Farmington Hills, Mich • San Francisco • New York • Waterville, Maine
Meriden, Conn • Mason, Ohio • Chicago

GALE
CENGAGE Learning·

LIBRARY OF CONGRESS CATALOGING-IN-PUBLICATION DATA

Names: Klassen, Julie, 1964-
Title: Lady maybe / by Julie Klassen.
Description: Large print edition. | Waterville, Maine : Thorndike Press, 2016. | ©2015 | Series: Thorndike Press large print Christian fiction
Identifiers: LCCN 2015037082 | ISBN 9781410485595 (hardcover) | ISBN 1410485595 (hardcover)
Subjects: LCSH: Large type books. | GSAFD: Christian fiction.
Classification: LCC PS3611.L37 L32 2016 | DDC 813/.6–dc23
LC record available at http://lccn.loc.gov/2015037082

Published in 2016 by arrangement with The Berkley Publishing Group, an imprint of Penguin Publishing Group, a division of Penguin Random House LLC

Printed in Mexico
1 2 3 4 5 6 7 20 19 18 17 16

Under three things the earth
trembles, under four it cannot bear up:
a servant who becomes king,
a godless fool who gets plenty to eat,
a contemptible woman who gets
married,
and a servant who displaces her
mistress. . . .
— PROVERBS 30:21–23 (NIV)

USEFUL COMPANION.

A lady, in her 24th year, anxiously desires a situation as above.

She is musical, a good reader, domesticated, and industrious, and can be well-recommended. She would be most suitable for an elderly lady.

Address to A. R. A., post-office, High Wycombe.

— ADVERTISEMENT,
THE TIMES OF LONDON, 1847

CHAPTER 1

Bath, England
1819

Lady Marianna Mayfield sat at her dressing table — clothed, curled, and powdered. She feigned interest in her reflection in the mirror, but in reality, she watched the housemaid behind her, packing away every last one of her belongings.

Early that morning, Sir John had come to her room and announced that they were leaving Bath that very day. He refused to tell her where they were going, fearful she would somehow get word to Anthony Fontaine. Nor was he allowing her to bring any of the servants, who would of course wish to know where they were headed, and might let slip their destination.

Marianna's stomach clenched. Did he really think another move would stop her? Stop *him*?

She shot to her feet and stalked to the

window. Pulling back the gauzy drapery, she frowned. There in the rear mews, the groom and coachman prepared the new carriage for departure — replacing the long, spring-loaded candles in its brass lamps, then checking the wheels and springs.

Now she knew why he had ordered a traveling chariot, custom built for long journeys. It was an expensive equipage, but a man like Sir John Mayfield would not blink at the cost. Not when he was determined to steal away with her, and leave any would-be followers behind.

Anthony will find me. Of course he would. He had done so easily the last time they moved, taking a house here in Bath. Still, she wished he might return early from London, before they departed. Perhaps he would finally stand up to Sir John, tell him what he could do with his futile scheme, and end this farce of a marriage once and for all.

A knock sounded on the open doorjamb. Frown still in place, she glanced over, expecting Sir John with another edict.

Instead it was the butler, Hopkins. "A caller for you, your ladyship."

Marianna's heart leapt.

"It is Miss Rogers," he added. "Are you at home, or shall I send her away?"

Marianna's momentary elation deflated, but not completely.

"Heavens no, don't send her away," she said. "Show her into the morning room."

"Very good, your ladyship." Hopkins bowed and departed.

The arrival of her former companion was certainly a surprise, considering how abruptly Hannah Rogers had left their employ a half year before — but not an unhappy surprise. Glancing at her empty drawers and wardrobe with sinking heart, Marianna left her bedchamber and made her way downstairs.

A familiar, willowy figure rose at her entrance, assailing Marianna with waves of nostalgic fondness — followed by betrayal that the woman had left without a word. She swallowed the bitter lump and began, "Hannah! My goodness. I never expected to see you again."

The young woman met her gaze, expression tense. "My lady."

Marianna smiled brightly. "You're a godsend, an absolute godsend — if I believed in such things. What timing! That you should come back now."

Hannah Rogers clasped her hands tightly, and lowered her eyes. "I . . . I never received my final allowance."

13

Companions received a modest salary referred to as an allowance, not vulgar "wages." Marianna had not expected the belated request, but didn't quibble.

"Of course you should have it. I never understood why you left without collecting your due." She rang a bell on the side table and Hopkins appeared.

"Ask Mr. Ward to bring in Miss Rogers's remaining allowance, if you please."

When the butler left the room, Marianna turned back to Hannah and asked, "How have you been keeping?"

"Oh . . ." Miss Rogers formed a tenuous smile. "Well enough, thank you."

Unconvinced, Marianna sat and studied her, taking in the wary eyes, pale skin, and sharp cheekbones — the hollows beneath more noticeable than she remembered.

"You appear in good health," Marianna allowed. "If a little tired. And thin."

"Thank you, my lady."

"Please, be seated. I would offer you refreshment, but Sir John has seen fit to dismiss most of the servants already. We're down to Hopkins, Mr. Ward, and one maid."

Hannah remained standing, but Marianna didn't press her. Instead, she tentatively asked, "And have you found another situation? I awaited word from you, or request for a character reference, but nothing ever came."

"Yes. I have another place, or did, until recently."

"Oh?" Hope rising, Marianna asked, "Are you not engaged at present?"

"No."

Marianna rose and eagerly took the young woman's hand. "Again, I say, what timing. For I am in dire need of a traveling companion."

"Traveling companion?"

"Yes. Sir John insists on uprooting us again. Just when I have begun to appreciate Bath society. But he will not yield, and so off we go." She laughed in artificial gaiety. "Say you will come with me as my companion, Hannah. He won't even let me take my lady's maid. He's already dismissed her."

He would probably refuse to allow Miss Rogers to go with them as well, Marianna knew, but she had to try.

Hannah shook her head. "I couldn't leave Bath, my lady. Not now."

"You must! I shall . . . double your allowance to convince you. If Sir John does not agree, I shall use my own money."

Hannah hesitated, then faltered, "I . . . I don't even know where you are going."

"Nor do I! He won't even tell his own wife

where we are bound. Isn't that a laugh? Thinks I'll tell a certain someone, which of course I would."

Again Hannah shook her head. "I couldn't leave at present. I have family here —"

"Your father lives in Bristol." Marianna reminded her. "And you left him when we moved here."

"Yes, but . . . that was different."

"Oh, I don't imagine it will be so much different," Marianna said breezily. "I doubt we'll go far. The last time we only moved from Bristol to Bath — as though a mere dozen miles would keep us apart."

She knew Hannah would understand the reference to her first love, whom Miss Rogers had met on several occasions.

Still Hannah hesitated. "I don't know. . . ."

"Oh, do come, Hannah. It won't be forever. If you don't like the place, or need to return to your family, you will be free to leave. You left before, after all, when it suited you." Marianna smiled to soften the words — jab and assurance rolled into one.

She continued, "I really can't bear this alone. Traveling with Sir John to some unknown place. No comforting presence between us. No familiar, friendly faces. He insists we hire all new servants when we arrive. We are not to take Hopkins or even

16

Mr. Ward."

As if on cue, the door opened and her husband's secretary entered. She noticed Hannah stiffen.

"Ah, Mr. Ward. You remember Hannah Rogers, I trust?"

The thin man with thinner hair and pock-marked skin turned expressionless eyes her way. "Yes, m'lady. Left without notice, as I recall."

"Yes, well, no matter. She has come for her allowance, which she is owed fairly, so no argument, if you please."

His eyes glinted with displeasure or perhaps rebellion. "Yes, m'lady. Hopkins did inform me."

He turned stiffly to Miss Rogers. "I've taken a penalty from your *allowance,*" he began in patronizing fashion, "for leaving without proper notice, along with the eleven days you missed that quarter. Here is the remainder."

Miss Rogers gingerly extended her palm, head bowed like a beggar. The man dropped several sovereigns and shillings onto her outstretched hand, smirking all the while.

"Thank you," Hannah mumbled.

He turned without a word and quit the room.

Watching him go, Marianna shivered. "I

cannot say I am sorry to leave him behind. Odious man. He is returning to Bristol to oversee Sir John's interests there."

Hannah glanced down at the coins in her hand. "I'm grateful for the offer, my lady. I am. But I . . . need to think about it."

Marianna Mayfield studied her. Something was different about Miss Rogers. What was it? "Well don't think too long," Marianna said. "We're leaving at four this afternoon, according to Sir John. Unless I can persuade him to forgo this idiotic notion. Jealous fool."

Hannah looked up at her, expression torn. Almost miserable. She said, "If I'm not here by half past three, don't wait for me. It means I'm not coming."

The hours passed all too quickly. The maid continued packing, and Marianna continued pacing. Still Anthony did not arrive. Nor did Hannah.

Marianna looked out the drawing room window toward the street. The traveling chariot had been moved to the front of the house, four horses now harnessed to it, the lead horse now and again stamping an eager hoof.

The maid, butler, and a hired lad stowed their belongings in the built-in imperial —

like a large, shallow valise atop the roof. More baggage rode in the rear, strapped in to the outside seat where two servants could have sat, had Sir John allowed her to take any with them.

At that moment, he strode into the room, imposing in his shooting jacket. He sternly insisted Marianna gather her hand luggage and prepare to depart so Hopkins could begin closing up the house. He turned on his heel and stalked away, his grim expression brooking no disagreement.

One of Marianna's friends had told her she was lucky to have a husband with such a decided, commanding manner. Marianna did not agree. But she knew further argument about staying would be futile. The house had already been sold. She glanced at her watch pin. Twenty after three.

Ten more minutes . . .

Still hoping her former companion would arrive in time, she gathered her things and stepped outside.

Beside the carriage, Sir John spoke with a hired postilion, who would ride the lead horse for the first stage of the journey. They were taking no groom or guard. As Marianna approached, Sir John reached inside and extracted a flintlock rifle from the chariot's concealed gun case. He checked

19

it, then returned it to its hiding place. Apparently, he would act as guard himself. Perhaps she ought be glad Anthony had not shown up after all.

Her gaze fell to her watch pin once more. Half past three. *Dash it.* She had so hoped Hannah would come.

Suddenly that very figure appeared at the end of Camden Place, where the crescent met Lansdown Street. Marianna's heart lifted. As she watched, a tall, dark-haired young man jogged after Hannah and snagged her by the elbow. They were too far away for Marianna to hear their conversation, but she saw Hannah shake her head and gently extract her arm from his grip. Resignation showed in her expression, but no fear. A suitor, perhaps? If so, no wonder Hannah hesitated to leave Bath.

Hannah turned away from the man and strode toward the carriage.

"John, look," Marianna said. "Miss Rogers has come to join us!"

Her tall husband stiffened and turned to stare, expression inscrutable.

Hannah Rogers hurried toward them, valise bumping against her leg.

Marianna beamed. "Oh, Hannah, how happy I am to see you! I dread making this journey, but I shall not mind nearly so much with you beside me."

"The offer still stands?" Hannah asked, panting to catch her breath.

Marianna ignored her husband's glare and smiled at her would-be companion. "Of course."

"And I may return if the situation doesn't suit?"

"Well you won't be a prisoner, Hannah. I wish I could say the same for myself." She sent Sir John a pointed look. Waited for him to refuse. To insist that they travel alone.

His jaw clenched, but he said nothing.

The hired lad strapped Hannah's valise with the others, and the three entered the carriage, settling themselves onto the velvet cushions of the plush interior. Marianna reached up and fingered the golden tassels of the rich blue window draperies and murmured, "What a pretty cage."

They rode through the night in uneasy silence, stopping to change horses at coaching inns along the way. Cramped and sleepy, Marianna sat as far away from Sir John as possible on the bench seat they shared. She leaned against the carriage wall and looked out the side window, avoiding his gaze.

The brass candle lamps glowed steadily beyond the windowpane. Eventually, night waned and dawn began to redden the sky, following their westward course along the Bristol Channel.

Miss Rogers, perched on the pull-down seat nearby, seemed to grow more restless with each passing mile. Brow furrowed, she bit her lip and twisted her long fingers again and again in her lap. Outside, a light drizzle began to fall, and if Marianna was not mistaken, her companion's eyes were damp as well.

As they entered yet another unknown hamlet and rumbled past its village green, the three of them stared out the window at a sobering sight: a pair of low-lying wooden stocks. Two women sat on the ground behind them, bound at the ankles. One woman scowled and swore at the jeering passersby. The other stared off into the distance with as much quiet dignity as the mortifying position allowed. Marianna wondered what each woman had been found guilty of. She was struck by how differently each faced the consequences of her actions, whatever they were. A chill passed up Marianna's neck. Would she face consequences for her own actions? She shrugged off the uncomfortable thought. Nothing would happen to her. It had not been her fault — or her idea. And after all, they had gotten away with everything for more than two years now.

Sometime later, they stopped at another coaching inn. To that point, they had traveled with a team of four, driven by a succession of mounted postilions. But this inn had only two horses available, and how mismatched they were. The weary postilion departed, replaced by a fresh young man of nineteen or twenty. He converted the chariot's front box into a coachman's seat and from there, lifted the reins.

"It won't be long now," Sir John said, continuing to survey the road behind them with wary eyes. "We're beginning the final short stretch of the journey."

As they left the inn yard, the drizzle swelled into a driving rain. The winds increased with each mile, howling and rocking the carriage.

They all lurched as the young driver pulled the horses to the side of the road and halted. He turned on his seat to face them through the front carriage window. Sir John opened the speaking flap to listen to what the young man had to say. Wind and rain garbled his words.

"The roads are awful bad, sir. And the storm is picking up. I don't think it wise to go on."

"Come lad, it cannot be much farther."

"Three miles, give or take."

"And no inn before?"

"No, sir. But a farmer might let us shelter in his barn."

"A barn — with these ladies? No. We must press on. I have a particular reason."

"But, sir . . ."

"I shall make it worth your while." Through the flap, Sir John handed the young man a small bulging purse. "And that much again when you deliver us there safely."

The young man's eyes widened. "Yes, sir." He wiped the rain from his face and turned forward, allowing the flap to fall.

Marianna protested, "John, the boy is right. It is foolish to press on and get us all killed."

Suddenly, Hannah sat up straighter. "Allow me down, if you please. I should not have come. It was a mistake."

Astonished, Marianna stared at her. As did Sir John.

"I need to go back," Hannah insisted, her voice nearly desperate.

Mouth grimly set, Sir John shook his head. "We are not going back."

"I know — I shall find my own way. Just let me out."

She rose and lunged toward the door, but

he blocked her way with a strong, out-stretched arm.

"I cannot in good conscience let you down here," he said. "Not on this lonely stretch of road during a storm."

"Hannah," Marianna pleaded. "You agreed to come with me. I need you."

"But I need —"

The coachman cracked his whip, the horses strained, and the carriage jerked into motion. To Marianna's relief, her companion had lost her opportunity to abruptly abandon them a second time.

Tears filled Hannah's eyes and rolled down her thin cheeks.

"See what you've done, John?" Marianna scowled at her husband. "You've upset her. My only friend in the world and you've upset her." She added sullenly, "It won't work you know. He shall find me anyway."

Sir John set his jaw and stared straight ahead, though there was little to see through the front window save the coachman's flapping greatcoat. Marianna glanced again at Hannah, noticing she kept her face averted to hide her tears.

Marianna wondered what had so upset the young woman, who had always seemed so stoic and self-contained in the past. But at the moment, Marianna had her own problems to think about. Turning toward the window, she stared at the lashing rain, the weedy verge between road and steep coastline, and the occasional glimpse of the grey Bristol Channel beyond. *He will find me,* she reassured herself again. *He did before.*

But Sir John had taken many new precautions this time, clearly more determined than ever. Well, *she* was more determined as well. Things had changed — she had their child to think of now. And she would love that child far more than her father had ever loved her. Her chest tightened at the thought. If only she had figured out some way to get word to Anthony. But it was too late.

Suddenly the carriage wheels slipped as though on ice, losing their traction on the muddy road. The vehicle lurched. The horses screamed. So did Marianna.

Hannah cried out, "God almighty, help us. Protect him!"

The carriage fell to one side. A great snap and whinny and the vehicle was flying, weightless. A second later, it fell. Over the edge, toward the channel. The side of the cliff rushed toward them. A huge crash scattered her mind and shook her bones. A wheel sailed past the window. The next moment they were airborne again, before the top of the carriage hit rock, the vehicle rolling, rolling until she lost all sense of up and down. The world shifted violently and ended in a blinding collision.

And she knew no more.

CHAPTER 2

Pain. Cold. Weight pressing. Struggling to breathe . . .

Peering through narrow slits, she saw slivers of shimmering color, like light through prism glass. Yellow-white sun. Blue water. *Water?* A flash of red. Then blue again. A glint of purple and gold. Confusion. A hand in hers, slipping away. Metal, biting into her fingers.

Why can I not awaken from this dream?

So cold. So heavy. Darkness descending . . .

"Hello? Can you hear me?"

A man's voice. *Must get out from under from this pressing weight.* She sucked in desperate, shallow breaths.

"Lady Mayfield? Can you hear me?"

Her eyes fluttered open and glimpsed faces floating above. More confusion. Why was the side window above her?

"It's all right. We're here to help you. I'm

a doctor. Dr. Parrish." The man nodded to the younger face hovering beside his. "My son, Edgar. We're going to get you and your husband out of there."

Your husband . . . She looked down and found Sir John lying limp across her body. Alive or dead? His hat bobbed lazily in the water filling the lower half of the carriage. His legs were sprawled, one bent at an unnatural angle.

There were only two of them in what was left of the carriage. Where was she? Turning her head, pain shot through her skull. She couldn't turn far, pinned as she was. Through the gaping hole where the roof had once been, she looked out into the choppy water of the channel.

The younger man above her looked in the same direction. He pointed. "Pa. Look. Is someone out there?"

The older man squinted. "Can't tell. Too far out."

But she could tell. A red cloak floated on the tide, drawing the form it shrouded farther from shore.

The older man looked down at her again. "Was there someone else with you?"

She nodded, pain searing her. She felt as though needles pricked her scalp.

The man reverently removed his hat. "Too

far to go after. Even if we could swim."

A roaring in her ears. It couldn't be.

"A servant?" he asked.

A companion was higher than a servant, she thought. A gentlewoman. She opened her mouth to explain, but no sound came. Her brain and tongue seemed disconnected. She pressed a hand to her aching chest and nodded again.

"There's nothing we can do for her. I'm so sorry. But let's get you out of there."

Darkness tunneled her vision once more, and she sank into it.

The next time she opened her eyes, the same face hovered above her, nearer now. The older face, looking not into her eyes, but at some lower part of her. Who was he? He'd said his name, but she'd forgotten it. She couldn't see much of the room without moving her head, but the bedchamber was not familiar. Where was she? How long had she been there? Her brain felt sluggish, addled, only partially aware of the rest of her.

"She's opened her eyes," said a woman's voice, one she did not recognize.

She tried to turn her head toward the woman, but pain flared before her eyes, momentarily blinding her.

The man's voice tensed. "My lady? How do you feel?"

"She's in pain, George," the woman snapped. "Even I can see that."

She parted her lips, tried to speak. "He . . . lay . . ."

He took her hand, eyes round in concern. "Sir John is badly injured, my lady. But he lives, so there is hope. You leave him to me, all right? Do not fret. You've sustained several injuries yourself, but you will recover."

"The . . . the . . . ?"

He grimaced as though he'd understood her. "I am afraid the coachman is dead. The harnesses snapped when the carriage fell and the horses ran free. The young man was not as fortunate."

She pressed her eyes closed. *Poor man,* she thought. Though she didn't really remember him.

"It's not your fault, my lady. You mustn't upset yourself." He shook his head. "We saw the horses running wild, harnesses flapping, and that's how we knew to look for the carriage in the first place. The crest confirmed who you were, though of course we were expecting you." He patted her hand. "Now. You just rest, and Mrs. Parrish and I shall take care of you and your husband."

Husband . . . She closed her eyes and pushed the uncomfortable thought away.

She lay, floating in and out of foggy wakefulness. The kind doctor had given her laudanum for the pain. A broken arm, he'd said. And a head wound — a gash and concussion. Now and again, someone gently lifted her head and pressed sips of water or broth to her lips, but she had little sense of time passing.

The woman's voice said, "Sir John is bad off indeed, and if he lasts the week I shall be very much surprised."

A second woman hushed the first. "Shh. She'll hear you."

In spite of the distance between them, she would never have wished such harm to befall him. *Poor Sir John,* she thought.

Lying there with her eyes closed, she tried to recall his face. Her thoughts slowly wheeled back until scattered images flickered through her mind. . . .

Sir John picking up a fire iron and poking at a log in frustration.

Sir John, looking at her, jaw clenched. "What I want is a wife who will be faithful to me. Is that too much to ask?"

Another flicker. Another image. His usually stern face softened and stilled in her mind like a portrait, captured in oils and cobwebbed recollection. A handsome face, she thought, if her memory could be trusted. Grey-blue eyes and strong, masculine features framed by light brown hair . . .

She had admired him once, she realized. What had changed between them? Had they ever been happy?

She tried to recall their lives before — where they had come from. Bath, she thought. And before that Bristol. Vaguely, she remembered when Sir John announced they were moving to Bath. She remembered feeling torn. Should she obey his wishes? Should she go?

He hadn't wanted to, but in the end he had taken them both. His wife and her companion. Just as he'd brought them both on this trip. Yes, she remembered Bath, the lovely house in Camden Place. And an ugly house in dreary Trim Street. Trim Street? What on earth would have taken her there . . . ? She grimaced, trying to think. But her mind remained a muddle.

She must have uttered some agitated sound, for a kind woman's voice crooned, "There, there. It's all right. You're safe." A gentle hand lifted her head. "Drink some of this now. . . ."

A cup rim touched her lips and she sipped.

"That's it," the woman said. "Very good, my dear."

The warm broth soothed her aching throat. The warm words soothed her troubled soul.

She knew it was a dream, but couldn't awaken. She dreamt she'd left a helpless baby in a basket on the shore of the Bristol Channel. She'd meant to return for the child directly, but instead she lay there as though paralyzed, unable to force her frozen body to move. The tide was coming in. Closer and closer, licking at the sides of the basket. A hand reached toward it — a woman's hand. But the woman was in the water, the tide pulling her, dragging her away, her waterlogged gown and cloak weighing her down.

She grasped the woman's hand, trying to save her, but the wet fingers slipped through hers. Remembering the child, she turned, but it was too late. The basket was already floating away across the channel. . . .

With a start, she sucked in a breath and opened her eyes. She blinked at her surroundings. The half-tester bed was not hers. The lace-trimmed dressing table was unfamiliar.

She squeezed her eyes shut and tried to

34

think. Where was she? What had happened? The carriage crash, that was it. They were not in Bath any longer. Nor in Bristol. Somewhere in the West Country, she believed, but had no idea where. Oh, what was wrong with her? Why could she not remember? It felt like a warm dark blanket lay over her mind's eye, blocking her memory, hindering clear thought.

One thing she knew with panicky certainty. She was forgetting something. Something important.

The door opened and the kind woman entered with a basin of water and folded cloths. "Good morning, my lady," she greeted warmly. She set the basin on a side table, then stepped to the washstand for soap.

"Good morning, Mrs. . . . I'm sorry, I forgot your name."

"That's all right, my lady. I often forget names myself. I'm Mrs. Turrill."

The kind woman was perhaps in her early sixties, evidenced by the many lines creasing her long, pleasant face. Her hair was still brown, though its center part was considerably wider than a younger woman's would be.

Mrs. Turrill helped her wash her face and hands and clean her teeth. Then she opened a drawer of the wardrobe and extracted a fresh nightdress and wrapper.

"What a blessing all your gowns were not spoilt in the accident, my lady. Your trunk must have been thrown clear."

Another flash of memory. Trunks and valises strapped in the rear seat. "Yes . . ." she murmured.

"It won't be long. In a few days you'll be up and about and wearing your pretty things." The housekeeper lifted the bodice of a gown of blue satin. "Oh, I like this one. Looks brand new."

Was it? It must be, for she could not remember seeing it before.

"And here is a lovely day dress." The housekeeper shook out a serviceable muslin and squinted at its neckline. "It's missing a button. I'm not terribly skilled with a needle, but I can manage that."

The day dress, in a pale wash of rose pink, did look familiar. She recognized it with relief. She hadn't completely lost her memory.

Lifting a hand to push a stray hair from her face, she stilled, captured by the sight of a ring on her finger. She stared at the hand aloft above her, as though it were a separate entity — someone else's hand. On it shone a gold band, with amethyst and purple sapphires. She recognized the ring at once and sighed gratefully. Things were starting to come back to her.

But again that heavy shadow fell over her. That nagging fear. Things might be coming back, but she was still forgetting something. Something far more important than a dress or ring.

The cheerful doctor stopped in that morning and found her still staring at the ring.

"Almost lost that," he said. "Found it clasped in your hand and slid it back on your finger myself."

She hesitated. "Oh. I . . . Th— thank you."

He studied her face. "How are you feeling?"

"Confused."

"And no wonder, my lady. What a shock you've had. The concussion you suffered could very well muddle your mind for some days to come."

Perhaps that explained her jumbled thoughts and elusive memories. His calm assurance eased her fear. She looked around the sunny room and asked, "Where am I?"

"Clifton House, between Countisbury and Lynton, in Devonshire."

Devonshire? Had she known he'd meant to go so far? The name "Clifton" meant nothing to her. She asked, "Is this your house?"

"Good heavens, no. It's your house. Been in your husband's family for ages, though he's never lived here before. My son has been caretaking the place since the former tenants left last year."

"I . . . see," she murmured, though she didn't see, really.

"Don't worry, my lady. It will all come back in time." He rubbed his hands together and beamed at her. "Well. I imagine you want to see your husband."

The smile of reply that lifted her mouth faltered, then fell. No, she did not want to see him. In fact, the thought filled her with misgiving. She hedged, "I . . . don't know."

"I understand. But he doesn't look too bad. Bruises and cuts on his face, head, and hands, but most of his injuries are internal."

Was she only reluctant to see his injuries, or was it something more? Sir John had never hurt her, had he? Then why was she afraid?

The doctor took her good arm and helped her rise. The room swam and tilted and she leaned against him for support.

"Dizzy?"

"Yes," she panted.

Mrs. Turrill came in with her sewing

basket and tut-tutted. "She is not ready to be up and about yet, doctor."

"So I see. I was only going to take her across the corridor to see Sir John. But I think we shall wait a day or two."

"I should say so. Besides, I'll want to brush her hair and get her dressed proper before she visits him."

"I'm afraid he shan't notice at the moment."

"Perhaps not," she said. "But a woman likes to feel pretty when she sees the man she loves."

Together they helped her back into bed.

She knew they referred to Sir John, but another face shimmered before her mind's eye. Settling under the bedclothes, she pushed away thoughts of Sir John, and tried to focus on the faint image of sparkling blue eyes and an affectionate smile. But other images kept pushing his face aside — a red cloak floating on the tide, a hand slipping from hers. . . . Had she only dreamt it, or was she remembering something that had actually happened?

CHAPTER 3

That next afternoon, Dr. Parrish came in and sat at her bedside. "And how are you feeling today, my lady?"

"Better, I think."

"Everyone treating you well?"

She nodded. "Mrs. Turrill is very kind."

He beamed. "I am happy to hear it. Sally Turrill is my cousin and I recommended her for the position myself. Though not everyone was in favor of the arrangement."

"I am grateful you did."

"You don't know how that pleases me. Men love to be right, you know." He winked at her. He then went on to explain that Mrs. Turrill had prepared the house for their arrival and, after the accident, had offered to serve as her nurse and lady's maid, as well as cook-housekeeper. He said, "Apparently, Sir John asked Edgar to engage minimal staff, but planned to select the rest of the servants after you arrived. But, well, as it is . . ." He lifted his hands in a helpless gesture. "Sally *has* hired a young manservant and a kitchen maid. Otherwise, she has been making do."

"I hope it isn't too much for her," she said.

"I've not heard a single word of complaint from her. Likes to be busy, Sally does."

His smile dimmed then. He clasped his hands over his knee and cleared his throat. "Now, um, there is something I need to tell you . . ."

A woman passed by the open door, and, seeing the two of them together, paused in its threshold. Sir John's chamber nurse, she believed, though she wasn't sure of her name.

The woman frowned at them. "It must be grand to sit and talk while others change bedding and bandages, and feed and tend your patients. I've had more than enough for one day, doctor. It's your turn."

The woman stalked away, her heels echoing down the corridor and clumping down the stairs.

When they were alone again she asked, "Is that Sir John's nurse?"

"Em, no." He gave a lame little chuckle. "My wife."

"Oh! I'm sorry. That is, I did not realize. . . ."

He lifted a hand to stem her apology. "Understandable misapprehension," he consoled. "Mrs. Parrish has, um, kindly agreed to act as chamber nurse. She tends Sir John during my absences, while I call on other patients. It's only temporary, until the nurse I usually employ finishes with her current patient."

"Ah, I see."

He rose. "Well, I had better go and look in on Sir John. We shall finish our talk later, all right?"

After several minutes had passed, Mrs. Turrill entered wearing an apron over a simple frock as usual, and carrying a dinner tray. "Hello, my lady. How are you feeling?"

"Better, I think. Thank you. Dr. Parrish and I were just speaking of you."

"Were you indeed? That explains the itch in my ear. Well, George is a good man, but if he tells you any tales about my wild younger days, I shall have to return the favor!" She grinned. "Known him since a lad, I have. What a scamp he was, too."

"But your accent is . . . familiar."

"You've a good ear, my lady! I was born in this parish, like George, but was in service in Bristol for many a year."

"Ah."

Mrs. Turrill helped her sit up in bed,

propped with pillows. She laid a linen cloth over the bedclothes and helped her eat soup and sip tea.

Afterward, the housekeeper reached into her apron pocket. "Edgar has been digging through the wreckage to see what might be salvaged." She extracted a black glove and held it near.

"Probably Sir John's," she said, and instinctively reached for it. She laid it on her lap and smoothed the soft leather. She felt her cheeks warm to see a man's glove on her leg, even if that part of her was covered in bedclothes. *Silly creature,* she told herself. She held the glove instead and tried to remember if she'd ever held Sir John's hand in hers.

A flare of memory flashed through her brain. Sir John taking her hand, almost roughly. She blinked. That couldn't be right. Oh, when would her brain cease its scattered state?

Mrs. Turrill searched in her pocket for another small object. "Do you recognize this?"

She held out a small piece of jewelry — a brooch. The pin bore a tiny painting of someone's eye under glass and framed by gems.

Mrs. Turrill said, "It's one of them lover's

eyes. Popular tokens, I understand. I thought it might be yours, seeing as it's set in garnets — red for love and all that. Sir John's eye, is it?"

Was it? She didn't recall wearing it, yet she recalled so little. She *had* seen it before, she thought. The thickness of the eyebrow suggested a man's eye, with a brown iris. She pressed her own eyes closed, trying to recall the color and shape of Sir John's eyes. She'd thought they were bluish grey. Was her memory still so faulty, or had the miniaturist got it wrong somehow? Or was this image not of Sir John's eye at all, but rather a lover's, as the name suggested?

Had she a lover? Was she that sort of woman? Heaven help her if her father found out.

"I . . . don't know," she murmured, feeling frustrated and confused.

Mrs. Turrill patted her hand. "Don't worry, my lady. It will all come back to you eventually."

The housekeeper gathered up the dishes. "When I have time, I shall try to find a few more things of yours, my lady. Might help you remember. And perhaps something of that poor girl's to send to her family."

"Yes . . . Poor girl." She echoed sympathetically. The young woman's smiling face shimmered in her mind a moment, then faded away. She was too embarrassed to admit that at the moment, she did not recall her name.

That evening, she was still sitting propped up in bed when Dr. Parrish returned to her room.

"How good to see you sitting up, my lady." He smiled at her, then announced, "I have taken the liberty of borrowing a wheeled chair we might use. Edgar is waiting downstairs to help carry it up if you are willing to give it a go. I thought we might use it to convey you to Sir John's room, as you are no doubt anxious to see him."

"I . . ." She licked dry lips. "I should like to see him, yes." She forced a smile for the kind man's benefit, unsure why her stomach twisted at the thought.

A few minutes later, father and son returned to her door, a wicker-backed invalid chair between them. The doctor puffed at the exertion, while his strapping son looked unaffected.

She smiled at the young man. "Thank you, Edgar."

"My lady." He shyly tipped his hat and took his leave.

The doctor rolled the chair into the room

45

and positioned it near the bed. Then he took her good arm and helped her rise. Again, the room swam and she leaned against him for support.

He looked at her in concern. "Still dizzy?"

She nodded, and settled with relief into the chair.

"Then we won't stay long and tire you out." He wheeled her through the door and across the paneled passageway. When they reached a door across the landing, Dr. Parrish stepped around the chair to open it, then eased her over the threshold.

The room was dim, the curtains drawn. An oil lamp burned on the side table.

Damp hands clasped in her lap, she looked toward the bed. Sir John lay there unnaturally still, fierce eyes closed, temple bruised, cheekbone swollen, mouth slack. So different than when she had last seen him, pugnaciously refusing to yield. He wore a simple nightshirt, open at the throat, instead of his usual elegantly tied cravat. His exposed neck lay bare, specked with new whiskers. How vulnerable he looked. How weak.

She whispered, "Will he live?"

The physician hesitated. "Only God knows. I have done all I can for him. Set and bandaged his broken ankle. Wrapped his cracked clavicle and ribs. I pray there is no internal bleeding." Dr. Parrish grimaced. "His head injury is what concerns me the most. I've sent for a surgeon from Barnstaple to give his opinion. He should be here tomorrow."

She nodded her understanding. She felt pity for Sir John. Perhaps even grief. But beyond that, she wasn't sure what she felt. She stared at the broken man before her, her emotions a confusing jumble. Did she love him? He didn't love her, she didn't think. She pressed her eyes shut, willing herself to remember a wedding, or a wedding night. Nothing.

Then . . . fragments of memory spotted her vision. Buttons and hairpins falling to the floor. Cool rain on her skin. Warm hands. A man sweeping her up into his arms. But in the memory the man had no face. Was it Sir John? She couldn't be sure.

The memory faded. A wedding would have pleased her father. Though it would have disappointed the other man. For there had been someone else, had there not? Again she winced and tried to remember, but could not.

Instead, she saw another scene in passing, as though she walked through a theatre and out again mid-performance. . . .

There she was, sitting awkwardly in the morning room of the Bristol house.

Sir John stood, arms crossed, looking not at her but out the window. "So, what do you think of the arrangement?" he asked. "Are you willing?"

"Yes," she replied, knowing her father would approve.

He winced and shook his head. "But . . . should I agree to it?"

"Only if you wish to."

"My wishes?" He barked a dry little laugh. "God doesn't often grant me what I wish for, I find."

"Then perhaps you wish for the wrong things."

He looked at her then, and his flinty eyes held hers. "You may be right. And what is it *you* wish for?"

The scene faded. Had it been real or mere fancy? She could not have said how she'd answered his question or even if she had. Nor did she recall the specifics of their arrangement.

She did remember what a tall, commanding presence he had been. But the figure shrouded in bedclothes before her seemed sadly diminished. She wondered what Sir John had wished for so earnestly. It seemed unlikely that it would be granted now. For certainly no one would have wished for a fate like this.

CHAPTER 4

The next day, Dr. Parrish and Mrs. Turrill came into her bedchamber together, bringing unusual tension with them. Something had happened, she thought. Or was about to.

"What is it?" she asked. "Is it Sir John?"

"No. His condition has not changed," the doctor assured her, without his customary smile. He sat at her bedside, asked how she was feeling, and then looked significantly at his cousin.

Mrs. Turrill turned to her and began, "Edgar has brought up a few more things from the wreckage, and I think we've found something of yours, my lady."

"Oh?" She looked at the woman with interest. "What is it?"

She held up an embroidered bag. "He found this among the rocks. It's a needlework bag, apparently."

Mrs. Turrill opened wide the bag's cinched

neck and extracted a ball of wool, and thin wooden needles still attached to a wad of knitting. She pulled it flat. "It's a baby's cap, I think," the housekeeper said. "Did you make it?"

She accepted the damp, lopsided half circle and studied its loose, uneven stitches. "I don't . . . think so." She wondered if it had belonged to the poor woman in the carriage.

Dr. Parrish glanced at Mrs. Turrill again, then tentatively began, "You see, Sir John mentioned you were with child when he wrote, but —"

"Did he?" she interrupted in surprise.

The doctor exchanged an awkward look with his cousin, then continued, "But when I examined you, I . . ." he paused, apparently struggling to find the right words.

But she wasn't really listening. She was staring at the small, knitted cap. She didn't recognize it, and yet — looking at it filled her with a panicky dread.

Had she been knitting that cap? Was she expecting a child? How could she have forgotten something as life-changing as that? What was wrong with her — was her brain damaged? Instinctively, she laid her hand on her abdomen. So flat. Too flat.

The doctor cleared his throat and contin-

51

ued, "I'm afraid I discovered you've . . . lost the child."

She stared at the man. "Lost him?"

With sad eyes, the doctor nodded and pressed her hand.

Grief pierced her, a dozen jabs with an icy knife of dread, deflating her heart, sending her soul into a dark well of pain. She forgot to breathe. Then — lungs searing hot — she opened her mouth and sucked in a sob-shaken breath.

She bit back the cry she longed to exhale, but there was no stopping the tears that spilled forth in its place.

Mrs. Turrill reached over and brushed a damp strand of hair from her face. "I am so sorry, my lady. It's a great loss, to be sure. I've lost a child of my own, and know the pain you must feel. But praise God, you and Sir John survived and may yet have other children."

She was vaguely aware of the doctor sending the woman a cautioning look, warning her not to raise her hopes, but she ignored it. Instead she recalled the dream — the baby in a basket, floating away from her. Had she lost her child? Lost him before he'd ever breathed? Then why did the sound of a baby's cry ring in her memory as familiar as her own voice?

Her mind whirled, set free like a globe knocked from its stand and sent spinning across the room.

Her tears stopped flowing then, and in their place pellets of memory fell like sleet — one stinging shard after another. She gasped aloud, relief and new pain enveloping her. She *had* lost her child. But that did not mean he was dead, did it? *Dear God, no.*

"My lady . . . ?" Mrs. Turrill asked, eyes wide and worried.

"I . . . I am all right," she managed. "Or at least I — we — shall be. I hope."

Footfalls hammered up the stairs and Edgar Parrish lurched through the open door.

"Pa, come quick," he panted. "The Dirksen boy took a bad fall from the tree in the churchyard."

Dr. Parrish stood immediately. "I'll get my bag. Have you alerted your mother?"

Edgar nodded. "She's in the gig already." The young man glanced at her sheepishly, his face reddening. "Sorry to interrupt, your ladyship."

She squinted up at him, confusion returning. "Not at all . . ."

The doctor turned to Mrs. Turrill. "Please look in on Sir John for me."

"Of course."

He looked at her and patted her hand.

"Now. You just rest, my lady. Mrs. Turrill will look after you and your husband until we return."

She nodded vaguely as he turned away. Watching them all go, her mind silently echoed, *husband* . . . ? She had no husband.

She felt her brow knit and her whirling thoughts snag and snarl at the doctor's words. Her muddled brain had refused to take it in before. His words, Edgar's, Mrs. Turrill's had all seemed like nonsense. As if they were addressing someone else behind her, just out of view. Now her brain abruptly quit spinning and their words, their deferential manner, the fine room, snapped into place in her mind. They thought *she* was Lady Mayfield. That she, Hannah Rogers, was Sir John's wife.

That night, Hannah tossed and turned for hours, trying to figure out how the misunderstanding had first arisen and how best to break the news. She dreaded to think how these respectable people would react when they learned the truth.

When she finally fell asleep, the dream revisited her. Her baby in a basket on shore. She'd meant to return for him directly, but instead lay there, unable to move. The tide was coming in. Closer and closer, lapping at the sides of the basket. A hand reached toward the basket — Lady Mayfield's hand. But how could that be? Lady Mayfield was in the water, the tide pulling her, dragging her away, her waterlogged gown and cloak weighing her down. Hannah grasped her hand, trying to save her, but the woman's fingers slipped from hers. Remembering her son, Hannah turned in alarm, but it was too late. The basket was already bobbing away across the channel.

The dream changed then — fearful imaginings replaced by fearful memory — a scene that was all too real. . . .

Hannah hurried to the old Trim Street terrace house where she'd spent her lying-in, and knocked on the door until the skin of her knuckles scraped raw. Finally, a narrow slit opened and a pair of irritated eyes appeared.

"Please, Mrs. Beech," Hannah said. "I need to see him."

"Have you got the money?"

"Not yet. But I will have."

"When?"

"Soon."

"You told me that yesterday and the day before, and the day before that."

Hannah strived to keep her voice calm. "I

know. I'm sorry. Please —"

"I'm out of patience. When you pay me what's owed, you may see him. But not before."

"You can't do that. I'm his mother. I need —"

"And I need what's due me. This is not a charity, girl. I've learnt how to deal with chits like you. Mercy gets me nowhere. It's a hard line that speaks to girls used to gettin' their way, wheedling another coin from some weak parent or sweetheart. Well I ain't your mother nor your sweetheart. Give me what's mine and I shall give you what's yours."

"But, you have no right —"

"I have every right." The eyes flashed. "Don't believe me? Go to the constable if you like. Tell him I'm holding your child and tell him why. Mr. Green has no sympathy for those who don't pay what they owe. See if you don't end up at the workhouse yet. Or debtor's prison."

Hannah gasped. "You wouldn't. . . ."

"Wouldn't I? I don't keep brats whose way ain't paid. And what would become of your wee babe then?"

Terror shot through Hannah. What was she threatening to do? Hannah could hardly believe this woman was the same benevolent

56

matron who had received her so kindly only months before. She rushed on desperately, "I have a new situation, but I won't receive my allowance until quarter's end. What would you suggest I do — beg in the streets?"

"No. Nothing so unprofitable. I am a businesswoman after all. Do what most girls in your situation do."

Hannah shivered. "I would never do such a thing, Mrs. Beech. Whatever you might think of me."

"Evidence to the contrary, perhaps now is the time to start. Tom Simpkins would set you up in no time, no doubt."

"Tom Simpkins is a —"

"Tom Simpkins is my brother, girl. Careful what you say."

"I'm sorry, Mrs. Beech. But please —"

The eyes moved away from the slit. "Come back when you've got the money."

She called after the woman, "Who is nursing him?"

"Becky."

Becky? Sweet, simple, unstable Becky.

Hannah swallowed. "I will get the money, I will. Every last shilling. But promise me you'll take care of him until I return. Please — it isn't his fault. Take good care of him, I beg of you."

"Every day you leave him here is another shilling. The rate goes up when you're in arrears." The slit shut with a metallic click. How very final it sounded.

Hannah winced. A shilling a day? It was practically all she earned. She would never catch up. She stood there on the stoop, frozen in dread. Her breasts stung with pinpricks of milk. She had wrapped her bosom when she took the new situation — sneaking away to nurse her son once a day and twice on Sundays. Her milk had already diminished, yet the build-up still ached. But that was nothing to the pain in her heart. . . .

With a start, Hannah opened her eyes. She drew in a long breath and blinked at her surroundings. Where was Danny? She looked to the right and to the left, pulse pounding. Then she recalled with a heavy heart that her baby was not with her. He was at Mrs. Beech's, out of reach.

Becky will look out for him, she told herself. *Becky will make sure he doesn't go hungry.*

Then Hannah remembered Becky's trembling hands, pale face, and wide vacant eyes when she'd first seen the bereaved girl wandering the streets of Bath, looking for her own child, forgetting or unwilling to accept that her infant daughter had died.

Her precious son's well-being was in this girl's hands? *Oh, God in heaven, protect him! Keep him in your safekeeping until I can return for him.*

Return. She had to return to him. Now. What had she been thinking to leave him? Had she any idea the Mayfields meant to go so far, she never would have agreed. And now with Sir John lying near death and his wife drowned, she wouldn't even receive the generous allowance Lady Mayfield had promised her. How then would she redeem her son?

Tears trickled from the corners of her eyes, down her temples and into her hair. She raised a hand to brush the tears away — a hand that bore a large ring. A gold band, amethyst and purple sapphires.

She recognized it again, only now she remembered why — Marianna almost always wore it. How had Lady Mayfield's ring ended on her hand? Fragments of memory tried to reassert themselves, but she saw only jumbled pieces through wavy, clouded glass. She had thought it only a dream. But had it really happened? Had she been sensible enough to grasp Lady Mayfield's hand before the woman was pulled out by the receding tide — and weak as she was, ended up with only her ring?

She blinked and blinked again. It didn't seem right. What a frightening, unsettling feeling, not being able to sift reality from dream.

But one thing she did remember and knew with all certainty. She needed to find a way to return to Bath as soon as possible, and with enough money to pay her ever-mounting debt to the matron who held her son's life in her hands. Though in reality both heartless Mrs. Beech and troubled Becky frightened her.

The gems of the ring caught the sunlight slicing through the window, sending shafts of colored light dancing on the ceiling.

A sign, or a temptation?

Surely a ring like this was worth a great deal. A ring Sir John, if he lived, would believe consigned to the tides, lost forever with his wife.

Dare she?

A short while later, Dr. Parrish and his wife stopped by to check on her. He cheerfully reported that the little boy who'd fallen from the tree was recovering nicely. "Little scamp dislocated his collarbone, but I've set it back in place. He'll be right as a trivet in no time."

"*If* his poor harried mamma can somehow keep him quiet in bed for a few days," Mrs.

Parrish added doubtfully.

Hannah formed a faint, dutiful smile, though her thoughts and stomach churned.

Tentatively, she began, "May I ask, Dr. Parrish. Are you . . . well acquainted with Sir John?"

He sat in the armchair nearby, clearly happy to stay and talk. His wife lingered in the doorway.

"Not at all," Dr. Parrish said. "Only by letters. Never met the man before and I suppose I still haven't. Not really."

"But —" She frowned in concentration. "I thought you said your son . . . ?"

He nodded. "Edgar met him when Sir John came out to look at the place a few months ago."

"That's right," Mrs. Parrish added. "Dr. Parrish and I were away delivering twins at the time."

"Sir John came alone?"

"Had a man with him, Edgar said. A man of business, I think, though I don't exactly recall." The doctor's eyes sparkled. "But you were not with him, my lady. Edgar made no mention of the charming Lady Mayfield. That I would recall."

Mrs. Parrish frowned and crossed her arms.

Hannah opened her mouth to correct him,

then stopped. The fact that a lady's companion would be sent packing once there was no lady in the house gave her pause. The valuable ring gave her pause. The very notion gave her pause. But her conscience rose up, urging her to tell the truth and find a way to redeem Danny honestly.

She asked, "Dr. Parrish, can you tell me how soon I will be well enough to travel?"

His eyes widened. "Travel? But you have only just arrived."

"I know. But I need to return to Bath as soon as possible."

Mrs. Parrish's frown deepened. "Why, if I may ask? If you forgot something, perhaps we might send for it."

Hannah shook her head. "I didn't forget anything." She winced at the irony of those words. "But I have left someone extremely important in Bath and I must return for him."

They both looked at her expectantly, awaiting an explanation.

She swallowed. "My son. I am ashamed to say I forgot him for a time."

The doctor's eyes widened once more. "Good heavens! When I examined you, I assumed you'd miscarried the child. Though considering, well, several things, I should have known you'd already delivered. I am so sorry I blundered in saying you'd lost the child. How incompetent you must think me!"

"Not at all," Hannah mumbled. "Remind me. How did you even know there was a child?"

"Sir John mentioned his wife was expecting in one of his letters."

"Ah." She lifted her chin in understanding, but inwardly her thoughts rebelled. How had she not noticed Marianna was in the family way?

"Praise God, you did *not* bring the child with you," Dr. Parrish continued. "I shudder at the thought of a wee one in that wreck. A son, you said?"

"Yes. I . . . left him with his nurse."

"Until you were settled and had readied the house?" Mrs. Parrish asked. "There is no proper nursery as yet. I'm surprised Sir John did not ask Edgar to have one fitted up for your arrival."

Hannah had no idea how to answer that. She had been about to tell the truth about her child and situation, only to find the Parrishes already quite aware "Lady Mayfield" had been expecting a child, though not this soon. Now her emotions were in turmoil, and indecision plagued her. . . . If it meant being able to rescue her son, dare she allow them to continue believing she was Lady Mayfield — just for a little while? Just long enough to have her baby boy back in her arms?

She faltered. "I . . . don't know why. All I know is that I need to return to my son."

The doctor nodded. "And bring him here as soon as may be. Yes, what a comfort he shall be to you in these uncertain days."

"A great comfort," she agreed.

"As eager as you are, I must insist you wait a few more days before undertaking such a journey. Allow that head wound to heal a bit more. I've set your arm with splints and soaked bandages. But the starch solution requires several days to dry thoroughly enough to immobilize the bone. If you rush things, it won't heal properly. You don't want to risk the use of the arm."

No, she could not afford to lose the use of her arm. How then would she be able to work to support herself and her son?

What if she allowed the misapprehension to continue for just a few more days? Then she would leave, sell the ring if she had to, collect Danny, and disappear, never to return.

Would God forgive such a deception? There was only one thing that would cause her to stoop to such a ruse — the well-being of her son. She would do anything — well, almost anything — to rescue him.

"Good morning, my lady," Mrs. Turrill greeted as she carried in the breakfast tray the next day. It was her customary greeting, but the words, the title, sounded suddenly jarring in Hannah's ears.

Today Mrs. Turrill wore a long-sleeved frock of deep plum, a ruffled neck scarf, and a long apron. She set the tray on a side table, then turned to her. "Shall we try sitting in an armchair today, my lady? If you feel up to it, that is."

Her voice was musical, with a broad range of tones depending on her mood. Hearing it made Hannah feel homesick. For while her mother had spoken with an upper-class accent and her father had lived in Oxford in his years as tutor and curate, most of her neighbors and childhood friends sounded like Mrs. Turrill. She wondered how long the woman had lived in Bristol, why she had returned, and about the child she mentioned she'd lost. But Hannah didn't ask. She did not want to compound her sins by forming friendships — or tempt the woman to ask personal questions in return.

So instead, Hannah managed a wan smile and said, "Yes, I think I can manage that."

Mrs. Turrill helped her from the bed and into an armchair, and there Hannah began her breakfast, Mrs. Turrill chatting cheerfully all the while.

How Hannah wished she might feign sleep and the insensibility that excused her falseness. But she had to prove herself recovering and well enough to travel as soon as possible.

Later that morning, Hannah was still sitting in the chair and staring out the window when Dr. Parrish stopped by her room with his medical bag.

He beamed at her. "How good to see you out of that bed."

He examined her head wound, declared it was healing well, and decided it was time to remove the stitches. Hannah bit the inside of her cheek to keep tears at bay during the unpleasant procedure, and exhaled in relief when he'd finished.

He patted her hand. "Well done, brave lady." He put his implements away, then asked, "Shall we try walking once more, my lady? I imagine you are anxious to see your husband again."

Hannah's throat tightened. "I don't know. Do you think it would be . . . safe?"

"Safe?"

She thought quickly. "With my arm, I mean."

"Yes, I think so. We'll take it slow, and be careful not to jostle your arm."

There was no graceful way to refuse to see her "husband," so she whispered, "Very well."

The doctor helped her rise. As usual, the room swam, and her legs felt weak and unstable.

He tightened his grip on her good arm. "Dizziness or weakness?"

She forced a smile. "A little of both."

"Then perhaps we should wait until to-morrow," he suggested. "Or we could use the wheeled chair again . . . ?"

She was tempted to claim fatigue and put off the visit to Sir John's bedside altogether. But she firmed her resolve, knowing the sooner she proved herself sufficiently recovered, the sooner she could leave.

"Just give me a moment." She inhaled deeply. "Yes, there. The dizziness is passing."

He waited patiently, studying her face. What did he see? Was he thinking to himself that he'd imagined a "lady" to be more beautiful? More genteel? She took a deep breath, then another. "All right. I am ready."

He cupped her elbow to support her and

gently led her across the room and out into the passage. Hannah's heart rate accelerated with each step. The nearer they drew to Sir John's bedchamber, the more her nerves jangled. She didn't know which she dreaded more: seeing the man broken and bruised and lying near death, or that he might regain his senses, open his eyes, and declare her a fraud.

When they reached the bedchamber door, Dr. Parrish opened it and ushered her inside.

The doctor's sharp-featured wife sat in a chair near the foot of the bed, knitting wool and needles in her lap, keeping watch over her husband's patient.

"Any change, Mrs. Parrish?"

"No change, Dr. Parrish."

Knowing it was expected of her, Hannah turned toward the bed, pressing her good hand to her abdomen. How cold, she thought, to be glad the man was insensible. He lay still as before, eyes closed. The bruises on his face were beginning to change color, his cheekbone perhaps a little less swollen, his mouth still slack. No one had shaved him, and whiskers darkened the lower half of his face in colors of bronze and silver. She had always thought him young for his age, but now he looked older than his forty years. Only his hair seemed the same — thick and brown with a faint silvering at his side-whiskers.

She was aware of the doctor beside her. Sensed his wife's expectant air. Having no idea what to say, Hannah mumbled, "He looks . . . different."

The physician nodded. "I imagine he does."

She whispered, "What did the surgeon say?"

Dr. Parrish regretfully shook his head. "He isn't keen on operating at present. He isn't convinced Sir John's brain has swelled to a dangerous degree. I am afraid he doesn't think your husband would survive an operation, even if he thought one necessary. He is too weak."

Sadness swept over her. "I see."

Mrs. Parrish tipped her head to one side. "Strange that he was so severely injured, while you were not, my lady. I suspect his body cushioned yours against the first violent impact before the carriage rolled."

Hannah recalled waking to find Sir John sprawled across her body. But if the woman's theory was correct, she felt grateful, and a little guilty, for escaping relatively unscathed.

Mrs. Parrish added, "The vicar has been

here to see him. I hope you don't mind my asking him?"

"Of course not," Hannah whispered.

"He prayed over you as well."

Hannah's head jerked up. "Did he? I don't remember."

"You were asleep. We didn't want to wake you."

"Oh." An uncomfortable feeling snaked up her spine at the thought.

Dr. Parrish said gently, "You may touch him, if you like, my lady. You shan't hurt him."

Hannah swallowed. She supposed a wife would want to touch her husband, smooth the hair from his brow. Squeeze his hand. Whisper in his ear that she loved him. But she was not his wife. And Hannah knew that Lady Mayfield herself would likely not do so either, had she been there. Besides, Hannah was reluctant to touch him under the watchful eyes of doctor and wife. It would be taking her "role" too far. Would they remember she had taken such a liberty after she left — after the truth was known?

As she stood there thinking, not moving, not touching, she felt Mrs. Parrish's frowning gaze on her profile.

Hannah bit her lip, stepped forward, and reached out a tentative hand. Would they notice it trembling? She touched Sir John's arm, lightly, afraid to wake him, before quickly stepping back.

Dr. Parrish stood beside her. "I hope and pray he will recover in time."

"As do I," Hannah said solemnly. And she sincerely meant it, though she planned to be well away before then.

CHAPTER 5

The next morning, Hannah announced to Mrs. Turrill that she would like to dress for the day, rather than remain in nightdress and wrapper. The woman smiled and said she thought that an excellent notion. The dress Hannah had been wearing the day of the wreck had been torn and stained, and she didn't see her own valise among the luggage piled in the corner. It had apparently been lost to the tide. Only her reticule on the bedside table had remained with her after the crash — its ribbons tied to her wrist. So Hannah asked the housekeeper to help her into one of Marianna's older day dresses of loose, stretchy muslin, which could easily be slipped over her wrapped arm. She did not want to wear any of Marianna's finer, fitted gowns, which would likely hang on her. And how presumptuous she would feel to do so.

She sat on the dressing stool while the

woman helped her on with stockings. Then Mrs. Turrill picked out a pair of pointy-toe leather slippers with small heels. Hannah sucked in a breath. "Um. Perhaps my half boots instead? The ones I wore when we . . . arrived?"

The housekeeper shook her head. "Oh no. Those were all but ruined in the channel, my lady. Salt water is so hard on leather."

She knelt before her and tried to wedge the shoe onto her foot, but it was too tight. Hannah held her breath, her heartbeat loud in her ears. Was she to be exposed already?

Mrs. Turrill bit her lip, staring down at the obstinate appendage. "Your feet are swollen, my lady. From the accident or lying abed, I'd wager. Shall I send these to the cobbler for a stretch?"

Hannah breathed a sigh of relief. "Yes, please."

In the meantime, Mrs. Turrill loosened the lacings of a pair of satin slippers and worked those onto her feet instead.

Then Hannah asked if she might go downstairs for breakfast. She was no longer an invalid, she asserted, who required a tray delivered to her bedchamber.

Mrs. Turrill said she was happy to oblige, and to see the sunny dining parlor put to use at last. She insisted, however, on taking her arm and helping her down the stairs.

A week had passed since the accident, and this was the first time Hannah had seen the ground floor of Clifton House. She admired the open, two-story staircase hall, and peeked into the green and white drawing room and mahogany-paneled morning room as they passed.

In the dining parlor, Mrs. Turrill pulled back a chair for her and introduced her to Ben Jones, a young manservant of perhaps seventeen, who opened the shutters and laid a fire in the hearth to dispel the lingering chill.

After the meal, Hannah thanked Mrs. Turrill and Ben. Then she went out into the hall and sat in an armchair to await Dr. Parrish — ready to state her case.

When the physician entered through the side door sometime later, he drew up short, rearing his head back. "Good morning, my lady. What a surprise to see you downstairs. You are looking well, I must say."

"Thank you. I am feeling perfectly well."

"And now that you have seen more of your new home, I hope it meets with your approval?"

"Yes, it's lovely, but I am anxious to return to Bath for my son. You can imagine how I miss him. If someone might drive me to the nearest coaching inn, I shall travel by stage from there."

"Of course you are eager to collect your little boy. I don't blame you. But I cannot allow you to travel alone. A lady like you . . . why, it simply isn't done."

"I appreciate your concern, Dr. Parrish, but I shall be fine. I have done the like before."

His brows rose high. "Have you indeed? I am surprised — surprised Sir John would allow it."

"It was . . . before I knew him."

"Ah. Yes. But you are Lady Mayfield now and I cannot in good conscience allow you to venture forth alone, especially after your concussion, not to mention a broken arm. I cannot go myself, for Mr. Higgerson is on his deathbed, poor fellow. But we'll hire a chaise from the inn and Edgar will accompany you. He has some medical knowledge, should you suffer a setback or any problems arise."

"Dr. Parrish, you are most kind. But I couldn't —"

"It's all right. The missus and I have been discussing the matter ever since we learned of the little boy. She thought you might not be comfortable traveling alone with a young man you barely know, so I've asked Edgar's intended to go along with you. Nancy is a sweet girl, you'll see."

"Really, it is not necessary."

He looked at her, clearly bewildered and hurt that she should protest so vehemently. "It is no bother. We insist upon it."

She felt trapped by kindness and good manners. By his expectation of how Lady Mayfield would graciously behave. If only they had known her!

"Then, I thank you, Dr. Parrish, though I am terribly sorry to put you all to so much trouble."

"Never mind that, my lady. That's what neighbors are for. Besides, I believe Nancy will greatly enjoy the excursion."

Hannah forced a smile. Now what was she to do? How was she to evade Edgar and Nancy once they arrived in Bath? For she could not take them with her into foul Trim Street. Her falsehood would be revealed instantly.

"May I also suggest, my lady," Dr. Parrish added, "that you might wish to contact Sir John's solicitor or man of business while you are in Bath? Or at least write to him and apprise him of the situation here?"

"Ah," she murmured noncommittally, lifting her chin to acknowledge the suggestions, though having no intention of doing either.

The trip was arranged for the following day. The journey there and back would be a lengthy one, so they planned to spend one night in an inn before returning. Mrs. Turrill prepared a hamper of food and gathered extra blankets, though the weather was mild. Hannah retrieved her own reticule and packed one small valise, ostensibly to see her through a night in an inn as well as a few things for the baby. In actuality, she took only the essentials for life on her own: a spare shift and gown, bonnet, toothpowder and brush, and the pair of stretched slippers. She wore her own half boots, stained and stiff as they were. And the ring beneath her gloves.

Early in the morning, the hired chaise and four, with a postilion mounted on the lead horse, clattered up the drive and halted in front of the house. From inside the chaise, Edgar pushed open the door and alighted, then turned to hand down a pleasant-looking young woman in plain, but neat traveling clothes.

Stepping outside to greet them, Hannah realized it was her first time out of doors at Clifton. She paused to survey the turreted stone house set amid blooming whitebeam trees and privet hedges. To feel the spring-time sun on her skin and breathe in the sweet smell of hyacinth and bluebells.

Mr. and Mrs. Parrish walked over from their house next door — the Grange — to bid them all safe journey.

Dr. Parrish drew her aside and asked quietly, "My lady. Have you sufficient funds for the journey?"

She hesitated, glancing at the ring bulging beneath her glove, and then made a show of perusing her reticule. She surveyed the few coins there, left over from those given her by the begrudging Mr. Ward. She had paid Mrs. Beech a portion of what she owed before leaving Bath with the Mayfields, and now only a small sum remained.

She murmured, "How much do you think I shall need?"

"You should carry enough for the inns, tolls, horses, and postilions, but not so much to invite trouble."

"I had not thought of all that." Hannah frowned. "I am afraid I haven't enough to cover those expenses."

The lines of his face deepened in concern. He said kindly, "With your permission, I shall retrieve ten pounds or so from your husband's purse, assuming he has that much ready cash."

She swallowed. It was a great deal of money. Travel by chaise must be expensive indeed. "If you think that would be . . . suitable."

"Ample sufficient, I am sure."

"Then, yes. Please do. Thank you, doctor." She ignored the twinge of guilt and the thought of how Dr. Parrish would react when he someday learned he had given so much money to a mere companion.

A few minutes later, money collected and good-byes said, Dr. Parrish gave Hannah a hand up, and she settled herself inside the carriage. Nancy sat beside her on the single, front-facing bench, Edgar on her other side. And Ben, their young manservant, sat on the rear, outside seat.

Hannah was not looking forward to sharing the cramped space with two people she barely knew and who knew her as someone she was not. She dreaded making small talk and increasing her chances of giving herself away. But it would be rude to remain silent for hours on end.

She asked Nancy about her family, and Edgar about the other properties he managed for absentee landlords — the Devonshire coast being a popular second-home site for artists and the upper class. In turn, she answered their questions about Bath and its attractions, but replied in vague terms to more personal queries.

Eventually, they stopped at a coaching inn to hire fresh horses. Hannah was glad for the respite — her wrapped arm throbbed from all the jostling it had suffered.

Edgar suggested they step inside for refreshment, and all agreed. As they sat in the parlor and sipped tea, he again politely attempted to engage her in conversation. But noticing her distracted reserve, he soon turned his attention to sweet, shy Nancy instead, who was thrilled to be venturing into neighboring Somerset for the first time in her life.

Later, back in the rocking chaise, Hannah spent the hours cradling her aching arm, feigning sleep to avoid further conversation, and trying to plan what she would do when they arrived in Bath. She certainly didn't want them to see what sort of establishment and in what neighborhood she had left her child. But how might she dissuade them from escorting her all the way to Mrs. Beech's door? Or how would she evade them if they did?

She decided to thank them for bringing her to Bath and then insist on retrieving Danny on her own. She would then pay a messenger to deliver a note to them in her stead, saying something unforeseen had arisen and one of her own family would escort her back to Clifton in a few days.

If Sir John had died, "Lady Mayfield" would be under no moral compulsion to return to that house in Devonshire, a place she had not even seen before the accident. She could say she was returning to her former home, to the succor of friends and family. But what sort of a wife would leave a husband alone near death? She shuddered to contemplate what they would think of her.

She hated all these lies. What if she were to confess to Edgar and Nancy that she was not who they believed her to be? But then . . . would she not be guilty of stealing from Sir John's purse, and possibly arrested for fraud or who knew what other fatal charges? And then what would become of Danny?

All Hannah wanted was to redeem her son from Mrs. Beech, and disappear. Leave Mrs. Beech, Sir John, and even kind Dr. Parrish and his family far behind. Though how she would support herself and Danny she did not know. Especially with her arm bound in splints. But she wouldn't think about that at present. She had enough money to get Danny back and that was all that mattered — for now.

Hannah prayed again that Becky would keep Danny safe until she got there. She knew the girl took a special interest in him. That thought reminded her of the day less than a fortnight ago when Becky had appeared at the home of Hannah's new employer. How drastically her life had changed since then. . . .

When Danny was about a month old, Hannah had taken a position as companion to a sour, elderly dowager. The widow lived near enough to Mrs. Beech's that Hannah could easily slip away to see him and nurse him from time to time. She'd hated to leave him, but felt she had no other choice.

One day, she had been halfheartedly perusing books in the dower house library, selecting several to read aloud to the far-sighted widow, when the prim housekeeper came to find her.

"There is a girl to see you at the servants' entrance, Miss Rogers. A Becky Brown."

Hannah's heart thumped in alarm. "Becky?" *Oh, God in heaven, please let nothing have happened to Danny.*

Murmuring thanks to the housekeeper, Hannah hurried belowstairs to the servants' entrance. There, Becky stood huddled by the door, shrinking under the speculative gazes of cook and kitchen maid.

"Becky," Hannah hissed, leading her into the quiet passage. "You weren't to come here. What is it? What's happened?"

"The Jones boy is took bad with a fever, and now little Molly is fussin'. I'm afeared. Afeared the fever will spread through the whole house."

Hannah's stomach clenched. "And Danny? How is Danny?"

"He's all right, I think. So far at least. Nursed well this mornin'. Hardly left any for the others. I nurse your babe first, you know. For you."

Wary gratitude filled Hannah. "Thank you, Becky. I do appreciate it. Greatly. But you're sure he isn't ill?"

"No, miss. Not yet. But I thought you'd want to know."

"Well, Miss Rogers."

Hannah whirled at the voice. She hadn't heard the shrewd housekeeper follow her.

Her eyes narrowed to glinting slits. "You'll be packing your bags, and sharp-like, when the mistress hears you've a babe, and you not married."

The housekeeper turned on her heel and marched up the back stairs.

Becky's face crumpled. "Sorry, Miss Hannah."

Hannah groaned. "I told you not to come here, Becky. You might have sent word and I would have met you somewhere."

"I'm sorry. I was just so worried." Tears filled the girl's eyes.

Hannah bit her lip to stifle another rebuke. "I know. It was good of you to think of Danny. And me. There now, don't cry. You meant well."

"But how will you pay Mrs. Beech if you haven't a post?"

Hannah blinked back tears of her own. "I don't know." One idea came to her. But it was a possibility she'd avoided resorting to before.

As the housekeeper predicted, the dowager dismissed Hannah soon after Becky departed, and vowed that Hannah wouldn't find another situation in Bath with any decent woman of her acquaintance.

Hannah swallowed back bile at the cruel words the woman had slung at her, words like "undeserving, deceitful," and worse.

Hannah packed her belongings into her valise, and left with a heavy heart, knowing what she must do. She had promised herself she would never return. Yet she found herself walking north, up Lansdown Street, and turning in to Camden Place. To that gate, that door, that house she had left a half year before.

She let herself in at the low wrought iron gate, hoping not to encounter Mr. Ward, who would likely greet her with a lewd offer or send her away with a harsh word before she'd even seen Lady Mayfield.

She hesitated to knock on the front door. She had to remind herself that she had not been in service — she had been Lady Mayfield's companion. A gentlewoman, though a poor one.

Without change of expression, the stoic butler, Hopkins, let her in, allowed her to leave her valise in the hall cupboard, and showed her into the morning room while he went to see if Lady Mayfield was at home to callers. Thankfully there was no sign of Mr. Ward. Still, Hannah wrung her gloved hands, fearing her former mistress might refuse to see her, especially as she had left her so abruptly.

A few moments later, Lady Mayfield burst into the room. "Hannah! My goodness. I never expected to see you again."

Marianna went on, exclaiming how pleased she was to see her. Then the woman surveyed her from head to toe, speculation gleaming in her brown eyes. "You appear in good health. If a little tired. And thin."

Oh yes, Hannah was considerably thinner now than she had been when Marianna had last seen her.

Hannah clasped her hands tightly together, pulse pounding to be in the presence of a Mayfield once again. Then she sheepishly asked for her final allowance.

Marianna agreed, and in short order Mr. Ward was summoned to bring it.

At the mention of his name, Hannah shivered. Mr. Ward, along with several other servants, had come with the Mayfields from their primary residence in Bristol. How she'd detested his leering glances and wandering hands.

While they waited, Hannah listened in stunned silence as Lady Mayfield begged her to accompany her as traveling companion, even going so far as to offer her double her former allowance. Hannah hesitated. It was a good offer. No — what was she thinking? She could not leave. She had a child now, though she hadn't the courage to tell Marianna Mayfield that.

But, could she afford to refuse such an offer? Especially when Marianna said Hannah could leave whenever she wanted — which would be just as soon as she earned enough. And at the offered rate, it wouldn't take long, assuming Mrs. Beech didn't raise her fees again. But what if Becky came to look for her with more worrisome news, and she was nowhere to be found? What if something happened to Danny before she could return? What then?

Mr. Ward came in with her allowance — minus what he'd subtracted for her early departure without notice. She avoided his cold eyes and laid out her palm, feeling like a beggar. *I earned this fairly,* she reminded herself, though the discomfort did not ease. He dropped several sovereigns and shillings onto her outstretched hand, careful not to touch her. He had not been so careful before.

When he left, Hannah studied the coins in her hand. It would help. It would reduce the amount she owed greedy Mrs. Beech. But it wasn't enough. It might buy her some time, though. Assure a measure of safety for her son, until she could earn the rest.

She told Lady Mayfield she was grateful for the offer, but needed time to think about it.

Marianna Mayfield studied her. "Well don't think too long," she said. "We're leaving at four this afternoon, according to Sir John. Unless I can persuade him to forgo this idiotic notion. Jealous fool."

Sir John had the right to be jealous, Hannah knew. She chewed her lip and considered. Dare she throw in her lot with tempestuous Lady Mayfield, her wily lover, and her imposing husband? She had promised herself she never would do so again. But had she any other choice?

"If I'm not here by half past three, don't wait for me," Hannah said. "It means I'm not coming."

From there, Hannah had walked directly to Trim Street. How stifling the air in that grim, narrow lane. No wonder the neighborhood was rumored to foster putrid fevers. Hannah's stomach fisted at the thought.

She reached Mrs. Beech's house and knocked on the door. When the eye slit opened, Mrs. Beech snapped, "Who is it?"

Hannah pushed the coins through the slot, and heard them clatter to the floor.

"I shall have more. Soon."

Mrs. Beech's eyes appeared in the slit. "Took my advice, did you?"

Hannah stifled a bitter retort. She could not afford to further alienate this woman. "I took another position. One that pays better."

"Obviously."

"Please, may I see Danny before I go? I may not be able to return for some time."

"Sorry. I told you before. Pay what you owe, or go without."

"I just want to see him. With my own eyes. See that he is all right."

The woman hesitated. Had she a heart after all? "Oh very well. But just for a moment. Becky! Bring the Rogers boy down."

Hannah waited for the door to open, but it remained closed. Through the peephole, she glimpsed skirt and apron as someone — Becky, she supposed — came down the stairs, a bundled babe in arms. Her body ached at the sight. It should be her arms holding him.

"Let her have a look at him. Through there," the woman ordered.

The slight body turned, repositioned the bundle, and then, there he was. That dear little face, awake, alert. The skin so fair that blue veins shone beneath his eyes, making the irises appear bluer yet. Little pursed lips working, already looking for his next meal. The smooth round cheeks, the fine tufts of hair. Hannah's heart swelled and her eyes stung. In reply, her breasts surged with pinpricks of life, of milk, though she was all but dry by now. Still she longed for him, the touch of him, the feel and smell of her little boy with her whole being.

"Hello, Danny," she cooed through the

slit, not caring how foolish she must look to passersby or the cruel matron. "Hello, my dear one. Mamma loves you. Never forget she does." Her voice cracked. "I shall be back for you soon. Just as soon as I can . . ."

"That's enough now, Becky," Mrs. Beech ordered. "Take the boy away."

The girl hesitated, then turned.

Tears streamed down Hannah's face but she remained bent at her waist, her eyes at the slit, hoping for one last glimpse of him. To tide her over. To feed her soul.

Glinting eyes reappeared in the slit instead, blocking her view. "And that's the last you'll see of him, until you pay in full."

With the echoing clack of Mrs. Beech's door slit still ringing in her ears, Hannah had trudged, weeping, to the Bath Abbey courtyard to see Fred Bonner, who stopped there twice a week on his delivery route from Bristol.

She found a bench and sat down to wait. Finally, Fred and his wagon appeared. Reaching the courtyard, he jumped down and tied his horse at his usual spot. She rose and walked toward him.

His face brightened when he saw her. "Hannah!" he called with a boyish grin and bounded toward her. But his grin faded when he neared and saw her tear-streaked face. "What is it, Han?"

"I need to speak with you." She steeled herself. She was almost as reluctant to ask him for help, as she would be to ask her father. Almost.

"That sounds serious." Fred eyed her valise with a frown.

"It is. I need help."

"You know I'd do anything for you, Han, if I could. Anything."

She did know. He had asked her to marry him more than once. If he offered to help her now, she would accept. She explained that Mrs. Beech was refusing to allow her to have Danny. And that fever was spreading through the house.

The tall young man listened, his brown, hound-dog eyes wide in concern.

"Freddie, I need money," Hannah said in conclusion. "It shames me to say so, but there it is. If you want to help me . . . us . . . then that's what I need. I have never asked you for a farthing, but now I'm asking."

He winced. "Oh, Han. I want to help you. Both of you. I *had* a few pounds put by, but I've sunk those into this wagon."

Tears filling her eyes again, she turned and walked away across the courtyard, but Fred followed after her.

"I'll make more with my own route, see.

As soon as I pay off Pa for the horse, all the earnings will be mine free and clear and then I can support you proper."

"When will that be?"

"Half a year. Give or take. And then we can be married. Say you'll marry me, Han. You know I love you."

She did know. Fred Bonner had loved her since they were children, growing up as neighbors in Bristol. But love wasn't enough.

"Oh, Freddie. I'm sorry. But Danny and I can't wait that long."

She turned leaden legs north, up Lansdown Street.

He called after her, "Would your father not help you?"

"No." Nor would she ask him to, if she could help it.

At the top of Camden Place, Fred grasped her arm, forcing her to pause.

"Let me go and talk to my pa then. Perhaps he might help us."

"Would he?" She turned to face him. "When you tell him everything?"

His jaw ticked, but he did not answer. In a lower voice, he asked, "What do you intend to do, Han?"

She gently pulled her arm from his grasp. "What I must."

She resolutely turned into Camden Place, leaving Fred standing there, downcast and alone. . . .

In the hired chaise, Hannah awoke with a start. She had fallen asleep and her memories had slipped into dreams. Her hand had fallen asleep as well. Beside her, Edgar snored softly. Nancy, however, sat wide awake, looking at her strangely. Hannah straightened on the bench, sending the girl a rueful smile. Had she muttered something in her sleep? She hoped she had said nothing to give herself away.

CHAPTER 6

When they reached the outskirts of Bath, Hannah's pulse rate accelerated. She'd only been gone a little more than a week, she reminded herself. Surely Danny would still be all right.

The postilion directed the horses into the yard of the Westgate, an old coaching inn near the heart of the city. There, hostellers relieved him of his duty and led the hired horses into the stables for a much-deserved rest.

Ben helped Hannah and Nancy down from the carriage. Both women were eager to stretch their legs after the many hours of confinement.

Edgar asked Ben to wait at the inn and keep an eye on the carriage, while he escorted the ladies. As Edgar gave the young man final instructions, Hannah looked about her, gaining her bearings.

She took a deep breath and said brightly,

"The baths are just there." She pointed across the street, then turned to Edgar and pressed several coins into his palm. "You cannot bring Nancy all the way to Bath and not show her the Pump Room and Roman baths. I shall go on my own to pick up Danny. I will want a little time alone to explain the situation and Sir John's condition before I return."

Edgar's brow furrowed. "But Papa said I was to deliver you directly and help with your things."

"And you have delivered me as promised and I so appreciate your help," Hannah said. "I am going just around the corner and won't have much to carry. Now you two go on, and have a nice time. I shall meet you back here in say . . . two hours time?"

Edgar frowned and seemed about to refuse, but Nancy took him by the arm and eagerly pulled him across the courtyard toward the Pump Room, grinning and chatting with excitement. Halfway across the courtyard, Edgar turned to glance at her over his shoulder, looking very much like his father at that moment with concern and uncertainty written on his face. Hannah smiled and waved encouragement and watched until they had disappeared through the arched doorway of the fashionable establishment.

Hannah surreptitiously scanned the courtyard and street beyond for Freddie, though she didn't think it was one of his regular delivery days. She was relieved not to see him or his wagon anywhere.

Satisfied, Hannah turned and walked briskly away. Her destination was not "just around the corner." It was seven or eight blocks away. She crossed Westgate Street and walked quickly up Bridewell, before turning into narrow Trim Street. Arriving winded, she knocked at the door of the old terrace house, her heart tripping from the rapid pace and the fear that Danny had taken sick with fever or met with some other dire fate during her absence.

A heavy tread shook the floor within. The door slit opened and a pair of eyes beneath bushy brows appeared. A man's eyes.

"Yeah? Whaddya want?"

Hannah blinked in surprise. "I am here to see Mrs. Beech."

His eyes roved her face and neck and suddenly the bar was thrown and the door swung wide. Hannah took a wary step back. Her nose wrinkled at the look and smell of the potbellied, unkempt man framed in its threshold.

"She ain't here." The man continued his

perusal of her face and figure. "But I wager I can help ya."

"Not here?" Hannah's breath caught. "But . . . she has my son. I am here to collect him."

"What's your name, girl?"

"Hannah Rogers."

"Ah." His eyes lit. "The girl what owes Bertha a great deal of money."

"I have it, sir. When will Mrs. Beech return?"

"She won't. But I'll take it in her stead."

Hannah was instantly suspicious. "Pardon me, sir. But my business is with Mrs. Beech."

"Then your business is with me. I'm her brother. Tom Simpkins is the name. Perhaps you've heard of me?"

A shiver of revulsion passed over her. The panderer who led desperate girls into a life of prostitution for his profit.

"She has mentioned her brother, but —"

"That's me. I'm running the place now."

No . . . She didn't dare trust him. But had she any choice? She had to get Danny back. At any price. She opened her reticule and handed him the money she owed.

He accepted it eagerly. "Is that all of it? Are you certain?"

It was all she was prepared to give the

man. She wasn't about to suggest he check his sister's books or mention she'd threatened to increase her rates yet again.

"Yes," Hannah said. "Now please bring me my son, or allow me inside and I shall collect him myself."

He pocketed the money and crossed his arms, leaning on the threshold. "I'm afraid I can't do that."

Panic and anger rippled through her. "Why not?"

Behind the leering man, Hannah glimpsed a woman in only shift and stays traipse past, pulling a man up the stairs behind her.

Simpkins shrugged. "He ain't here. None of them brats are. Wet nurses neither. I told you this is my place now. Bertha landed in a spot of trouble, see. Spending a bit of time in the lockup at present, awaitin' trial."

Hannah stared, uncomprehending. She could believe Mrs. Beech had been discovered for the corrupt matron she was, but this? She sputtered, "But where are the children?"

"Oh, parceled out here and there."

Her heart pounded. "But where? Where is Daniel Rogers? Surely you have a record?"

"Nope. All I know is, her charges has been split up. Some sent to the Walcot Poor House on the London Road. Some to the workhouses in Bradford or Bristol."

Hannah lifted her chin. "I don't believe you." She pushed past the greasy man, and stormed through the hall and up the stairs to the nursery. She threw back the door, and recoiled at the sight of a man and woman in bed. No cradles. No babies.

Nerves jangling, she ran to the next door and did the same. Inside, a frowsy woman gaped up at her from a dressing table. Her lined face was heavily powdered and rouged, in an effort to look younger — and less used — than her years.

"Where are the children?" Hannah asked her. "The babies?"

The woman shook her head. "No babes here, love. This is Tomcat's place now. Did he not tell you?" She surveyed Hannah with bloodshot eyes. "I hope you're not looking for work. You're no great beauty, but he'd replace me in a heartbeat for someone young and fresh like you."

"I am only looking for my child."

"You're too late, love. The last stragglers left this morning."

Too late? God in heaven, no . . . Oh, why had she dawdled? Why had she taken Dr. Parrish's advice and waited? What was an arm compared to her child . . . her flesh and blood, her life?

Trembling in terror, Hannah hurried back down the stairs and past the grinning menace at the door, ignoring his offer to stay and enjoy a life of luxury in his care. She had to get out of that house before she was sick. Before she lost her last thread of self-control and fell into a heap of futile sobs on the man's nasty floor.

She all but leapt from the front stoop, and dashed around the corner of the house into the alleyway between two tenements. She drew in desperate breaths of fresh air, trying to stay the nausea, but it was no good. Her stomach wrung with molten dread, and bile climbed her throat. She bent over to wretch.

For a moment afterward she stood hunched there, clammy with perspiration, mind whirling. *Now what?* She could walk to the poor house on the London Road, but she didn't think the place took in such young inmates. The workhouse in Bristol had a nursery, she believed. Would she have to accept a ride home with Fred, confess all to her father, and beg him to help her? She would if she had to, to save her son. Though she doubted her father would come to their aid. How mortified he would be to do so.

Oh, Danny, where are you? Who has you?

How confused he must be, how abandoned he must feel. *Oh God, is this my punishment? Forgive me! I deserve it, but Danny does not. He is innocent; please preserve him. Please help me find him.* Hannah's lungs burned, shrank, until she could hardly breathe. Silent shudders wracked her body.

She heard something then. . . . Sobbing. For a moment she thought her own grief had burst forth. But no — it was coming from somewhere farther down the alley. Another mother who had discovered her child gone? How many women were crying at that moment?

Hannah looked down the dim alley and saw a figure sitting huddled on a back stoop, head bent, hugging her knees.

A flicker of recognition penetrated Hannah's grief. Tentatively, she called, "Becky?"

The trembling figure looked up, her face pale in the shadowed doorway. Becky's eyes widened. Her shaking stilled.

Hannah walked toward the girl, a tendril of hope rising in her battered heart. Perhaps Becky would know where Danny was.

"Becky, I've just come from Mrs. Beech's. Where is Danny — do you know?"

The girl's mouth parted, but she said nothing. Hannah took a few steps nearer and saw the girl hugged not only her slender self, but also a swaddled bundle.

Hope tangled with revulsion. Had the girl reverted to carrying around a swaddled doll to deal with the loss that sometimes unhinged her grip on reality?

"Becky . . . ?" she prompted.

The girl rose to her feet. "Miss Hannah, I . . . I didn't think I'd ever see you again," she faltered. "Mrs. Beech said you wouldn't come back."

"I said I would return and here I am." Hannah pointed at her splinted arm. "I was injured in a carriage accident, or I might have come sooner."

But Becky didn't seem to notice her arm. "He's my favorite, you know," she said, staring vacantly ahead. "Mrs. Beech said I weren't fit to take care of a child and that's why God took mine away. Said the workhouse would be far better for 'im."

Hannah's raw stomach twisted again. "She took Danny to the workhouse? Which one?"

"Planned to. But I took 'im afore she could. Played up like I was gonna work for that Mr. Simpkins and they let me back in."

The bundle in her arms whined and Hannah's pulse leapt. *Danny?* Hannah hesitated. How should she handle this — how could she pry the child from the girl's arms without injuring either of them?

She forced a smile. "Becky, have you rescued Danny for me? Is that what you've done?"

The girl stared at her.

"Oh, Becky!" she enthused. "Mrs. Beech was wrong — see how good you are with children! Why, you have saved Danny."

She held out her arms to embrace Becky, heedless of her tender limb. Becky stiffened. Hannah gingerly wrapped her arms around the slender girl, Danny between them. At least she prayed it was Danny. She had yet to get a good look at him.

"Dear, dear Becky. How will I ever thank you? When I returned to Mrs. Beech's and found all the children gone — I thought my heart would tear in two. You remember how that feels, I know, poor dear. Having lost your own little girl."

"My little girl," Becky repeated.

"Yes. Gone to heaven. Safe with God. And now you have saved my son. My Danny. How grateful I am."

Becky looked down at the child, now squirming in her arms.

Hannah's heart surged to glimpse the dear face. "Hello, Danny! How glad I am to see you again. What good care Becky has taken of you. Let me see how big you are." She placed tentative hands on each side of the little body, clamped tightly to Becky's mid-riff.

For a moment the thin arms remained locked.

"He must be growing heavy, Becky. I'll give you a rest, shall I?" Again she forced a smile and inserted her fingers between child and slender girl.

Finally, Becky yielded and Danny was in her arms at last. Ignoring the pain, Hannah held the boy awkwardly in the crook of her splinted arm and turned him toward her, hungry for a good look at him. His face, pinched in discomfort, his nearly bald head, and blotchy cheeks were a masterpiece of beauty to her. It was all she could do not to crumple to the ground in relief. *Thank you, God, thank you, God, thank you, God.* She molded his small warm body to hers, patting his back, instinctively beginning to sway in the ancient dance of comfort. *Thank you!*

A glance at Becky dampened her euphoria. The girl, barely more than a child herself, now hugged herself alone. Face blank, eyes haunted.

Compassion tugged at Hannah. "Becky, what will you do now? Where will you go?"

The girl shrugged. "Don't know."

For the first time Hannah noticed the small carpetbag at the girl's feet. Likely all her worldly possessions. "Will you try to find a new place?" Hannah asked.

Again the shrug. "Mrs. Beech gave me no character. Perhaps I'll work for Mr. Simpkins yet."

"Becky, no . . ." Hannah urged. She thought a moment, then bit her lip. "Is your milk still flowing?"

Becky nodded. "I fed Danny, didn't I? Fed him first so he'd not go hungry."

Cupping Danny's bottom with her good hand, Hannah reached out the other, extending from the sling, and awkwardly patted Becky's arm. "And I am truly grateful."

What should Hannah do? A part of her wanted to distance herself from this pitiful girl as soon as possible. To be on her way, just her and her son. But the reality was her own milk had dried up. And she could ill afford to buy milk to feed Danny. Let alone feed herself.

She didn't even know where she was going or how she would support the two of them. How on earth could she support a third person as well?

Becky looked up at her, the anticipation of disappointment dulling her small dark eyes. "And you, Miss Hannah? Where will you go?"

"I don't know, either."

Becky waited a moment longer, brows high. When Hannah said no more, she deflated, shoulders slumping.

What should she do? Find Fred and ride with him back to Bristol and show up at her father's door — likely only to be turned away? Or go to one of the same poor houses or workhouses where the other children had gone? She shuddered at the thought of any of those fates.

Hannah took a deep breath. "You may come with me, if you like, Becky. I can't guarantee we'll eat or where we'll sleep, but if you're sure you won't be able to find another situation here. . . ."

"Oh, thank you, Miss Hannah. Thank you!"

The girl's face lit as though Hannah had offered her something worthwhile. Becky bent and picked up her threadbare piece of luggage. Hannah hoped she had a spare nappy or two inside.

They had barely stepped from the alley when Hannah gasped and drew up short. There was Edgar Parrish, Nancy trailing behind.

She froze. What to do now? Turn and run . . . with child in arms? Confess all?

"My lady. There you are." Edgar exhaled in relief.

She stood in place, breathless. Caught. "Edgar. What are you doing here? Why are you two not at the Pump Room?"

"After you left, I . . . didn't feel right about you going off alone. I knew Pa wouldn't like it. I was afraid I wouldn't find you. I almost didn't look down this street. . . ."

She forced a light tone. "Yes, well, you needn't have done so."

His gaze shifted to the child in her arms. "Is this your boy?"

"Yes, this is Daniel."

His expression softened. "A handsome lad."

"Thank you."

Edgar looked expectantly at her companion, and then back at her.

Hannah pressed her dry lips together, then said, "And this is Becky Brown. My son's nurse."

He nodded. "Ah."

"Becky, this is Edgar Parrish and his . . . friend, Nancy Smith."

The two young women bobbed curtsies to one another.

Edgar frowned over his shoulder at the ill-kempt house with its peeling paint. "This isn't where you lived, surely."

"No." Hoping to explain the grim neighborhood, Hannah fabricated, "Becky was visiting a poor relation near here. That's why it took me a little longer to find her."

"I see. Is your nurse coming back with us? I can sit on the rear seat with Ben for the return journey; it's no trouble."

Hannah looked from Edgar to Becky. "I . . . am not certain. We were just discussing that very thing."

"But I am coming with you!" Becky's voice rose in a panicked shrill. "You said I could."

But that was before I knew I'd be caught and might have to return to Devonshire, Hannah thought, but she said, "I know, but — you must understand that Lynton is a long way off. Are you sure you want to leave Bath and everyone you know?"

"I have no friends here. Not any more."

Hannah was trapped. Hemmed in on both sides. "Will you excuse us a moment, Mr. Parrish? I wish to speak with Becky in private, before she makes such a big decision."

Edgar pulled a face. "She didn't know where you and Sir John had moved to?"

"I . . . just want her to be certain she wants to come with us."

"We'll wait right here." Edgar held out his arms. "I'll hold Danny for you. Pa wouldn't want you straining that arm."

"Oh." She hesitated. "Thank you, but I don't mind. I've missed him." Had he seen the intention to flee in her eyes?

"Just while the two of you talk," Edgar said. "Give us the chance to become acquainted." He gave a good-natured grin. "I won't have liberty on the way back, as I'll be sitting outside."

How could she refuse him? Biting her lip, she begrudgingly handed over her son. Nancy quickly crowded close, cooing and smiling into Danny's face.

Hannah took Becky's arm and led her several yards away, pausing beside an abandoned barrel.

She spoke in a low voice. "Becky. If you are to come with me, with them, there is something you need to know. Remember the carriage accident I mentioned?"

Vaguely the girl nodded. "Is that how you hurt your arm?"

"Yes. I was traveling with my former employer and his wife. She died in the crash. The doctor who found us thought I was the man's wife. I was insensible for a time, and wasn't even sure who I was for days. Eventually I realized they thought I was the lady of the house. . . ."

"Is that why he called you, 'my lady'?"

"Yes."

"I did wonder."

"I haven't corrected them. It was the only way I could think of to return for Danny. At all events, they all think I am Lady Mayfield. If you come with us, you mustn't give me away. Or use my real name. Ever."

The girl's brow furrowed. "But you can't fool them forever."

"I know. I don't want to. I only want to take care of Danny." The reality of Hannah's situation dawned on her as she spoke. "But here, as myself, I have no post, nowhere to sleep and nothing to eat. In Lynton, I am Lady Mayfield, with a house to sleep in, a position to offer you with wages, and all the food you, Danny, and I need. It will only be until my arm mends and I can find work and someplace for us to live. But I know what I am doing is deceitful and wrong. And I will understand if you want nothing to do with it. If you want to stay here, stay. I would not blame you. But please say nothing to anyone else about this — promise?"

Becky frowned in confusion. "But the husband. Surely he knows you're not his wife."

Hannah shook her head. "He hasn't awakened. The doctor didn't even know if he would live at first, though now he hopes he will."

"But as soon as he wakes up . . ."

Hannah nodded. "Then you and I and Danny will have to leave immediately. I don't think you would get into any trouble for going along with this, but I certainly shall."

Becky thought. "Perhaps we might find new posts a'way out there where nobody knows us."

"That's what I'm hoping. But first you will return with us as Danny's nurse. If you still want to come."

"I've nowhere else to go."

Hannah glanced over at her son in Edgar Parrish's arms. "Neither, it seems, do I."

She turned toward the waiting Edgar and forced a smile. "Becky will be coming with us after all. I hope that is all right."

"Of course. Do we need to go and pick up his belongings?"

She said breezily, "Never mind that. We have sufficient for the journey and will purchase what he needs when we arrive."

For a moment both Nancy and Edgar stared at her, confusion wrinkling their brows.

"A fresh start in his new home," Hannah said brightly. She turned and strode away in the direction of the coaching inn before either of them could ask further questions, though she heard Nancy whispering to Edgar as they walked. Probably something about the wasteful ways of the wealthy. Better that, Hannah thought, than suspecting the truth.

When they arrived at the Westgate, rested horses were harnessed to the hired chaise. When all was ready, Ben helped her, Becky, and Nancy, into the chaise.

Edgar handed Danny in to her. "Now, then." He smiled. "Let's get this fine lad home."

Home . . . The word echoed through Hannah's mind. Lynton was not her home. Nor was Bath. Her father's house in Bristol had once been, but no longer. Would she and Danny ever have a home of their own?

Hannah held her son on a small rug on her lap. As the sun lowered in the sky, they stopped for the night at a coaching inn. Before joining the others for a late supper, she excused herself and stepped into a nearby shop to purchase baby linen for Danny — a clean nightgown, cap, and cloth for nappies. She once again considered leaving young Mr. Parrish and his sweetheart. But the inn was on the outskirts of a small village that did not look promising in terms of employment. Besides, her arm was not yet fit for work. And then there was Becky to consider. Hannah had to resign herself to the uncomfortable notion of returning to Lynton — to the house of Sir John May-field — and taking her chances there.

What if Sir John had awakened? She winced at the thought of Dr. Parrish inform-ing Sir John that his wife had returned to Bath to collect their child.

"Collect our child?" He would say, stupe-fied. "Our child has yet to be born."

After that would follow questions, descrip-tions, and the stunning realization that his wife's companion had the audacity to as-sume his wife's identity. And that his own wife was gone. How hurt and disillusioned kind Dr. Parrish would be, and how furious Sir John. Would she return "home," only to be cast out, or worse, arrested as the fraud she was? What would happen to Danny then?

CHAPTER 7

Back on the road the next day, they passed the village where they'd seen the two women in the stocks. Now the stocks were empty. Even so, a shiver crept up Hannah's spine.

As they passed through Countisbury and neared Clifton, Hannah's palms began to perspire and she found herself breathing shallow and fast. Here, the road seemed to hug the cliffs more tightly, and the chaise seemed to careen too close to the edge. She winced as snatches of memory flashed through her mind — tumbling down, crying out, whipping red cape and whirling windows, glimpses of the channel beyond. . . .

Hannah tensed and searched for a handhold.

"Is this where the accident happened?" she asked, a little catch in her voice.

Nancy looked out the window, studying the passing terrain. "Yes, my lady, very near."

Another shiver passed over Hannah and she held Danny closer.

When the chaise reached Clifton at last, Hannah's heart beat so hard she feared Nancy would hear it. The postilion slowed the horses and brought the chaise to a stop in front of the house. Ben opened the door for them and let down the step. Edgar extended his hand to help Nancy alight. When it was Hannah's turn, she stepped from the carriage on shaky legs, then reached back to take Danny from Becky.

Child firmly in her arms, Hannah turned toward Clifton, holding her breath, pulse tripping unevenly, ready to bolt if need be. Becky stepped down beside her, hovering near. She felt Becky's uncertain gaze return again and again to her profile, but was too anxious to offer any reassurances.

Out from the house came Dr. and Mrs. Parrish, followed by the housekeeper, Mrs. Turrill. She could not make out their expressions — accusation or welcome?

Nancy waved and Edgar lifted a thumb high.

"Here you are," Dr. Parrish called. "You must have made an early start. We were just beginning to look for you."

Her throat tight, Hannah asked, "How is Sir John?"

The physician looked at her, his expression grave . . . but not, she thought, angry.

"About the same. I had hoped for more improvement by now, some good news to welcome you home, but —"

"He has not awakened?"

"I'm afraid not."

Relief. Had she smiled? She hadn't meant to, but she realized Mrs. Parrish was looking at her askance. Hannah hastened to add, "But he lives and that is good news in itself. You can't know how I worried what might await me."

That was perfectly true.

"Yes, we can thank God for that." Mrs. Turrill smiled. "For while there is life there is hope." She came forward and held out her arms. "And here he is, the little man. Hand him over, my lady. I've been waitin' to get a good look at 'im."

Reluctantly, Hannah handed Danny to the housekeeper.

The older woman beamed. "Hello, lover! Aren't you the handsome one? Looks like his mamma he does. Oh, and there's a bit of his pa around his nose and mouth."

Hannah felt heat creep up her neck at the words. She reminded herself that the woman would naturally assume he was Sir John's son.

Mrs. Turrill turned toward the door, carrying Hannah's boy into Sir John Mayfield's house. At the thought, Hannah's knees suddenly wobbled and her head swam.

Dr. Parrish was at her side in an instant. "Steady on, my lady."

Mrs. Parrish added, "Careful Dr. Parrish, she looks ready to swoon."

"I'm sorry," Hannah murmured, embarrassed. "I'm fine, really. I —"

"And no wonder. Such a long journey so soon after your injuries. Come inside, my lady, and let's get you settled. A good meal and a good night's sleep in your own bed, that's what I prescribe."

My own bed, she silently echoed. *The bed I've made for myself, and now must lie in.*

The Parrishes invited her to join them for dinner at the Grange, their quaint thatched house adjacent to the grounds of Clifton. But Hannah claimed fatigue and politely declined. She thanked Edgar and Nancy warmly for helping her retrieve her son. Then, with a chorus of "welcome homes" and "you rest now," Mrs. Parrish, Edgar, and Nancy departed.

Dr. Parrish remained to check on Sir John once more. He opened the door for the women and followed them inside. Danny still in her arms, Mrs. Turrill surveyed

Becky's scrawny figure and ordered her down to the kitchen for tea and toast.

Dr. Parrish invited Hannah to accompany him upstairs to look in on Sir John. Knowing it would be unnatural not to want to see her "husband," she took the doctor's arm and allowed him to help her up the stairs and into Sir John's bedchamber. There, she met the new chamber nurse, Mrs. Weaver, who had arrived while they were gone. Hannah smiled wanly at the woman, who then excused herself to give them privacy.

Dr. Parrish approached the bed, but Hannah held back, watching from a distance as the physician performed his usual routine, checking Sir John's eyes, his heart rate, his breathing.

When he finished, Hannah stepped nearer and looked down at the injured man. His whiskers had grown a little longer, while his swelling had subsided somewhat. Even if it was wrong of her to be relieved he had yet to regain his senses, she was sincerely glad he still lived. *It's all right,* she said to him silently. *I've got my son back. You can wake up now.*

Dr. Parrish turned to her. "I'll have a look at your arm, if you don't mind. Make sure nothing's gone awry during the journey."

"Very well." She sat in the chair he indicated while he checked the condition of the stiff bandages, the circulation in her hand, and palpated her upper arm above the sling.

"Still tender?"

She bit back a yelp. "A little."

He tilted her chin and looked into her eyes. "Any headaches?"

Her head had pounded with tension all day. "A small one."

"I'll give you something for it. Take it the next time you eat something and try to get a good night's sleep."

"I shall. Thank you."

He smiled at her, patted her good arm, and then took his leave, following his family home.

Hannah went to find Danny. Belowstairs, she found Mrs. Turrill and the kitchen maid filling a small tub with warm water. Together they bathed her son and dressed him in the clean things Hannah had purchased. If the housekeeper had noticed that Danny had smelled less than sweet, she'd been too polite to comment.

"We shall have to do some sewing and shopping," the housekeeper said. "Get this lad a few new things. I've taken the liberty of bringing in my old cradle I'd stored away in the cottage I share with my sister. No doubt you'll want to get something finer, but for now . . ."

"I am sure it will do perfectly well, Mrs. Turrill. Thank you so much." She was glad the housekeeper did not press her about why they had not brought more supplies nor asked her to prepare a nursery before their arrival. Apparently the kind woman assumed Sir John's decision to bring no servants also explained why they had brought no furnishings and scant clothing for the child. How strange and thoughtless she must think them.

While the kitchen maid dumped the water, the other women went upstairs to the small room Mrs. Turrill had begun fitting out as a nursery. There, she had arranged the cradle, along with a side table, dressing chest, and rocking chair. She asked Ben to help her carry in a single bed for Becky. White lace curtains and a cheerful braided rug brightened the room.

"It's lovely, Mrs. Turrill. Thank you."

"Becky, why don't you put your things in this dressing chest as well. Or if you prefer, we can bring in another from one of the other rooms."

Becky shook her head saying timidly, "That's all right. I don't want to be no trouble."

"No trouble at all, Becky. This room is

yours and Danny's now. Or, if you'd like your own room, there is a spare one just next door."

"A whole room, just for me? Oh, no. I wouldn't know what to do with myself."

Again Hannah found the housekeeper studying Becky. She then shifted her gaze to Hannah, her brows high with questions.

Hannah ignored them.

Once they had put away Danny's few things, Mrs. Turrill asked Becky to run downstairs to fill the pitcher for the basin. When the girl had hurried from the room to do her bidding, the woman turned to Hannah and asked, "My lady, I am curious. A girl like Becky. Sweet to be sure but a little . . . well, simple. Lost. How is it you came to engage her as Danny's nurse?"

Hannah's pulse quickened. Though living a lie, she hated each falsehood she uttered. What could she say that was truthful without mentioning the maternity home? Recollecting the haunted look on Becky's face when she found her in the alley, Hannah swallowed and said, "Becky needed us . . . needed Danny . . . as much as we needed her."

Mrs. Turrill considered her reply, expression somber. "Her wee one died, is that it?"

Hannah nodded. "A little girl."

The housekeeper nodded her understanding. "She's barely more than a girl herself. I'm surprised her family could part with her."

"She hasn't any family that I know of. I believe she is all alone in the world."

The housekeeper's dark eyes misted. "Well, she is not alone any longer."

Late that afternoon, Hannah ate a simple meal in the dining parlor alone. She had offered to eat her meals in the small servant's hall with the others, but Mrs. Turrill would not hear of it.

Afterward, Hannah went upstairs and kept Becky company while she nursed Danny. When the girl began repositioning her dress, Hannah rose and gently took Danny from her.

"You go to bed, Becky. I'll rock Danny until he falls asleep."

"But I'm the nurse; I'm to do that. Mrs. Turrill says I need to learn the duties of a proper wet nurse."

"And you shall. But tonight you look ready to drop from exhaustion. You go to bed and get some rest."

Becky complied. While Hannah gingerly gathered Danny in her good arm and settled into the rocking chair, Becky stripped down to her shift and climbed into bed. Hannah made a mental note to provide Becky with a nightdress as soon as she could.

Pulling the bedclothes up to her chin, Becky said wistfully, "Mrs. Turrill is nice, isn't she?"

"Yes. Very."

"It's strange to hear her call you 'my lady' or 'Lady Mayfield.'"

Hannah quickly glanced toward the door, then whispered, "Becky, you mustn't speak of it, remember. That is my name here. You, too, must call me 'my lady' or 'ma'am.'"

Becky sighed. "I'll try, Miss Hannah." She closed her eyes and said no more.

Heaven help me, Hannah thought. Her secret was in this poor girl's hands.

The night passed uneventfully, and Hannah began to breathe a little easier. She enjoyed her breakfast in the sunny dining parlor, strolled through the garden, and then returned to check on Danny. A short while later, Mrs. Turrill came up and found her in the nursery, where Hannah sat rocking Danny and talking quietly to Becky.

"A gentleman is here, my lady," she began, her usual smile absent, "asking, or rather demanding, to see the lady of the house."

Hannah started. "Who is it?"

"He refuses to give his name. Shall I send him away?"

Who would refuse to identify himself, and why? Hannah wondered. She felt Becky's panicked look, but ignored it, forcing her own voice to remain calm. "Did you tell him about the accident? That Sir John is . . . incapacitated?"

"I told him nothing, my lady. He never asked about Sir John. Only you."

"How odd." Hannah's thoughts whirled. "What does he look like?"

She shrugged. "Dark curly hair. Handsome, in his way. He's dressed like a gentleman." Mrs. Turrill sniffed. "Though his manner contradicts that impression."

Hannah's stomach churned. Could it be? The description, though not specific, could easily describe Lady Mayfield's lover, Mr. Anthony Fontaine. If so, how had he discovered where they'd gone, and relatively quickly, too? Hannah knew she could not refuse to see him, for Marianna would never have done so. And he was unlikely to leave after one refusal. He would probably assume Sir John was preventing his wife from seeing him, and dig in his heels.

Did Mr. Fontaine deserve to know his lover had died? Hannah owed him nothing, yet she didn't want the man hanging about, causing trouble for them all.

She rose and handed Danny to Becky. "I shall see him, Mrs. Turrill."

Mrs. Turrill studied her face. "Shall I go in with you?"

"No, thank you. If it is who I think it is, it is best that I speak to him privately. Find a way to gently tell him about the accident. The . . . drowning."

Her expression softened. "A friend of that poor girl's, is he?"

"If it is who I believe it is, yes."

Mrs. Turrill followed as far as the drawing room. Hannah peeked through the narrow crack between the double doors. Inside, facing the windows stood Anthony Fontaine, unmistakable in profile. Roman nose, dark curls falling over his brow, brooding, yet undeniably attractive.

Hannah faced Mrs. Turrill. "It's all right," she whispered. "I know him." She hoped the woman would not eavesdrop at the door.

She waited until Mrs. Turrill nodded in reply and turned away.

Standing there, Hannah thought back to the times she had been in Mr. Fontaine's company. Usually Lady Mayfield went out on some pretense to meet him. But on the rare evening Sir John was at his club or away at one of his other properties, Marianna often invited friends over. Usually female friends or a couple. But on a few occasions, she had been brazen enough to invite *him* to Sir John's Bristol house.

Hannah recalled one evening only too well. . . .

When Hopkins announced his arrival, Mr. Fontaine bowed to Lady Mayfield as though a mere acquaintance. "Good evening, Lady Mayfield. Thank you for your gracious invitation."

"And where is Mrs. Fontaine?" Marianna asked.

"My dear wife is at home and plans to go to bed early." With a glance at the footman arranging decanters on the sideboard, he added, "But she insisted I come. How rude it would be, she said, were we both to disappoint Lady Mayfield when she so kindly, and unexpectedly, invited us."

"I do hope Mrs. Fontaine is not unwell."

"A trifling malady, I assure you. A cool drink and a warm bed are all she longs for on this chilly night."

Lady Mayfield coyly dipped her head. "All she longs for?"

Hannah rose to excuse herself, but Lady Mayfield insisted she stay. Hannah knew why — so the servants wouldn't spread gossip of their tête-à-tête from servants' hall to servants' hall. If they did, all of Bristol would soon know she had entertained a man alone in her husband's absence. There were enough rumors about Lady Mayfield and Anthony Fontaine as it was.

Hannah had begrudgingly complied, sinking back into her corner chair and picking up her needlework once more. But it was difficult to concentrate. Her gaze flitted over to the couple more often than it should have. The two sat close together on the sofa, sipping from glasses of port, heads bent near in private conversation. Had he just kissed her cheek . . . her ear? Hannah looked down and realized she had made a mess of her last several stitches and would need to pick them out.

Mr. Fontaine's hand lifted from the arm of the sofa to stroke Lady Mayfield's gown-covered knee. Marianna's eyes flashed to Hannah and caught her looking, but she did not scowl or demand her to leave. Rather she grinned, mischief dancing in her big brown eyes.

Hannah looked away first.

Lady Mayfield was not only beautiful, but well-endowed. A fact emphasized by the low neckline of her evening gown and her excellent stays. When Hannah next looked up, she noticed Anthony Fontaine's gaze linger on her bosom. Then a finger followed suit.

Hannah rose abruptly. "I am sorry my lady, but I would like to retire."

"Oh come, Hannah. What a prude you are. Very well, if you must. But slip through the side door so the servants don't see you leaving."

Anthony Fontaine winked at her.

Blindly Hannah slipped from the room. She retreated to her bedchamber upstairs, trying hard not to imagine what was happening in the room below. . . .

And now Anthony Fontaine was here in the Clifton drawing room. Hoping to see Marianna. How could he fail to expose her? Heaven help her, this would not be easy.

Taking a deep breath, Hannah opened the double doors, closed them behind her, and faced Lady Mayfield's lover. She was glad she wore a nondescript muslin, and not one of Marianna's more memorable gowns.

Mr. Fontaine turned, surprise crossing his handsome face. "Miss Rogers?" He frowned, then bowed dutifully. "I did not expect to see you here. I asked for the lady of the house."

Hannah put a finger to her lips. "Please, keep your voice down."

"Where is she?" he demanded, hands on hips.

"Won't you sit down?"

"I will not." He ran an agitated hand through his forelock. "Does he forbid her to come down?"

"If by 'he' you mean Sir John, he forbids nothing." For some reason, Hannah was reticent to reveal Sir John's weak state to this particular man. His foe. "She cannot come, because she is not here."

He scowled. "Don't try to fob me off. I know this is where he brought her. I have already been to his other properties. Go and tell her I am here."

"Please, sit down."

"I won't. Not until you tell me where she is."

Hannah took a deep breath. "I'm afraid there has been a terrible accident."

His eyes flew to hers, alert. Tense.

"On the journey here, we drove through a storm. The carriage slipped from the road, fell over the cliff, and landed partway into the sea."

"Good heavens." He visibly stiffened, preparing for a blow.

Hannah dreaded telling him. "The doctor says she likely died on impact and did not suffer."

He gaped at her, then slowly sank to the sofa, crumpling the hat brim in his hands. Then abruptly his eyes hardened. "Are you fabricating this tale to trick me into leaving?"

She lifted her splinted arm, then pulled back the hair from her brow to reveal the jagged line on her forehead. "No. The accident was all too real."

He looked down at his hands. When he next spoke, it was in a whisper. "Where is she?" The same words, but now seeking a different sort of answer.

She hesitated. "I am afraid her body has not yet been recovered."

His head snapped up. "Then how do you know she is dead?"

"The doctor and his son saw a figure floating away as the tide receded. A figure in a red cloak. Marianna wore hers that day, I remember. They believe she was thrown from the carriage as it fell, or that the tide drew her from a broad hole in its side."

His mouth parted, incredulous. "And where was *he*?" His lip curled. "Probably threw her over the cliff himself."

She shook her head. "Sir John was insensible as was I. In fact . . ." She hesitated. "Sir John has yet to awaken."

"But . . . it's been what — eleven or twelve days?"

She nodded. "About that."

"Will he live?"

"The doctor hopes so, but is not certain."

His handsome face contorted. "I hope he dies. I hope he suffers for all eternity."

Several moments passed in strained silence broken only by the ticking of the long-case clock.

Then he glanced at her, sullen. "She did not mention you. When did you return?"

"The day they left Bath."

He nodded, looking across the room at nothing. "I am glad you were with her. She was always fond of you."

Guilt pricked Hannah. She could not say the same.

He rose, still twisting the hat brim, unable now to meet her eyes. "It's his fault, you know. Not mine. It's not my fault."

Strange that he should feel guilty, though she supposed he *was* at least in part to blame for the move in the first place, the hurry, though not the wreck itself. But who was she to absolve anybody?

He turned toward the window, countenance bleak. "Marianna can't be . . . gone. I would know it. In my heart, I would know it."

She was surprised at how genuine his grief appeared. Perhaps it had been more than an affair after all — more than physical attraction. Though Hannah resented this man for Sir John's sake, he had done nothing to her personally. She said softly, "I am sorry, Mr. Fontaine. Truly."

He stood there, staring blindly through the wavy glass, making no move to leave.

Tentatively, she asked, "May I offer you some refreshment before you go? You must be tired after your journey."

"No. I could not eat or drink." He fumbled for a card in his coat pocket and gave it to her with trembling hands. "If you hear anything. If her — If she is found. Please write and let me know."

Hannah didn't plan to be there much longer, but she could not very well refuse the stricken man's request. "Very well."

"Thank you," he whispered, and stumbled from the room and out of the house looking dazed and lost.

Hannah stood at the front windows watching him wander away toward town. Mrs. Turrill joined her at the window. "Took it hard, did he?"

"Yes," Hannah agreed. "Very hard."

CHAPTER 8

The next day, Hannah awoke to find Mrs. Turrill folding back her shutters. Then the housekeeper turned, opened the wardrobe, and began perusing its contents.

Hannah sat up in bed, favoring her wrapped arm. She noticed the tray of hot chocolate and toast on her bedside table.

Mrs. Turrill followed her gaze. "I thought you might like a little something straight away. You ate so little yesterday."

"Thank you. You do too much for me, Mrs. Turrill." Hannah sipped her chocolate.

"Yes, I do." The woman gave her a saucy wink. "It's why I have engaged a housemaid to start tomorrow. Her name is Kitty. I hope you don't mind."

"Of course not. You need the help, managing the house and helping to care for me as you do." Hannah nibbled a bite of toasted bread.

"It's been my pleasure." She looked back

133

inside the wardrobe. "My lady, you've been wearing those same two frocks since you've been up and about. Let's try one of your other pretty gowns today."

Marianna's pretty gowns, Hannah reminded herself. Since the accident, she had rotated between two of Marianna's older, simple day dresses — insisting they were the easiest to slip over her wrapped arm.

Mrs. Turrill pulled forth a dress of lilac sarcenet. "How about this frock? It must look so well with your coloring."

Hannah eyed the crossover bodice warily. "Oh. That's all right, Mrs. Turrill. I have no need to dress especially well today."

"Now, I insist. Mrs. Parrish and the vicar's wife are coming for tea this afternoon, remember?"

Were they? How had she forgotten? "I . . . I am not sure. . . ."

"Oh, do humor me, my lady. It is a pity to neglect such pretty things."

Hannah climbed unsteadily from the bed and began washing for the day. She allowed Mrs. Turrill to help her lace her stays and tie her stockings. When the housekeeper lifted the lilac dress, Hannah tried to demur once more. "Really, I don't think the gown will suit me. I . . ."

Ignoring her protests, Mrs. Turrill slid it

over her head and shoulders. Nervously, Hannah put her good arm through one sleeve, then Mrs. Turrill helped her carefully and gently manipulate her wrapped arm though the other. Hannah stood, facing the mirror, as Mrs. Turrill began working the fastenings behind.

Hannah's palms began to perspire. She knew that she and Lady Mayfield were not the same build. Hannah was slightly taller and more slender, while Marianna had been far curvier. The nightdresses, shifts, and adjustable stays were forgiving, but this formfitting dress, made for and tailored to Marianna's measurements would surely give her away.

"I have not worn this gown before," she mumbled. Perfectly true.

Mrs. Turrill asked, "Recently made, was it?"

"Mm-hm."

Finished with the fastenings, Mrs. Turrill looked over Hannah's shoulder into the long cheval looking glass. She pulled at the ribbon-trimmed waistline and at the extra material crossing Hannah's small chest. "It doesn't fit you very well, my lady." She frowned. "Have you lost weight since your last fitting?"

"Since giving birth, yes. In the bosom,

especially."

The housekeeper's brow puckered. "I'm not a dab hand with the needle, I fear. Not with something so fine."

"Never mind, Mrs. Turrill. I shall give it a go as soon as I regain use of both hands. But for now, perhaps the sprigged muslin? That one will . . . still . . . fit me, I think."

Later that morning, Edgar Parrish knocked on the open nursery door. In his arms, he carried a box of baby things, saved from his own childhood — tiny gowns, caps, and stockings, a finely knit blanket, and a gnarled stuffed rabbit.

Hannah protested, "But you'll want these for your own children someday."

"Someday, my lady. But not today."

"That is kind of you, Edgar. But I'm afraid we'll spoil them."

He shrugged easily and glanced around the nursery. "I know it's been hard for you to set up a place for Danny here, what with your arm and your headaches."

Must they all be so kind to her?

Hannah said, "I hope your mother doesn't mind."

A flicker of hesitation crossed his face. "No . . . Though she didn't think a lady like yourself would accept such humble offerings."

"Of course I will. And gratefully."

She smiled at him and he returned the gesture.

When he left the room a few minutes later, Becky stepped to the window to watch him go. "Edgar is surely handsome, ain't he?"

"I suppose so." Hannah began sorting through the articles in the box. When Becky remained silent Hannah looked up. The wistful expression on the girl's face disquieted her.

She said gently, "Becky, you know he and Nancy are courting, don't you?"

Becky shrugged her thin shoulders. "Well, they ain't married yet."

"No. Not yet."

"Not ever, if I have my way." She gave a little giggle.

"Becky, be careful. The Parrishes have been very kind to us."

"What has that to say to anything? Mrs. Parrish don't approve of Nancy. It's plain as day she don't. So who's to say they'll marry?"

Mrs. Parrish doesn't approve of anyone, Hannah thought. But she said only, "Becky, we shall not be staying here much longer.

Don't go forming attachments that cannot last."

Perhaps she ought to take her own advice, Hannah thought, for she was already fond of Dr. Parrish and Mrs. Turrill, and knew both of them doted on her. She hated the fact that she would soon disillusion them, disappoint them, and sink in their estimations. But would it not become only more difficult the longer she allowed this act to go on? Oh, if only her arm would heal so she could leave. But Dr. Parrish thought it might take six weeks to heal fully and two had barely passed. Even then, would she really just steal away with Danny and Becky without a word of explanation to anyone? How Dr. Parrish and dear Mrs. Turrill would worry. Probably even gather a search party. No. At the very least she would need to leave behind a letter, explaining. Apologizing. And hope they might understand and somehow forgive her.

But a letter seemed so cowardly. How much better to come out with it, to explain, to admit she had been wrong, but hope they could see that her motivation had not been self-gain, but the preservation of her child. How Mrs. Parrish would gloat and rail. Edgar would be hurt, as would his father. Mrs. Turrill? She had no idea how the kindly

138

woman might react, but somehow Hannah thought she would be the most understanding of them all. At least she hoped she would be.

After wrestling with herself all morning, Hannah made her decision. She would confess all to Dr. Parrish. She hoped to catch him in the hall, but by the time she gathered her courage, she heard the door to Sir John's bedchamber open and close. Taking a deep breath, she left her room and walked across the landing. She knocked and let herself in.

Dr. Parrish was bent low, ear pressed to Sir John's chest, listening. He glanced up when she entered.

Hannah grimaced in apology and waited near the door. From there, Sir John looked much the same as he had before, his eyes still closed.

A few moments later, Dr. Parrish lifted his head and straightened. "Hello, my lady. Come to see how Sir John fares this afternoon?" He turned to search for something in his medical bag. When she made no reply, nor moved to join him at the bedside, he looked at her over his shoulder. "Did you need something?"

She licked dry lips, heart pounding.

He turned to face her, expression concerned, clearly sensing her anxiety. "Is everything all right?"

"No." She swallowed and shook her head. "Dr. Parrish, I need to tell you something."

He tucked his chin. "Oh?"

She clasped her hands tightly. "Do you remember finding us — Sir John and me — in the overturned carriage? Rescuing us?"

"Of course I remember. Far better than you do, I imagine." He smiled.

"Yes, of course. But do you remember when you first called me 'Lady Mayfield'?"

His brow puckered in thought. "I don't recall exactly. Though I know I did call down to you to let you know Edgar and I were there to help."

"Yes. You see, you kindly assumed that I was Lady Mayfield, when I . . ."

Her words fell away, her breath hitched. She stared past Dr. Parrish into the eyes of Sir John Mayfield.

"When you were . . . what?" Dr. Parrish prompted kindly.

But Hannah could not remove her gaze from Sir John's. She grasped the doctor's arm. "His eyes are open."

He whirled toward the bed.

"My goodness. You're right! Well, hello, Sir John." Dr. Parrish stepped forward, then turned his head. "My lady, I wonder if you would be so good as to introduce us?"

"Oh." Hannah hesitated. "Of course. Sir John, may I present Dr. George Parrish, who has been caring for you since the accident. Dr. Parrish, Sir John Mayfield."

"How do you do, sir?" Dr. Parrish smiled, but she noticed how his eyes roved his patient's face, gauging his reaction. There wasn't one, at least nothing she could see.

"If I may, Sir John, I am going to take your hand." The doctor did so. "If you are able, please squeeze my hand in return."

Sir John's eyes did not move to follow the doctor's movements. They seemed fixed on her — or was he merely staring blindly in her direction? She wanted to move away from that disconcerting, blank gaze, but felt rooted to the spot.

Apparently Sir John did not perform the doctor's request.

"That's all right. There's plenty of time for that later. We are very happy to see you open your eyes. You have been, shall we say, asleep, for nearly a fortnight."

Was that the slightest flicker of his eyes, or merely an instinctive blink?

Hannah whispered, "Is he aware, or . . . ?"

Dr. Parrish raised a hand and snapped his fingers before Sir John's eyes. No reaction.

"It doesn't seem so. Perhaps the muscles

141

of his eyelids simply contracted, opened, of their own accord." As if on cue, Sir John's eyes drifted closed once more. "Still, it is something new. A good sign, I think."

Dr. Parrish continued his examination, while Hannah chewed her lip . . . and her options.

He straightened. "Well, I must go tell his nurse and Mrs. Parrish. If you wouldn't mind sitting with him until Mrs. Weaver returns? I'll send her up directly." At the door, he turned back. "I'm sorry, my lady. What was it you wanted to tell me?"

Hannah's lips parted, then she pressed them together once more. "Um. Never mind. In light of this, it was nothing. I shall tell you later."

He gave her a distracted smile and hurried away.

Hannah had lost her opportunity. And her courage.

Perhaps it was a sign, Hannah decided. A sign she should leave a letter instead of trying to tell Dr. Parrish in person.

But first, Hannah had to face a visit with Mrs. Parrish and an introduction to the vicar's wife. Hannah had suggested Mrs. Turrill join the ladies for tea — she was a relative after all — but Mrs. Turrill said it wasn't her place.

At the appointed hour, the ladies arrived and were seated in the drawing room. Mrs. Turrill quietly served the tea, ignoring Mrs. Parrish's patronizing smile, and quickly departed.

The vicar's wife, Mrs. Barton, seemed a pleasant, timid little thing, Hannah decided. A perfect foil for confident and outspoken Mrs. Parrish.

The ladies sipped tea and chewed dainty bites of butter biscuits. Then Mrs. Barton said, "My lady, may I ask which church you attended in Bath?"

"Oh . . ." Hannah hesitated. "I . . . that is, I'm afraid we rarely attended in Bath." Hurrying to redeem herself, she added, "But as a girl I spent a great deal of time in church in Bristol. My father was a . . ." She stopped, realizing she was about to answer as herself, and not as Marianna. "A churchgoer," she finished lamely.

"Ah . . ." Mrs. Barton nodded faintly, clearly unsure what to say to that.

Mrs. Parrish rolled her eyes.

After that, Hannah spoke as little as possible, afraid to make another mistake, no doubt disappointing her guests and proving herself a poor hostess.

Mrs. Parrish took over the conversation,

explaining that she had a few friends in Bath, and was sure Lady Mayfield must have heard of them.

"Lady Mayfield" had not. Hannah could, at least, speak with confidence about their former life in Bristol, and the area of Bath where they had resided — the fashionable Camden Place. But could she not tell them of the previous season's famous newcomers and social events? No, she was afraid she could not.

After an hour of tedious conversation about her supposed life and Bath society, Hannah's nerves were frayed and she felt exhausted. Perhaps realizing this, the vicar's wife changed the subject, asking if she might meet her son. Relieved to oblige, Hannah brought Danny down from the nursery, and the ladies politely praised him. They soon after took their leave.

When they had gone, Mrs. Turrill asked her, "How did it go?"

"I failed to impress them, I'm afraid."

"There's no need to impress anyone here, my lady. Just be yourself."

Ah. If only she could.

Hannah went to bed early that night, suffering from her worst headache in days.

The next morning, Hannah began her letter.

Dear Dr. and Mrs. Parrish, and Mrs. Turrill,
I have left Clifton and taken Danny and Becky with me. You will no doubt be surprised, but please do not be anxious. . . .

Hannah paused. Why should they not be anxious? She was certainly anxious. She still didn't know where they were going. Where might she find work — and work that paid enough for lodgings as well as food?

Someone knocked sharply at her door. She jumped and quickly hid the letter under the blotter.

"Lady Mayfield?" Dr. Parrish's voice. "It's Sir John. His eyes are open again. He seems more responsive."

Dread snaked down her spine and pooled in her stomach. Why had she not confessed to Dr. Parrish before? She stood on shaky legs and opened her door. "He's awake?"

"Come and see."

He gestured for her to precede him across the passage with such hope in his eyes. Every instinct told her to flee, to turn and run the other way. To gather Danny and

Becky and leave Clifton that very moment before Sir John could denounce her. Instead she numbly allowed Dr. Parrish to usher her into the sickroom. To her unveiling.

Again, the chamber nurse excused herself. Much as before, Sir John's eyes were open and vaguely focused.

"Good. His eyes are still open," the physician began. "I am not certain if he is fully sensible or not. He has yet to speak, but he did seem agitated when I first arrived."

Hannah fisted her good hand, nails pricking her palm. She would have remained several feet from the bed, had Dr. Parrish not gently urged her forward.

"Here she is, Sir John. Here is your wife. You see she is well. Nothing to worry about save getting better yourself."

Hannah's throat tightened. Sir John's eyes shifted to her, and her heart pounded in fear. She pressed a damp hand to her abdomen, and told herself to breathe.

She would try to explain. Not to excuse herself, but to apologize . . .

He stared at her with eyes a changeable silvery blue, like a deep, cold lake. A flicker of a frown tinged his brow, then as quickly passed. Displeasure, confusion, or both?

She held herself stiffly, every muscle tense, waiting for him to scowl and say, *"She is not my wife."*

"Come, my lady," Dr. Parrish urged. "Come and speak to him."

She faltered. "I . . . I don't know what to say. Why does he not speak?"

"Perhaps he cannot. His brain is not yet fully recovered. Perhaps he is still fighting to regain his memory as you did. Encourage him. Remind him who he is. Who you are."

What different words she would have spoken had Dr. Parrish not been standing there — confession, begging forgiveness, for secrecy until she might steal away . . .

"You are Sir John Mayfield," she began instead. "Lately of Bath and before that Bristol. Do you remember Bath? The lovely house in Camden Place? And Bristol — the house on Great George street? That was where I first became acquainted with your . . . household."

He only stared at her dully.

"Remind him who you are," Dr. Parrish whispered.

She hesitated. "And of course you know me," she uttered feebly. The words *"I am your wife."* Or, *"I am Marianna, Lady Mayfield,"* refused to come. She felt that if she forced out those words, she would lose her breakfast in the bargain.

Dr. Parrish leaned nearer Sir John. "And of course you know this is Lady Mayfield, your wife."

Sir John's eyes moved slowly from her face to the doctor's without change in expression.

The doctor turned back to her. "Tell him about Danny, how he fares, that he is here. . . ."

"Oh." She swallowed. Must she? Sir John didn't even know of the child. "Yes. You see, I have returned to Bath and collected little Daniel and his nurse. I was so relieved to find him."

She felt Dr. Parrish's stunned gaze on her profile, and hastened to add, "In good health. To find him in good health and faring well. I am so thankful he is here with me, with us, once again. Mrs. Turrill has taken quite a liking to him, but then, you are not yet acquainted with our housekeeper, so I will say no more of her for now."

How inane she was! Her mind felt as unfocused as Sir John's glassy stare.

"Perhaps we should bring in wee Danny to see his father?"

She hesitated once more. "Um . . . he is napping at present. Perhaps another time."

"Ah, yes. I'm afraid we have tired Sir John as it is." He patted the man's arm. "You rest now, sir. And don't worry. The human brain is a marvelous thing and you will no doubt be right as a trivet in no time. And when you are, your wife and son will be here to welcome you back."

Dr. Parrish smiled up at her and Hannah forced a half smile in return. But she was quite certain neither wife nor child would be there if and when Sir John returned to himself.

She thanked Dr. Parrish and returned to her room, trembling all over. She had escaped the noose for now. A scapegrace, by every measure. *Oh, God. Will you ever forgive me?* she asked silently. *What shall I do?* For she knew very well she wouldn't avoid discovery much longer. Every hour she stayed, she compounded her crime and worsened the fate that awaited her.

CHAPTER 9

Hannah went upstairs to the nursery to talk to Becky. To begin easing the way toward their inevitable departure. But when she entered, she found Mrs. Turrill in the room as well, Danny in her arms, bouncing him gently and smiling into his face.

Becky turned as she entered. "Hello, Miss Hannah."

Hannah froze. She locked stunned gazes with Becky, and the girl's face paled.

Mrs. Turrill turned to frown at the young nurse. Whatever she saw on Becky's face made her frown deepen. "Why do you call Lady Mayfield 'Miss Hannah'?"

Becky stood there blinking, mouth ajar.

"We don't call our betters by their Christian names, unless we've been invited to do so. Besides, I believe Lady Mayfield's given name is Marianna."

Becky faltered, "I . . . I forgot."

Hannah's mind rushed to formulate a

plausible explanation. "Did she say Hannah?" she asked lightly. "I thought she said, 'Anna.' Short for Marianna, perhaps, or . . . was Anna the name of your little girl, Becky? Is that it? Were you thinking of her and said her name by mistake?"

Now Mrs. Turrill's perplexed frown shifted to Hannah.

Hannah's pulse pounded. What a muddle.

"Anna?" Becky murmured, as if trying the name on her tongue and seeing how it tasted. "Anna is a pretty name and would 'ave suited her. Never saw a more beautiful creature than my wee girl."

"And you will see her again, Becky. In heaven." Hannah soothed. "She's in God's care now, healthy and happy."

"How can she be happy? Without me?" Becky's chin quivered.

Oh, dear. She had said the wrong thing. Hannah added quickly, "Because she knows she will see you again someday. How she must look forward to it."

"Then perhaps I should join her soon," the girl said. "Perhaps I —"

"No, Becky. Never say so. We need you *here,* Danny and I."

"And I," Mrs. Turrill added earnestly. "Like my own daughter you are."

Becky turned to the woman, wide-eyed.

151

"Really? How kind you are, Mrs. Turrill. Never was my own mum half so kind as you are. Though I oughtn't to speak ill of the dead, I know."

"Come now, Becky dear. Let us speak of only happy things for the rest of the day, shall we?" Mrs. Turrill squeezed her arm. "And you may be the first to taste my fresh batch of toffee."

"May I? Oh, thank you."

Hannah released a ragged breath. The second noose dodged in as many days. Though the speculative look in Mrs. Turrill's eyes had unsettled Hannah. She wasn't sure the housekeeper had been fooled.

Stepping from the room, Hannah nearly ran into Mrs. Parrish in the passage. *Oh no.* Her heart sank. How long had the woman been standing there?

"Just letting you know I'm heading into town, if you need anything." She glanced through the door at Becky and then back again.

Hannah forced a smile. "No, we have all we need, thank you."

Mrs. Parrish nodded and turned toward the stairs, leaving Hannah to wonder how much the doctor's wife had overheard.

Either way, Hannah knew it was time to plan their escape, arm healed or not.

Part of Hannah dreaded the prospect of setting off for an unknown future. Another part of her was as anxious to leave as a goose with its neck stretched on the chopping block.

Over the next two days, Hannah took in the waist of one of Marianna's spencer jackets to fit her, and discreetly began to gather the things she would take with them when they left. Only necessities and as few of Marianna's belongings as possible. If her own things had not been lost, she would take nothing for herself that had not belonged to her. But she could not leave without proper clothing. Besides, Marianna no longer had need of them.

The next afternoon, Mrs. Turrill knocked and announced through the closed door, "There's a man to see Sir John, my lady."

Hannah's nerves jangled in alarm — had Mr. Fontaine returned? With her shoe, Hannah nudged the partially filled valise under the bed and went to open the door. She gestured Mrs. Turrill inside and closed the door behind her.

"The same man as before?" she asked.

"No. A Mr. James Lowden."

Lowden? The name rang a distant bell in Hannah's memory, but she could not place it. Surely it wasn't anyone of their acquaintance. Had not Sir John kept their destination a secret? Of course, Mr. Fontaine had managed to find them, and fairly quickly.

"Did you tell him why Sir John is unable to receive him?"

"No, my lady. I thought it best coming from you."

She wondered if this Mr. Lowden was acquainted with Lady Mayfield.

"Please tell Mr. Lowden Sir John is unable to receive him at present and ask his business, if you please."

Mrs. Turrill hesitated, a slight frown creasing her brow, likely wondering why her mistress didn't ask him herself, but too polite to ask. "Very well, my lady."

While the housekeeper was gone, Hannah paced. Now what? Why hadn't she left earlier as she knew she should have?

Mrs. Turrill returned a few minutes later and handed her a calling card. "Says he's Sir John's solicitor. From Bristol."

Hannah's thoughts whirled. Had Sir John informed his solicitor of their whereabouts? Or had the accident been reported in the newspaper and the man had come on his own initiative? She asked, "How did he hear of the accident?"

"I don't think he has. Says he's come on

some matters of business. He seemed perplexed when I told him Sir John was unable to receive him, and asked to see you instead. By the way, he rode his own horse, so Ben's tending to it in the stable. Heaven knows if there's even any feed in there. We shall have to borrow some from the Parrishes. . . ."

But Hannah wasn't really listening. Instead, she stared down at the card, heart thumping hard.

JAMES LOWDEN
MESSRS. LOWDEN & LOWDEN,
ATTORNEYS AND SOLICITORS
7 QUEEN'S PARADE, BRISTOL

She squinted at the print, as though to conjure the man's face on the card. Had she met Sir John's solicitor? Again the distant ring of the memory bell. She believed she had glimpsed the solicitor back in the Mayfields' Bristol house, but only the vaguest recollection remained. An older gentleman, well-dressed. Had he seen *her*? Not likely. Would he have met Lady Mayfield? Very likely.

Now what?

There was no way she could gather Danny and Becky and their things from the nursery and sneak off now, not with Mrs. Turrill standing there regarding her anxiously, and Mr. Lowden waiting downstairs.

There was nothing for it. "Very well, Mrs. Turrill. I will see him." She cloaked her fear and said as casually as she could, "I hope he will not regret coming all this way in vain."

Mrs. Turrill nodded and opened the door for her.

Hannah slowly descended the stairs, pulse pounding double time. As she entered the drawing room, she pressed a hand to her chest and took a shaky breath.

The man who rose when she entered was nothing as she'd expected. He was neither old nor silver-haired nor vaguely familiar. She was quite certain she had never laid eyes on him before in her life. He was a handsome man in his early to mid-thirties with golden brown hair, darker side-whiskers, and striking green eyes. He wore riding boots, dark coat . . . and a frown.

For a moment he simply stared at her, hard. Did he know she was not Marianna Mayfield?

Her throat dry, she said, "Mr. Lowden. How do you do?"

He winced in apparent disbelief. "Lady . . . Mayfield?"

She cradled her wrapped arm with her

free hand. "I'm afraid you have come to us at an unfortunate time."

"Your housekeeper mentioned Sir John was indisposed. Ill, I take it? Nothing serious I hope."

"Unfortunately I must disappoint you. We were in a carriage accident on the journey here. Sir John has suffered terrible injuries. He only opened his eyes a few days ago. And has yet to speak."

The man looked thunderstruck. "Good heavens. Why did no one tell me? Will he recover? Has a physician been called?"

His questions tumbled out one after another and Hannah answered them quietly and carefully.

At last Mr. Lowden exhaled a long breath. "Thank God no one was killed."

Hannah hesitated. "Actually . . . the driver was killed. And —"

"Is that how you injured your arm?"

She looked down at her ungainly limb. "Yes. I was left with a broken arm and a head wound, which has all but healed." She self-consciously touched her temple. The gash had faded to a jagged red line, but would definitely leave a scar. "Nothing to Sir John's injuries."

His mouth hardened into a grim line. "Yes. Sir John is always the one left hurt, isn't he?"

She stared at him, uncertain of his meaning. Then she asked, "Have we met before, Mr. Lowden?"

"No."

"I did not think so."

He explained, "My father was Sir John's solicitor for years, but he passed on two months ago."

"Ah, I thought I recalled Sir John's solicitor being an older man."

His green eyes glinted. "And I recall my father describing you, Lady Mayfield." The solicitor's tone was not complimentary.

"Oh?"

"You are not at all as I expected."

"I am sorry."

One fair brow rose. "Are you — why?"

She amended quickly, "Sorry for your loss."

He nodded slightly, studying her with disconcerting directness and, if she was not mistaken, disapproval.

She asked, "How did you find us?"

He shrugged easily. "Sir John informed me he was coming here to Lynton and asked me to call at my earliest convenience."

"Did he?" Should she admit she — or at least Marianna — had thought it all a big secret?

"That surprises you?" he asked.

"Well, yes."

He watched her closely. "He confided in me about this move and the reasons behind it."

She swallowed the lump in her throat, feeling as guilty as if she really were the unfaithful Marianna, though her guilt stemmed from another source. "I see."

She redirected the conversation. "Did Sir John know about your father's passing?"

"Yes, I informed him, and he wrote back to ask that I continue to look after his interests in my father's stead."

"Did he?" *How unfortunate,* Hannah thought.

His frown deepened. "If you don't believe me, I can show you his letter."

"Why should I not believe you?"

"You may not wish to, once you hear what he asked me to do in that letter."

"Oh?"

"But never mind. We need not speak of that now. May I see him?"

She quickly considered his request. "I see no reason why not. But would you mind waiting a few minutes? His doctor, our neighbor, usually comes to check on him about now and I would like to ask his opinion first."

"Very well."

She settled herself in a chair and he reclaimed the sofa. For a few moments they sat in awkward silence, Hannah self-consciously entwining her fingers and smoothing her skirt. Finally, she could stand it no longer and rose. "I shall call for some refreshment. You must be tired and thirsty after your journey."

"I would not decline a cup of tea. Thank you."

She nodded and went to the door, wishing she had thought to offer refreshment earlier. She might have simply pulled the bell cord beside the fireplace, but at the moment, she wanted nothing more than to escape the piercing, measuring gaze of Sir John's solicitor.

A quarter of an hour later, tea poured and nervously sipped, Hannah was relieved to hear Dr. Parrish arrive at last. Apparently an ailing yeoman farmer had required more of his time and care than he'd anticipated.

Hannah introduced the newcomer. "Dr. Parrish, this is Mr. Lowden. Sir John's solicitor from Bristol."

"Ah, so you did contact him as I suggested. Good."

She formed an unconvincing smile, ignored Mr. Lowden's lowered brow, and continued, "Dr. Parrish and his wife are our neighbors and have been kindness itself to us since we arrived. Dr. Parrish and his son are the ones who found us after the accident. They rescued us, carried us here to the house, and have taken care of us ever since."

"That was good of you, sir," Mr. Lowden said. "Very noble."

Dr. Parrish tucked his chin, clearly pleased at the praise. "How I thank God we saw those runaway horses. I shudder to think what might have happened to them had we not. The same fate as the poor driver and maid, I fear."

Mr. Lowden's head snapped toward her. "Maid? You did not mention a maid."

"Did I not?" she murmured. "Actually, she was a lady's companion." She was lying to a solicitor now? Heaven help her.

"Poor girl drowned," Dr. Parrish replied. "Carriage fell from the Cliff Road and landed half in the water."

Mr. Lowden said, "Sir John wrote nothing about a maid or a companion in his last letter. He mentioned he planned to engage all new staff."

Hannah said, "He did. But I — It was a last-minute arrangement."

"Has the woman's family been informed?"

Dr. Parrish said, "Lady Mayfield knew nothing of her family, but I did send a notice to the Bath papers."

"And the driver's family?"

"Yes," Dr. Parrish replied. "Him I knew. His parents own the coaching inn at Porlock. I carried the young man back to them in my own cart." He grimaced. "Bad business. Terrible distraught they were, too, of course."

Mr. Lowden frowned at her. "How did this *accident* happen? Were you being pursued by someone Sir John wished to avoid?"

Hannah shook her head. "No one pursued us. It was an accident, Mr. Lowden. There was a violent storm. But Sir John was eager to press on."

"Yes, he had reason to leave Bath and quickly." He gave her a pointed look, then turned toward the physician. "May I see him?"

"Of course," Dr. Parrish agreed. "And have you met young master Mayfield?"

Mr. Lowden's brow furrowed. "Master Mayfield?"

"Sir John and Lady Mayfield's son?" the doctor clarified.

Mr. Lowden's lips parted. "Son? I know nothing of a son."

162

Seeing the doctor's astounded expression, Hannah hurried to explain. "Mr. Lowden has only lately taken over as Sir John's solicitor after his father's death, and is not acquainted with every recent event."

"Ah."

Mr. Lowden's frown deepened. "He did mention his wife was expecting a child, but I thought . . ."

Dr. Parrish interrupted with a nod. "I thought the same. Surprised I was to hear the young master had already arrived. And what a bonny lad he is. You will want to see him."

Mr. Lowden held her gaze, challenge glinting in his eyes. "Indeed I shall."

Dr. Parrish led Mr. Lowden upstairs, the two men speaking in low voices as they went. A part of Hannah thought she ought to go in with them, in case Sir John should awaken again and say something to expose her. She would then be alerted to imminent danger. Instead, she remained in the drawing room. Mr. Lowden, though not a judge, was a solicitor. He was attached to, familiar with, and represented the law. Having him appear increased the risks to herself and therefore to Daniel as well. She would need to tread wisely, extract herself more carefully.

Several minutes later, Mr. Lowden came back downstairs alone, his expression pensive.

She rose, fiddling with the sling with her free hand. "How did you find him?"

"Very bad indeed. It is quite a shock."

"Yes. This has all been deeply shocking."

He stood there, making no move to pick up his hat from the side table nor to take his leave. Did he expect her to invite him to stay? She supposed she should. Probably would have, were she Marianna Mayfield, who enjoyed nothing more than a handsome man's company. But she did not want this man under the same roof, watching her every move, measuring and noting her every word to use against her later. To catch her leaving . . .

Mr. Lowden cleared his throat. "Pardon me for asking. But did your husband happen to mention that he invited me to stay here when I came to Devonshire?"

Her stomach fell. "No. I'm sorry. He didn't even mention you were coming."

"I did send a letter to him here; did you not receive it?"

She shook her head. "We've received no post since we've been here, that I know of."

"How strange. I wrote to apprise him of when I would arrive and to thank him for his invitation to stay at Clifton."

Hannah hesitated, then swallowed nervously. "Well then, of course you must stay here, Mr. Lowden. I will ask Mrs. Turrill to prepare one of the guest rooms. I should warn you that we have only minimal staff at present. With the accident, we have yet to hire more."

"It's not a problem; I am used to doing for myself. But I don't wish to trouble you. If it is not convenient, I suppose there might be an inn somewhere nearby . . . ?"

"Never mind, Mr. Lowden." She forced a smile. "Of course you must stay here. I am not hungry, but I shall ask Mrs. Turrill to send up dinner on a tray."

She wanted to ask him how long he planned to stay, but did not wish to appear impolite. Might it be wiser to wait to make her escape until after he had gone?

A few minutes later, Mrs. Turrill showed the man to a guest room, but Hannah waited for Dr. Parrish. She caught up with the physician near the side door as he was readying to take his leave.

"Dr. Parrish, I have a question. Mr. Lowden mentioned that he had sent a letter to Sir John here, informing him of his arrival. But I have seen no post since we arrived. Do you know anything about the postal arrangements for Clifton?"

He pursed his lips in thought. "We receive our post regularly enough. And I am quite certain Edgar informed the postmaster of the names of the new tenants. I am going into the village first thing tomorrow and shall speak to Mr. Mason myself."

"Only if it is no trouble."

"No trouble at all, my lady."

"Thank you, Dr. Parrish. You are very kind."

He tipped his hat. "My pleasure."

Chapter 10

The next morning, Hannah rose early, dressed with Mrs. Turrill's help, and slipped downstairs to the dining parlor, hoping to eat her breakfast alone before Mr. Lowden came down. But she had barely helped herself to coffee and toast from the sideboard when their houseguest entered, newspaper tucked under his arm.

"Mr. Lowden, good morning." She forced a smile. "I trust you slept well?"

"Perfectly well as always. But then, I have the benefit of a clean conscience."

Hannah's smile stiffened.

He filled his own plate and cup and sat down. The two ate in awkward silence, every replaced lid and scrape of cutlery seeming as loud as a clanging cymbal. He refilled his coffee cup and unfolded the newspaper, sipping while he read.

"Perhaps you might use the morning room as your office while you're here," she offered, hoping he would take the hint and retreat there now. Instead, Hannah waited impatiently for Mr. Lowden to finish his third cup of coffee, ready to make her escape as soon as politeness allowed.

Dr. Parrish appeared in the threshold, and Hannah sighed in relief.

"Sorry to disturb your meal," he began.

"Not at all, doctor. We have just finished. May I offer you something?"

"No, thank you." He raised a small stack of letters. "I have taken the liberty of collecting your post while I was in town. Mr. Mason was reluctant to hand it over. According to him, when Sir John visited before the move, he requested that all post be held for him. He asked that it not be delivered to the house, but said he would collect it himself, in person. But after I explained Sir John's condition, he begrudgingly gave way. Extremely dedicated, our postmaster." He extended the letters. "Here you are, my la—"

Mr. Lowden interrupted him. "Doctor, since Sir John obviously had reservations about whose hand the post ended in, perhaps I, as his solicitor, should peruse it first."

Dr. Parrish frowned. "I didn't read it, if that's what you're thinking. I imagine Sir

John only wanted his post held until his family was in residence. Surely her ladyship can give you anything she thinks Sir John would want you to see to."

"But what if *she* is the person he did not want reading his post?"

The doctor frowned. "His wife? Really, Mr. Lowden. That is unkind." With a defensive glare at the newcomer, he handed her the letters.

Mr. Lowden craned his neck to see them. "The one on top is from me to Sir John. There is nothing in it you need see."

Ignoring his outstretched hand, Hannah slid it to the bottom of the pile. She flipped past the next letter, and with a jolt recognized the handwriting of the third, before sliding all the letters into her lap.

She smiled at their neighbor. "Thank you, Dr. Parrish. I greatly appreciate your help."

Hannah excused herself from a glowering Mr. Lowden and accompanied Dr. Parrish upstairs to check on Sir John.

"That man seems to have taken against you."

"You noticed that, too? I find it strange. Especially as I never met him before he came here."

In the bedchamber, Sir John slept deeply and turned his head away from the doctor's attempts to rouse him. "Even that is a response, my lady. Another good sign."

He greeted the nurse then went on to explain that Mrs. Weaver had begun a regimen of massage and stretching to keep Sir John's muscles from becoming atrophied while lying abed night and day. The treatment seemed to render him more responsive overall.

"About that, doctor," Mrs. Weaver interrupted gently. "May I have a private word before you take your leave?"

"Of course."

Hannah excused herself to give the two privacy and slipped into her room to read the post. She first opened the letter in the familiar hand, fingers trembling. How in the world had Freddie learned even this much of their direction? It was addressed to Sir John Mayfield, Lynton Post Office, Devon.

Dear Sir,

I read in the newspaper an account of the death of one Hannah Rogers. The news report said only: "A maid, Hannah Rogers, lately of Bath, drowned. Anyone knowing the whereabouts of her next of kin, please write in care of the Lynton Post Office."

I could not rest without telling you.

Hannah Rogers was more than a maid, sir. And more than a lady's companion. She was a dear friend. A clever, educated young woman. The daughter of a parson and a gentlewoman. The owner of a lovely singing voice. A kind neighbor, a loyal friend, and a loving mother. Describing her as merely a "maid" does not do her justice. She will be missed not because she is not there to tote and carry for your wife, sir. No offense. But because the world is a darker place without her, the future no longer full of hope.

I have hand-delivered the news to her father in Bristol, who received it with much distress and grief. If Hannah left any belongings, please forward them to Mr. Thomas Rogers, 37 Hill Street, Bristol.

Sincerely,
Fred Bonner

Oh, Freddie . . . Tears blurred her vision. Poor man. She had not stopped to consider how the news of her "death" would affect him — nor anticipated that he would take the news to her father. Poor Fred. He did not know it wasn't true. How could he? Of course he had told her father, thinking he would want to know, even though they were estranged. Had her father really been distressed and grieved? Her eyes filled anew at the thought.

For the truth of her situation would bring him little comfort.

She next eyed Mr. Lowden's letter. Should she return it to him unopened? Or place it in Sir John's bedchamber for when . . . if . . . he fully regained his senses? Then she recalled the solicitor's discomfort at seeing the letter in her hands. What had he written that he didn't want Lady Mayfield to read? Swallowing sour guilt, she pried up the seal and read.

My dear sir,
I am in receipt of your letter and accept your commission with gratitude. I appreciate the confidence you place in me based on my father's recommendation when we are so little acquainted.

I will travel into Devonshire at my first opportunity, which is unlikely to occur before the end of the month. I'm afraid there is a great deal to do in arranging my father's affairs, both personally and professionally. Your condolences and understanding mean a great deal to me at this time.

My father was very careful about cli-

172

ent privacy and had not shared with me any details about the situation you mentioned in your letter. However, since you asked me to assume the management of your affairs, I have taken the liberty of reviewing the files and the past correspondence between yourself and Mr. Lowden, senior. I am sorry the situation has so deteriorated, as are you no doubt, and of course will do everything in my power to assist and protect you and your estate should the worst happen as you fear.

Thank you for the offer of accommodation whilst I visit Lynton. I will look forward to deepening our acquaintance.

I am,
Yours sincerely,
James Lowden

Hannah rubbed her eyelids with forefinger and thumb. At least the man had told the truth about Sir John's offer of a room. It wasn't so much that she hadn't believed him; she simply had not wanted him there. She read in the veiled, tactful words that Mr. Lowden had been apprised of Lady Mayfield's . . . proclivities. She felt shame tingle along her spine and heat her cheeks and had to remind herself again that Marianna's shame was not hers. She had her own to bear.

She opened the last letter, also addressed to Sir John Mayfield, and posted quite recently.

Sir John,

I come to your house in Devonshire and Miss Rogers tells me Lady Mayfield has perished. But I have seen no announcement of her death in the Bristol or London newspapers. Are you waiting to recover her body, or have I been lied to? You may think me a fool, but you, sir, are the fool if you think to put me off so easily. I will discover the truth. And if I find you are to blame for any harm that has befallen her, I will kill you myself. As I should have done long before now.

A. Fontaine

Goodness. How rash he was. And to put such a threat in writing! She recalled how devastated Mr. Fontaine had been when she'd told him the news. Now he had grasped on to a branch of hope . . . and was eager to bludgeon Sir John with it.

What if Mr. Lowden had read this letter? She'd be bound for jail in no time. What

174

should she do — burn it? She was sorely tempted. But for some reason she hesitated. The threat seemed important . . . perhaps evidence against the man should he return and attempt to harm Sir John, or saw the same notice Freddie had seen in the Bath newspaper, and tried to use it against her. She would have to hide it carefully. But where could she hide it that no one cleaning — or searching — the room might stumble upon it? Her bedchamber seemed the safest place, near at hand and in a room no man should enter, save her "husband," who was currently bedridden.

She considered the books in the bookcase — too few, too easy to flip through and find. The urn atop the dressing chest . . . too obvious. Between the tick and bed ropes . . . too easily found while changing the bed linens. Perhaps inside Lady Mayfield's bandboxes? She rose and went to the stack of hatboxes beside the wardrobe. She opened the middle one and extracted a hat with a tall crown circled with wide ribbon. *Yes* . . . She slid the folded letter beneath the wide band, repositioned a hat pin through it and regarded the hat from all angles. Yes, someone might look in the box and inside the hat and not notice a thing. It would do.

The letter from Fred was less incriminating — quite flattering actually. Though her ears burned in shame to think of the high regard in which he held her compared to her current deception. She deserved not his fair praise in life nor in "death." Still, she did not want Mr. Lowden to have her father's address. So this letter she tucked beneath her underthings in her dressing chest.

She contemplated the one from Mr. Lowden. . . . She didn't want Mrs. Turrill or the new maid to read it and think the worst of Lady Mayfield, to look upon *her* with a jaundiced eye. She was guilty of her own immorality, yes, but did not relish taking on Marianna's as well. This letter she would put with Sir John's things in his room.

When she returned to his bedchamber to do so, she was surprised to find Dr. Parrish still there, quietly conversing with the chamber nurse.

"Ah, my lady." Dr. Parrish looked up and gave her an apologetic smile. "I am afraid Mrs. Weaver has had to give notice. She will be leaving us at the end of the week."

The woman went on to explain that her daughter was nearing the end of her confinement and she wanted to be on hand for the birth of her first grandchild.

"I understand," Hannah said. "Though of course we shall be sorry to see you go." She thanked Mrs. Weaver for everything and wondered uneasily who would take over her duties. Would Mrs. Parrish return, or would she be expected to do so herself? Hannah quailed at the thought.

Hannah went back downstairs and found Mr. Lowden at the desk in the morning room, bent over a sheaf of papers. He had obviously lost no time in making himself at home there.

He smirked up at her. "Anything *interesting* in the post?"

She met his challenging look with a cold one of her own. "Not especially, no."

"And my letter?"

"I have left it in Sir John's room."

"You read it?"

"I did."

"And the others?"

"Nothing to concern you." But was that really true? Hannah turned to leave the room, her conscience plaguing her. For had a man not threatened Mr. Lowden's client?

"Love letters from Mr. Fontaine, I suppose?" he called after her.

She whirled back around. So much for

veiled tact.

"I assure you there were no love letters."

"You know Sir John hoped to keep Fontaine from discovering where you had gone."

Dare she tell him? "Then his plan was unsuccessful, sir, for Mr. Fontaine has already been here."

His eyes flashed. "Has he indeed? And I wonder how he found you so quickly."

"I have no idea."

The man scoffed. "Right. And what was the outcome of his visit?"

"He left. Disappointed."

"Did he?"

"Yes."

"Or is he merely . . . waiting?" he asked, his green eyes glinting like fish scales in sunlight.

"Waiting?"

"Now that Sir John's fate is uncertain. Why rush off without a penny, when one believes an inheritance awaits if only one is patient?" His lip curled in disdain.

She stared at him, slowly shaking her head in disbelief.

He asked, "Do you know what Sir John has asked me to do?"

"You have yet to tell me."

"He asked me to change his will."

Hannah shrugged. "What is that to me?"

"Everything."

Perhaps to Marianna but not to her. Oh, why had she stayed?

She asked, "Change it how?"

"I imagine to exclude you from it. To eliminate any benefit to you were he to suddenly perish through *accidental* means."

"You are not suggesting I would do anything to harm Sir John?"

"Can you deny you have hurt him gravely already?"

"Not physically. Never that. You cannot believe . . . anyone . . . would do such a thing."

"I think he believed it possible. Perhaps even feared that very thing. That you or Mr. Fontaine would be tempted to rid the world of the only man who stood between you."

She stared at him, thinking of Mr. Fontaine's threatening letter. Was it possible? Had Mr. Fontaine and Marianna contemplated such a thing? Surely no one could have manipulated that carriage crash.

"I don't believe it," she murmured.

"Here. Read Sir John's letter yourself."

Curious, she accepted the letter, carrying it to the window to read in better light.

Dear Mr. Lowden,

Allow me to express my deepest condolences on your father's passing. He was the best of men and it was my privilege to call him advisor and friend these many years. You and I are not well acquainted, but your father had every confidence in your abilities, and therefore, so have I. I hope you will carry on as my solicitor in his stead.

There are a few matters I wish to discuss with you. Unfortunately, circumstances are such that I have decided we must quit Bath immediately and cannot come to your offices before we depart. I hope you will do me the honor of traveling to see me at your convenience once your own affairs — and your father's — are settled and your deepest mourning past. I have told no one else where we are going and of course Lady Mayfield does not know for reasons that should be evident if your father apprised you of my situation. If he has not, suffice it to say, my wife has carried on a relationship with a Mr. Anthony Fontaine, a bad connection which was, to my grief, not severed at our marriage nor when we moved from Bristol to Bath. The man has followed and I know full well, will try to follow again. To complicate matters, Lady Mayfield is expecting a child.

For the time being, we shall relocate to Clifton, a house I inherited but have never before occupied. I'm sure all the details are in your father's records, but in simple terms, the property is located in Devonshire, 12 miles west of Porlock, between Countisbury and the twin villages of Lynton & Lynmouth. The house is just south of the Cliff Road before the descent into Lynmouth. If you have any trouble, note that we are neighbors to a well-known physician, Dr. George Parrish. Inquiring of his residence will lead you to ours.

To keep our destination quiet, I have decided not to bring along any of our present servants, who might understandably wish to allow relatives and friends to know where they were going. We shall hire new staff in Devonshire. The property manager, our neighbor's grown son, will engage minimal staff to sufficiently ready the house for our arrival.

When you come, I wish to revise my will, among other things, so please bring along whatever documents are necessary to accomplish this. Of course, I will compensate you for your time and reimburse your traveling expenses. Do not consider lodging. The house has several spare rooms and you are more than welcome to stay with us during your visit.

Until then, I depend upon your discretion and remain,

Sir John Mayfield, KCB

"He says nothing about fearing for his life," Hannah observed. "What a vile imagination you have."

Though what Sir John had written was condemning enough, Hannah secretly allowed. No wonder James Lowden looked at her the way he did. She had to remind herself he did not see *her,* he saw or thought he saw Marianna — unfaithful, manipulative, selfish Marianna. The woman who broke his client's heart and perhaps, intended to do him some fatal harm, though Hannah doubted the woman capable of such evil. Mr. Fontaine? She did not know him well enough to judge. Yet, had not desire and jealousy driven men to violent acts throughout history? Oh yes.

She detested the thought of Mr. Lowden holding such a low opinion of her. But what could she do? Was the truth of who she was and what she had done any better?

Mrs. Turrill came down the stairs, Danny in her arms and a doting smile on her face.

"Here's your mamma, little man."

Handing the letter back to Mr. Lowden, Hannah crossed the room to take Danny. The housekeeper settled the child in the crook of her good arm.

Mrs. Turrill whispered, "Hope you don't mind. Becky is not herself this morning. Has awful cramps. I've got her bundled up in bed with a hot-water bottle."

"That's fine, Mrs. Turrill. I never mind having Danny with me."

"That's what I thought. You're a good mother you are, my lady." She said this with a pointed glance at the solicitor, before retreating belowstairs.

Mr. Lowden rose and took a few steps nearer. "This is your son?"

"Yes. This is Daniel."

He studied the little face with a critical eye. "He looks like you." Mr. Lowden sent her a sidelong glance. "Does he also look like his father?"

She weighed the implications of the question, but thought it wisest to say nothing.

Mr. Lowden resumed his seat. "I still don't understand why Sir John did not mention in his letter that his wife was to deliver a child so soon."

"Perhaps he was mistaken or unaware of the child's due date."

"Had you some reason to mislead him in that?"

She frowned at him. "You are very rude, Mr. Lowden. How did your mother raise you?"

For a moment he seemed taken aback. Then his eyes narrowed. "My mother was a good and godly person. She cared little for appearances. She did not raise me to pretend to approve of someone when I did not."

"You judge someone you have never met, never spoken to, never even seen?"

"Did I need to? When my client has made it clear he does not trust his wife. That he has reason to believe the child his wife carried was not his own?"

Hannah stilled. Was it true? Was Marianna carrying Anthony Fontaine's child? If so, did Mr. Fontaine know? She wondered briefly if and how Sir John knew for certain, but guessed she knew the answer.

CHAPTER 11

James Lowden was not certain what to think or what to do. It was a condition he rarely found himself in and did not like it. He was usually a man of sharp judgment, of accurate first impressions, and of swift action. Now he felt off-balance, strangely unsettled and unsure how to proceed. He had traveled to Devonshire with a clear idea of what was expected of him: come to the aid of the betrayed husband, take legal steps to assure she and her lover gained nothing by his future death, beyond the jointure agreed to in the original marriage settlement. Of course he had never expected to find Sir John lying insensible and close to death already. Even if he drafted a new will for him, Sir John could not sign it, nor could he honestly say his client was presently of sound mind. Yes, he had Sir John's letter in which his intention to otherwise disinherit his unfaithful wife seemed clear. But the man had written with a modicum of discretion, to protect himself from more scandal should the letter be misdirected, James supposed. Such a letter could be presented to a judge in court, but it was unlikely to take precedence over Sir John's last signed will and testament. Especially when so much money was at stake. Sir John Mayfield was a wealthy man. He had formerly been in trade in Bristol, where he had made his fortune and been granted the honor of knighthood by the king.

Yet it was not only Sir John's condition that surprised James, but Lady Mayfield herself. He had come expecting a certain kind of woman. Vain and spoiled and manipulative. Beautiful, but easy to despise. Why did he have this vague memory of a friend describing the new Lady Mayfield as a dark-haired beauty? Had the man been mistaken or had he forgotten? For the woman's hair was reddish brown. She had fine, blue-green eyes and pale, lightly freckled skin. Not unattractive, but certainly not what he would describe as a "dark beauty." With her coloring and high cheekbones, she appeared of Scottish descent or perhaps Irish, though her speech was as fine as any Mayfair lady's. She was a bit younger than he'd expected as well. Perhaps three or four and twenty —

though he realized she might be older than she looked. He had expected her to be flirtatious, but she kept her distance when she could, and behaved with cool reserve when she couldn't. She dressed modestly, tucked lace or high necklines, with her hair pulled back simply and little or no cosmetics. She clearly wasn't out to seduce him. Perhaps she knew why he'd come before he mentioned the will. She didn't seem resentful, but defensive? Yes. She was definitely hiding something.

And how she doted on her child. He had heard her singing sweetly to the boy the previous night. She certainly did not appear the spoiled hoyden, leaving the care of her troublesome brat to others. What was she up to? Was it a ploy to win him to her side? He reminded himself that she was known for her ability to lure and manipulate men. Perhaps her ability to appear sweet and gentle was part of her deceptive charm. He must be careful to steel himself against her. His role was to protect Sir John and his interests. Not to begin second-guessing him. Or himself.

Hannah knew she could not skip dinner again, and avoiding Mr. Lowden would only make him suspicious. But how she dreaded the hours alone in his company.

The meal itself, served earlier in the West Country than in the city, passed uneventfully. Now and again Mr. Lowden opened his mouth as if to ask her something, but then hesitated, his glance veering to Mrs. Turrill as she laid the courses or quietly directed Ben to carry away this serving dish or that. In the end, he remained silent, except to ask for something to be passed or to compliment the cook-housekeeper on the excellent meal.

Afterward, Hannah rose in relief and withdrew to the drawing room, where Mrs. Turrill had laid out a coffee service. She hoped Mr. Lowden would linger in the dining room over port and a cigar or whatever it was men partook of after meals. In fact, she hoped he smoked a whole box of cigars. But instead he followed her into the drawing room and poured them each a cup of coffee.

She would stay while he finished one cup, she told herself, and then she would claim fatigue and excuse herself to retire early. Hannah sat in an armchair, sipped her coffee, and then set the cup and saucer on the side table. She picked up a novel to discourage conversation, but could not concentrate on the words. She felt him watching her over its pages. When she looked up at last, he smiled at her as if she'd just delivered the cue he'd been waiting for.

"Although I did not meet you until coming to Clifton, you are acquainted, I believe, with an old friend of mine."

Hannah was instantly on her guard. Would she expose herself by not remembering this supposed acquaintance?

She turned a page and affected a casual air. "Oh? And which friend is this?"

"Captain Robert Blanchard." He watched her face intently. "Tall thin chap. Curly blond hair? A cousin to Lord Weston, or so he claims."

"I . . . am sorry. I don't recall."

"No? Apparently he had the pleasure of making your acquaintance in Bath last year. At a rout Lord Weston hosted."

Hannah thought back. Marianna *had* gone to Lord Weston's rout alone, she recalled, while Sir John was away on business. And later she'd pouted that Mr. Fontaine had not made an appearance, so she'd had to make do with other entertainment. Flirting with an officer was certainly the type of diversion Marianna had enjoyed, though as far as Hannah knew, she'd never taken a lover besides Fontaine.

"Perhaps your friend mistook me for

someone else," Hannah hedged. "There were . . . many people there."

Mr. Lowden glanced over his shoulder to make sure they were alone, then said, "But you made quite an impression on this particular man. I saw Blanchard not long afterward and he told me he'd met the enchanting Lady Mayfield, with 'eyes that drew him like siren song.' And how she flirted with him, stroking his lapel and whispering in his ear. He seemed quite certain that if he'd had the nerve to ask her to leave the party with him, she would have."

Hannah's stomach soured and her mind worked quickly. If she decried the charge as out of the realm of possibility, he would never believe her. But if she agreed to this particular charge, it might be a trap. And even if true, how mortifying to own such illicit behavior to Sir John's solicitor.

When she remained silent, he slyly prompted, "A cavalry officer . . . ?"

Hannah knew she had to step carefully, and answer as Marianna might. "Oh, a *cavalry* officer," she drawled. "You might have said so sooner. I admit I admire a man in uniform, but I am afraid I don't recall this particular man. Blanchard, was it?"

His golden brows rose. "You flirt so blatantly with every officer you meet?"

190

"I . . . like to show my appreciation for brave military service."

He smirked. "How patriotic of you."

Hannah forced a tight-lipped smile and returned her focus to her book, hoping he would change the subject.

He did not.

"Well, Blanchard remembered you. And how he extolled your unmatched beauty."

"There, you see?" she said lightly. "He must have been speaking of someone else."

His gaze roved her face, her neck, her décolletage. . . . Mortification seared through Hannah, and heated every inch of skin grazed by his critical eye.

"Yes. I see your point," he said. "I suppose it's possible he made a mistake. He admitted he was in his cups that night. Often is."

Instead of feeling vindicated, personal insult had been heaped upon her borrowed shame. She bent her flushed face over her book.

Mr. Lowden persisted, "But you *do* have a reputation for being a notorious flirt. Or are you going to deny that as well?"

She looked up at him coldly. "I would not bother to deny it. You have already made up your mind about me — and pronounced judgment without benefit of trial."

He gave her a self-satisfied grin. "Who said you were not on trial?"

At that, Hannah rose and excused herself to go upstairs to the nursery. After she checked on Danny, she went down to her room to gather her wits. Mr. Lowden put her on edge like no man she had ever met. The way he had looked at her, the things he had said in that sly, baiting tone . . . She would hate to face him in a courtroom.

From the corridor, she heard footsteps and low voices — Dr. and Mrs. Parrish arriving to look in on Sir John. Hannah took several more deep breaths, waited until her hands had stopped shaking, and then went to join them. Inside Sir John's bedchamber, she found Dr. Parrish and his wife in earnest conversation over their patient's prone figure.

Dr. Parrish glanced up. "Ah, my lady. My good wife and I were just discussing Sir John's care with Mrs. Weaver soon to leave us. Mrs. Turrill has offered to take over some of her duties, now that you are less in need of help. And the new housemaid will assist her. But as far as treatments to moderate his loss of strength . . . that's where you come in."

"Oh?" Nerves prickled through Hannah. "I am afraid I am unfamiliar with such treatments."

"As are most people." Dr. Parrish stroked his chin and explained, "You see, at the teaching hospital where I studied, a physician with the East India Company taught us the benefits of massage, or 'medical rubbing' as it is sometimes called. As well as a regimen of stretching exercises to keep muscles from becoming atrophied. Now that Mrs. Weaver is leaving, I thought Mrs. Parrish might perform the technique in her stead. But Mrs. Parrish wisely points out that it might be more appropriate for you to do so. I promise you it will help your husband if, as we all hope, he regains his senses and his health in time."

Hannah lifted her sling, relieved to have an excuse. "But unfortunately, with my arm as it is . . ."

"I've thought of that. But there is still a great deal you can do with one hand, until I remove your bandages."

"I . . . see." She swallowed. "I have never done the like before, doctor. If Mrs. Parrish has experience, and wouldn't mind —"

"It isn't that I mind, my lady," Mrs. Parrish said with a thin smile. "But I have my own house and family to take care of, not to mention helping Dr. Parrish with difficult birthings and the like. Whereas you . . . well, you have more time to dedicate to the practice. Who better than his own wife? One flesh, and all that."

Hannah looked away from the woman's challenging look, to the doctor's kind face. "Is it difficult?" she asked.

"Not at all. I shall show you now, if you are amenable, and then I will check on your progress from time to time to see how you get on. All right?"

How could she refuse to help "her husband"?

"Very well."

He lifted the bedclothes from Sir John's left arm. "Another of my professors trained in Sweden. Quite progressive, the Swedes, in their use of exercises and medical rubbing."

How nice for them, Hannah thought, less than charitably.

As Dr. Parrish began demonstrating how to stretch and massage the muscles, Mrs. Parrish excused herself to prepare a late supper at home.

Hannah relaxed once the woman had left. She didn't know why the doctor's wife did not like her. Did Mrs. Parrish suspect she wasn't who she said she was?

Dr. Parrish, however, was very easy to be with, good company, and a good friend. If only she might have enjoyed his friendship as herself. As it was, she was soon to lose his friendship, and so much more.

She followed Dr. Parrish's example, removing the bedclothes from Sir John's other arm, stretching the hand, massaging fingers and muscles. Then she braced herself and moved on to his uninjured leg. Using her good hand, she gently pushed Sir John's toes toward his ankle to stretch the calf, then kneaded the muscles. It wasn't too difficult, though it would certainly be easier with two hands.

After a time, Dr. Parrish stepped back and collected his bag. "Well, you have the way of it now. I shall leave you to it."

"Thank you, doctor."

She continued kneading Sir John's calf muscle, feeling warm and self-conscious. She reminded herself she was acting as a nurse, a medical "rubber," and tried not to focus on the fact that her hand was on Sir John Mayfield's bare leg.

As she stood there, the sight spurred a long-forgotten memory. . . .

She and Lady Mayfield had been out walking through Bristol and stopped at a millinery. On their way home, Marianna suggested an alternate route and led the way.

They strolled past brick buildings and shops that catered to gentlemen — tobacconists, newsagents, barbers, and a fencing club.

When Marianna stopped walking, Hannah turned to see what had arrested her attention. The muffled clang of metal striking metal drew her gaze to the windows of a nearby building. Inside, two men fenced back and forth.

Marianna grinned. "This is Sir John's fencing club. Let's go in and take a peek."

"No, my lady," Hannah hissed. "The sign says, *Gentlemen Only*."

Marianna huffed. "You are a spoilsport, Hannah. Just like Sir John." She sniffed and stepped nearer the windows.

Hannah crept to her side, feeling self-conscious and hoping no one of their acquaintance would pass by and see them there — especially not her father.

The men inside wore fencing costumes — padded linen jackets, leather gloves on thrusting hands, and wire mesh masks concealing their faces. The competitors advanced and retreated, lunging and striking again and again at a grueling pace. They were so focused on their bout that they remained unaware of their audience.

Hannah admired their skill and agility, and the way their leg muscles strained against snug white pantaloons with each low lunge. Hannah had once heard Sir John say that fencing helped him stay fit and vent his frustrations. Standing there, she could understand how it might do so.

The taller man scored a hit, acknowledged by the other, and the bout ended. The men saluted one another, shook hands, and removed their masks. Hannah felt her lips part in surprise. The taller man was Sir John Mayfield. He was breathing hard and perspiring, but he looked young and masculine and strong. His opponent stepped away, but Sir John remained, unfastening and removing his jacket. The second man tossed Sir John a towel, and with it he wiped his face and torso. Hannah could not help but stare at Sir John's muscular chest, abdomen, and shoulders. She hoped Lady Mayfield could not read her thoughts.

Beside her, Marianna breathed, "Isn't he something?"

Hannah was surprised to hear the admiration in her voice, though she silently agreed. But when she glanced over, she found Marianna's gaze glued not on Sir John, but rather on his opponent. . . .

Memory fading, Hannah replaced the bedclothes over Sir John's leg. No wonder he had fenced so often, she thought. He'd had a great deal of frustration to vent.

On his way to the morning room the next day, James hesitated outside the threshold of the drawing room. He heard Marianna Mayfield within, cooing softly to the little boy — Anthony Fontaine's little boy?

"Ah, my dear one. Mamma loves you. Yes, she does."

He glanced around the doorjamb. She sat in a chair with the child on her lap, his head on her knees, his legs straight up, gently clapping his feet together. "Pat a cake, pat a cake, baker's man. Bake me a cake as fast as you can. Pat it and prick it and mark it with a D. And put it in the oven for Danny and me."

He stepped inside. "I wonder, my lady. Would you dote on him so were he Sir John's son?"

Her head snapped toward him, clearly startled by his presence and his words.

"And a good morning to you, too, Mr. Lowden." With a defensive little lift of her chin, she added, "And, yes, I would." Her face flushed.

He was surprised to see his words had embarrassed her. Was she admitting the child was not Sir John's? That surprised him as well.

She looked back at the little boy. "Uh-oh. Someone's nappy needs a change." And instead of calling for a servant, she rose, and carried the child upstairs to tend him herself. Or perhaps, simply to get away from her husband's mean-spirited solicitor.

He knew she employed a wet nurse, but evidently Lady Mayfield often changed and coddled the child herself. Which was the real Lady Mayfield? The unfaithful wife or the devoted mother?

Apparently, it was quite possible to be both.

CHAPTER 12

At dinner that evening, James Lowden again sat at table with his client's wife. It was a bit awkward, just the two of them, but he looked forward to another opportunity to speak with her alone. Though of course, a servant or two would be on hand to lay the courses. Even so, he would have her undivided attention. He relished the notion. For he had a few more questions he wished to put to her.

Lady Mayfield had dressed for dinner in a gown of emerald green, ribbon trim at high waist and sleeves. She looked reserved and dignified. Her hair was pinned at the back of her head as usual, but tonight there were curls at each temple. The effect softened Lady Mayfield's features, he decided. And the color must flatter her complexion, for she looked quite pretty tonight. Or perhaps it was the glass of Madeira he'd helped himself to before dinner.

After they had finished their soup and begun the fish course, he asked, "What can you tell me about your companion who died?"

Her fork stilled midway to her mouth. "Why?"

"I am only curious."

"What would you like to know?" She set down her bite of fish, untasted.

He sipped his wine. "Why was she with you in the first place? Sir John wrote specifically that he planned to take no servants from Bath. And, do you not find it odd that no one has responded to the death notice Dr. Parrish sent to the *Bath Journal*? Unless you have received something in the post you did not mention?"

With a nervous glance at Mrs. Turrill at the sideboard, Lady Mayfield said, "I already told you it was a last-minute decision. Miss Rogers was my companion in Bristol. She moved with us to Bath, but left us soon after. We had not seen her for some time when she appeared at our door. I all but begged Sir John to allow her to come along. I had always been fond of her and I hated the thought of going who-knew-where with no companion."

James waited until Mrs. Turrill left the room with a tray of dishes, then leaned forward. "Your husband was not companion enough?"

"Mr. Lowden, you cannot pretend ignorance about the nature of the relationship. You showed me the letter, remember. The marriage was not a love match."

"On the contrary, I have reason to believe it was a love match, at least on Sir John's side."

The woman bit her lip. "I would prefer not to discuss marriage with you, Mr. Lowden."

"Very well; back to Hannah Rogers. Sir John acquiesced and allowed her to come along?"

"Yes, as should be obvious."

"Had she no family? No one who might be wondering what has become of her? No one to come here in hopes of visiting her grave — or to mourn her loss?"

"First of all, there is no grave to visit, as her body has yet to be recovered. As far as her family, I understand there is only one parent living and the two of them were estranged."

"Have you written to this parent? To inform him of his daughter's fate? Estranged or not, he would want to know."

She cocked her head to one side. "How do you know it is a father I speak of?"

He shrugged. "An assumption."

She looked as though she didn't believe him. She said slowly, "I have not written personally, but I do know that the parent has been informed."

"Oh? How?"

"We did receive one letter from a friend of Hannah's who saw the notice. He wrote to say he delivered the news to her parent in person."

"What friend is this?"

"I hardly think it would matter to you."

"May I see this letter?"

She narrowed her eyes. "Your curiosity astounds me, Mr. Lowden. Apparently, you have a great deal of time on your hands."

He made no rebuttal but watched her closely, studying her irritated face. The mantel clock ticked once, twice, thrice.

Finally, he shook his head. "How much you conceal, my lady. One wonders why."

The next morning, Hannah brushed out her long hair, thinking back to her dinner with Mr. Lowden, as she had done for much of the night. In fact she'd had difficulty falling asleep because their conversation kept repeating itself through her mind. He was clearly suspicious of something, but she did not think he guessed that the lady's companion he'd asked so many questions about had been seated directly across the table from him. She hoped her replies had laid his questions to rest. But somehow, she doubted it.

She went upstairs to the nursery and was surprised to find Danny alone, with no sign of Becky. Danny lay awake in his cradle, contentedly cooing and kicking his legs. At the sound of her voice he turned his head and smiled his gummy grin. Love surging through her, Hannah scooped him up as gracefully as she could and changed him herself, though without full use of both arms, the task took twice as long as it should have.

Afterward, she carried him downstairs to look for Becky. As she passed, she heard voices coming from the morning room. James Lowden's voice and Becky's. What in the world?

He was saying, "How did you become a nurse, Miss Brown, if I may ask?"

Becky faltered. "I . . . in the usual way, I suppose."

Hannah glanced around the doorjamb and saw Becky looking down, clearly embarrassed.

"Let me rephrase that. Where did Lady Mayfield find you?"

"Find me?"

"Through an agency, or . . . ?"

She nodded vaguely. "Mrs. Beech's."

"And your own child . . . ?"

Silence, then a small whisper. "Died."

"I'm sorry. And had you been a nurse before, for another family?"

"No, sir. No other family. But I did nurse several —"

"Mr. Lowden," Hannah interrupted, stepping across the threshold. "What is the meaning of this?"

"Meaning? I am only speaking with Miss Brown."

"Interrogating her, by the sound of it."

Becky shook her head. "I didn't tell him nothing, honest I didn't."

"Of course you didn't, Becky. There is nothing to tell. Nothing that need concern Mr. Lowden. Becky, why do you not take Danny into the garden for a bit of fresh air while I speak with Mr. Lowden?"

"Yes, miss — er . . . my lady." The girl took the child from her and all but ran from the room.

James Lowden looked at his client's wife. Lady Mayfield's thin mouth cinched tight, her eyes flashed, her prominent cheekbones shone in high color. She clenched her hands

205

and waited until they could no longer hear the girl's retreating footfalls.

"Mr. Lowden. If you have anything to ask, you may ask me directly. You need not go behind my back and question the servants. Do you not realize how hurtful such questions can be to a girl in Becky's situation? She lost her own child — her little daughter — shortly after she was born. How do you think wet nurses become wet nurses? Their newborns either die, or she gives up her child to nurse some other woman's infant. Either way, these are not happy stories women are proud and eager to speak of. How insensitive you are. How cruel."

Her words pricked his conscience. "I take your point, and I apologize. I did not think it through. I will apologize to Miss Brown as well."

"I shall convey your apologies to her myself, Mr. Lowden. You make her nervous, and no wonder."

"The girl's emotional state is questionable. So why, may I ask, would you engage her to nurse your own child?"

Lady Mayfield seemed to hesitate. "Because she . . . needed a place, and we needed her."

"Could you not nurse your child yourself?"

She gaped. Her face mottled red and white beneath her freckles. "How dare you?"

"Forgive me; that was rude. I of course realize many ladies prefer not to —"

"It had nothing to do with *preference,*" she snapped. "If I could have nursed Danny myself, I would have. I did so for the first month of his life, but then, circumstances changed and I was no longer able to do so, to my great regret."

Her anger, her deep distress and guilt stunned him. He had obviously struck a nerve. "Again, I apologize for my insolence," he said. "I should not have asked such a thing. I have no right to judge you or anyone."

"Yet you do so at every turn, it seems to me. You who have had every advantage in life, everything handed to you — your career, your livelihood."

He stared at her, incredulous. "What are you talking about? You know nothing about me. Yes, I was educated, but I had to work hard to earn my degree. Then my father thought I needed worldly experience, and released me from the firm. I took a position with the East India Company and lived abroad — China, India. And for the last several years, I worked at the London headquarters. I'd be there yet, had my father not died. And even now I am not handed my father's practice, for his clients do not know me nor trust a younger man. Many have opted to engage more established solicitors. Sir John is in the minority in retaining my services. Why do you think I was able to leave the practice in my clerk's hands and come here?"

"I did not realize."

"Of course not. How could you. It is not something I trumpet about. Not something a lady like you, a pampered only child from a wealthy family, would understand."

Her mouth parted. Would she try to refute his charges? Instead she said, "Thank you for telling me. But perhaps you ought to return to your practice. I will let you know when Sir John is able to communicate his wishes to you."

"Will you? Now that you know what he asked me to do?"

"Yes, I will."

He smirked at her. "Are you telling me I've worn out my welcome already? Are you asking me to leave?"

He noticed her fisting her hand.

"Of course not, Mr. Lowden. I merely think your interests would be better served by returning to Bristol."

"And what of Sir John's interests?"

"Do you not think Dr. Parrish capable? Do you doubt Sir John is in good hands?"

"It is not Dr. Parrish's hands I worry about."

For a moment they stared at one another. Lady Mayfield's cheeks singed red with embarrassment or anger or both. She took a deep breath, clearly fighting to maintain self-control.

"If you will excuse me, Mr. Lowden. I am going to check on my son. And his humiliated nurse."

Face fuming, Hannah swept out of the morning room and walked briskly out to the garden to find Becky and Danny. To reassure the girl that she had done nothing wrong. And to gently remind her what not to say. But she saw no sign of them in the garden.

She returned to the house and climbed the stairs. Becky must have slipped inside and up to the nursery without Hannah noticing, so heated was her discussion with Mr. Lowden.

But she found the nursery empty, the whole floor quiet. She checked her room, Sir John's room, every room, as she made her way back downstairs. Her pulse began to accelerate with each empty room she passed.

She hurried down to the housekeeper's parlor. "Mrs. Turrill, have you seen Becky? She took Danny out to the garden but they're not there now."

The older woman looked up in concern. "Have you checked the nursery?"

"That's the first place I looked. I've checked the whole house except here belowstairs."

"Probably wandered over to the Parrishes'. Shall I send Kitty round to check?"

"Please. I'll check the garden again and the little wood beyond. Becky liked the bluebells there I remember."

Mrs. Turrill nodded. "My fault I'm afraid. Told her they were my favorite." She rose. "I'll check the rest of the house again."

Dread seeped through Hannah's veins. A knowing. A fear . . .

She ran back outside and through the garden, calling for Becky. Remembering the girl's distraught face as she had last seen it, Hannah prayed, *Please, God, don't let her do anything foolish.*

Mr. Lowden followed her out of the house, looking at her in concern, brows drawn low. Only then did she realize tears ran down her cheeks.

"What is it?" he asked. "What's happened? Is it Sir John?"

"No. Have you seen Becky? She took Danny into the garden when you . . . while you and I spoke and now I cannot find them."

"Have you checked inside? And the Parrishes'?"

She nodded. "The maid's run over to the Grange, and Mrs. Turrill is searching the house again."

The young manservant, Ben, came out of the nearby stables, leading a saddled roan. "Here's your horse, sir. All ready for your morning ride."

"Thank you, but Becky Brown has gone missing, her young charge with her. Have you seen them?"

"No, sir," Ben replied, eyes round.

"Borrow a horse from the Parrishes and ride the coast road toward Countisbury," Mr. Lowden said. "I'll ride toward Lynton. Ask anyone you meet if they've seen her. Make haste."

One glance at her teary face and the young man turned and sprinted toward the Grange. Mr. Lowden swung himself up onto his horse.

He looked down at her. "Stay here in case she returns."

Hannah shook her head. "I can't stay and do nothing. Mrs. Turrill is here. I'm going to search the wood."

"I'll ride a few miles and if I seen no sign of them, I'll circle back and meet you there."

She nodded and turned, jogging downhill and into the nearby wood with its carpet of bluebells. *Dear God in heaven, please let Danny be all right. Help me find them. Oh, God, please have mercy. Please.*

Hannah opened her mouth to call out, then hesitated. Might the girl bolt at the sound of her name, fearing she was in trouble? Perhaps a quiet approach would be better. Continuing on, Hannah stepped on a dry branch and it snapped as loud as gun shot in the quiet wood. So much for stealth.

She called out, "Becky!"

Hannah hurried on, panic rising. What had the girl gone and done? What had *she* done by allowing Becky to leave the house with her son? If something happened to him, she would never forgive herself.

In the distance, she heard Mrs. Turrill's voice call out, "Becky! Becky my girl!"

Hannah squeezed her eyes shut. She had not been found in the house nor at the Parrishes'. Hannah trudged on, stepping over logs and pushing away branches, looking this way and that for any sign someone had passed that way.

Listen, a voice in her mind whispered. Then repeated once more, *Listen.*

Hannah paused where she was. She closed her eyes and focused all her attention on hearing.

What was that sound? The gentle whirring of a dove? No. Of running water. She followed the sound, not sure why, but having no other idea which way to go.

The Lyn River ran nearby on its way toward Lynmouth and the Bristol Channel. Would Becky be drawn to the water? It was unlikely she could swim. Water and a baby . . . the two words struck terror in Hannah's heart. She blinked away images of Danny floating away as Lady Mayfield had. Or simply sinking . . .

"Becky!" she called all the louder.

Hannah tripped over a bramble and went sprawling. Pain shot through her injured arm. She heard a familiar whimper and looked up from her prone position, belly on the ground. She tried to cry out, but the fall had knocked the air from her lungs and the cry lodged in her throat.

Ahead, Becky stood on the riverbank, Danny in one arm, the other outstretched for balance. She reached her slippered foot toward a rock amid the rapidly flowing river.

Hannah sucked in a wheezy breath and called out, "Becky, stop! What are you doing?"

The girl turned. "Taking him somewhere safe."

Hannah lumbered to her feet and started forward. She would never reach the girl in time. . . .

Suddenly, Mr. Lowden stepped out from behind a tree. Becky shrieked and leapt from the bank onto the rock. Hannah gasped as Danny bobbled in her grasp.

"There you are, Becky. I am glad I found you," Mr. Lowden said, placating palms outstretched. "I wanted to apologize. I'm sorry I was rude to you before. I hope you will forgive me."

Becky looked from him to a rock farther out, uncertain.

Mr. Lowden calmly went on, "Master Daniel looks to have enjoyed his walk in the wood. Well done. Let us return him to Lady Mayfield."

Becky frowned at Mr. Lowden. "Ain't Lady Mayfield's child."

Panic seized Hannah. She called, "Becky, Danny is my son. You know he is! You are only upset."

Mr. Lowden soothed, "Becky, look at him. No one could look at this handsome lad and not know who his mother is."

Becky looked down at the baby.

"Let me help you," Mr. Lowden said, reaching toward her. "That's it, take my hand."

With a glance toward Hannah, Becky tentatively placed her hand in Mr. Lowden's. He held it and steadied her as she leapt back from the rock onto solid ground.

Hannah released a shaky breath.

"Shall I hold him for you?" Mr. Lowden asked. "How tired your arms must be from carrying him so far from the house."

Becky's face crumpled. "I never meant him no harm, honest I didn't."

"Of course not." He gently took Danny from her. "I will be happy to carry him home for you. Perhaps you would like to sit atop my horse?"

"Your horse, sir? I ain't never rode a horse in my life."

"Well, there's a first time for everything. Perhaps Lady Mayfield might prefer to hold Danny and I shall lead you by the reins? Though you must promise to hold on tight. I shouldn't want any harm to befall you. I know Lady Mayfield depends upon you. In fact, she was just telling me after you left, how much she and Danny need you."

"Was she?"

Hannah walked near, brushing the dirt from her hands. She met James Lowden's gaze, saw his subtle nod.

"That's right, Becky," she agreed. "We need you. You gave us such a fright when you strayed so far from the house alone. Promise me you shall never do so again. If you wish to walk in the wood, I shall be happy to accompany you in future."

"Very well, miss — Um, my lady."

Over the girl's head, Hannah mouthed the words "thank you," to Mr. Lowden, feeling at the moment that she would like to throw her arms around him in gratitude. However, better sense and a throbbing arm kept her from acting on the foolish impulse. She prayed she had not broken her arm all over again.

Remembering Becky's, *"Ain't Lady Mayfield's child,"* Hannah wondered if more than her arm had been damaged. Or had Mr. Lowden believed her explanation of Becky's blunder?

When Hannah and Becky returned Danny to the nursery, Mrs. Turrill was there to meet them. She hugged Becky to herself. Then Danny in his turn.

"Sorry I'm so stupid," Becky said, chin quivering. "I didn't mean to scare everyone.

Honest."

Mrs. Turrill's brow furrowed. "You're not stupid, Becky. Whoever told you that?"

Becky shrugged. "Everybody. My mum, Mrs. Beech, and them what . . ." The girl's words trailed away and a haunted look shadowed her face.

"Them . . . who?" Mrs. Turrill asked, expression pained, jaw tight.

Becky looked away from the housekeeper's wide eyes. "Them men what . . ." She bit her lip. "Never mind." She shrugged again. "I'm sure they was right."

Mrs. Turrill shook her head, eyes glinting. "They were not right. They were wrong. Mean-spirited and wrong. You are not stupid, Becky Brown. You are intelligent, and good, and valuable. Do you hear me?"

"Aww . . ." Becky said it as though she didn't believe the words — as though she barely heard the words, really. Like a slinking pup who recognized an encouraging voice when it had known only undeserved blows. Becky touched a finger to the woman's cheek and whispered, "That's why I love ya."

CHAPTER 13

That evening, Hannah and Mr. Lowden sat
near the fire in the drawing room after dinner, somewhat more companionably than
before their shared trauma. Mr. Lowden
read a book by lamplight and Hannah
sewed as best she could with one hand
restricted by a sling. Earlier, when they'd
returned from the river, Mr. Lowden had
insisted Dr. Parrish reexamine her arm. The
physician had done so, and applied new
starched bandages as a precaution, although
he assured her the bone was knitting nicely.

Now, Mr. Lowden apparently grew restless, for he laid the book aside and rose. He
paused beside the game table with an inlaid
chessboard made from squares of oak and
maple. He picked up the queen, then looked
from the piece to her. "I recall my father
mentioning a visit you and Sir John once
paid him."

She glanced up from her needle, instantly

wary. "Oh?"

"Yes, he invited you both to dinner, I believe, soon after your marriage."

She looked at him, waiting for him to continue. Wondering what he was up to.

"I was in London at the time, at the company headquarters. But I seem to recall him telling me later that he had challenged you to a game of chess. And that you beat him quite handily. Is that true?"

She stared at him, thinking quickly. Dare she assent to remembering the occasion? James Lowden had not been there; it was only the hearsay of his deceased father. But then she thought again. She didn't recall ever seeing Marianna play chess and she barely tolerated any card game that required more than luck. But . . . why would Mr. Lowden recount such a tale if it weren't true? Was it a trick? And what if she agreed and he challenged her to a game?

She said, "I'm afraid I don't recall that, Mr. Lowden. Perhaps your father was being overly chivalrous . . . or forgetful."

For several ticks of the long-case clock James Lowden held her gaze. Then he replaced the piece. "Actually, I am the one being forgetful. Now that I think about it, it was another client's wife he referred to. You don't play chess, I take it?"

"Not well, no."

"Ah. My mistake."

He regarded her with a strange glint in his soft green eyes, the color of pale moss. The corner of his mouth quirked in a knowing grin that seemed to say, *You have passed another test, but it shan't be the last.* The grin emphasized the deep brackets on either side of his mouth. Not dimples, but long grooves, masculine and appealing.

Stop it, Hannah, she reprimanded herself. She could not trust this man. Heaven help her if she began to admire him.

Hannah was massaging Sir John's calf muscle with one hand as Dr. Parrish had instructed, when the physician came in to pay his daily call.

"Ah, how diligent you are, my lady. Well done. It will help him, you will see."

She looked up to acknowledge his encouragement and froze. Sir John's eyes were opened. He was staring at her. And not with the vacant look they had seen before. He was looking *at her.*

"Well, well!" beamed Dr. Parrish. "Look who has returned to us at last! Thank the Lord and pass the glass! Hello, Sir John."

The patient's gaze slowly slid toward the physician, then returned to look at her.

She self-consciously began lowering the bedclothes over his exposed leg. "He must wonder what I am doing. How strange to wake up and find someone rubbing his leg."

"Oh, I don't think any man would object to that!" The good doctor winked at Sir John. "Would he, sir?"

There was no change in Sir John's expression.

"Ah! I forget you don't know me. You may not remember meeting me earlier, but I feel as though I've come to know you quite well. I am George Parrish, your physician and neighbor. My son Edgar showed you about the place when you first visited."

The barest flicker of comprehension shone in Sir John's eyes before returning to Hannah.

The doctor gestured toward Hannah and smiled. "And you know this lovely creature, of course."

When his patient failed to respond with word, smile, or even nod, the doctor asked him to follow his finger, to blink one for yes and two for no, or squeeze his hand.

"Now, there's no rush, Sir John. You speak whenever you like. No hurry. You are healing nicely and no doubt will be your old self soon."

The doctor brightened. "I know! Perhaps

you would like this dear lady to read to you. She has a fine reading voice. In fact, I heard her reading to Master Daniel only last evening." He turned to her. "Has Sir John a favorite book?"

Hannah hesitated. "I . . . shall find something."

"I think reading to him for an hour or so each day an excellent idea. Stimulate his brain. Help him rediscover words again, which have apparently somehow left him."

Hannah read to Sir John that very afternoon. She'd been pleased to find the first volume of *The History of Sir Charles Grandison* among his salvaged things. Her own copy was lost forever, along with her valise.

She sat in the armchair near his bed and began reading. Sir John opened his eyes and watched her as she did so. His bruising and swelling continued to fade, and his marled brown-and-silver beard to thicken.

Half an hour or so later, Mrs. Turrill knocked and entered with a tea tray. "Shall you have your tea here with Sir John, my lady? Ah! He is awake, bless my soul, he is."

"Sir John, have you met Mrs. Turrill, our housekeeper?"

Mrs. Turrill dipped her head and smiled. "What a happy day this is. Well, I shall leave you. Anything else you need, my lady, you just ring, all right?"

The phrase, "my lady," which she had begun to grow accustomed to, sounded like a trumpet blast in Sir John's presence. She winced.

"Thank you, Mrs. Turrill."

The housekeeper left, closing the door behind her.

For a moment, Hannah kept her gaze on the closed door, all the while feeling Sir John's scrutiny on her profile. Slowly, resignedly, she turned. Damp hands clasped in her lap, she faced her begrudging employer, her former mistress's husband, her first infatuation — although he'd never known it. His expression remained inscrutable.

She sighed, and quietly began, "When they found us alone together in the carriage after the accident, they assumed I was Lady Mayfield. At first I was insensible, as you have been. And when I regained my senses and realized . . . well, I should have corrected them, but I did not. I have a child to think of. And with my arm broken, there were few or no posts I would be suited for. I felt I had no choice but to remain here. With Lady Mayfield gone, who was I to be companion to? I would have no position, no place to sleep, and no way to provide for my son or myself. So I allowed the misapprehension to continue. It was wrong of me, I know. I plan to leave as soon as my arm is sufficiently healed and I might find work somewhere. In the meantime, I hope you will forgive me."

His eyes narrowed, his brow furrowed, but whether his expression spoke of anger, or confusion, or deep thought, she was not certain. Did he even remember her?

Good heavens. She realized she had said, "with Lady Mayfield gone." Was this the first he was hearing of his wife's fate? This was not the way to break the news, bound up in her own confession. But it was too late now. And who else besides her would tell him his wife was dead?

"Yes. I am sorry to have to tell you. Lady Mayfield perished in the accident. Dr. Parrish doesn't think she suffered." Lacking the courage to meet his gaze, she closed the book and arose. "Well. Again, I am sorry. Sorry for your loss. For everything."

She turned and quit the room, knowing it was only a matter of time until he regained the power of speech and ordered her to leave. Or worse.

Mr. Lowden would surely return to Bristol soon. He couldn't abandon his practice for long. As soon as he did, she would depart as well. If she left now, the solicitor might suspect what she had done and send someone after her. She thought again of the two women they had seen in the village stocks and shivered, knowing she would pay a high price for her deceit.

The next day, James Lowden entered Sir John Mayfield's bedchamber, closing the door behind him. He stepped toward his employer's bed, not feeling as charitable toward the man as he should.

Sir John watched him approach, recognition flickering in his eyes. Apparently he was more sensible than during James's earlier visits to his bedside.

"Hello, Sir John. How are you feeling today?"

The man lifted a limp hand in a weak, so-so gesture.

James said, "As you are not yet able to discuss your wishes regarding your will, I think I ought to return to Bristol for a few days and take care of things there. But if you wish me to remain, I shall."

Again the man lifted his hand, this time in an apparent wave of dismissal.

"You are . . . comfortable . . . being alone here — well, not alone exactly, but without me to watch out for you and your affairs?"

Sir John nodded.

"Of course, Dr. Parrish is here daily as is Mrs. Turrill. An excellent woman," James said. "I have asked the good doctor to send word as soon as you regain your ability to speak or write your wishes. I will return by week's end either way."

Again, the slight nod.

James gave a cursory bow and turned to go. Hand on the door latch, he looked back over his shoulder. "I wish you a speedy recovery."

It wasn't completely true.

James had nothing against his employer, but a part of him wanted a little more time alone with Lady Mayfield. He had enjoyed their conversations in relative privacy, which would evaporate if and when her husband regained his mobility. The woman intrigued him, though she was clearly hiding something. And he wanted to figure her out, like a complicated legal case. Like a mystery.

James Lowden had never felt this way about a married woman before and didn't like himself very much because of it. He was attracted to Lady Mayfield, even as he reminded himself again and again that she was another man's wife — though not a faithful one. He wasn't even sure what drew him. He had met women more beautiful, more skilled in flirtation, more tempting. Was it the challenge she represented? Did he not want to be the one man she did *not* flirt with? He hoped he was not so shallow.

Did he see mutual attraction mirrored in her blue-green eyes, or did he fool himself? She probably had this effect on most men, Anthony Fontaine most of all. Probably engendered such feelings to suit her ends. But she didn't seem like that sort of woman, for all he'd heard about her.

Yes, he had some business to attend to in Bristol. But he also knew he ought to remove himself from Lady Mayfield's presence before he said or did something stupid — something they might both regret. He also wished to find the family of the lady's companion, Hannah Rogers. There were several nagging questions and loose ends he wished to lay to rest with her. While he was there, he might also inquire into the whereabouts of Anthony Fontaine.

James packed his things and carried his valise down to the dining parlor where Lady Mayfield sat near the window finishing her breakfast. Sunlight shone on her, bringing out the red highlights in her wavy russet hair.

She looked up when he approached.

"Good morning, Mr. Lowden." Her gaze fell to his valise and her eyes widened. "You are leaving us?"

"For a week or so. I am leaving my horse and traveling by stage. I have asked Dr. Parrish to send word if Sir John speaks and asks for me sooner."

"I see. Apparently you don't trust me to do so."

He hesitated. "Not completely, no. Even so, I regret my rudeness to you and I apologize."

She rose and stepped around the table. "I understand, Mr. Lowden. No hard feelings. And thank you again for your help in finding Danny and Becky that day."

"I was happy to be of service." Still he hesitated, turning his hat brim in his hands.

Abruptly, she held out her hand to him. One of his hands immediately abandoned his hat to capture the delicate fingers in his.

"Farewell, Mr. Lowden, and safe journey," she said. "I hope your practice thrives and many new clients realize your competence and skill despite your youth. I wish you a long and happy life."

How earnest, how sober her expression.

"My goodness," he said with a half grin. "I am only leaving for a week. I shall see you again."

She blushed, and ducked her head. "Of course."

Chagrined to have embarrassed her again, he pressed her hand. "But I thank you. Your well wishes mean a great deal, especially considering we got off on the wrong foot together."

She gave him a regretful little grin, but then lowered her eyes once more.

Unable to resist, he lifted her hand to his lips. He pressed a kiss there, lingering a second too long for propriety but not caring. What did a woman like her care about propriety anyway? Or was that only with a certain other gentleman?

"Good-bye, Mr. Lowden," she said.

His gaze locked on hers, then she slipped her hand from his.

"We shall just say 'until we meet again,' all right?"

She formed an unconvincing smile.

Why did he feel that she was saying good-bye for good?

Chapter 14

The next day, Hannah read another chapter to Sir John. She glanced over at him, lying flat, staring at the ceiling, eyes open. Being a tall man, his heels extended past the end of the bed. He seemed to be listening, but it was difficult to gauge his reaction or how much he understood.

Did he even remember giving her this book for Christmas two years ago? *The History of Sir Charles Grandison* was the only gift she'd received, save a length of ribbon from Freddie. It was not unusual for an employer to give a few coins or a token gift on Boxing Day, but one so personal and thoughtful? Unusual indeed.

When she'd unwrapped it, he'd explained, "I know you enjoy novels. I don't read many, but this is a favorite. The main character is a good, honorable man one actually admires."

Like you, she remembered thinking at the

time. But she was a clergyman's daughter, and knew better than to covet another woman's husband, so she had endeavored to stifle her admiration for the man. And for the most part, she had succeeded. It helped that he gave her no encouragement.

Remembering those feelings now made her feel almost disloyal to Marianna's memory. Regardless, she still thought him a good, admirable man. Even now. After everything.

A quick knock sounded and Mrs. Turrill came into the room, Danny in her arms. Hannah laid aside her book and quickly rose to intercept her, but the housekeeper was already approaching the bed, angling Danny toward Sir John.

"Look who I have here."

Sir John slowly turned his head toward them.

"Now, you know who this fine handsome lad is, don't you?"

Sir John stared, slack-mouthed. His head moved left, right, in the slowest of shakes.

"Why this is Master Daniel. And if you don't recognize him, I shouldn't wonder, growing so fast as he is." She looked from Sir John to the child and back again. "Is there not a marked resemblance, I ask you?"

Hannah held her breath.

Again, Sir John's head turned side to side.

"He looks like his mother of course, but also like his father," Mrs. Turrill persisted. "Don't you see it?"

Here it comes. . . . Hannah thought, fidgeting nervously.

Sir John's gaze shifted to her. He rasped out his first word since the accident. "No."

Her heart pounded. What had she expected?

She felt Mrs. Turrill's uncertain gaze on her profile. The woman obviously sensed something amiss. Hannah wondered if she guessed what it was. If only she could brush it off with a smile, and say easily, *"Sir John has always insisted Danny takes after my side."* But she couldn't do it. The lies she had told had begun to rot and stink and sicken, and she could not bring herself to utter another to this dear woman.

Hannah stepped near the bed and held out her hands to take Danny, but the housekeeper kept hold of him, her smile unnaturally bright. "How good to hear your voice, Sir John."

Mrs. Turrill insisted *she* would take Danny back up to the nursery for his nap. "You go on with your reading. It seems to have helped Sir John already, for has he not just spoken? That is good news indeed."

Not for me, Hannah thought. It was only a matter of time now. . . .

She stood there, uncertain what to do as Mrs. Turrill left, shutting the door behind her. Longing to flee the tension in the room, Hannah turned from the bed, but Sir John snagged her arm.

She gasped and looked down at his hand on her wrist, as surprised as if a crab at the seashore had leapt onto her arm. She blinked and risked a look at Sir John's face. His expression was turbulent, bewildered, questioning. But angry? She wasn't sure. He stared into her eyes, and she stared back. When his grip weakened, she pulled her hand from his and hurried from the room.

Hannah avoided Sir John's bedchamber for the rest of the day. She asked Mrs. Turrill to look in on him for her, claiming a headache — the headache was real, though not the reason she avoided Sir John. She imagined Mrs. Turrill and Dr. Parrish thought it strange and uncaring of her.

While Mrs. Turrill was busy in Sir John's bedchamber, Hannah went upstairs to see Becky.

"Becky, quietly gather your things. I'll gather Danny's. It's time for us to leave."

"But I like it here," Becky pouted. "And

Mrs. Turrill says I'm like a daughter to her."

"I know, and I'm sorry. But Sir John is beginning to speak. Our time here is at an end. I told you we wouldn't be staying forever."

"But where will we go?"

"Exeter, I think. It's a sizeable town. Lots of work there, I imagine."

Becky's chin trembled. "But I don't want to go. . . ."

Hannah forced a smile and patted the girl's arm. She couldn't afford for Becky to erupt in a fit of pique. "There, there. Never mind, Becky," she soothed. "You just lie down and rest, all right? We'll talk about it another time."

Becky nodded in relief.

Hannah left her and went down to her room to finish packing. She pulled the partially filled valise from under the bed, tucked a few more things inside, and was about to retrieve the letter hidden in the hatbox when Mrs. Turrill knocked and stuck her head in the door.

"Sir John is asking for you, my lady."

Hannah's heart slammed against her breastbone.

"Dr. Parrish is in with him now. Talking quite well he is, too. He wishes you to join them."

Mrs. Turrill watched her closely. "He also asked that you bring Danny."

"Did he?"

"Yes, though he referred to him as 'the child,' not by name. . . ."

How concerned the woman looked. Had she guessed the truth?

Hannah forced a smile. "Thank you, Mrs. Turrill. Just give me a few minutes to freshen up."

Five minutes later, Hannah set her packed valise beside her door and went up to the nursery for Daniel. Over her day dress she wore Marianna's long pelisse, since her own had not survived the accident.

She dressed Danny in the small clothes she had purchased during the journey, and a wool jumper Mrs. Turrill had knit for him. She left all the baby things the Parrishes had loaned her — clean and pressed — in the nursery. Becky, napping peacefully on her small bed, slept on, undisturbed.

Hannah had decided to leave Becky at Clifton, knowing how attached she had become to Mrs. Turrill and Mrs. Turrill to her. She knew the troubled young woman would be in better hands with the kindly housekeeper than with her. Danny would have to be weaned more abruptly than she'd like. But thankfully, he'd already begun taking a bit of thin gruel and mashed fruit. Becky continued to nurse him, but Hannah had noticed that the nursings did not last as long, and that Danny grew restless and popped off her breast more quickly than before. Yes, the end was near. In more ways than one.

Hannah returned to her room for her valise. She would have to hold it in her good hand and Danny in the crook of her bandaged arm. It couldn't be helped. She would simply walk downstairs, out the side door, and to the nearest coaching inn. There, using the money she had left from the trip to Bath, she would put as much distance between herself and Clifton as she could.

She stepped across the threshold. *But to leave with no word of explanation or apology?* She hesitated in the passage, pulse pounding. On the left, the stairs and freedom. To the right, Sir John's bedchamber.

Face him, a quiet voice whispered in her mind. Her own voice, God's, or the devil's, she couldn't be certain.

I am afraid, Hannah thought in reply.

As well she should be.

Freed of indecision, she set down the valise and shifted Danny to her other arm. She turned not to unknown freedom but across the landing to Sir John's bedchamber, to sure condemnation.

She heard their voices before she reached the door, left ajar. Sir John's low raspy voice now and again responding to Dr. Parrish's loquacious one. Were they talking about her? Had Sir John already told him?

Dr. Parrish turned when she entered. His face lit up at the sight of them. "Ah, here is your family now. Your lovely wife and fine healthy son."

Clearly, Sir John had yet to disillusion him.

Hannah swallowed. "Dr. Parrish. I am glad you are here. There is something —"

"Always glad to be of service, especially to my neighbors," the doctor went on. "And I've grown quite fond of this lad, I don't mind telling you. Just look at him. My goodness, what a resemblance."

"Resemblance to whom?" Sir John asked, voice scratchy from disuse.

Dr. Parrish's brows shot up. "To whom! That's a good one, sir. To you, of course. Mayfield nose and all."

"That's not who I see."

It was now or never, Hannah realized. To explain her side, to apologize. Better to confess voluntarily than to wait to be exposed and then try to defend herself afterward.

She began hurriedly, "You see, Dr. Parrish. When you found us in the wrecked carriage and saw only the two of us within, you quite naturally assumed that we were . . . that I was —"

"What a sight it was, too," Dr. Parrish interjected. "I shall never forget it. What a picture of tenderness amidst tragedy. For even though the both of you were injured and insensible, your wife tenderly cradled your head in her lap."

Why must the man always interrupt? Hannah took a breath and pushed on. "Dr. Parrish, you are very kind. But it was only the way the carriage landed, the positions the fall thrust us into."

"The positions *fate* thrust you into!" he insisted. "Do you think such things happen by chance?"

"Fate? Tenderness?" Hannah shook her head, incredulous. "I don't know how you could find such a scene anything but horrid."

The doctor sighed. "Well, I had not yet come upon the coachman, who was thrown some distance from the wreck. Nor had we spied the poor creature carried away on the tide."

Sir John winced. He murmured through a crackling throat, "My fault. All mine."

Dr. Parrish said, "And your wife suffered her injuries, too, but look how well she has recovered. Her head injury — show him, my lady, if you would. There. I put in the stitches myself and later removed them. I'm no surgeon mind, but there isn't one for miles, so the missus and I did our best. There will be a scar I fear, but nothing a little carefully arranged hair cannot conceal. And her arm is knitting nicely. She needs to regain the strength of it, just as you will need to regain the use and strength of your limbs."

Hannah squeezed her eyes shut. It was so tempting not to go on. Not to admit the truth. She exhaled an angst-ridden sigh. "Dr. Parrish, please let me finish. I need to apologize. You misunderstood the situation and I allowed that misapprehension to continue. I am not —"

"My lady," Sir John slanted her a look. "Are you not well?" He turned toward Dr. Parrish. "Doctor, might her head wound have left her confused? For my wife does not seem herself."

Hannah stared at him, feeling her mouth sag open. She glanced over her shoulder. Had Marianna miraculously appeared? Was he seeing an apparition? She turned back and met his unwavering gaze. Had his head

wound left *him* confused, or . . . ? Or what?
My wife does not seem herself. What did that
mean? Was he blind, or off in his attic? But
the eyes that locked on hers held a disconcerting, knowing glint. Was he telling her
not to reveal her identity to Dr. Parrish?
Why should he?

As though for clarification, Sir John asked,
"The poor creature carried away on the tide
. . . ?"

Dr. Parrish replied, "Your wife's companion. Hannah Rogers."

Hannah had mentioned the death before,
though she wasn't sure how much he'd
comprehended.

Sir John lifted his chin in understanding.
"Ah. Of course."

Dr. Parrish added, "And as sad as that is,
we can at least be thankful that you and
Lady Mayfield were spared."

Hannah opened her mouth in one last attempt, but the words evaporated under the
intensity of Sir John's gaze. He reached out
and grasped her free hand. It likely appeared a comforting gesture, but to Hannah
it felt like a warning.

As if sensing her unease, Danny began to
whine and chafe, kicking painfully against
her arm.

Sir John said with a casual air Hannah

240

found unsettling, "The child is restless, my *dear*. Perhaps you ought to lay him down and get some rest yourself. But do come and see me again in an hour or so."

He wanted to speak to her alone, was that it? To avoid scandal to the Mayfield name? And no doubt to tell her exactly what he thought of her in private.

She returned in an hour's time as bid, curious to learn why Sir John had not exposed her, even as she feared it. Surely he would not knowingly cover for her, would he? No, she was foolish to hope. But when she peeked in at the door, she saw that the man was asleep in his bed and hadn't the heart — nor the courage — to wake him.

She thought back to their first private meeting, the one in which they had discussed the terms of her employment as lady's companion. Sir John offered a generous allowance, though he clearly had reservations about engaging a companion for his wife in the first place. She recalled sitting awkwardly in the morning room of the Mayfields' Bristol house, while Sir John stood across the room, looking not at her but out the window. "Are you willing?"

"Yes," she replied.

He winced, indicating her reply didn't

241

please him, though she wasn't sure why. He said, as if to himself, "But . . . should I agree to it?"

"Only if you wish to."

"My wishes?" He barked a dry laugh that sounded anything but jovial. "God doesn't often grant me what I wish for, I find."

She said earnestly, "Then perhaps you wish for the wrong things."

He looked at her then, as though for the first time. "You may be right. And what is it *you* wish for?"

Challenge lit his silvery blue eyes and for a moment she sank into them, feeling tongue-tied and intimidated.

Before she could fashion a suitable reply, he crossed his arms and continued, "It would be unfair to ask you to report where Lady Mayfield goes and whom she meets, but I can at least hope you will be a good influence on her." He added dryly, "Unlike most of the company she keeps."

She lifted her chin. "You're right, sir. I cannot be her companion and your spy. But I will offer friendly advice when I can to keep her from harming her own reputation or her marriage."

"Ha," he'd scoffed, his cool eyes icing over. "Too late."

If she'd known everything that would happen in that house, would she have agreed to the arrangement? How naïve she had been to think she could curb Marianna's behavior with men. She had not even succeeded in controlling her own.

Curiosity piqued, Hannah decided not to leave until she heard what Sir John wanted to say to her in private.

The next evening, Hannah quietly slipped into Sir John's bedchamber while Dr. Parrish repacked his medical bag. He lifted a hand to acknowledge her presence, then returned to his task. She sat stiffly in the chair she had occupied to read to Sir John, but did not pick up the book. Instead she clasped nervous hands in her lap and wondered what awaited her. Sir John wore a fine dressing gown over his nightshirt and his hair was combed. He had likely been blond in his youth, but now at forty his hair was light brown and at the moment, in need of a good cutting.

He flicked a peevish look in her direction. "I asked you to return last night."

"I did. You were asleep."

Not appearing convinced, he turned his calculating gaze to the doctor. "The, em, medical rubbing my *kind* wife has been performing so ably . . . Is there any reason not to continue with that?"

Hannah cringed at the biting irony in his voice, but the good doctor did not seem to notice.

He shook his head. "None at all. Not until you are on your feet and taking exercise on your own."

"Excellent." Sir John sent her a challenging look. "And doctor, one more thing?"

"Yes?"

"Any reason I cannot resume my . . . conjugal duties . . . with my wife?"

Hannah gasped and ducked her head, cheeks flaming.

The doctor's mouth parted, clearly taken aback. He glanced from one to the other, then fiddled with his case. He ended with an indulgent dimple. "Sir John, you jest, I think. You enjoy teasing Lady Mayfield, I see. But you have embarrassed her, my good sir, and must endeavor to be more discreet in future."

Sir John did not return the man's grin. "I am not jesting. I am in earnest."

Hannah's mind whirled. What was Sir John doing? Embarrassing her as a form of punishment for her deception? It was not like him. Had the crash damaged his mind and character as well as his body? Did he somehow really believe her to be his wife?

The doctor faltered, "Well. I . . . that being the case, I would prefer to speak in private about such matters."

"Why? Does your answer not affect her as much as it does me?"

Dr. Parrish frowned. "Not exactly, no. For she is all but recovered and you are not, though you progress daily. I think with your ribs and that ankle of yours, any . . . strenuous . . . activity will be quite uncomfortable at present. Painful even." He shook his head. "No, in my professional opinion, it is not advisable at present."

"No? Pity. What about sharing my bed. For simple comfort and affection? Is there any harm in that?"

"Sir John!" Hannah protested. "You push too far."

Sir John coolly studied her face. "Apparently, Lady Mayfield is concerned she would injure me in the night."

She recognized the sarcasm in his tone even if the physician did not. Dr. Parrish pursed his lips in thought.

Please say no, Hannah silently pled. Even if she had admired Sir John in the past, at the moment all she felt was fear and mortification. He had never spoken to her so coarsely nor been so cavalier.

"If she is careful not to jostle you too

245

much, I see no harm," the doctor decided. "And no doubt it would be a welcome change for both of you after such a long parting. Yes, I think that would be all right."

Hannah sputtered, "But, I — I can't."

Both men turned to stare at her.

She faltered, "I mean . . . What will Mrs. Turrill say? She will know I have not slept in my own bed and —"

Dr. Parrish interrupted gently, "My dear lady. We are not such proper city folk. Here in the West Country, a man and wife may share a bed without raising eyebrows, I assure you."

"Ah, what a relief," Sir John said with a patronizing smile. "There, my lady, those objections dealt with and the matter settled."

"But Sir John —" she began.

He cut her off once more. "Thank you so much, Dr. Parrish. You have earned your stipend today indeed."

The trusting man looked from one to the other with some bemusement, perhaps noticing Sir John's sarcasm at last, but unsure of its cause or meaning. He was clearly aware of "Lady Mayfield's" discomfort, but likely assumed it was due to modesty and not any real unease or fear of her changeable husband.

When Dr. Parrish had taken his leave, Sir John said archly, "I'm sure you will want to change into your nightclothes."

She slowly shook her head. "Why are you doing this?"

"Because my memory is beginning to return. And with it my imagination." His sardonic tone followed her out the door. "Don't be long, *wife.*"

She walked stiffly from the room and forced her legs down the passage. How had it come to this? What was she to do — refuse and cause a scene? Gather up Danny and walk out the door as darkness began to fall? Surely, he did not really expect her to share his bed. Had seeing Danny and realizing she'd had a child out of wedlock given him ideas? Just because she had fallen in that way once before did not mean she would do so again.

For several minutes, Hannah stood in her bedchamber, uncertain. Then a quiet knock pulled her around.

There stood Mrs. Turrill, questions in her eyes. "I hope you don't mind, but Dr. Parrish mentioned Sir John's request. I thought you might like me to help you change."

"Thank you, Mrs. Turrill." The kind woman helped her into her nightclothes and brushed her hair.

"Are you certain you will be all right?" The light in the woman's eyes, her cautious expression, made Hannah wonder just what she was asking. Just what she knew. Or suspected.

Hannah forced a smile. "Yes, of course." *I will just sleep in the upholstered chair near the fire,* she told herself. In the same room, to appease Dr. Parrish. Near enough to Sir John, she hoped, to appease him and whatever strange test he was giving her. If he wanted to provoke her into confessing who she was, why had he not simply allowed her to do so before? Was he trying to force her to blurt out the truth, and bolt?

She was tempted to do just that.

But where would that leave Danny?

When she entered Sir John's room, she noticed he had slid himself over — or Mrs. Turrill had helped him — leaving space for her in bed. Yet, she did not miss the surprise flash in his eyes when she returned in her nightclothes. Apparently, he had not expected her to agree.

But a moment later his expression hardened once more, and he patted the bed beside him. "Come, *wife.*"

"Sir John . . ." She ducked her chin in reproof.

"You're the one who started this. If you

prefer to leave, go. It's not as though I could chase you."

His eyes flickered over her nightdress and wrapper. She expected a leer or amorous glance but she was mistaken, for he winced as though in pain.

"Those are Marianna's, are they not?"

So he did remember his wife after all.

Hannah looked down at the ivory lawn with its pink ribbon trim. All of Marianna's nightclothes had pink trim, she recalled. She'd insisted upon it.

"Yes. I'm sorry, but my things were lost in the accident."

He turned his face, looking up at the ceiling instead of her. His lips pressed together, working. "So much lost."

Her heart unexpectedly lurched for him. He had shown no grief over Marianna before now. She had begun to believe he didn't feel any. She had been wrong.

"I'm sorry," she repeated, the words heavy with new meaning.

She saw tears brighten his eyes before he blinked them away.

His voice hoarse, he asked, "Is she really gone?"

Hannah whispered, "Yes."

"Gone . . . or dead?"

She looked at him sharply, stunned by the

question.

He glanced over, before returning his gaze to the ceiling above. "Come now. You cannot pretend to know she was daily hoping for a way to be rid of me. A chance to leave me and return to her *lover*." He spat out the final word like spoiled meat. "How the two of you must have mocked me, laughing behind your hands at the honored knight whose own wife was repulsed by him."

Hannah shook her head. "I never mocked you, sir."

"Tell me the truth," he went on. "Did you help her plan her escape? Apparently you at least went along with it, since you are here, pretending to be her."

She gaped at him. "Is *that* why you are doing this? I promise you, sir. I had nothing to do with it. It was an accident. A terrible, unforeseeable accident."

He held her gaze as if measuring her honesty. Then he blew out a breath. "If she really is dead — drowned — then I am cruel indeed to voice such a thing, to even think it. And I apologize. But knowing her as I did. How she despised me. I cannot help but wonder."

Standing there awkwardly, Hannah said, "Sir John, I don't know what to say. Dr. Parrish believes she may have already been dead when the tide drew her from the cracked carriage. Or perhaps that she was thrown into the channel when the carriage crashed, but I don't think that can be true."

He frowned at her. "Why?"

Hannah closed her eyes, trying to capture the fleeting memory, but it scurried from view. "I don't know. I think I may have seen her drifting away. . . . Dr. Parrish and his son tell me they saw her floating, slowly sinking, without struggle. They assured me she did not suffer."

Should she tell him about the ring? If she did, would she not have to return it directly? She did plan to return it, once she found a paying position. But the ring was her insurance. If it was between Danny going hungry or without medicine if he needed it . . . then she would sell the ring or pawn it. She hated the thought of stealing. Knew it was wrong. But she was loath to give up the only thing that might stand between her son and starvation until she found a way to support them.

"I was in and out of my senses," she explained. "I remember only a few flashes of the accident and what came after. But I have a vague memory of trying to grasp her hand, to pull her back, but I had not the strength."

251

He gave a shiver of a nod. His eyes remained distant, as though trying to visualize the scene for himself.

"Not your fault," he whispered. "Mine. All mine. I should never have insisted we drive on."

"Perhaps, but it was an accident. You could not have known what would happen. That we were so near the cliff. Had you known, of course you would have made a different decision."

"Would I? You have more confidence than I do. All I cared about was getting her away from him. Wanted no delays to give him opportunity to catch up. I was determined to separate the two of them forever." He uttered a dry laugh and his voice cracked. "Apparently, I succeeded, didn't I?"

Again, her heart went out to him. To suffer such a loss was hard enough. But to couple that loss with the guilt of feeling responsible for your wife's death? It could cripple the strongest of men. She briefly wondered if his serious injuries added to the torment, but then realized they probably served as some sort of consolation. Had he escaped unscathed, his guilt would likely be tenfold.

She was tempted to ask him why he had not exposed her, why he had allowed her false identity to stand, but was afraid she would not like his answer. He looked so weary, so grief-stricken at the moment that she could not bear to press him. Nor did she want to goad him to return to his baiting callousness.

Tomorrow would be soon enough to ask. Cautiously she stepped toward the bed she had been afraid to approach a quarter hour before. She did not know what she intended to do. Not to lie in it, no. But to offer some sort of comfort.

He watched her, eyes wary.

"Water, Sir John?" she asked, nodding toward the jug and glass on the side table.

He slowly reached out his hand, elbow propped on the bed.

She poured a glass with trembling fingers and held it out to him, but he did not take it. He only looked at her, arm upraised. He moved his hand away from the glass, but left it extended toward her.

"No?" She set down the glass and nervously eyed him. She recalled holding his glove found after the wreck, and wondering if she'd ever held his hand. Tentatively, she slid the fingers of her good hand over his and gave them a gentle squeeze. She waited anxiously, but he did not grab tight or pull her into his bed. Nor repeat his request that she join him there. For a few moments more they remained as they were, she standing, he lying, gazes touching, fingers entwined.

Then she said, "I shall sit here by the fire and keep you company until you fall asleep, shall I?"

With a slight nod of resignation, he released her hand and lowered his arm.

She sat in the cushioned chair near the fire, but angled the chair to better see Sir John. She gathered a lap rug over her legs and settled back. "You sleep now, Sir John."

"That's all I do is sleep . . ." he murmured, but already his eyes were drifting closed.

She awoke with a start many hours later, surprised to see dim dawn light seeping in through the transom and between the shutters. She looked over at the bed and found Sir John watching her, an extra pillow propped under his head.

Self-consciously, she straightened in the chair, wincing at her stiff neck and numb arm. She glanced down at herself, relieved to find her nightclothes were not askew, and still covered her modestly.

"I . . . didn't intend to sleep here all night."

"I'm glad you did," he said. "I liked having you here, though it cannot have been comfortable."

In more ways than one, she thought, rising gingerly.

He added, "I'll have that water now, if you don't mind."

She hesitated. If he had managed to place a second pillow under his head, he could likely slide over and help himself to a glass of water.

She walked forward slowly. She didn't mind helping him, but she was wary of his motives. Or was he simply accustomed to being served?

She handed him the glass and this time he took it and sipped. His eyes dropped to her hands. Only then did she realize she was unconsciously rubbing one hand with the other, trying to restore feeling and dispel the prickling numbness. Her efforts were somewhat hindered by the stiff bandage.

He handed back the glass and she returned it to the side table.

"Sit," he commanded.

"What?"

"Just sit." He nodded toward the bed. Nervously, she obeyed, sitting gingerly on the edge, ready to bolt at the first sign of danger.

"Your hand." He laid open his palm to receive it.

Thankfully, she was not wearing his wife's ring. Even so, she hesitated. Did he simply want to hold it again, as he had the night before? It seemed childish to refuse him when she had complied once already, but somehow in the light of day, the act seemed more awkward and forward.

She swallowed and tentatively laid her numb hand in his. He raised his other hand as well and began kneading and gently massaging her palm and fingers.

Needles of pleasure and pain shot up her arm. Embarrassment followed. "Sir John, you needn't do that. It had only fallen asleep. I —"

"Hush. It is the least I can do after all your ministrations to me."

She wanted to pull her hand away. Knew she should. But the pleasure, the relief, were too sweet, and she failed to do so.

So that was how Mrs. Turrill found them when she came in with the breakfast tray. Hannah sitting on the bed, her hand in Sir John's. She felt embarrassed at being caught so close to him, and tried to pull her hand away, but he held it fast.

Mrs. Turrill smiled a closed-mouth smile, dimples in her cheeks. For a second, Hannah saw the scene as though through the housekeeper's eyes. What a sweet domestic picture they must make. Husband and wife, hand in hand. If only she knew the truth of it. How her smiles would fade then.

CHAPTER 15

Hannah returned to Sir John's bedchamber the next evening. Not to sleep in his bed, nor in the uncomfortable chair again, but to talk with him for a time before bidding him good night.

She was surprised to find him propped up with pillows — a portable writing desk in his lap, and quill in hand.

"Good evening, Miss . . . my lady. What a pleasant surprise."

She ducked her head, embarrassed to hear him call her by the title. "If you are busy, I shall leave you."

"Not at all. Come and talk to me. What a pleasure that will be." His warm tone seemed sincere. Was he?

She walked closer. "May I ask what you are writing?"

"A letter to Mr. Lowden."

"Ah." Hannah felt an odd twinge at the sound of his name.

Sir John set aside his writing things and patted the edge of the bed. "Please. Come and sit by me. I promise to behave myself." The words rumbled low in his chest. She had almost forgotten what a rich, baritone voice he had.

Tentatively, Hannah sat on the edge of the bed. He took her free hand in his, interlacing their fingers. Had she not once longed for such a gesture?

"How is Danny?" he asked.

"He is well, thank you."

"I am glad to hear it." He hesitated, then said gently, "How surprising to find you'd become a mother. We had no idea."

She avoided his gaze. "I know."

"I . . . don't suppose it would be polite to ask about . . . the child's father?"

Hannah felt her cheeks heat. Instead of replying, she asked the question that had been on her mind for some time.

"Pardon me for raising a sad topic, Sir John. But I was surprised to hear from Dr. Parrish that Lady Mayfield had been with child."

He flinched. "Yes, a physician in Bath confirmed it."

"A double loss for you then."

Sighing, he said, "Of course I am sorry for any loss of life, especially of one so young and innocent. But when I think it was in my power to prevent it . . ."

"Sir John, you don't know that."

"But the child Marianna carried was not mine," he went on evenly. "Couldn't be. But as she and I would have been married at the time of its birth — the child, if a son, would have legally been heir to my entailed property. And, if Marianna had but asked me, I would have forgiven her and loved that child as if he or she were my own flesh and blood."

A wistful ache ran through her at the words. "What did Marianna say, when the doctor confirmed the news? She must have feared you might realize the child was not yours."

"She was not repentant, if that is what you think. She said, 'What did you expect?' "

Hannah shook her head. "But still you hoped to keep her from Mr. Fontaine? Hoped coming here would bring her back to you?" She heard the incredulity in her voice but felt powerless to curb it.

"She was my wife. And I her husband. Before God. For better or for worse. Though I never imagined how much worse — how that vow would test me like no words I had spoken in my life."

Sir John pulled a face and continued.

"What did I do to make Marianna so despise me, did she ever tell you?"

Hannah hesitated. "I don't know that it was anything you did, Sir John. I think she already had strong feelings for Mr. Fontaine when you met her."

"Then why did she marry me?"

Hannah had wondered that herself, and had pieced together at least a partial answer from things Marianna had confided. "You know her father wielded a great deal of influence over her while he lived," she gently began. "And you are a man of far more consequence than Mr. Fontaine — wealth, property, title. It's little wonder Mr. Spencer was so strongly in favor of the match."

Sir John nodded thoughtfully. "And Marianna agreed, believing there would be no hindrance to continuing her affair with Fontaine on the side."

Hannah shrugged. "I don't know if she intended to continue seeing him from the beginning, or not."

"In either case," Sir John said, "I am quite certain she didn't foresee the lengths I would go to prevent that happening." He rubbed his free hand over his eyes. "I thought if I could just get her away from him, away from his influence, she might give me, give us, a chance. But she never did."

He looked down at their entwined fingers, then sent her a sidelong glance. "How hypocritical you must think me now."

"I'm sorry, Sir John."

"How can you be sorry? After everything I've done? It is I who should be begging your forgiveness."

How self-conscious Hannah felt, sitting there, her small hand in his large one. Yet she could not deny the sensation a pleasant one. They sat that way, silent for several minutes.

Then Hannah took a deep breath, dreading his reaction to what she was about to say. "By the way," she began. "While you were still insensible, Mr. Fontaine came here, demanding to see Marianna."

His brows lowered ominously. "The devil he did."

"Yes. About a week and a half after the accident. He demanded to see Marianna, but of course I told him that was not possible. And why."

"What did he say?"

"He was shocked of course. And . . . clearly devastated."

He took this in, thoughtfully chewing his lip.

"Of course he recognized me," Hannah added. "But he only stayed for a short time,

and no one referred to me as Lady Mayfield while he was here."

He nodded his understanding.

"But if he should return . . ." Hannah let
her timid words trail away.

"Why would he? Now that she is gone?"

"I hope you are right," Hannah said. For
she hated to think what Fontaine would do
when he learned she'd been impersonating
his dear departed lover. But for now, she
pushed that thought away.

Sir John ran a thumb over her knuckles.
"You know, I'm surprised some handsome
suitor like Fontaine hasn't claimed *your* af-
fections by now. I would say I was sorry to
learn you had not married after you left us,
but that would be a lie."

"Perhaps I should have. For Daniel's
sake." Again she wondered whom Sir John
had meant when he said, "that is not who I
see" when he looked at Danny. He had
never met Fred Bonner, she didn't think.
Had he noticed the way his secretary, Mr.
Ward, had looked at her, and suspected
him? She hoped not.

Sir John released her hand and traced a
finger around the delicate skin of her inner
wrist, sending a feathery tingle up her arm.
"A place without freckles," he observed.

He ran his hand up her arm, bare to the

puffed sleeve high on her shoulder, then back down again. "You are a beautiful woman, Hannah. I hope you know that."

She managed a little shrug. She thought herself rather plain, but Fred had often told her how pretty she was. He'd admired her, even asked her to marry him. At the moment she was glad she declined.

She said, "Nothing to Marianna, I know."

"She was a rare beauty, it is true," he allowed. "In face and figure."

Hannah felt his gaze linger on her neckline and felt self-conscious and insecure. Marianna had been endowed with a generous bosom. A generous . . . everything.

Suddenly she sucked in a breath. For his palm pressed lightly to her bodice. His gaze however, remained on her face. "You are beautiful, Hannah. Just as you are. Never doubt it. Slender and feminine and graceful."

Heart thumping, Hannah sat there stiffly on the edge of his bed. Torn between fleeing, and leaning closer.

He removed his hand, and she released the shaky breath she'd been holding. Awkwardly, she rose. "Well. Good night, Sir John."

"Leaving?"

"Yes. I think it's best, don't you?"

He slowly shook his head, eyes glinting. "I don't think you want to hear my answer to that."

Hannah found herself singing to Danny the next morning, feeling the closest thing to happiness she had felt in a long while. As she looked into her son's precious face, irrational hope rose in her heart, and she found herself entertaining an unrealistic dream.

Later, she left Danny in Becky's care and went downstairs to find a children's book to read to him, and a simple book for Becky, who had confided that she didn't know how to read. Hannah would have liked to go outside as well and pick some flowers to brighten the nursery and Sir John's room, but at the moment rain fell steadily outside.

She was passing the vestibule when someone knocked at the front entrance, so she answered it herself. She opened the door and stared, for a moment her vision and mind not connecting. She'd forgotten how tall he was. How strange, how surreal to see him here, out of his usual element. He was from her past life — how had he managed to step onto the stage of her present one?

"Hannah," Fred breathed, eyes wide. "I knew it. I knew you could not be dead."

"Shh. Freddie. Not here. Let's go out into the garden."

He hesitated, mouth parted. "It's raining."

"I know, but . . . We used to like the rain, remember?"

"We were children then, Han."

She grabbed an oil-coat from a peg near the door and swung it around her shoulders. Rangy, dark-haired Fred turned up his collar, replaced his hat, and followed her back outside.

She led the way along the stone path, stopping beneath the arched, vine-covered trellis — a doorway of sorts between Clifton and the garden, with a path to the Grange beyond. The thick, interwoven vines and leaves protected them from the worst of the rain.

"What happened, Han," he asked. "Why are you here? You do know they put it about that you had died. It was in the newspaper."

"I know. I received your letter."

"*You* received the letter? But I wrote to Sir John. . . ."

She explained about the crash, the drowning, Sir John's injuries and her own, and the doctor's assumption that she was Lady Mayfield.

He stared at her in disbelief, dark eyes pained. "And you let them go on believing

266

it? And let me go on believing you were dead? I told your father you died! How could you do that, Han?"

"I needed a way to get Danny back. I could think of nothing else to do."

"Nothing?" His eyes flashed. "Nothing but lying and pretending to be dead? Deceiving people into believing you are another woman — another man's wife?" Incredulity warred with the anger in his voice.

"What should I have done, Freddie?" Her voice rose. "You could not help me. I would never have been able to earn enough on my own and especially not while my arm was broken."

"What about your father?" he challenged. "He would have helped you."

"Would he? Even if he had the money, would he really . . . when he knew everything?"

Fred considered, then his gaze skittered away. "He might."

For a moment they stood there in uncomfortable silence, the rain pattering against the glossy leaves of the trellis.

Finally Fred asked, "Is Danny all right? I didn't know if you'd taken him with you or not. I was so worried when I went to that house in Trim Street, but found no children there."

"Yes, he is with me and well, thank God."

"What will you do when Sir John wakes and realizes what you've done?"

"He has regained his senses. And he has not exposed me."

"What? Why on earth not?" Suddenly Fred's mouth tightened, and his eyes dulled. "I don't think I want to know."

"It's not like that," she said, hoping it was true. Sir John's acceptance of her charade felt almost . . . protective. Might it mean more? She gripped her old friend's arm. "Look. I am sorry, Freddie. For all of it. But it has gone too far. I know I cannot pretend to be Marianna for much longer, but I can't just walk away. Not yet. Not until I figure out Sir John's intentions, and how to provide for Danny."

His gaze lifted to the grand house beyond. "Seems like you've figured that out well enough."

She winced. "Please, let it lie for now, Fred. I will tell my father in my own time. Though really, might it not be easier for him to go on thinking I'm dead? Might that not be easier to bear than the truth of all I've done?"

He ran a hand over his face. "I don't know." For a moment he stared blindly across the dripping, green garden. Then he said, "By the way, a man came around, asking questions about Hannah Rogers, and why she had left the Mayfields' employ. I don't remember his name. A solicitor, I think he said."

Her heart thudded. "What did you tell him?"

"Nothing."

"Good." From the other side of the trellis, movement caught Hannah's eye. A flash of green cloak and black umbrella. A sharp-featured face. *Oh no.* Mrs. Parrish. Had she seen her there, speaking to a strange man in private? No doubt she would think the worst and waste no time in spreading it about the county.

She turned back to Fred. "I would invite you in for a meal after your journey, but I hate to ask you to pretend you are only a friend passing by."

"Whose friend?" he asked, lip curled. "Me, Lady Mayfield's friend? That's a laugh."

"Well at least come to the kitchen door and I'll wrap up something for the journey home."

"The kitchen door like a beggar? No, thank you, Hannah. Or should I say, my lady."

His sarcasm cut her. "Fred, please . . ."

Suddenly he gripped her arms, big brown eyes pleading. "This is insane, Hannah. Come away with me. Right now. Go collect Danny and I'll take you home. We'll marry. My father will help us and so will yours, perhaps."

For a fleeting second she considered it, allowed her mind to travel down the path of possibilities. What she would gain, what she would lose. She was fond of Fred, but Sir John was a widower now. Was there any hope . . . ?

She felt his scrutiny. Did the shame show in her heated cheeks, her difficulty in meeting his gaze?

His entreaty turned into a scowl. "You don't want to marry me. Why should you give up all this" — he gestured toward the house — "to be a simple carter's wife? I never would have thought it of you." He shook his head. "Better to be a rich man's trollop than a poor man's wife?"

She gasped and her vision blurred. She felt dizzy and ill. Never had dear Fred spoken to her with such venom. She momentarily considered slapping his face as a maligned lady might. But truly, what else was he to think? Had she any virtue, any honor left to defend?

He bit his lip and his eyes softened. "I'm

sorry, Han. I didn't mean it. I'm just shocked. Disappointed."

"I understand," she murmured. She took a long steadying breath, then asked, "Why did you come here, Fred?"

He shrugged. "I couldn't believe it was true; that you were gone. I had to come and see where it happened. Learn if anyone had witnessed the accident, and if your body had yet been recovered. Ask the Mayfields if any of your belongings had been salvaged that I might take to your father. Or keep for myself, to remember you by." He shook his head. "How foolish I am."

She squeezed his arm, tears filling her eyes. "Not foolish — dear."

"Not dear enough, it turns out." He sighed deeply. "If you won't change your mind, I'll leave. But I warn you, Han. When people find out they've been deceived, there'll be the devil to pay."

She nodded, fearing and believing that very thing. "I know." If only she had not allowed people to think she was Marianna. What a trap she had made for herself.

He reached a hand toward her, hesitated midair, then dropped it. "Good-bye, Han. Again."

With a sad smile, he turned away. He passed through the archway, out of the

271

garden, and out of her life. Leaving her standing there on the threshold. Alone.

CHAPTER 16

Hannah spent the rest of the afternoon second-guessing herself and praying she had not made yet another mistake by not leaving with Fred. Sir John's wife had just died. It was far too soon to expect anything from him. Was she foolish to remain a little longer, and increase her risk of discovery? Especially knowing that Mr. Lowden was in Bristol asking questions about her. Who knew what information he might uncover and bring back with him? In the meantime, she curtailed her visits to Sir John's bedchamber. Because if the servants or the Parrishes thought their relationship had become intimate, how much worse it would be when the truth came out. . . . She shuddered at the thought and pushed it away once more.

A few days later, Sir John issued a formal invitation for "his lady and son" to join him for dinner in his room. Mrs. Turrill grinned like a schoolgirl and eagerly planned a meal as festive as a picnic.

Kitty enthused, "So romantic of Sir John. You are a lucky woman, my lady."

Hannah wasn't sure about that, but managed a nervous smile, wondering what Sir John was up to now. She hoped he wasn't trifling with her for some reason. She thought again of his compliments, the way he had touched her, and the fact that he'd asked Dr. Parrish if she could share his bed. . . . Might Sir John want marital "rights" from this pretend marriage of theirs?

The housemaid insisted on curling Hannah's hair again and touching a little rouge to her cheeks. As if her face wasn't red enough between her self-consciousness and her freckles.

Becky bathed Danny and dressed him in a fresh gown and cap, while Hannah wore an ordinary white muslin dinner dress — gently but firmly refusing to wear one of Marianna's more elegant gowns. She remembered too well Sir John's reaction to his wife's nightclothes.

At the appointed hour, Hannah carried Danny into Sir John's bedchamber. The days were longer now, and the room was bathed in golden, late afternoon sunlight. Someone had helped Sir John into the wheeled invalid chair and he sat at a small tea table laid with linen, china, and fresh flowers. He was dressed in an open banyan jacket and loose cravat. Instead of a waistcoat, his ribs were bound in thick bandages. His hair had been cut, by Mrs. Turrill, she guessed, and brushed back from his face. His beard had been neatly trimmed, which accentuated his cheekbones and masculinity. He looked handsome, and for a moment, reminded her of a pirate.

"Good evening, my —" He stopped, bit his lip, then abruptly held out his hands to take Danny.

A blanketed basket sat on the floor near her chair, so she might lay the child down to better eat her meal, but Sir John insisted on holding him.

She sat down, wiping damp palms on her table napkin. She surveyed the meal spread before them: veal-and-ham pie, roast chicken, salad, stewed fruit, and biscuits. "Mrs. Turrill has outdone herself," she said.

He nodded. "Indeed she has." He held Danny in the crook of one arm while he ate with the other, now and again feeding the boy bits of biscuit or stewed fruit. It was apparent Sir John was already regaining strength with the help of Mrs. Turrill's excellent cooking.

After several bites, he began, "May I ask how have you been occupying yourself? You have been somewhat scarce these last few days."

"Have I?" Hannah thought back quickly. "Oh, well, I . . . have undertaken to teach my young nurse to read. I found her staring at your copy of *Sir Charles Grandison.* And when I said she could read it when we were through, she confessed she could not read. So I have begun teaching her."

"That is good of you."

She ducked her head. "I am not doing so to boast, nor to impress you."

"Though perhaps as an excuse to avoid me?"

A dry crust caught in her throat, and she hurriedly took a sip of lemonade. Setting down her glass, she picked up a basket near at hand and offered it to him. "Bread roll, Sir John?"

He took the hint and didn't press her, instead turning his attention to Danny, talking quietly to the child and gently bouncing his knee to keep him content.

With relief, Hannah focused on her meal. The pie was delicious and she savored every bite. Next she attempted to cut a piece of roast chicken, but found it difficult to employ both knife and fork with her arm in its sling.

Danny nodded off to sleep in Sir John's arms, and he gently bent low and laid the boy in the basket. Then he reached for her knife. "Here, let me help you with that."

Hannah flushed. "No, really, I am not a child."

He placed his warm hand over hers, stilling her efforts, and looked into her eyes. "You are a woman, as I am very much aware. But I am at least partly to blame for your injury, so please allow me this small thing."

She gave in then and watched as he cut her meat, feeling like a helpless little girl and not liking the sensation.

Finishing, he set down the cutlery and asked, "Does your arm pain you a great deal?"

"No. Hardly at all."

"And your forehead?" He reached his hand toward her.

She recoiled in surprise and, seeing the flash of hurt cross his eyes, instantly regretted her reaction.

He said, "I only wanted to see it. To assure myself you are healing well."

"I am. I promise."

He extended his hand again. This time she sat still as he gently brushed back the hair that Kitty had so carefully arranged to hide the red mark.

"See? It's nearly healed," she said.

He frowned. "That will leave a scar." He regretfully shook his head. "Another injury at my hands."

"Sir John, it's nothing."

"And the other?"

Hannah's throat felt suddenly dry, and she found the words stuck there as the crust had been moments before.

In his basket, Danny let out a cry. Glad for the diversion, Hannah reached down for him. "Probably wet his nappy."

She rose. "Thank you for the dinner, Sir John, but I had better to take him back up to the nursery."

Sir John gave her a knowing look. "Making your escape already, Miss Rogers? I knew it would only be a matter of time until you did."

The next afternoon, Hannah was on her way downstairs after settling Danny for his nap and giving Becky a reading lesson, when she heard the door open below and Mrs. Turrill greet a visitor. Hannah tensed. Had Fred returned?

She descended the final pair of stairs on tiptoe and paused on the half landing to survey the vestibule. There, James Lowden handed his hat to Mrs. Turrill. He looked up, and his green eyes locked on hers, his expression difficult to decipher.

Mrs. Turrill turned her head to see what had arrested his attention. "Ah. My lady, look who's here."

"You're back," Hannah breathed in some surprise.

"Yes. I said I would return in about a week. Do you not recall?"

"Oh. It's just . . . well, the time passed quickly." And she had not departed as planned.

"You are not . . . happy to see me?"

"On the contrary, you are very perfectly welcome."

He studied her face, his brows low in curiosity — or suspicion?

She looked away first, and found Mrs. Turrill watching her, worry evident in her soulful dark eyes.

The housekeeper excused herself, leaving the two alone in expectant silence.

Hannah said awkwardly, "Your former room is ready for you. And the morning room is at your disposal. Everything is the same as before."

He tilted his head to the side, eyes glinting. "Not everything."

She swallowed, unsure of his meaning and afraid to ask. What had he learned about her while he'd been away? She forced a smile. "Well, I shall leave you to get settled. We're to have roast duck for dinner tonight, I understand. I hope you like duck?"

His mouth quirked. "Domesticated or decoy?"

She blinked. "I . . . have no idea."

"Poor hen," he said. "Trapped in a decoy snare of her own making." His cold eyes belied his sympathetic tone.

Hannah was taken aback by the odd exchange, stung by the innuendo. She hoped she was imagining it.

He tugged off his gloves and said, "Well, I shall go up and greet Sir John if you don't mind. Assuming he is still alive?"

"Of course he is," she defended. "In fact, you will find him greatly recovered and speaking for himself."

"Well. Good." He slapped his gloves onto the sideboard and took himself upstairs.

James Lowden walked up the stairs, irritation coursing through him. He was vexed with himself, with her, and with Sir John. How much should he tell his employer of what he'd learned in Bristol? He paused at the bedchamber door, took a deep breath, and knocked.

"Come," Sir John called.

His strong reply surprised James. It was the first time he had heard the man's voice since the accident.

James entered the room, surprised again to find his client sitting upright in bed in a fine burgundy dressing gown, though a counterpane covered his legs. He wore a beard, neatly trimmed. And someone had cut his hair. He looked younger than when James had last seen him.

"Hello, Sir John."

"Mr. Lowden. Welcome back."

James shook his head. "You wrote to say you were recovering, but — my goodness, how well you look." He did indeed. James knew he should be glad.

"Thank you. Good journey?"

"Oh, the usual tedious, spine-jarring experience. No accidents or anything if that's what you meant."

"I did not."

James felt his neck heat. What a callous thing to say. "I did not mean . . . I was not referring to —"

Sir John waved away his apology. "Never mind. As you see, no harm has befallen me during your absence. You worried for nothing."

"Did I?"

"Yes, as it turns out."

"And . . . why is that?"

"Why? Because the lady in question means me no harm, I assure you."

"Does she not?"

Sir John shook his head. "In fact she has been quite kind in ministering to me body and soul."

Body and soul? Flummoxed, James faltered, "But you still wish to revise your will, I trust?"

"Let's hold off on that at present."

"But —" James bit his tongue. He cleared his throat, wishing he might clear his confusion as easily. "Well, that is your prerogative of course, but I must say I am surprised."

But was he — was he really?

"Go and get settled Mr. Lowden. We shall have plenty of time to talk later."

That evening, Hannah ate dinner with Mr. Lowden in awkward formality, the roast duck tasting like sawdust in her mouth. Their former, fledgling camaraderie seemed to have vanished. He had changed toward her, she realized. During his absence, had he learned something unsavory about Lady Mayfield . . . or about Hannah Rogers?

Near the end of the meal, Mr. Lowden

picked up his wine, but instead of sipping, held his glass midair.

"You once told me you received a letter from a friend of Miss Rogers, who took it upon himself to inform her father of her death."

Sending a nervous glance to Mrs. Turrill, dishing out their rice pudding at the sideboard, Hannah nodded.

He asked, "Was this 'friend' a Fred Bonner?"

She snapped her head toward him, instantly on her guard.

Not waiting for her to answer, he added, "And was her father a Mr. Thomas Rogers, formerly of Oxford, now curate of St. Michael's on the outskirts of Bristol?"

She only stared at him, heart racing.

"Hannah Rogers's mother, a Mrs. Anne Rogers, died ten years ago of the influenza, I believe," he continued. "Hannah had two elder brothers, both gone to sea. Did you know the eldest, Bryan Rogers, has passed his lieutenancy examination?"

Mutely, she shook her head.

"Apparently, I know more about this bosom companion of yours than you do, my lady."

Hannah faltered, "How did you . . . ?"

"When I returned to Bristol, I unearthed

a letter Sir John wrote to my father last year, while he was living in Bath, asking him to look into the matter of his wife's missing companion. As you yourself told me, Hannah Rogers left abruptly, which apparently concerned Sir John, as she had always been a steady, reliable sort before. According to my father's notes, Sir John feared some harm may have befallen her, or that someone in his household had done something to cause offense, or to cause her to fear for her safety — something significant to cause a dependable person to act in such an uncharacteristic manner."

Hannah's mind whirled. Sir John had worried about her? Who in his household did he think had done something to offend or frighten her — Mr. Ward, Marianna and Mr. Fontaine, or he himself?

Mr. Lowden continued, "My father asked Sir John if this Miss Rogers had stolen something or if anything had gone missing. But he assured my father it was nothing like that. He seemed to trust her thoroughly."

"Did he?" she murmured, surprised and pleased to hear it.

"Yes. I reviewed what little correspondence I could find pertaining to Miss Rogers. Apparently, my father did not pursue the matter very far. So I decided to do so myself. I went to her father's house, but Mr. Rogers had not seen his daughter since she'd moved with the Mayfields to Bath. I also met a friend of hers, a Fred Bonner. He seemed quite reticent to speak with me. It was obvious the young man had been fond of Miss Rogers, perhaps even loved her, and mourned her loss. It was also clear he was hiding something about her past. It made me wonder if Hannah had got herself into trouble with this young man. If she had left the Mayfields' employ to conceal a certain . . . condition."

Hannah's throat tightened. "Why would you think that?"

"Just a guess. A suspicion. Did no one notice anything unusual about her? Had Miss Rogers confided anything about a young man, or her future plans? Had she been ill in the mornings? Gained weight?"

Hannah felt her neck heat. "These are not things spoken of in polite company."

A spoon clanked and she glanced over, only then realizing Mrs. Turrill was still in the room. Hannah pressed her lips together. "That will be all, Mrs. Turrill. Thank you so much."

"Yes, an excellent dinner," Mr. Lowden added. "Thank you."

With a concerned look at one and then

the other, Mrs. Turrill backed from the room and closed the door behind her.

Mr. Lowden continued, "I asked for a description of Hannah Rogers." He pulled a small notebook from his pocket and flipped past several pages. "Would you like to hear how she was described?"

"No."

He read from his notes as if she had not spoken. " 'Slender. Reddish brown hair. Fair eyes. Modest in dress and comportment.' That was from Mr. Rogers. And this one from Fred Bonner. 'A pretty girl with dark ginger hair and freckles. A lovely smile.' "

Tears bit her eyes, but panic burned them away. She had no idea what to say.

He looked up at her. "Is it an accurate description?"

Instead of answering, she asked, "Have you shared this information with Sir John?"

"Not yet. Do you think he will find it interesting?"

"I have no idea." Very little of it would surprise him, Hannah thought. Then why was she so frightened?

James Lowden leaned back in his chair and surprised her by changing tack. "Sir John is in good spirits. He tells me you've been 'ministering to him body and soul.' What did he mean by that?"

She licked her dry lips. "I . . . suppose he means that I have undertaken a regimen Dr. Parrish ordered to help him strengthen his limbs after lying in bed so long. Simple stretches and the kneading of muscles. That's all."

"Is that all?"

She blinked away images of Sir John holding her hand. Brushing the hair from her brow. Touching her bodice.

Mr. Lowden watched her face. "Very . . . wifely," he allowed. "Very intimate. I must say I am surprised."

"It isn't *intimate,*" she defended. "Not in that way."

The housemaid knocked once and poked her head into the room. "Excuse me, my lady. But Sir John wishes to know if you will be visiting his bedchamber again tonight?"

Heat suffused her neck and face. She could not meet Mr. Lowden's startled gaze.

Hannah did go to Sir John's bedchamber that night, but she went earlier, before she had changed into her nightclothes — determined not to stay long. Mr. Lowden's return had been a cold splash of reality, making her tenuous situation seem less hopeful and more tawdry. She knew he had gone up to see Sir John again after dinner. She wondered if he had confided any of his findings — his visit to her father, or his theories about Fred Bonner and Hannah. Should she?

She once again found Sir John sitting up in bed with a portable writing desk in his lap, and quill in hand. He looked up at her with a ready smile. Then his gaze flicked to the mantel clock before returning to her, sweeping over her emerald green evening dress — one of Marianna's older ones she'd altered to fit her slighter figure.

"Good evening, my lady. You're . . . early."

"Hello, Sir John."

She approached the bed without being asked and stopped beside it.

He looked at her, taking in the lower, evening-gown neckline. Her pinned hair. Her wary face. "The color suits you. You look beautiful," he said quietly. "Beautiful and sad."

She ducked her head.

Nib in hand, he lifted the quill, tickling under her chin. "Look at me," he said gently. "What is it? Is Danny all right?"

"A little colicky, but otherwise fine." She looked up and braved a small smile. "Thank you for asking."

Holding her gaze, he slowly lowered the

quill from beneath her chin, down the column of her throat, down her breastbone, toward the hollow beneath.

She jerked away, stepping back from the bed. His familiarity, which had previously warmed her, now put her on edge.

He frowned. "Forgive me, I thought . . . What's wrong? Has something happened?"

"Mr. Lowden is with us again, and it's . . . awkward. He's asking questions."

"About us?"

"About . . . Hannah Rogers."

"Ah . . ." He considered this, then said quietly, "Remember, my dear. Mr. Lowden works for me. You have nothing to fear from him."

He tilted his head to the side and regarded her cautiously. "Or is fear not what you feel for him? Is there . . . more to it?"

"I don't know," she whispered. "He took against me at first, but then we seemed to come to a truce. But now . . . he's changed toward me. He knows, or at least suspects the truth."

"Leave him to me. Unless . . ." He studied her face. "Have you developed feelings for my solicitor?"

She stared at him, stunned by the suggestion, and yet . . . could she honestly say she felt nothing for the man? "I . . . We . . .

Nothing of that sort is going on. But he seems . . . angry with me, or at least suspicious."

He nodded and said in his low, rich voice, "Perhaps he cannot reconcile the Lady Mayfield I wrote about, with the modest, gentle woman he met here. A woman twice as ladylike as Marianna Spencer ever was."

She relished his praise, even as dread cramped her stomach. She had been living in a dream these last few days. An unrealistic, unattainable dream.

He held out his hand to her. She hesitated, then placed hers in his. But then someone knocked on the door and Hannah jumped back, embarrassed. She didn't want James Lowden to find them in anything resembling an *intimate* position.

But it was not James Lowden. Mrs. Turrill entered carrying Danny, dressed in a little nightshirt and cap, his face red and pinched in pain.

"Sorry to disturb you both," Mrs. Turrill said. "But it's the colic again. Becky couldn't settle him and nor can I."

Hannah took the baby from the housekeeper and began gently bouncing him, her wrapped arm bearing more weight now without pain. "Thank you, Mrs. Turrill. I'll take care of him. Why don't you retire for the evening — you look exhausted. I'll be up soon, but Becky can help me change."

"I am worn off my feet, I admit," the woman said. "Very well. If you're sure."

"I am. Good night, Mrs. Turrill."

"Good night, my lady. Sir."

When the housekeeper had departed, Hannah turned back to Sir John. Danny continued to whine. "Well, I won't keep you. I'm sure you don't want to listen to him fuss."

"Nonsense. Here." He set aside his writing things and opened his arms. "Give him to me."

What was Sir John doing? What was *she* doing? Opening her heart to foolish hopes and dreams again, that's what. Still she could not refuse his offer, his warm expression, and outstretched arms.

She handed Danny to him and he laid the boy on his lap, feet toward him. He slowly, gently lifted the child's knees toward his abdomen and then repeated the movement several times. It reminded her somewhat of the stretching movements she had performed for Sir John.

At first Danny's face continued to pucker, but after several more repetitions, her little angel broke wind. Hannah was embarrassed and relieved both. The boy's small abdomen became less distended as the pressure eased.

Sir John smiled. "There we go. That's better, ay, little man?"

Danny relaxed and Sir John lowered the boy's legs, keeping his large hands on her son's pudgy white feet. Danny looked up at his deliverer and cooed.

It nearly broke her heart.

Chapter 17

James lingered over breakfast the next morning, waiting for the lady of the house to join him. When she finally entered the dining parlor, she hesitated at seeing him, no doubt unsure what sort of reception to expect. He couldn't blame her for not being happy to see him after their recent conversation.

"Good morning, Mr. Lowden."

"Morning." He sipped tepid coffee and waited while she poured her own cup at the sideboard and helped herself to bread and butter.

She sat across from him, and he noticed her fingers tremble as she picked up the delicate china cup.

He studied her, sitting with such perfect posture, little finger raised, the picture of a poised lady. It annoyed him.

She took the tiniest bite of her bread and chewed daintily. The silence between them stretched.

He drummed his fingers on the table, scowling. Glancing around to assure they were alone, he said in low voice, "I understand why you did it, but what I don't understand is . . . why does Sir John go along with it?"

He looked at her, waiting for her to enlighten him. Wondering if she would deny knowing what he was talking about.

She sighed, and whispered, "I am not certain."

"You haven't asked him?"

She shook her head.

He rose and stood at the window, squinting into the morning sun. "Why would a man allow another woman to take his wife's place?"

When she made no reply, he said, "Unfortunately, I can think of several reasons." He frowned, turning back to her. "But what about the child — Dr. Parrish mentioned you returned to Bath for him after the accident. Has Sir John said anything about him?"

"Only that he sees no resemblance between Danny and himself."

James felt his brows rise. "Did he? When was this?"

"Soon after he awoke. Mrs. Turrill and

Dr. Parrish both went on about how Danny looked like him, but on both occasions Sir John said he saw no resemblance."

"That must have been awkward."

"Yes, it was." She lifted her chin, eyes sparking defiantly. "Any other questions, *counselor*?"

His gaze lingered on her bright eyes, her high color, her tight lips. . . . "Only one. For now. How far do you plan to take this?"

She exhaled deeply. "I don't know. I never planned to take it this far. All I wanted was to get Danny back. I never expected Sir John to do more for us. I thought I would remain until my arm mended. But Sir John awoke before I could leave. And he did not expose me. In fact, he seemed to encourage the pretense."

"Why?"

"At first I thought it was his head wound, that he was confused. But now . . ." Her words trailed away on a shrug.

James wondered if there was more to the story than she was willing to tell him.

"Does he love you?" he asked.

"He has never said so, no."

"You don't think he would marry you." James heard the derision in his voice. The incredulity.

She lifted her chin. "Am I so far beneath

him? Would that be out of the question?"

"If I have anything to say about it, yes. Especially after this whole charade of yours."

She paled. "Meaning you will counsel him against it?"

Meaning I want you for myself, James thought, stifling the illogical words. After what he'd found out he ought to despise her. He could not seriously contemplate marriage to a woman like her. It could only lead to scandal, which would in no way help his struggling law practice.

But all he said was, "Yes. I will counsel him against it."

She screwed up her face. "Why do you care?"

"I don't," he lied. "But my duty is to protect my client's interests."

"By protecting him from me?"

"Yes."

"I see. Well. Thank you for being honest with me."

He held her gaze. "You ought to try it sometime."

She looked away first, but he felt little victory. For he hadn't been fully truthful with her, either.

Mrs. Parrish and the vicar's wife were due

to call again that afternoon. Hannah forced a smile when Mrs. Turrill reminded her of the engagement, and fastened an overdress of embroidered lawn over her sprigged muslin, in which to receive callers. But inwardly, Hannah dreaded it. How could she face them, *pretend* for them, especially with Mr. Lowden there under the same roof?

Mrs. Parrish arrived first. Hannah waited until Mrs. Turrill had shown the woman into the drawing room and stepped out again.

Then she took a deep breath and began, "Mrs. Parrish, I am glad for a moment to speak with you alone. I know you saw an old friend of mine who stopped by last week — just to say hello as he passed through the area, and I wouldn't want you to think —"

"Old friend?" the woman interrupted with a sly smile. "Very friendly indeed from the looks of it."

"It isn't what you think, Mrs. Parrish. It was only a brief, friendly call. Perfectly innocent."

"If you say so. But then . . . why hide in the garden like secret lovers?"

Hannah forced herself to hold the woman's challenging gaze. But what could she say to that?

Nothing.

Mrs. Parrish's eyes gleamed in triumph.

A moment later, Mrs. Turrill showed the vicar's wife into the room. Greetings were exchanged and the conversation turned light and bright while Mrs. Turrill served refreshments.

Personally Hannah thought Mrs. Parrish paid calls at Clifton not because she enjoyed her company, but because the proud physician's wife enjoyed having her husband's cousin wait on her hand and foot.

Mrs. Parrish had brought with her a copy of the *Bath Journal,* mailed to her by one of her friends who lived there. Mrs. Parrish enjoyed reading about the comings and goings of the ton in Bath, the little sister city to London. She also brought the local newspaper, with its accounts of runaway apprentices, ships into port, obituaries, and notices.

"Listen to this," Mrs. Parrish said, sipping noisily at her teacup before returning it with a clink to its saucer.

"On Monday died Mr. Robert Meyers Jr., a wealthy butcher. He dined last Friday with some friends at a tavern, on mock turtle, when two of the company wantonly put a quantity of Jalap in his plate, which operated so violently as to occasion his death."

"No!" responded the timid little vicar's wife, looking suitably shocked.

Mrs. Parrish nodded somberly. "I could have predicted such an outcome. Jalap is a known cathartic, which of course I know, being Dr. Parrish's helpmeet all these years."

"Ahh . . ." the vicar's wife murmured, clearly impressed. "If only you had been there to warn them."

"Very true, Mrs. Barton. Very true." She turned the broadsheet over. "Bankruptcies. Always a sobering reminder to be thrifty." She ran her finger over the names as she pronounced them with barely concealed relish.

"BANKRUPTS. Robert Dean, of Stamford, Innholder. William Castle, of Chichester, Brazier. John Keates, of Stanwell, Papermaker. Anthony Fontaine, of Bristol, Gentleman."

Here Mrs. Parrish snorted. "Gentleman indeed. No longer, now that he's passed through the gazette."

Mrs. Barton covered her mouth, tee-heeing discreetly behind her tiny hand, like a little girl who knew it was naughty to laugh at the misfortune of others.

But Hannah paid them little heed, her mind still echoing with the name *Anthony*

Fontaine. Could Marianna's Mr. Fontaine be bankrupt?

Mrs. Barton nibbled a biscuit. "Pray, do read on, Mrs. Parrish."

"Very well." The doctor's wife perused another column.

"Oh, dear. What a pity. *LOST betwixt Bristol and Bath, a GOLD RING, inlaid with amethyst and purple sapphires, engraved with the Maker's Name, John Ebsworth, London. Whoever has found the said Ring, and will bring it to the Printer, shall receive One Guinea Reward.*"

"One guinea reward for such a ring?" The vicar's wife tuttutted. "I doubt such a valuable piece shall be returned when it might be sold for far more."

"I am afraid you are right, Mrs. Barton. Human greed being what it is."

The vicar's wife nodded. "Unless God chooses to intervene in the heart of whoever finds it."

Mrs. Parrish turned to Hannah. "Amethyst and purple sapphires . . . Isn't that very like your ring, Lady Mayfield?"

Hannah swallowed and nodded. "A family ring, yes."

"Who made it, do you know?"

"I don't."

Mrs. Barton said, "Wouldn't that be

300

something if it were made by this same John Ebsworth of London?"

"I suppose there are many similar rings about the country," Hannah said lightly, faking a sip of tea.

Mrs. Parrish frowned in thought. "Was that the ring Dr. Parrish found in your hand after the accident?"

"Yes. He put it on my finger so it wouldn't get lost."

"Odd that it was in your hand and not on your finger already." Mrs. Parrish eyed her speculatively.

Hannah shrugged, squirming under the women's scrutiny. "I recall so little of the wreck."

When the uncomfortable visit finally concluded, Hannah went upstairs to her room and retrieved the ring from a little box in her valise. Standing next to the window to capture the sunlight she read the fine, tiny engraving inside the band. Her heart lurched. *John Ebsworth, London.* No doubt just a coincidence. Surely no one had reported this particular ring lost. Many such rings were likely made. Hadn't she said as much to her guests?

While the lady of the house entertained visitors, James took the day's correspondence up to Sir John's room. There he found the man sitting in a wheeled chair, reading.

James handed him a letter from Mr. Ward, his secretary, keeping him abreast of the household accounts at the Bristol property, and requesting a bank draft to cover a few unforeseen expenses. "Shall I take care of that, sir?" James offered.

"Yes, if you would. Thank you."

James hesitated. "Are you ready to talk about your will?" *The reason you brought me out here in the first place,* he thought to himself.

"If we must. I have decided not to change it."

"You no longer wish to disinherit your wife beyond the marriage settlement?"

"I do not."

"But —" James turned away and ran a hand through his hair. He went to the door, made sure no one was loitering about, and shut it once again.

"Sir John. I think I should tell you that I know the young woman in this house is not Marianna Mayfield. She is Hannah Rogers, your wife's former companion. I suspected something was amiss when last I was here, and have taken it upon myself to look into the matter. I spoke to her friends and to her father in Bristol. I've heard her described in great detail — from her slender figure to her freckles."

James took a deep breath, then continued, "Her father knows nothing of the child, and nor did I tell him. The two had become estranged and apparently Miss Rogers kept the news of her pregnancy and birth from him, for obvious reasons."

Sir John said nothing, but James saw a pulse tick in his jaw. James went on, "And while I can understand why she might pass herself off as Lady Mayfield to secure shelter for herself and her son, I cannot in good conscience allow it to go on."

Sir John frowned. "Who asked you to 'look into' these matters, as though they are any of your concern?"

James felt his defenses rise. "You wrote and asked my father to look into her whereabouts after she left your employ," James said. "And now, as your solicitor —"

"That was nearly a year ago," Sir John said. "And only to learn what had become of her. Not to ferret out information better left buried."

James reeled back, flummoxed. "Does she have some sort of hold on you, sir? For you to go along with this? Is she extorting money from you somehow, or . . . ?"

"Heavens, no. What an imagination you

have, Mr. Lowden. And how you do see criminal intent where none exists. Perhaps you missed your calling. A career as a runner or perhaps judge and jury might have better suited you."

"Sir. I don't know what to say. You know she is not your wife."

"Of course I know she is not Marianna Mayfield. I am not blind, nor insane."

"Well, you were out of your senses for quite some time, so I thought —"

"You thought wrong. It was Dr. Parrish who assumed Miss Rogers was Lady Mayfield when he found us alone in the wrecked carriage. And she allowed the misapprehension to continue only because she was concerned about how she would support her young son."

"And she could think of no way beyond impersonating her dead mistress?"

Sir John winced. "You exaggerate, Lowden. It wasn't as bad as all that."

James shook his head. "I don't understand you, sir."

"I'm not paying you to understand me. As I said, let's leave the will for now."

"But what about the child?"

"Good point — include the child as well."

James fisted his hands. What was the man playing at? Was he really willing to risk this woman's illegitimate child becoming heir to his estate? "But you said it yourself, Sir John. You see no resemblance between yourself and the boy."

He narrowed his eyes. "Who told you that?"

"His mother told me herself. I gather she heard you say as much to both Mrs. Turrill and Dr. Parrish."

"That's true, I did."

James felt as though he were repeating things to a young child . . . or a simpleton. "You admit he looks nothing like you, Sir John. That's because he —"

"Yes, but he looks a great deal like someone I once knew."

"Mr. Fontaine?" The words were out of James's mouth before he could think the better of them.

Sir John scowled at him. "No. *Not* Fontaine."

Seeing the anger in Sir John's expression, James thought it wiser not to hazard another ill-advised guess.

Dr. Parrish found Hannah in the nursery and asked her to assist him in Sir John's bedchamber. "Today is the day, my lady. Sir John is going to attempt his first steps!"

Mixed emotions filled her. Would he be

able to walk, she wondered, after lying in bed for so many weeks? She and Dr. Parrish, along with nurse Weaver, had tried to maintain some level of strength and agility in his legs — especially the one with the sound ankle. But the other? She hoped he would not be disappointed.

When she arrived, Sir John slid himself to the edge of his bed. Dr. Parrish took one arm, and looked at her expectantly. "My lady?"

"Oh, of course." Hannah stepped to Sir John's other side and grasped Sir John's elbow.

"All right, Sir John. Whenever you are ready. We're here to help steady you. We'll expect no dashes, sir. Just a simple stand-up is our only goal for today. Are you ready?"

Sir John gritted his teeth, sliding himself farther forward, and spacing his feet shoulder-width apart. "Ready."

"On three. One, two, three . . ."

Together, she and the physician helped Sir John rise. Hannah felt a tremor pass all the way up his body and through the arm she held. Hannah repositioned her own weight to strengthen her hold, thinking, *Please, God, help him stand.*

"You've done it, Sir John!" Dr. Parrish enthused, and he and Hannah shared a private smile. "How is the ankle — does it hurt?"

"Not bad," he gritted out. Then his legs began to tremble violently.

"There now, sit down. Easy does it."

"I want to walk."

"Tomorrow is another day, Sir John. Mustn't rush things."

"Must she be here?" He jerked his head toward her.

"Your wife? I would think you would want her here to support you."

"I . . . don't like her seeing me like this. So cursed weak."

"Weak? Why the injuries you suffered would have been the end of many a man half your age. I see nothing weak in you, sir. Do you, my lady?"

"No. Nothing. Sir John has always been a strong man. Physically and otherwise. And will be so again."

For a moment Sir John's eyes met hers. And she was touched by the vulnerability there as he gauged her sincerity. She squeezed his hand. "I am proud of you."

His eyes shone with something else then. Something deep and arresting. Hannah looked away first.

From a deep sleep, James woke abruptly,

startled by a rapping on his door. His room was still dead-of-night dark. Alarmed, he threw back the bedclothes and climbed from bed. Before he could retrieve his dressing gown, the door creaked open and a figure appeared carrying a candle.

"Mr. Lowden?"

Miss Rogers stood in his threshold, clad in nightdress and shawl, hair in a thick plait over her shoulder. His heart leapt. For one illogical moment desire flared. But a closer look at her pale, wide-eyed face told him this was no amorous visit — something was wrong.

"I'm sorry to wake you, but it's Danny. And Becky. They're both terribly hot and restless. Becky has grasped onto Mrs. Turrill in a panic and won't let go. I've sent Kitty for cool cloths, but I hoped you might —"

He grabbed his dressing gown from the back of a chair. "Shall I run for Dr. Parrish?"

"Please. I hate to leave Danny for another moment."

"I understand. Go back to him. I'll bring the doctor as soon as may be."

"Thank you." In the flickering candlelight, her earnest eyes held his. Then she turned and disappeared from view, the patter of her bare feet quickly treading up the stairs.

He pulled on a pair of trousers and shoes. Wrestling a coat over his nightshirt, he hurried downstairs, out the side door, and ran to the Grange.

Ten minutes later, Hannah sat in the rocking chair, a whining Danny in her arms. She dabbed a damp cloth to his face and neck, trying in vain to cool and comfort him. Across the room, Mrs. Turrill administered the same treatment to Becky, praying over the girl in low tones as she did so. Kitty, having delivered the cloths, stood helplessly by, twisting her apron in her hands.

Hannah hoped Dr. Parrish would hurry. Surely he would know what to do. Her fears rose, jumbling her innards and tormenting her imagination. What if there was nothing he could do? Might Danny succumb like those poor children at Mrs. Beech's? Was this the same fever — had it somehow lay dormant in Danny and Becky, only to strike now when she had thought them well and truly free of the effects of that place?

She heard footsteps clumping up the passage and relief filled her. One set of footsteps. Had Mr. Lowden returned to his room once he'd summoned Dr. Parrish?

But it was Mr. Lowden himself who

knocked and then let himself into the nursery.

"Where is Dr. Parrish?" Hannah asked, alarmed. "Is he coming?"

Mr. Lowden grimly shook his head. "He and Mrs. Parrish have been gone all night, attending a difficult birth. Edgar Parrish has gone on horseback to bring him back or at least his instructions until he can come himself."

"Oh, no."

Mr. Lowden knelt before the rocking chair. He laid his wrist on Danny's little forehead and frowned.

"He's too hot. Get that blanket off of him." He rose. "And let's open some windows." He shrugged off his greatcoat and began throwing back shutters. He was dressed in only trousers and shirtsleeves, his hair tousled.

Mrs. Turrill spoke up from Becky's bedside. "Won't they take a chill?"

"I don't know. All I know is that we need to get their fevers down."

He surveyed the room until his eyes landed on the housemaid, standing huddled in the corner.

"Bring all the cold water you can carry. Is there any ice remaining?"

"Maybe a little, sir. Mostly straw by now."

"If there is any, bring it quickly."

Kitty scuttled off to do his bidding. He returned and knelt once more before Hannah's chair. This time he lifted his hand toward her. She recoiled in surprise before she realized his intention. His mouth tightened but he made no comment as he laid cool fingers on her brow.

"You are overly warm yourself. Not a fever, I don't think, but overheated from nerves no doubt. You will only make him warmer."

"What do you suggest?"

"A cold bath. He shan't like it, but it will help him."

"How do you know?"

"I've been down this path before, I'm sorry to say."

"Oh?"

"My younger sister."

"I didn't know you had a sister."

"I don't. Not any longer. We learned only after the fact what we should have done."

"I am sorry," Hannah whispered.

"So am I."

For a moment their gazes locked in fearful empathy.

From the bed, Becky groaned and cried out, "Hannah, Oh, Miss Hannah. It's the fever!"

Mrs. Turrill, sitting on the edge of the cot, looked across the room at her mistress, her eyes glistening in confusion and pity.

Hannah soothed, "Shhh . . . there now, Becky. It's only the fever talking. You're all right."

Mrs. Turrill picked up the thread. "That's right, Becky dear. Mrs. Turrill is here with you. Nothin' to fear. There now, sip this." She lifted a cup to the girl's lips.

Hannah felt Mr. Lowden's knowing look on her profile but avoided his gaze.

She peeled the blanket off Danny, and then pulled his small fists through the sleeves of his nightdress.

Becky thrashed side to side. "It's the fever what took the Jones boy and little Molly. We've got to get out of here."

He asked softly, "Where does she think she is?"

"The place where her own child died."

Hannah dipped the cloth once more into the basin of tepid water, wishing the maid would hurry with the ice. If Becky kept this up, Mrs. Turrill would realize who she really was, as Mr. Lowden had. Maybe she already knew. But at the moment all Hannah cared about was helping Danny. She hoped God would not strike him down as punishment for her many sins.

Again Mrs. Turrill's troubled gaze met hers, then moved to the solicitor. "Mr. Lowden. Perhaps you would be so good as to ride to my sister's in Lynmouth? The little yellow cottage at the bottom of the hill past the livery? I just remembered she might have some fever powder, left over from our mother's last illness."

"Does she?" He straightened. "Excellent. I shall go directly."

He turned without another word, grabbed his coat, and hastened from the room. Hannah looked at Mrs. Turrill and their gazes locked as the closing of the door reverberated through the room. If the woman now knew or guessed the truth, she didn't say a word.

"Thank you," Hannah whispered. And she was thanking her for far more than medicine.

Morning dawned bright and clear, and with it Hannah's mood. Mr. Lowden had delivered the fever powder, which they gave to Becky but hesitated to give it to Danny, not knowing how it might affect his small body. Instead, she had taken Mr. Lowden's advice and subjected the miserable little boy to brief submersions in the tin tub of cool water, which made him howl, but eventually lowered his fever.

When both patients progressed from sweating to shaking, Mr. Lowden had closed the windows and brought up wood and coals with Ben's help, stoking the fire with rolled-up shirtsleeves as though he were a manservant himself.

Mr. Lowden and Ben had left to retrieve more wood when Dr. Parrish finally jogged into the nursery huffing and puffing, red-faced and dog-tired. Even so, he ably took the situation in hand, affirming their actions so far, and recommending liquids and another dose of a fever powder of his own concoction.

Hannah breathed a prayer of thanksgiving, relieved to place Danny and Becky in the doctor's capable hands.

Leaving the room for a brief respite, she found Mr. Lowden sitting in a chair in the passage, elbows on his knees, head in his hands.

He rose when she stepped out. "Is Daniel all right?"

"He will be, yes."

Mr. Lowden exhaled a relieved breath. "Thank God."

The concern on his face, the kindness and help he'd delivered, weakened Hannah's reserve. Tears filled her eyes.

314

Instantly, his hands cupped her shoulders and his eyes searched hers. "What is it? Are you all right?"

She nodded, tears running in hot trails down her cheeks. "I was so afraid."

And then his arms were around her, holding her close in a comforting embrace.

"I know. So was I."

For several moments Hannah stood there, pressed to his chest, feeling the solid warmth of his body beneath her cheek. Savoring the feel of his arms around her, gathering her close. She wanted to stand there forever.

Instead, she stepped back, and wiped at her eyes. Her voice tremulous she said, "Thank you, Mr. Lowden. I don't know what I would have done without you."

But she knew all too well she would soon have to figure out how to do just that.

James Lowden returned to his bed, feeling torn and unsettled. He was surprised at himself. He had not meant to take Miss Rogers in his arms. He'd been surprised, too, at the surge of tenderness that had swept over him, the desire to protect her and comfort her. A few weeks ago, he would have declared such feelings inconceivable. He reminded himself that even though the woman he'd met at Clifton was *not* Marianna, unfaithful wife, Hannah Rogers was no bastion of virtue herself. She was apparently just as willing and able to deceive as her mistress had been. He could not and should not trust her. Or get too close.

He still wasn't completely sure why he was attracted to her. She had lovely thick hair and striking eyes, yes. But her nose was too long, her mouth too wide. And then there were her freckles. . . . But when he remembered how it had felt to hold her in his arms, he was almost ready to throw both logic and caution to the wind. He could still feel her slender figure through the nightdress, the marked curve of her waist, the press of her small bosom.

Stop it, he told himself.

He flinched to recall the foolish nurse moaning about "Miss Hannah" and whatever wretched place they had come from. He'd seen the suspicious look on the housekeeper's face. It was only a matter of time before she realized who Miss Rogers really was and that she had lied to them all. Did he really want to be mixed up in all of that? What would happen if people learned that he had known the truth yet remained silent? Would he be complicit in her fraud? What would that do to his legal practice and reputation?

Use your head, Lowden. He would be wise to keep the woman at arm's length — quite literally.

CHAPTER 18

Hannah spent the next several days remaining close to the nursery — close to Danny. She needed to watch over him. To assure herself he was improving. To think.

Dr. Parrish called often, and declared both patients well on their way to recovery. Concerned, Sir John asked to see the child, but the doctor hesitated, just in case the fever was catching. He didn't want to risk it when Sir John was regaining his strength at last. Mr. Lowden, meanwhile, had ridden to the larger town of Barnstaple, to acquire a bank draft to send to Mr. Ward. The hours passed slowly in his absence. Hannah had seen him only in passing the last few days.

Now that Mr. Lowden knew and Mrs. Turrill surely suspected, Hannah knew she should stop pretending to be Lady Mayfield and leave, but still she hesitated. The reality of her situation washed over her anew. Danny's fever had made it painfully clear. If . . .

When . . . she left, how alone she would be. How vulnerable. No Sir John to house them. No Mrs. Turrill to bring them meals. No handsome solicitor to rush out for fever powder. What would she do if Danny fell ill while she was in some squalid inn or boarding house? No gentleman-physician would come calling then. And apothecaries and surgeons did not work for free. The truth was, she was frightened to leave. Especially with Danny still listless from the fever, and her arm still tender. What if he had a relapse? Moreover, did she really want to disappear from Sir John's life again? Or from Mr. Lowden's, for that matter?

Mrs. Turrill came up to sit with her one evening while a storm brewed off the coast. She studied Hannah's face, her dark eyes filled with concern. "You look so weary and ill at ease, my lady. The fever is past and all is well. I'm sure of it."

"Thank you, Mrs. Turrill. I am sorry to be out of sorts."

"Not at all. It's only natural — what a trying few days you've had." Her eyes lit. "I know. A nice warm bath is what you need. I'll have Ben and Kitty bring the tub to your room and start heating the water. You go and lie down while you wait."

"That is not necessary, Mrs. Turrill. I

don't want to put everyone to extra work. You are already taking care of Sir John along with everything else."

"Nonsense. It's no trouble. Sir John had a nice long soak yesterday and it did him a world of good."

"Did it? I confess it does sound heavenly, but I hate to ask."

"You're not asking. I'm telling." Mrs. Turrill winked. "Go on with you now."

An hour later, Hannah found herself sitting in the large tin tub, knees bent, submerged in warm, wonderful water up to her chest, her bandaged arm resting on the edge of the tub. Usually she made do with a sponge bath or a wash in the small hip bath, but she realized Mrs. Turrill had been right. She felt the tension easing from her body. She washed with lilac and lye soap, then Kitty came in and washed her hair. Scrubbing away at her scalp felt so good, and she felt her fears wash away with the rinse water. "I think I'll soak a little longer, if you don't mind, Kitty."

"You go right ahead, my lady. I shall help Mrs. Turrill batten down the shutters against the storm. But I shall come back to help you soon."

"No hurry."

The girl left, shutting the door behind her.

Outside the wind howled. But she was warm and safe indoors. And so was Danny. She leaned back and rested her head against the cloth folded over the end of the tub. *Ahhh* . . .

The door banged open and Hannah started, sitting upright with a gasp and covering her bosom with one arm. She turned to see who had so boldly entered, but the threshold and passage beyond remained empty. The wind, she realized. Someone must have opened a window or the front door, sending her own door flying open in response. She waited a minute, assuming Kitty or Mrs. Turrill would have heard the bang, come to investigate, and close the door for her. She waited a few minutes longer, feeling self-conscious sitting there, her upper body partly exposed and quickly cooling.

No one came. With a sigh, she rose, using her good arm to help herself up. With her wrapped arm, she held the small towel she had rested against, covering her torso as best she could. The larger linen towel was out of reach on a chair several feet away.

She gingerly stepped out of the tub, placing one foot on the braided rug, then the other.

Footsteps sounded in the passageway

outside. At last! She turned toward the door to hide her exposed backside.

She looked up, a self-conscious grin on her face ready to explain to Kitty what had happened. Instead, she sucked in a breath and gaped at James Lowden.

He drew up in surprise and froze where he was, hat in hand, greatcoat hanging open, hair windblown. His mouth parted but he did not redden, or turn, or smile. His gaze began on her face and slowly moved down her neck, her shoulders and unbound hair, past the too small towel, to her long legs. . . .

Hannah found herself unable to move, barely able to breathe. She felt a blush burn down her entire body.

He stepped across the threshold, and her heart thumped hard. What would he do? For a moment he stood there, staring at her. His expression almost . . . disapproving — jaw clenched, lips tight. If he found her comely at all, he certainly did not show it.

"Be careful, my lady," he warned, voice low and dangerous.

"The wind blew it open," she defended.

His eyes glinted. "It's an ill wind that blows no one good."

He reached out his hand, and she gasped. But he only snagged the latch and retreated from the room, slowly pulling the door toward himself. He stood there in the threshold, eyes burning into hers, until the door snapped shut.

The next morning, Hannah rose languidly. She had slept deeply the night before — thanks to the relaxing bath, no doubt — despite that strange and embarrassing encounter with Mr. Lowden. Since he had come to their rescue during the fever, her heart had warmed to him. Meanwhile he flashed warm then cold in unpredictable turns. Did he wrestle with his feelings as she did? She was probably flattering herself. Perhaps the man had no feelings. For her, at any rate. Which was probably for the best, considering she was still posing as Sir John's wife.

Kitty helped her into the pale rose-pink day dress, and then Hannah sat at the dressing table to brush her hair. Her freshly washed hair felt soft and thick and clean, and in the sunlit mirror, red highlights shone more brightly than usual.

After a solitary breakfast she went up to the nursery and cuddled Danny. Becky declared she felt quite her old self and was ready for another reading lesson. Hannah agreed and, laying Danny in his cradle, sat beside the girl on the made bed. Becky opened *A Little Pretty Pocket-Book* and began reading the simple rhymes for each letter of the alphabet.

"My lady?" Becky asked sometime later. She tugged on Hannah's arm and repeated more loudly, "My lady?"

"Hm? Oh, sorry."

"What is it? You seem . . . different. Is it that Mr. Lowden? Or are you taking sick? Is everything all right?"

"Nothing for you to worry about, Becky. But thank you for asking."

A short while later, Hannah left Danny napping peacefully and Becky reading. She glanced through the open door of Sir John's bedchamber and saw him in the wheeled invalid chair, positioned near the window with a book. Mrs. Turrill was likely busy in the kitchen, and she believed Mr. Lowden was out riding. With everyone seemingly content for the moment, she decided she could take a little time for herself.

She strolled outside and into the garden, drawing in the warm fragrant air. Many decisions spun through her mind, but for a few moments she didn't want to think or worry or plan. She only wanted to be, and to breathe.

Mr. Lowden came striding over from the

stable. Seeing him, Hannah felt embarrassment nip at her. What sort of reception could she expect from him after last night? Even so, she could not help but admire his confident bearing, the gleam of his riding boots, the formfitting cut of his coat, and the beaver hat that shadowed his face. He looked up as if sensing her appraisal and lifted a hand in greeting. She liked his face, the deep vertical grooves along either side of his mouth, the straight nose, the full lower lip.

"Hello, *my* lady."

Her eyes flashed to his. The sound of his voice, the emphasis on the word "my" caused her heart to thrum. She had thought he might begin calling her Hannah or Miss Rogers now that he knew the truth. A part of her was relieved he had not. Another part longed to hear him speak her real name.

"Mr. Lowden." She dipped her head.

He lowered his voice. "I am sorry about last night."

"It was not your fault."

"No, but I might have handled it in a more gentlemanlike manner." He cocked his head to one side and gave her a lopsided grin. "Or less of one."

Embarrassment nipped again. And perhaps an ounce of pleasure.

She changed the subject, "Good ride?"

"Excellent, thank you." His moss-green gaze slowly traced her face. "You're looking lovely, if you don't mind my saying."

"So are you," she replied before she could think the better of it, and felt her cheeks heat.

"Thank you. I think." He grinned and the brackets in his cheeks deepened.

Then he squinted off into the distance and said, "Riding — motion — helps me think."

She nodded. "Walking does the same for me."

His eyes glinted. "Would you like to know what I was thinking about?"

The look he gave her unsettled her. "No. I don't believe I would."

Around them the wind picked up, scattering dandelion seeds and swaying the heavy hydrangea blooms on their stalks. He removed one of his gloves, reached out and captured a tendril of her hair floating on the breeze.

For a moment he looked at it. "All the colors of autumn," he murmured, grinning again. He hooked the strand behind her ear, his fingers lingering on her cheek.

He was close. So close. His gaze caressed her face, sinking into her eyes, then lowering to her mouth. She held her breath. Was he going to kiss her? Right then and there, in full view of their nosy neighbor Mrs. Parrish or anyone who might be looking from the windows? A part of her wished he would. Longed to lean near, to press her lips to his. Then, with a little stab of guilt, she remembered Sir John.

As though guessing her thoughts, Mr. Lowden glanced over her shoulder up at the second level of windows. His grin faded. "We appear to have an audience. So I shall bow and politely bid you good day."

"Sir John?" she asked.

He nodded, bowed, and left her standing there alone.

Standing in Sir John's doorway later that day, Hannah looked on as Dr. Parrish addressed his patient, still seated in the wheeled chair.

In his hands, Dr. Parrish held a carved, wooden cane. He said, "I've taken the liberty of bringing this for you. One of my favorite patients carves them in his spare time. Paid his medical bill with two of these fine specimens. And it would be my privilege to give one to you."

He angled the handle nearer Sir John. "See the intricate carving?"

"I see an invalid's cane," Sir John snapped.

"What an old man I shall look."

"Oh now. Just imagine it is one of those fine walking sticks sported by London gentlemen."

"Then I shall be a dandy."

"Better a dandy than an old man."

Sir John grimaced. "Touché."

Personally, Hannah thought Sir John was looking younger and more fit each day, except, that is, when he scowled, as he was at the moment.

Dr. Parrish noticed her in the doorway. "Ah. My lady. Just in time. You stand there and Sir John shall endeavor to walk to you."

Sir John's mouth twisted bitterly. "I am not an infant, man, toddling to his mother."

"Of course not, Sir John. But what better incentive than your dear wife's arms to urge you onward."

Hannah felt her cheeks heat.

Sir John looked up at her, eyes twinkling. "Do you hear that, my lady? You are to hold out your arms to me as incentive."

His teasing was playful, Hannah realized with relief — and not taunting as before.

He said to the physician, "I am more likely to bowl her over than sweep her off her feet."

"Just do your best, Sir John," Dr. Parrish said. "Even one step will be a victory."

Face furrowed in concentration or pain or both, Sir John took step by laborious step across the room. One hand white-knuckled the cane, the other supported by Dr. Parrish.

Hannah was tempted to take a step or two forward, to shorten the gap.

As if guessing her intention, Sir John stopped her with a determined lift of his chin. "Stay where you are."

Brow sweating, he pulled his hand from Dr. Parrish's grip. "I'll manage these last few steps on my own."

"But I want to be near at hand, should —"

"If I fall, I fall."

One foot slid forward — weight transferred, balance regained, cane thumped. Then the next foot, each step arduous and small. Hannah feared he would collapse before he made it. Sweat glistened at his neck now.

"Just one more," she said. "That's it. You've almost made it!"

Impulsively, Hannah extended her arms, thinking she might help support him, though doubting she would be able to catch him should he fall. He had lost a stone or more since the accident, but he was still a large man.

An ironic grin curled his lip. His eyes glinted with humor and determination.

The final step. Hannah reached out and held his arms, trying to steady him as he swayed on trembling legs.

Dr. Parrish applauded. "Bravo. I'd say that deserves a kiss, wouldn't you?" Dr. Parrish winked at Hannah.

"Here, here," Sir John agreed. "If only I can catch my breath long enough to enjoy it."

"I . . ." Hannah swallowed self-consciously. "Don't you want to sit down?"

"Oh, go on, my lady. I shall look the other way." Dr. Parrish grinned impishly.

Suddenly as breathless as Sir John himself, Hannah said, "Very well."

She reached up on tiptoes and aimed a friendly kiss toward Sir John's cheek. But he turned his head at the last moment and she met his lips instead.

She blinked in surprise. The firm warmth of his lips on hers was unexpected and unexpectedly . . . welcome. Mixed emotions stirred through her: confusion, loyalty, disloyalty, guilt. It was only a chaste kiss, she told herself. For the doctor's benefit. Was it not? Whatever it was, she was glad James Lowden was not there to see it.

Dr. Parrish clapped again. "Now that's

more like it. A good day's work indeed."

Sir John's eyes shone as he held her gaze. "Indeed."

That night, Hannah struggled to fall asleep. When she closed her eyes, she found her thoughts spinning from Mr. Lowden to Sir John — their faces revolving through her mind again and again.

Hannah did not sleep well, and was late coming down for breakfast the following morning. Kitty mentioned Mr. Lowden had already eaten and gone out for his ride.

After her meal, Hannah put on the altered spencer jacket and returned to the garden once more. She strolled past the flower beds, enjoying the fragrances of the colorful blooms and the temperate breeze in her hair. Secretly, she hoped for another private moment with James Lowden. Though she supposed if she were wise, she would keep her distance and avoid a private meeting with the man.

Hannah had just convinced herself to return to the house when he came riding through the gate.

She paused behind a wide yew tree as Ben come out and took his horse. How furtive and wanton she felt, hoping to shield herself from any prying eyes at the house windows.

She hoped James wouldn't guess her motives. Or did she?

Entering the garden, he removed his hat and smiled as he neared. "Hello, My . . . Hannah. May I call you Hannah?"

She warmed to hear her name on his lips. "Yes. I miss hearing it."

He reached out and ran a finger down her cheek. "Hannah. Sweet Hannah . . ."

Her pulse skittered.

He glanced about, and seeing they were alone, he leaned toward her. His mouth neared her cheek, his breath tickling her ear. "I have been trying to keep my distance from you. Especially here, under Sir John's roof. But seeing you the other night nearly did me in. One day, I hope to kiss every single one of your freckles. . . ."

Her breath caught and a flush ran over her body.

Suddenly, rain blew in off the channel in a pelting shower.

She squinted up at the sky in surprise. "Oh no . . ."

"Come on." He took her hand and together they ran toward the house, him all but pulling her behind him.

They dashed inside, laughing. Her wet shoes slipped on the polished floor and his arm quickly came around her, catching her before she could fall. Even after she was steady on her feet, his arm remained.

She smiled into his face and saw a leaf plastered to his cheek like the golden imprint of a kiss. She lifted her hand and peeled it off, her fingers tracing the admired groove as she had longed to do for days.

"A leaf," she explained, showing him the offending thing — her excuse for touching him.

His eyes darkened, and again he leaned near.

Suddenly a flicker of movement, a squeak of sound, drew her attention upward. There behind the stair rail sat Sir John in his invalid chair. Her heart twisted to see him through the balusters as though he were trapped behind bars — a prisoner above stairs. He watched them, face tense, eyes hard. She realized how they must look, standing so close together, James Lowden's arm lingering at her waist, her hand touching his face. Instinctively, she stepped back from James.

He followed the direction of her glance and his smile faded. "Hello, Sir John. We were caught out in the rain."

"So I see."

Caught. It seemed a very appropriate word.

"Did you need something, Sir John?" Hannah asked, stepping to the bottom of the stairs.

For several moments, his eyes held hers from above. "I thought I did, but I was wrong."

After she had dried her face and hung up her damp spencer, Hannah went up to the nursery to check on Danny. Then, she went back downstairs and knocked softly on Sir John's door.

"Yes?" came his muffled reply.

Inhaling deeply, she cracked open the door. "May I come in?"

He sat in his wheeled chair near the window, staring out at the lashing rain. He did not turn to greet her. She stepped in anyway and shut the door behind her, closing the tension in the room and making it hard to breathe.

She slowly crossed the room and stood beside his chair. She stared unseeing out the window, waiting for him to speak. Fearing what he would say.

Several moments passed, punctuated by the tick, tick, tick of the mantel clock and the spit, spit, spit of rain against the wavy glass.

Finally, he began, "I thought we had an

understanding, you and I."

Chagrin filled her and not a little surprise. She drew in a deep breath and asked weakly, "Have we?"

She felt his gaze shift toward her, but when she looked down, he was already looking out the window once more.

"I realize," he said slowly, "that we have never spoken of it directly. It is — well, an awkward subject to say the least."

"Yes," she breathed.

He lowered his voice. "I thought you wished to be known as my wife."

Her heart thumped painfully. Did she? How shocking to hear him say the words outright. She felt embarrassed anew at her presumption.

He asked, "Was I wrong?"

Again she felt his gaze on her profile. She shook her head. It was what she wanted, wasn't it? For Daniel's sake. For her own. Yet James was nearer her own age, attractive, and unencumbered. Might he offer her a real marriage instead of pretense? Real love? Neither man had spoken of love, she realized.

He said, "I did not think you would perform Marianna's role so admirably — down to the infidelity."

Her face burned hot. "That's not fair."

"Is it not?"

She turned and met his eyes. "No."

He studied her closely. "I am glad to hear it."

The eye contact grew too intense. Hannah looked out the window once more, as though the cool rain could soothe the heat from his scorching gaze.

A few moments later, he spoke again, his voice gentle. "May I ask why you have stayed here?"

She nodded. "At first, I only wanted to find a way to rescue Daniel. To provide for him. I dared not dream of a happy home for him."

"And now?"

"I . . ." How could she express her jumbled thoughts?

When she hesitated, he sent her a flinty glance from beneath his lashes. "Waiting for a better offer to come along?"

She flinched. "No."

He said patiently, "I understand what you want for Danny. What about for yourself?"

She considered, then shrugged. "How can I separate the two? If he is happy and healthy and safe, then I am content."

"You are a mother, Hannah, yes. But you are also a woman, a person with your own thoughts and feelings and dreams."

His words surprised her. "Am I?" she murmured. She felt as though she had given up her dreams long ago.

"Has Lowden offered to marry you?"

"No." But she wondered if he would.

Sir John expelled a sigh of relief. "Listen to me, Hannah. I don't want you to stay with me out of financial need alone. Or as your cross to bear to provide for your son. If you want to leave me, leave. If you want to stay . . . I realize that is unlikely, yet I hope. . . ." His words faded away.

She swallowed, wondering exactly what he was asking of her. The implication of his words prickled through her body in a combined chill and flush. She whispered, "What is it *you* want, Sir John?"

She felt his fingers entwine with hers, and looked into his face.

Voice hoarse, he asked, "Is that not obvious?"

She shook her head, stunned by the intensity of his expression, his voice.

His eyes sparked with fire. He pulled her toward him and down until she was seated on his lap. Before the intimate position fully registered, he cupped the side of her face with one of his large hands, tilting her mouth toward his. His other circled her waist and drew her near. He pressed his lips to hers, hard and passionate. When she did not pull away, he angled his head and deepened the kiss.

His ardor overwhelmed her and she was stunned by the desire that flowed through her in response. What sort of woman was she that she could be drawn to two men at once?

He pulled her tight against him, moving his mouth over hers — firm, warm, delicious. Slowly his lips caressed, savoring this corner of her lips, then the opposite, then the sweet center. He lifted his head to look into her eyes, to regard her mouth as though the most desirable prize in the world before descending again.

She remembered being kissed like this once before. It had been too long.

She lifted her free hand, spreading her fingers to hold his face, the heel of her hand cupping his jaw, feeling the bristle of beard below and smooth cheekbone above. Her thumb fanned up from his chin, to the sensitive corner of his mouth. Then she slid her hand around his neck, splaying it against the back of his head and threading into his thick hair.

"Hannah . . ." he breathed.

She kissed him again.

A knock sounded on the door. Hannah

338

leapt from Sir John's lap as though a scalded cat.

Mrs. Turrill entered with a tray bearing a chocolate pot and two cups. She hesitated, her smile fading as she looked from one embarrassed face to the other.

"I've brought chocolate," she said, setting the tray down with an agitated air. "It's very hot." She retreated to the door, then turned back once more. "Be careful you don't burn yourselves."

CHAPTER 19

Through Mrs. Turrill, Sir John invited Hannah to join him for tea in his bedchamber. Hannah wondered if he wished to continue the previous night's activities. But sitting across from him that afternoon, the atmosphere was more that of a business meeting — or a courtroom — than a social call.

He sat in his invalid chair pulled up to the small table. A tray of tea things lay between them.

Hannah poured for them, and then sipped. But in her unease, she barely tasted the tea.

Sir John stirred his own tea and began, "You mentioned yesterday that you stayed to rescue Danny. You have done so and yet remain here. May I ask why?"

Hannah set down her cup. "I wish I had some more honorable answer to give you. But the truth is I had nowhere else to go."

"Could you not return to your father in Bristol?"

"My father believes I am dead. And I doubt he would be relieved to learn I am alive, yet have born a child out of wedlock. You must know what a shameful thing that is, especially to a clergyman like my father."

She thought, then added, "I don't intend to make him sound a harsh man. He is not. And perhaps he would be relieved to know I am alive. But that does not mean he would allow his fallen daughter and illegitimate grandson to live with him. He would likely lose the curacy were it known. And it would break his heart."

"What about Bath? Where did you go after you left us?"

Hannah took a deep breath and replied, "I went to a maternity home I had seen advertised in the newspaper."

She paused to collect her thoughts. "The neighborhood was not ideal, but the matron was all warmth and kindness. At least, at first. When she realized I was a gentlewoman, she offered me a reduced rate for lodgings if I would help with sewing and correspondence and the like. I agreed, and the time passed quickly. After Danny was born, and I had recovered, Mrs. Beech offered me two options. I could stay on as a wet nurse. Or, I could leave Danny with her, and for a fee, he would be cared for by one of the nurses in her employ."

"Is that where you found Becky?" Sir John asked.

"Yes. Poor girl had lost her own child and Mrs. Beech kept her on as wet nurse. Becky is good-hearted and sincerely loves Danny, though I once feared she was not quite sound of mind. But she seems much better since coming here."

Hannah sighed, then continued. "At all events, as much as I wanted to stay with Danny, I knew that if I was ever to support the two of us, I would need to find a better situation. So, I took a position as a lady's companion to an elderly dowager, and slipped away when I could to visit Danny. The arrangement worked fairly well for a time, except that Mrs. Beech began raising her fees beyond what I had agreed to, and before I knew it, beyond what I could afford. When I fell behind in my payments, she refused to allow me to have Danny, or even to see him. . . ."

He winced. "I wish you had come to me. I would have helped."

She shifted uneasily. "I feared you would be obligated to confide my secret to your wife, or even to Mr. Ward, if finances were involved. Both had many connections in Bristol. I doubted a week would have passed before everyone in my home parish had heard of my fall — my own father among them."

"That's why you said nothing. We were concerned when you left so suddenly. I tried to find you, but to no avail."

She nodded. "Mr. Lowden mentioned that."

He shook his head in regret. "You were in a terrible situation. When I think of all you've gone through . . . I am sorry indeed."

Hannah paused to relish the sweet salve of that acknowledgement. Then she said, "You should know that Dr. Parrish gave me ten pounds from your purse for the journey to Bath to collect Danny. I used it to pay what I owed, and of course for traveling expenses. But that is all I've taken from you, besides food and shelter."

He held up his hand. "Don't give it another thought — or try to pay it back."

"I won't." She managed a weak chuckle. "I couldn't."

"I wouldn't want you to." He took a sip of tea and avoided her eyes. "May I ask how long you plan to stay here?"

"I planned to stay only until my arm healed and I could find a new position. Who would hire me with my arm in a sling?"

"I see." He bowed his head, drumming

343

his fingers on the table, before looking up at her once more. "Then why not remain in your . . . present position?"

Hannah felt her mouth fall open. Was he really suggesting they allow the ruse to continue indefinitely? She asked, "What are you saying?"

Sir John tented his fingers and regarded her earnestly. "If you continue on as Lady Mayfield, Danny would be my heir."

Heir? She had never considered such a possibility.

Sir John went on, "But if it were known that you and I were not married at the time of his birth, then that would not be possible. Worse yet, you would be exposed as a fraud."

Hannah cringed. "I will be anyway, as soon as we return to Bristol."

"Why return then?"

"Even if we don't, someone will come here eventually. Someone who knows I am not Marianna."

"Perhaps." Sir John exhaled and drew his shoulders back. "Well. Leave it with me for now. I will talk to Mr. Lowden about the options and legalities and draw up some sort of plan."

Talk to Mr. Lowden . . . Just as she'd feared he'd do.

344

Sir John sipped, then paused, looking at her over his teacup. "In the meantime, don't . . . go anywhere, all right?"

Hannah picked up her own cup, noticing her hand tremble. She managed a vague smile but made no promises.

Emboldened by Hannah's recent warmth toward him, James returned to Sir John's bedchamber that afternoon to talk sense to the man. He was his solicitor, after all. And part of his duty was to counsel his clients, and help them steer clear of ruinous decisions. Though James privately acknowledged that he was no longer an objective party in the situation.

He found Sir John seated in his wheeled chair at a large oak desk, busy over correspondence. James had overheard Edgar Parrish and Ben Jones discussing how they would elevate the man's desk on blocks, so the arms of his wheeled chair would fit under it, but this was his first time seeing the result of their handiwork.

Sir John was fully dressed, his hair and beard were neatly trimmed, and his eyes held a keen light. He certainly no longer looked like an invalid.

"Hello, Sir John."

"Mr. Lowden." Sir John set his quill back

345

into its holder and regarded him, then nodded toward the armchair in the corner. "Have a seat."

"No, thank you." James drew himself up. "Forgive me, but I think it my duty to counsel you against your present course. It can only end in scandal or heartbreak or both."

Sir John gave him a wry glance. "Your professional powers now extend to matters of the heart?"

The room felt suddenly warm and stifling, but James took a deep breath and reminded himself to remain calm. He said, "Have you asked yourself — or Miss Rogers for that matter — why she has remained?"

"I do not answer to you, Mr. Lowden. Nor does she. But I will tell you that she only planned to wait until her arm healed, and she could find a situation elsewhere."

"Are you sure that was all she was waiting for? For her arm to heal, so she could find work as someone else's scullion? When she had tasted the life of a lady?"

Sir John frowned. "What are you suggesting?"

"Perhaps she was waiting for you to die, Sir John. I hate to say it so bluntly, but there it is. If you had died, she might have inherited everything, well, she and her son. Why leave for paltry wages elsewhere, when the chance at a great inheritance awaited?"

"I am surprised at you, Mr. Lowden," Sir John said. "I thought you liked her."

"I did. I do. But I cannot ignore the possibility."

Sir John shook his head. "I don't believe she ever thought of that. Not for herself. If she thought of her son's future, I cannot blame her."

"Can you not?" James stared at the man, frustration mounting. "What has happened to you, sir? I begin to doubt you are of sound mind after all. Do you hear yourself? A woman poses as your wife, passes off her by-blow as your son, and you 'cannot blame her'?"

Sir John's hand flew out and grabbed James by his cravat, yanking a fistful of linen and jerking his face down to his eye level. "Never say that again, do you hear me? If I ever hear you call the boy such a name again, I will dismiss you instantly, do I make myself clear?"

Stunned, James managed a slight nod and his employer released his grip.

He had overstepped, he knew. And what if Hannah had heard the words he'd just spewed? "Forgive me," James said. "I ought not to have questioned your competence

347

nor condemned Miss Rogers." James lowered his voice. "But, sir. Why would you make him your heir? What is he to you? He is not your son."

"On the contrary, Mr. Lowden. That is exactly what he is. My son. My flesh and blood. *Heir of the body* — my body."

James Lowden gaped at him, speechless.

Sir John continued, "Why do you think Miss Rogers left our employ in the first place?"

James made no reply. A wave of nausea curdled his stomach and he feared he would be sick.

"It is not something I'm proud of," Sir John said. "But don't you see? It is my chance to do something right. To redeem, in a small way, all the wrong I have done."

James's mind refused to accept it. "But you said the boy looked nothing like you — you saw no resemblance."

"To myself, no. But he looks exactly like my brother, Paul."

"Your brother? Surely you are not suggesting Miss Rogers and your brother —"

Sir John scowled. "Thunder and turf, man. Paul died at sea years ago. I wasn't suggesting any such thing. Only that when I look at Daniel, I see the picture of my younger brother. Make no mistake, the boy is a Mayfield."

James shook his head. "Not legally."

"No, not legally, unless she continues on as Lady Mayfield." Sir John crossed his arms over his chest. "You are my solicitor. I'm sure you can find a way to make it work."

"Not ethically." James forced out the dreaded question, "Do you mean to marry her?"

"We are already married in the eyes of everyone here."

James shook his head. "First we must have Marianna declared dead. Then and only then can you marry Miss Rogers legally, if that is what you really intend to do."

"But then her son could not be my legal heir, if it is known his mother and I were not married at the time of his birth."

"Not for your entailed property, no. But you have more than sufficient funds should you decide to sponsor him through university or something along those lines."

"But Miss Rogers would be exposed as a . . . as not being whom others believe she is."

"Whom she *allowed* others to believe she is," James clarified. "She may not have started the lie, but she certainly perpetuated it." Even as he said it, James wondered how he could lash out at the woman who had captured his heart. Was it really only to extricate her from Sir John's good graces?

His client's eyes glinted. "How bitter you sound, Mr. Lowden. And here I thought you had feelings for her yourself."

James made no reply.

"I wouldn't worry if I were you," Sir John said, an ironic twist to his mouth. "Women don't stay with me. No doubt Miss Rogers will prove no different than the rest. She will be looking for her escape any day now and there you will be — ready to rescue her."

Mind in turmoil, James went downstairs and found Hannah alone in the drawing room, staring out the window at yet another coastal storm. For a moment he stood there gazing at her profile, remembering how his heart and body had burned when he'd seen her step from her bath, when she'd touched his face, and when her pupils had darkened and dilated after he'd promised to one day kiss all her freckles. . . . Now his heart cooled and he tasted ashes in his mouth.

He cleared his throat. "Hannah . . . em, Miss Rogers."

She turned and looked at him. For several ticks of the long-case clock she studied him in silence. His shock and worry must have shown in his expression, because she whispered, "He told you then?"

"Yes." Betrayal snaked up his spine. "Why didn't you?"

She shook her head. "I have never told anyone. Never spoken of it. Never would have, if Marianna still lived. In any case, I never dared imagine he might acknowledge Danny as his son. And I would never try to force him."

"Regardless," James said. "You don't have to do this. You don't have to stay here and pretend any longer."

She made no answer, turning away and staring once again through the rain-streaked window.

"You don't owe him anything," James insisted. "Or at least, not *everything*. And don't tell me you plan to continue living under another woman's identity. That cannot stand. Marianna Mayfield's death must be recorded."

"Why?"

"Because it's the law. And because you are *not* her."

"I know that. But I am Daniel's mother. And like it or not, Sir John is his father."

Bile soured his throat. "You will stay with him, because he — a married man — took advantage of you while you were in his employ? That is the sort of man you want?"

"It wasn't like that. I'm not saying it was right, but it wasn't like you make it sound."

Grasping her arms, James turned her to face him. He looked into her beguiling blue-green eyes and pain and longing washed over him. "But you want me. I know you do." His whole body tensed with frustration. Why would she not admit it?

His gripped her shoulders, his voice a low growl. "Hannah, tell me the truth. I need to hear you say it."

Composure crumbling, she whispered, "James, I . . . You're right, I do . . . have feelings for you. But —"

His arms whipped around her and he crushed her to him, pressing his mouth to hers, swallowing her words. For a moment she kissed him back, meeting and returning the bruising fervor of his kiss. Then she wrenched her mouth free and tried to pull back.

"James, stop. You didn't let me finish."

He buried his fingers in her hair and pressed his lips to her temple, her cheek, her throat. "You love me," he whispered into her ear. "What else is there to say?"

"A great deal." She lifted her palms to his chest and pushed a few inches of space between them.

"James." She drew in a shaky breath. "There is more to life than feelings or desire."

He shook his head. "Nothing is more important."

"Yes. There is self-control, and doing the right thing even when it is painful."

"No," he growled. "You shall not be the sacrificial lamb here. I won't let you do this."

He turned abruptly and strode from the room.

CHAPTER 20

Long after James had stalked away, Hannah remained, staring out the window at the lashing rain, wind-bent trees, and grey sky as evening darkened. Yet she saw not that storm, but another stormy night, last spring. When she had been snug and dry in the Mayfields' Bristol house. . . .

Hands clasped before her, Hannah glanced around the drawing room. Lady Mayfield's customary armchair was empty. She had gone out. Again. Meeting her lover, no doubt. Sir John stood before the hearth, imposing in evening clothes, one hand resting on the high mantel, the other propped on his hip. He stared at the fire, expression brooding.

Outside, lightning flashed and rain lashed the window panes. To go out on such a night? How desperate she must be to see Anthony Fontaine. Hannah recalled unsettling images of Marianna and Mr. Fontaine flirting, caressing, and stealing kisses in this room not long ago, but blinked them away. It seemed almost a betrayal to think of the two of them in her husband's presence.

Hannah and the Mayfields often sat there together in the evenings after dinner. Marianna in an armchair or dreamily playing the pianoforte, her mind far away while Hannah sat in the corner, quietly sewing or reading by candlelight. Sir John standing at the fire as he was now, lost in his own thoughts, or perhaps sitting on the sofa reading. Now and again, Lady Mayfield would engage him in a game of draughts or cards. If he was unwilling, she would turn to Hannah and urge her to play in his stead. Hannah complied because she was paid to do so, not because she cared for either game. When she was in one of her restless moods, Lady Mayfield might call for wine and two glasses and insist Hannah play cards with her into the wee hours.

But Hannah was unaccustomed to being alone with Sir John.

She hesitated. She never remained long in the room when it was only Sir John. He never showed any interest in her company and it would be awkward to attempt polite conversation with him — pretend that they

355

were not both aware of the missing person, and where she likely was and in whose company.

"Lady Mayfield has gone out," he announced, unnecessarily.

"On such a night . . ." she murmured.

"She would rather face foul weather than her foul husband it seems." He picked up a fire iron and began poking at a log, causing the languishing fire to smoke.

"Well. I think I shall turn in early. Good night, Sir John." She turned to go.

"Please stay, Miss Rogers. I find I cannot bear the solitude tonight."

She turned back. His eyes were still on the dying fire.

"Very well," she said quietly, and stepped toward her customary chair in the corner.

"It is cold tonight," he said. "Come and sit by the fire, if you will. I do not bite, no matter what my wife may have told you."

Hannah hesitated, then complied, walking over to sit on the sofa near the fire, but on the end farthest from him. "She has never said such a thing I assure you," she murmured, not sure if she was defending her mistress or him.

The Mayfields had been married a year and a half at that point. Still in their honeymoon period — or they should have been.

And Lady Mayfield was not discreet in her little jabs about her husband ever panting after her, confessing she could not stand his hands touching her. In fact, she had confided to Hannah that she had not allowed him to share her bed since their first wedding anniversary. Hannah had thought perhaps Lady Mayfield was exaggerating the matter, boasting to her companion as though it were something to be proud of. But judging by her husband's defeated expression, it was all too true.

He asked, "Has she told you what I have done to so offend her?"

Hannah shifted, feeling uncomfortable. She should not be having this conversation with Marianna's husband. He must be tormented indeed over his marriage to ask his wife's paid companion for advice. A companion he had not wished to engage in the first place.

When she made no reply, he stepped to the sideboard, poured two glasses of port, and carried one to her.

Murmuring her thanks, Hannah accepted the glass and sipped the ruby liquid. She thought again of Marianna Mayfield and Anthony Fontaine sitting on this very sofa, his hand on her leg, his finger on her décolletage, her sparkling eyes, her eager smile. . . . Marianna was certainly interested in intimate relations, just not with Sir John.

He downed his drink. "If she found me disgusting before our marriage, she certainly hid it well. What am I to do?" he asked, still not looking at her. Was he asking her, the fire, or God?

He continued, "I could bring a suit against her lover in a civil trial. But I have no desire to expose her or myself to scandal. Nor do I want a ruinous divorce. What I want is a wife who will be faithful to me. Is that too much to ask?"

"No. It shouldn't be," she quietly agreed.

"I don't suppose there is anything I can do to win back her affection?"

What could he do? Lady Mayfield didn't seem to worry about the rumors, his threats did not affect her, nor did his pleading and wooing. Knowing Marianna, the only thing that might move her was another woman's interest in her husband — ideally a woman more beautiful and more bewitching to turn his head. But Hannah doubted such a woman existed.

What *should* Sir John do: Make a pretense of flirting with another woman? Begin an immoral affair of his own? Sink to her level? No. He was a married man who wished to live honorably. Perhaps Marianna would respond if he simply stopped trying so hard. Hannah wasn't sure if neglect would have much effect on spoiled Marianna, but it might be worth a try.

When Hannah did not answer, he glanced at her. "A lost cause, is it? I am too old and too serious, as she never tires of telling me."

You are not old, Hannah thought, *though serious and reserved?* Yes. He would never be accused of being the life of the party — that had always been Marianna's role. But he was well-respected and gentlemanlike and attractive. . . . Inwardly she reprimanded herself, *Stop it, stop it, you foolish girl.*

She cleared her throat and said, "Perhaps you ought not try so hard. Ignore her for a time. Make her come to you. That might gain her attention."

"And watch six months of alienation turn into six years? If I left her alone, I think her only reaction would be one of relief."

Very likely, Hannah thought, but did not say such an injurious thing.

"I was engaged to be married once before, but the young lady broke things off. Apparently I am quite repulsive."

She glanced up and found his gaze on her. What vulnerability etched that face. A handsome face, in her view. Sir John might be fifteen years her senior but to her he had always seemed younger. He was tall, his shoulders broad, his body lean. Fine lines crinkled the corner of his eyes and between his brows, but otherwise his skin was smooth and taut. He kept himself well-read, well-groomed, and well-dressed. Sir John Mayfield was also a wealthy man, knighted by the king. Personally, Hannah didn't understand why Marianna found him unattractive . . . or at least not as attractive as Anthony Fontaine.

"No, sir."

He smiled dryly. "That answer was long in coming. You needn't be polite."

"I am not being polite. It is true. I do not think you repulsive."

He touched his heart, a mocking light in his grey-blue eyes. "What a compliment. I am in your debt, madam."

"I did not mean —"

"Never mind, Miss Rogers. It is kind of you to try."

She felt the urge to lay a comforting hand on his arm, to reassure him. She rose. His gaze snapped over, watching her in some surprise. How inappropriate such consolation would be coming from her, she realized. Courage failing her, she stepped to the window instead. She pretended to survey the storm, the swaying branches, the lightning slicing the ominous sky.

She felt his gaze on her profile.

"It's getting worse," she observed.

"Yes, it is," he muttered, and went back to poking the fire.

She glanced at his despondent expression. He was not a perfect man. No one was. But Hannah had lived in that house long enough to know that the lion's share of the blame lay with Marianna.

Courage returning, she stepped from the window to his side, and — with a nervous swallow — laid her hand on his arm. He gave a little start and looked down at her pale bare fingers on his dark sleeve. He looked from her hand to her face almost warily.

"Sir John, forgive me for speaking out of turn. But there is nothing wrong with you. You are kind and gentlemanlike. A bit quiet, perhaps, but intelligent, well-respected, and honorable. I don't know why she finds such fault with you. I think perhaps it is simply that you are not Mr. Fontaine."

He inhaled, then slowly released the breath. "Well, there is nothing I can do about that." He patted her hand awkwardly. "Still, I thank you, Miss Rogers."

She smiled apologetically and removed

her hand. "You're welcome."

In the hearth, the fire sparked to life at last.

She watched it for several moments, then sighed. "Well, I think I shall retire."

He nodded. "I shall follow soon after. Good night, Miss Rogers."

"Good night, sir."

She slipped from the drawing room, but one of the footmen, waiting in the corridor, waved her over. "Evenin', Miss Rogers."

She nodded. "Jack."

"I heard her ladyship's gone out for the evening."

Was the man fishing for gossip?

"She has," Hannah officiously replied. "Sir John was just lamenting the fact that she had a prior engagement on such a night as this."

"I imagine that was a bit awkward, just the two of you in there. Alone."

If she wasn't careful, Jack would be gossiping about her next. She bit back a rebuke and feigned nonchalance instead. "Not too bad," she said with a shrug. "I believe he thought I missed her company, so he conversed with me to pass the time. Kind of him, but we have so little to talk about."

"Does he really believe her ladyship is out at some charity meeting or whatever lie she fed him? Douglas hated having to take the horse and carriage out in this, I can tell you. Charity meeting, my eye."

"I have no idea. Well, good night, Jack."

"Miss."

She had neglected to bring a lamp up the stairs with her, but the candle on the landing guided her well enough. Besides, she knew the way by rote. She passed Lady Mayfield's room, then Sir John's dressing room and bedchamber, before a sound drew her back.

What was that banging?

She followed the repetitive clatter back to Lady Mayfield's room. She knocked at the open doorjamb, though she was quite certain Lady Mayfield had yet to return, then inched the door open. Lightning flashed, lighting up the room, and in an instant she identified the problem. The windows had been left open and the shutters not lashed down. Rain and wind were blowing into the room. Hannah ran forward, and began drawing in one window then another, latching them closed. The rain was coming in at a nearly horizontal angle — fat droplets splattered her face and neck.

Suddenly, Sir John appeared beside her, clearly drawn inside by the banging shutters as she had been. Or perhaps in hopes his wife had returned. Setting down his candle lamp in haste, he began latching the upper shutters, while she closed the lower halves. They worked together, passing closely, hands accidentally brushing as each reached for the last shutter.

"To leave open the windows on such a night . . ." Hannah muttered. Suddenly aware of her wet face, she grinned ruefully. "Here I thought we were the ones safe and dry indoors tonight."

He remained silent, jaw tense.

Nervous to be alone with him in Lady Mayfield's bedchamber, she prattled on, "I shall ask Mrs. Peabody to remind the housemaids to be more careful in future, shall I?"

He merely stood there, looking at her.

She asked, "Is the carpet wet? Perhaps I should gather a few bath towels, and —"

"Leave it."

She turned back in surprise, regarding him by the light of his candle lamp.

He said, "I don't care about the carpet, but you are damp through." He withdrew a clean handkerchief from his pocket, then lifted it toward her face. "Allow me." With one hand, he lightly took her chin between thumb and fingers. With the other he gathered a corner of the thin cloth and softly brushed her forehead, then her cheeks, her nose. . . . Her heart began to accelerate, nerves tingling at his touch.

"I hope your freckles will not rub off."

She chuckled mournfully. "If only they would. The bane of my existence."

He tilted her chin to better regard her complexion in the lamplight. "They're charming. You're quite beautiful."

"Ha." She shook her head. Pretty, maybe. But no one besides her mother had ever called her beautiful. "With this long nose and wide mouth? Hardly."

He ran the cloth down her nose. "Distinctive." Then he slowly ran it across her lips and whispered, "Desirable."

Their eyes met and locked. His fingers within the gauzy cloth lowered to her neck and trailed along her clavicle bones, stroking the bare skin above the modest neckline of her gown. She could hardly breathe. How wide the blacks of his eyes were in the flickering light. Intense with longing, yet tinged with uncertainty.

She didn't move.

He lowered his head slowly, gaze flicking over her eyes, her face, her lips. She didn't run or step away. She barely even blinked. He touched his lips to hers, softly, tentatively. A rush of sweet, heady longing filled her.

When she did not object, a spark flared behind his eyes. He pressed his lips to hers more fervently, wrapped his arms around her, and pulled her against him. How tense his body was. How nearly frantic his endless kiss.

Suddenly he tore his mouth away, grabbed her hand almost roughly, and opened the adjoining-room door. He paused only long enough to turn back for the candle lamp, then pulled her along behind him through his own dressing room and into his connecting bedchamber — a room she had never been in before. He shoved the door closed behind him with his foot and then he was kissing her again.

A small voice within her whispered this was wrong. That it was not too late. She could tell him to stop, break away, and retreat to her own room. But she gave the voice little heed. Perhaps it was the sweet port, the violent storm, his wife's callous infidelity, or the fact that she could give him something he had been refused for far too long. Something he deeply, desperately wanted. Or perhaps she simply allowed herself to be swept away in the moment, on a foreign feeling of power and desirability.

His hands slid up under her arms, then slowly downward, following her curves, her rib cage, the deep indentation at her waist and slight flare of slim hips. He sighed deep in his throat, as though the feel of her feminine shape was somehow satisfying. He tilted his head the other way, renewing his kiss with ardor.

The youthful stolen kisses and timid touches she had once shared with Fred seemed like child's play in comparison. She stood on her tiptoes — he was so much taller than she — allowing her shy fingers to touch the hair at the nape of his neck. Then she slid her hands tentatively down his shoulders to his chest. Without breaking their kiss, he pulled his arms away and struggled out of his formfitting coat. He ripped off his waistcoat, sending buttons clattering to the floor. Heedless, he grasped her hands and laid them on his chest. He still wore a white shirt, but the fine cotton did not conceal the hard muscle beneath. She ran her hands up over his shoulders and down the ropey muscles of his arms before returning to his chest. She had never touched a man before, except Freddie many years ago. His skinny, wiry frame had felt nothing like this.

Sir John lowered his head, kissing her

neck, her shoulder. His hands once again ran firmly up her sides until the heels of his hands brushed the swell of her and she gasped. He returned his mouth to hers, perhaps afraid she was about speak reason into the unreasonable, and stifled any protest with his kiss.

Suddenly he reached down, placed one arm beneath her knees, the other behind her back, and swept her up into his arms with apparent ease. He carried her to his canopied four-poster bed.

He laid her down atop the bedclothes and covered her with his warm weight. Propping himself on one elbow, he brushed away a lock of hair from her brow and looked into her eyes. "Beautiful Hannah . . ."

Had he called her his wife's name by mistake, or no name at all, she might yet have resisted him. But the sound of her given name in his deep voice, said with such feeling, such warmth . . . She was lost. She wrapped her arms around his neck, leaned up to kiss him, and held on.

Hannah awoke with a start sometime later. Outside, the storm had subsided, but it was still dark. What had awakened her — had a door slammed? Had Lady Mayfield returned home at last? Then suddenly she remembered. Where she was. With whom. And what they had done. All the desire and heady power dissolved into guilt and shame. And fear.

Pushing Sir John's arm gingerly from her waist, she swung her legs over and climbed from bed. She still wore her stays and shift, though he had worked her gown off her shoulders and tossed it onto the chair. She stepped into the gown and pulled it up over her shoulders and straightened her skirts as best she could. Her hair was down, the pins who knew where. She hoped whichever housemaid found them would assume they were Lady Mayfield's. Hannah crept around the room until she found her stockings and shoes. She slid on her shoes barefooted and bunched the stockings in one hand. She went to the main door, listened, and hearing nothing, slowly opened it. She allowed herself one last look at the slumbering Sir John, but could see little save a dim outline in the dark room. The candle lamp had long since burned itself out.

She slipped from the room, quietly closing the door behind her. She tiptoed toward her own room at the far end of the corridor and had nearly reached it when a shadowy figure carrying a candle appeared from around the corner. She stifled a gasp.

It was Mr. Ward. Mr. Ward, who often looked at her in a manner that made her uncomfortable, now glanced significantly from her, down the dark corridor. Had he any idea which room she had come from? She prayed not.

He looked at her with suspicion in his small eyes, or something even less flattering.

"Miss Rogers . . . What are you doing wandering about in the dark?"

She hoped he did not notice the few buttons at the back of her frock were not fastened. Hopefully her unbound hair covered the omission. "I . . . I thought I heard a door shut," she faltered, trying in vain to keep her voice steady. "Is . . . Lady Mayfield home at last?"

He studied her expression by the light of his candle. "Yes, which you would know if you had been to her room."

"I did not go in. I did not wish to wake her."

"I doubt she is asleep. Her poor lady's maid has just been called from her bed to undress her. For the second time this evening no doubt."

She despised the man's leering innuendo. Though he was probably right.

"Then she is in good hands," Hannah

said, attempting a casual tone and reaching for her door latch. Suddenly his hand shot out and descended over hers like a claw. She looked up at him in alarm.

He stared boldly into her face, as if daring her to protest. "Miss Rogers. Hannah. Perhaps we should . . . talk. In private."

Did he think he held some power over her? Was he threatening her, or simply hoping to take advantage of this unexpected encounter in the middle of the night?

"It is late, Mr. Ward," she said coolly. "Anything you have to say to me can wait until morning. Now I must bid you good night."

She wrenched the door open, stepped inside, and quickly shut it behind her, turning the key in the lock. She pressed her ear to the wood, hearing nothing over the loud beating of her heart. One minute . . . two . . . Finally she heard his footsteps retreat.

But she feared she had not suffered the last of his advances.

She did not see Sir John until the next afternoon. One of Marianna's female friends called, and while they were ensconced over tea and gossip in Marianna's boudoir, Sir John discreetly sought out Hannah in the library. Her stomach tensed at the sight of him. What would he say?

He closed the door behind them and began quietly, "Miss Rogers, I am deeply sorry about last night."

She ducked her head, ears burning. "As am I."

"I should have found the strength to stop myself. But I acted selfishly, and I apologize."

She managed a wooden nod. What was she supposed to say? What could she say? The more he regretted it, the more her own regret mounted.

He stepped closer. "I have never done the like before. You are a gentleman's daughter — a clergyman's daughter — which makes it all the more inexcusable. Were it in my power, were I not a married man, I would do the honorable thing. Since that is not possible, I am at a loss as to what to do. If there is anything you need. Mon—"

She cut him off. "Do not offer me money, I beg of you. That would make me feel even worse. Like a payment for services rendered."

"Oh . . ." He hesitated. "I see. Well. I did not intend it that way."

A single knock sounded and the door was opened before Sir John could reply. Mr.

Ward stuck his head in, like a jack-in-the-box. It might have been comical save for the timing and his suspicious expression, as he looked from one to the other.

Sir John said evenly, "Miss Rogers and I are discussing a few things, Mr. Ward, but is there something you needed?"

"Ah . . . No, sir. That is, I can wait. If you are in the middle of something . . . pressing." His brows lifted in expectation.

A weasel, Hannah decided. The man looked like a long-necked weasel.

"Not at all." Sir John crossed his arms. "What is it?"

Hannah spoke up, forcing a polite formality. "Thank you, Sir John. I will make a note of it. Now, if you will excuse me, I shall leave the two of you to your business."

Hannah didn't know if companions in most houses ate dinner with their mistress and her husband, but Lady Mayfield insisted upon it. It gave her someone to talk to, she said. And the presence of a third party forced her stern husband to remain polite and dissuaded him from engaging in serious conversation, like asking her where she had been and with whom, and confronting her behavior. Then again, it was not very common for a married woman to hire a companion at all. But there was little common about this marriage.

The three of them sat at table together as usual that evening. Sir John at the head, Lady Mayfield to his right and Hannah across from her. Most of the time, Lady Mayfield directed her chatter across the table at Hannah, effectively ignoring Sir John. Occasionally, she directed a question his way, or a bit of news, or a barb.

That night, however, Marianna Mayfield's gaze swung like a pendulum from Sir John to Hannah, brown eyes speculative above her raised wineglass. "You two are certainly quiet."

Neither replied for several moments.

Then he said, "I suppose it was the storm. Neither of us slept well last night."

Her arched brows rose high. "Neither of you?"

"Well, I don't know how anyone could sleep through all that thunder and lightning," he clarified. "Did you, Miss Rogers?"

Hannah licked dry lips. "No, I did not fall asleep until quite late, I'm afraid."

"Pity." Marianna smiled. "I slept like a lamb."

Hannah felt Lady Mayfield's gaze linger on her profile. When she glanced up, the woman was watching her curiously. "Perhaps that was what Mr. Ward meant. He told me he thought you . . . missed me . . . last night. He said he found you wandering the corridors quite late in search of me."

"I heard your shutters banging, and went to shut them."

Her brows shot up once more. "Really?" She glanced at her husband, eyes sparking with mischief, but not, Hannah thought, suspicion. "Sir John mentioned *he* shut them."

Hannah felt her cheeks warm, but strived for a casual air. "We . . . did so together."

"The shutters made quite a racket," Sir John added. "Which you would know. Had you been here."

Another course was laid, and Marianna changed the subject, to Hannah's great relief.

Likely to avoid more such awkward encounters, Sir John took himself away for a time, visiting his other properties. His absence gave Marianna the freedom she relished, but it added guilt to Hannah's already aching conscience — that he should have to leave on her account.

He returned several weeks later. Hannah saw little of him, for he spent the majority of his time in his study or in Mr. Ward's office. She wondered what sort of business or arrangements kept the two men so busy.

She found out soon enough.

Marianna stormed into the drawing room that afternoon, eyes blazing.

"I cannot believe what Sir John did."

Alarm jolted Hannah. Had Marianna found out somehow?

"Has he not mentioned it to you, either?" Marianna asked.

Hannah stared at her mistress. "Mentioned . . . what?"

"He has let a place in Bath. Do you know how I longed, how I begged to live in Bath when we first married? But no, he would deny me. And now, now that I wish to remain here, now he says we will go, whether I like it or not."

"Why should you not like it," Hannah murmured distractedly, her mind spinning with the news and what it would mean for her.

"Don't be coy, Hannah. You know perfectly well why."

"But would you not enjoy all the entertainments Bath affords?"

"I admit the plan has some appeal, if only for a few months. Bristol is so dreary in the winter. In Bath, there are balls in the assembly rooms, and concerts. And the very best people come for the Bath season. I should enjoy more variety in society. It won't be the same as the London season, of course, but might prove diverting. . . ."

"I am sure it shall, my lady."

Marianna inhaled an audible little gasp. "I shall have to order new gowns!"

How quickly Marianna had resigned herself to the move. Far more so than Hannah.

On her way upstairs to change for dinner, Sir John caught her in the hall.

"Miss Rogers, may I have a word with you in my study?"

Her breath hitched. "Of course, Sir John."

Swallowing hard, she followed him across the hall and into the masculine chamber.

"Leave the door open, if you please." He gestured her forward toward his desk. Quietly, he said, "Less chance of gossip if we leave the door open. And I shall be able to see if anyone nears the door while we talk."

Was gossip all he was hoping to avoid? Was further temptation to be avoided as well? Or did he find her revolting now that she was ruined?

She clasped her hands and waited.

He looked down at his desk as if gathering his thoughts, his fingers rolling and unrolling a scrap of paper. "I hope you will not be offended," he began, then looked up at her. "I have taken the liberty of finding another situation for you, Miss Rogers."

She stared at him in surprise.

"A friend of mine, Mr. Perrin, has a widowed mother in need of a companion. She is an old dear, and I have spent many a happy hour in her company. I would not have arranged it, if I did not think the two of you would suit one another. I honestly think you would enjoy the post. It will be far less . . . complicated."

She bit the inside of her cheek to keep tears at bay. *Irrational creature,* she inwardly chastised herself. For it felt like a rejection.

His eyebrows tented in apology. "Please know I am not dismissing you. Not in that sense. Not for anything you've done." He glanced toward the door. "Rather for what I fear I might do should you remain."

The mantel clock ticked and ticked again. He did not find her revolting after all. It was small comfort.

Her throat tight, she managed, "I understand."

"I hope Bath will be a new start for Marianna and me. What sort of a hypocrite would I be if I did not forgive her indiscretions and offer her a second, third, hundredth chance?"

She forced a wooden nod.

"I hope putting a little distance between her and a certain man will help, yes. But I also plan to make full use of the Bath season, and escort her to all the entertainments, all the pleasures of youth she has no doubt missed in my quiet company. I don't know if it will help. But I must try."

Again she nodded, heart aching, the words she longed to say fading away. After all, he was a married man. She had already refused his money, and really, what else could he offer her? He and Marianna had enough problems as it was. She wouldn't drive another wedge between them.

"She is my wife," he said, as if reading her thoughts. "I took vows. For better, for worse."

Unable to speak over her burning throat, Hannah bobbed a shaky curtsy, turned, and slipped from the room.

After dinner that evening, Sir John remained in the dining room over a glass of port, while the two women withdrew to the drawing room.

Marianna glared at her. "Sir John says you have no wish to go with us to Bath. Is that true?"

She delivered her prepared explanation. "It is not that I don't want to go with you, but that my father is here." *My father is here . . .* Hannah thought, *the very reason I should leave! Before he realizes and breaks his heart.* For though little more than a month had passed, Hannah already suspected the truth of her situation.

Marianna's lip curled. "Nothing says you have to remain near your father. I never wanted to see mine once I moved out, I can tell you. Come, Hannah. Whomever shall I find to replace you? I need you. You cannot be so disloyal."

"It isn't a lack of loyalty, my lady. I assure you. But Sir John has found a suitable position for me here — very kind of him really — so I might stay. You won't need me — you shall have a whole new retinue of friends and so many dances and concerts, you won't even miss me."

"Of course I will. Why don't you want to come — really?"

"My lady, if your husband thinks it best that just the two of you go together, then we must bow to his wisdom and preference in this matter. Perhaps he wants to keep you for himself, to have more time with just the two of you. It is quite romantic, really."

"Keep me to himself, yes. Romantic, no."

Sir John walked past the drawing room at that moment.

Lady Mayfield tilted her head and waved her hand. "John! Hannah thinks you don't want her anymore and are casting her off."

He stepped back and paused in the threshold. His gaze flicked to Hannah before returning to his wife.

Hannah's face burned. She said hastily, "I did not say that, my lady. Please do not put words in my mouth. I only meant that we should comply with Sir John's wishes in this regard."

"John. I said I would try and I intend to. But I had no notion you meant to deprive me of Hannah as well. To drag me to a new city with no companion? I shall be terribly lonely."

"And your husband will not suffice in this role, I take it?" he asked dryly.

"Have you ever? Take no offense, John, but you are not much given to conversation, or society, or games, or fashion, or any of the things I like."

"I will try."

"John. I don't mean to be difficult, but I think it only fair to warn you. Who knows from what quarter I might have to seek solace if Hannah isn't there — whom I should turn to for companionship?"

The sweet doe-eyed words carried an edge of threat.

Sir John locked gazes with his wife, then turned to Hannah. "Apparently, my wife cannot live without you, Miss Rogers. Nor be accountable for her actions if you do not accompany us to Bath. Will you come? I cannot force you, of course. You are free to refuse, to take the other situation I arranged for you. But if you wish to come . . . you are welcome." The veiled message seemed clear. The invitation delivered with little enthusiasm. He wished her to refuse.

Hannah ducked her head, not meeting his eyes. "I will come," she said. She accepted, though not for the reasons either of them probably thought.

Hannah had her own motives for getting out of town, away from the eyes of people who knew her best. But she wouldn't be able to stay with the Mayfields forever. Her loose, high-waisted gowns would conceal her secret for several months. Maybe longer, since Sir John now avoided looking at her, and Lady Mayfield was self-absorbed. But eventually Hannah knew she would have to leave them, before they discovered the truth. . . .

And several months later, her small savings

in hand, Hannah did leave them. And tried to leave behind those memories, those feelings, and that vain hope . . . Now it all came flooding back. Did she have to lock it all away in the hidden trunk of her mind where she usually kept it? Or could she finally lay it all it to rest . . . along with Marianna Mayfield?

CHAPTER 21

The next day Mr. Lowden rode again to Barnstaple on business for Sir John, and some of the tension in the house departed with him.

But not all.

To thank his neighbors for all they had done for him and his "family," Sir John had invited the Parrishes to dinner, and it was too late to rescind the invitation now.

Mrs. Turrill had hired extra kitchen staff and two footmen for the day, and oversaw the preparation of a fine meal, sure to impress even her cousin-in-law, Mrs. Parrish.

Hannah gave in to Mrs. Turrill's urgings and wore one of Marianna's prettiest gowns — an evening dress of white gauze striped with blue, pinned and tacked-in at the bodice to better fit her for the occasion. She also asked Kitty to curl and arrange her hair.

It would be the first time Sir John would

walk downstairs and preside over his own dining table. He left the invalid chair behind, trapped above stairs as he had once been, and made his way downstairs with Ben's help. Sir John wore evening clothes that now hung loosely on him. But he looked elegant even so, in Hannah's estimation.

At the appointed hour, he stood at the door, leaning on his cane, to welcome his guests. Hannah saw the strain in his tight jaw and knew he was in pain.

Mrs. Parrish entered, wearing a matronly, dark blue evening gown snug at bosom and upper arms and somewhat creased, as if she had not worn it in a long while. Nancy looked pretty in a dress of gossamer net over a pink satin, white flowers pinned in her hair. The doctor and Edgar wore Sunday best.

Greetings were exchanged, wraps taken, and everyone moved into the dining parlor.

"May I offer you something, Dr. Parrish?" Sir John indicated the decanter on the sideboard.

The doctor patted his chest as though for answers. "I . . . well yes, I think I will. Just a spot. Special occasion and all."

Sir John poured a small glass, and Hannah noticed his hand was not quite steady.

"Come, Sir John. Let the footmen do their work," she said gently, taking his arm. "Your place at the head of the table awaits."

"Quite right, my lady." Dr. Parrish nodded, sending her a look of understanding. "A place that has been empty too long, I'd say. I thank God you sit among us tonight, sir. Cause for celebration indeed."

"Here, here," Edgar echoed.

The six of them took their seats at the table. Mr. Lowden was not due back from Barnstaple until quite late, which, Hannah thought, was just as well. She was anxious enough as it was, sitting there at the foot of the table, facing Sir John at its head as though she really were mistress of the house, as though she really were Lady Mayfield. Nerves prickled through her and when she lifted her glass, her hands were not quite steady, either.

They began the first course of oxtail soup and red mullet. As Hannah dipped her spoon, she noticed Becky standing just outside the door, Danny in her arms. The baby — two fingers in his mouth and drooling away as usual — seemed content, so why had Becky brought him down? But the girl's eyes were not seeking hers out. Rather they seemed fastened on Edgar Parrish, a dreamy smile on her impish face. Edgar did not seem to notice, his attention fully engaged by Mrs. Turrill's excellent soup. But Nancy noticed. And frowned.

Oh, dear. Inwardly, Hannah sighed.

She tried to catch the girl's eye. And when Becky finally glanced her way, Hannah gave a little jerk of her head, signaling — she hoped — for the girl to move away from the door and stop ogling another woman's man. Not that she had never done the same . . . Instead one of the eager new footmen mistook it as his cue to lay the next course, though most were still spooning their soup. As the young man reached for Sir John's bowl, Hannah quickly lifted a hand to forestall him, sending him an apologetic smile for good measure. Not a promising beginning.

Across the table, Mrs. Parrish smirked at her. Or perhaps Hannah was being overly sensitive.

To cover the mistake, Hannah opened the conversation, as perhaps Sir John should have done as host. She looked at Edgar and Nancy and asked brightly, "So, you two. What are your plans?"

It was the wrong question, evidently. Nancy turned to Edgar, who glanced at his mother. Seeing her dark expression, he looked into his soup. "Ah, we . . . No specific plans at present. I have my hands full managing the properties and putting money aside, and . . ."

"Really, Lady Mayfield," Mrs. Parrish said. "Don't go putting ideas into their heads. They are still so young."

"Don't forget, my dear," Dr. Parrish spoke up. "You married me when you were only a slip of a girl. Barely eighteen."

Mrs. Parrish gave him a sour look. "I was too young to know my own mind. Just because my parents allowed me to rush headlong into marriage does not mean I must encourage my one and only son to follow the same, rash course."

Sheepish looks were exchanged, followed by silence as thick as clotted cream.

Nancy looked up first, her brave smile belying tear-bright eyes. "And what about you, Lady Mayfield? Why do you not tell us how you met Sir John and about your courtship and wedding?" She gazed at Hannah hopefully.

Hannah appreciated the girl's tact in trying to rescue the conversation, but she did not appreciate the specific question.

"Ah. Well." She darted at glance at Sir John, hoping he might rescue her. He coolly met her gaze from the head of the table. Apparently not. "I . . . am afraid there is not much to tell."

"Come, my dear," Sir John said. "If you won't tell, then I shall have to do the honors."

Did she hear gallantry in his tone, or threat?

When she said nothing, he began, "We met at a public ball in the Bristol assembly rooms."

Then he did remember, Hannah realized. It was not a flattering memory for either of them, so they had never spoken of it.

Picking up the story, Hannah said lightly, "He refused to dance with me. Or at least ignored the extremely overt hint that he should do so, from the man who introduced us."

Sir John shrugged. "I never cared for dancing. Good thing." He tapped his cane on the floor for emphasis and grinned wryly. "I suppose that's one benefit of being lame — I shall finally have an excuse to decline that amusement."

"Oh now, Sir John." The doctor tucked his chin in gentle chastisement. "One never knows. With God and plenty of exercise . . ."

Nancy interrupted eagerly. "Did you know right away he was the one for you? Did he sweep you off your feet?"

"Oh, em . . . Not then, no."

From the vestibule came the sound of the front door opening and closing. Everyone turned to look. A moment later James Lowden passed by the dining parlor on his way through the house.

He drew up short at the sight of the well-lit and crowded room. "Oh. Sorry to interrupt. I forgot the dinner was tonight. You all go on with your meal."

"You're back early," Hannah said.

"Yes. We concluded our transactions more quickly than anticipated."

Hannah glanced at Sir John's placid expression, then smiled politely at the newcomer. "You must join us, Mr. Lowden. I am sure there is room for another place. Is that not right, Mrs. Turrill?"

Mrs. Turrill hesitated. "If you wish it, of course, my lady. And plenty of food."

James waved a dismissive hand. "That's all right. I'll have something later. I need to wash and change after being on the road."

Sir John looked from her to his solicitor. "Come, Lowden. Join us. You may even sit by Lady Mayfield if you like."

"Yes, do tell us the news from Barnstaple, Mr. Lowden," Mrs. Parrish urged. "I don't get there as often as I should like."

James surveyed their expectant faces. "Very well, if you insist. But only if you promise not to delay courses on my account. I don't want Mrs. Turrill's excellent cooking to go cold. You proceed and I shall join you in a few minutes. . . ."

He returned a short while later, having changed and combed his windblown hair. He sat down in time for the main course — croquettes of chicken, boiled tongue, and vegetables.

He picked up his table napkin and smiled at the cook-housekeeper. "Thank you, Mrs. Turrill. Looks delicious."

"And what took you to Barnstaple, Mr. Lowden?" Mrs. Parrish asked from across the table, forking an asparagus spear into her mouth.

He answered pleasantly, "Just some business for Sir John."

"Oh?" Mrs. Parrish leaned forward, eyes sparkling. "What sort of business? Must have been important for you to undertake such a journey again so soon."

He glanced at his employer, then away. "Not especially, Mrs. Parrish, just banking and the like — too tedious for dinner conversation."

"If you say so." The doctor's wife lifted a heaping spoon from her saltcellar and sprinkled it liberally over her entire plate. Then she glanced at Mrs. Turrill, quietly directing the footmen near the sideboard. "Mr. Turrill's business often took him to Barnstaple as well, I believe. Did it not, Mrs. Turrill?"

Hannah looked over and saw the housekeeper's face grow rigid — it was the first time Hannah had heard a *Mr.* Turrill mentioned.

"Yes," the housekeeper agreed with a brittle smile. "As well you know."

Mrs. Parrish returned her focus to the solicitor. "At least you returned from Barnstaple, Mr. Lowden. Not all men do."

The doctor's mouth fell ajar. "Mrs. Parrish . . ." he breathed, sending a concerned look at his cousin.

"I am only making conversation," she insisted, sending a veiled glance toward her hostess. "It is the polite thing to do. And what was the news in Barnstaple, Mr. Lowden?" she went on, unaffected by her husband's tone or the tension in the room.

"Nothing much," James replied. "High prices bemoaned, the summer fair anticipated. The usual sort of talk." He glanced at George Parrish. "I brought those things you wanted from the apothecary, doctor. Don't let me forget to give them to you after dinner."

"Thank you, Mr. Lowden. Saved me a trip."

Mrs. Parrish sawed at a slice of boiled tongue with exaggerated effort and then chewed it laboriously. She said with philosophic air, "Tongue that is boiled too long always tends to be tough. So difficult to time it correctly."

Sir John regarded the woman evenly. When he spoke, the glint in his eye belied his pleasant voice. "One can learn to bite any tongue, Mrs. Parrish, no matter how tough or bitter, if one tries."

James bit back a grin and lifted a forkful of meat in salute. "Better a boiled tongue than a loose one, I always say."

Mrs. Parrish formed a feline smile and countered, "And either one is preferable to a forked tongue." She gave Hannah a pointed look.

Around the table, uneasy looks were shared — or avoided.

From the sideboard, Mrs. Turrill abruptly announced, "Now who is ready for their desserts?"

The dinner continued and with it the stilted conversation. Hannah sat there, barely tasting Mrs. Turrill's lovely strawberry tartlets or orange jelly. The evening had clearly demonstrated to Hannah what life would be like if they allowed the deception to go on. It would mean continuing to lie to dear people like Dr. Parrish and Mrs. Turrill. And increasing her chances of discovery by people like Mrs. Parrish.

No. James was right; it could not be borne. Or risked.

She would have to gather her courage and talk to Sir John about ending the ruse. Danny didn't need to be his heir. His protection, and hopefully someday his love, would be enough. Would Sir John bear the scandal and offer to marry her? If not, would James still want her? She doubted it.

With a heavy heart, she realized she would probably lose them both.

The next day Hannah gathered her courage and took herself to Sir John's bedchamber to discuss the matter.

Mrs. Turrill was just coming out, men's shaving kit in hand, and greeted her warmly. "Ah, my lady. You're just in time. Sir John just asked me to find you."

"Did he? Well . . . good," Hannah murmured, even as her palms perspired.

Mrs. Turrill's eyes twinkled. "Wait 'til you see him — some of my best work, if I do say so myself." She grinned and walked away.

Hannah crossed the threshold and drew up short, arrested by his appearance.

Sir John Mayfield sat in a regular chair at his desk, his wheeled chair left in the corner. He was fully dressed in shoes, trousers, waistcoat, frockcoat, and cravat, hair groomed and face clean-shaven. He looked younger without the beard — handsome, serious, and masculine. She could hardly believe this was the same man who'd lain bedridden for weeks. He looked far more like the man who had once swept her into his arms and into his bed. She drew a shaky breath, and tried to blink the memory away.

A sheaf of papers lay on the desk. He raised a hand and gestured toward the chair on its other side.

Hannah walked forward, hands nervously clasped together, and sat down. "Before you say anything," she began. "I need you to know that after last night, I have decided we cannot go on as we are. I will not continue to lie to everyone. Or to myself."

"I thought you might say that." He bowed his head, inhaling deeply. "In time, I could try to have Marianna declared dead. But it seems premature at present."

She pursed her lip in surprise. "Because you would need the Parrishes to testify, and they think the woman they saw floating away was me?"

"Not only that. Though that will pose a problem."

She frowned. "Then why — because her body has not been found?"

"Oh, I doubt she will ever be found." A strange light shone in his eyes. "But we cannot be certain." He held her gaze. "Will you wait? Remain here with me until we can sort this out one way or another?"

Why did he want to wait, Hannah wondered, and what exactly was he asking of her? He had not come out and asked her to marry him nor, she reminded herself, had he ever told her he loved her. Did he want her as a lover but not a wife? Or dread marrying a woman enmeshed in scandal?

Once, she had wanted nothing more than to live as husband and wife with the father of her child. To know she and Danny would be taken care of. But that was before. In those old unspoken dreams, she had not tainted her chances by assuming Marianna's identity, nor had she met James Lowden. . . .

She faltered. "I . . . don't know that I should stay that long."

Disappointment flitted across his face, but he didn't press her. Instead he opened a desk drawer and extracted his leather purse, and from it drew out several bank notes.

She watched his actions warily. "What are you doing?"

"Here is enough money to set yourself up — you, Danny, and Becky — in a place of your own while you figure out what you wish to do next."

She stared at him, not reaching for the notes. She whispered, "You want us to leave?"

He shrugged. "You will leave anyway, eventually. Why extend the charade any longer than necessary?" He laid the money on the table between them.

She whispered, "The charade of being Lady Mayfield, you mean?"

His eyes glinted. "The charade of caring for me."

"I . . . do care. And I don't want your money." She pushed the notes away. "Not like this. It feels like . . . a bribe to ease your conscience."

"And what if it is?"

"Then I think you truly cruel . . . and not merely callous and cynical as you pretend."

"Ah, Hannah. You are the cruel one. Raising my hopes when I knew better."

"How did I?"

"I thought I had finally found a woman who actually *wanted* to be my wife."

She stared at him, stunned by the open

vulnerability in his eyes. Again she felt the stir of feelings she'd long ago laid to rest as futile and wrong. "Sir John, I —"

Then his eyes shuttered and his mouth hardened. "Never mind. We all know what a poor judge of character I am where women are concerned."

Hannah felt as though she'd been slapped.

He glanced at her, and sighed. "Forgive me. It's only that I am well aware money is all I have to offer. I am a broken-down man who can barely walk. Why else would you want to stay?"

Again, he held up a hand. "No. Don't answer that. I am not fishing for compliments." He turned to the sheaf of papers and briskly pulled forth several bound pages. "I have asked Mr. Lowden, against his better judgment and adamant counsel, to draw up a legal document — a trust for Daniel to provide for his needs and future education. I guessed you would not accept money for yourself. But I hope you will not refuse for Danny's sake."

She stared at the legal document and the generous figure, speechless.

Then he leaned back in his chair and crossed his arms over his chest. "Now that your son is provided for, Miss Rogers, what do you want for yourself?"

Hannah's mind whirled. She didn't know. She honestly didn't know.

She licked dry lips. "May I think about it?"

His eyes dimmed but he set his jaw. "Of course. Let me know what you decide."

Hannah wandered downstairs in a haze, thoughts and stomach churning. She found herself at the open door of the morning room without consciously deciding to go there.

James rose and came around the desk, looking somber. "He showed you the papers then? The trust?"

She nodded and drew in a long breath. "I never dared believe a future with Sir John possible. But now . . . if he is willing to support my son . . . Danny will have security. Education. Life without the worry of where his next meal will come from."

James gripped her arms. "None of us have a secure future, Hannah. Not in this life. Sir John could change his mind. Lose his fortune. Decide you are not worth the scandal. For there will be a scandal, make no mistake. Even here, far from the hub of society. When people learn who you really are . . ."

His fingers on her shoulders dug hard, the

399

grooves bracketing his mouth deepened. "But, Hannah, it's more than that. I don't want you to pretend to be his wife. I want you to be mine. In reality. Legally, morally, forever. No ruse, no lies. Don't you want that, too?"

His words were jabs to her heart. The pain in his face a guilt-tipped arrow.

Tears filled her eyes. "James. If things were different — If I could go back and make different choices . . . But I cannot. I have to live with where I am and who I am now."

"You are *not* Marianna Mayfield."

"I know that. That's not what I meant." She squeezed her eyes shut. "He says in time he will report her death, so we can be together." She refrained from mentioning that Sir John had not directly asked her to marry him.

James frowned. "If he's serious, why put it off?"

"I think he wants to wait until her body is recovered. To avoid having to ask Dr. and Edgar Parrish to testify."

"There is no guarantee it will ever be found."

"I know that. But in the meantime, if Sir John is willing to stand by Daniel and me, then I cannot turn my back on that. On him."

His green eyes bore into hers. "I would stand by you, and raise Daniel as my own."

"You wouldn't love him as your own."

"I would. In time, I will come to love him as my own flesh and blood."

"He *is* Sir John's flesh and blood, and Sir John loves him already."

James glowered, looking away for a moment, but he did not deny it. "You would forgo your own happiness for his?"

For Sir John's happiness, or for Danny's? she wondered. But she didn't ask. The answer was the same.

"Yes," she whispered. Though she hoped she would find some measure of happiness, in time.

"And what about me?"

"You are young. You will find someone else. Someone not dragging a sordid past behind her."

His mouth twisted. "Is it because he is rich? Titled?"

Pain lanced her. "You know it is not."

"Oh yes, the poor, selfless girl who has to stay with the rich knight. Selfless indeed."

His words, his sneer, cut deep and she turned away.

He grasped her shoulders from behind. "Forgive me, Hannah. I didn't mean it. I am only . . . angry. Hurt."

"I know."

"I should never have allowed myself to hope. In my heart of hearts, I knew you'd choose him."

She stared out the window, seeing other windows, shutters slamming in a storm. . . . "I chose him a long time ago, whether I knew it or not."

She drew herself up, turned, and resolutely met his gaze. "I am fond of him." Should she tell James she had long admired Sir John Mayfield? Admit she had struggled to suppress her unrequited feelings for her employer while Marianna was alive? Or would it only hurt him more?

She said simply, "And hopefully in time he will come to care for me as he does Danny."

Oh, how she prayed that was true.

CHAPTER 22

After breakfast the next day, Mr. Lowden asked Hannah to join him in the morning room.

His eager eyes and secretive air indicated something important was afoot.

"I've had a letter from a friend of mine in this morning's post," he began as he ushered her inside. "Remember that Captain Blanchard I mentioned?"

"Yes?"

Checking the hall to be sure no one else was near, James closed the door. He gestured her to take a seat, and then lifted the open letter from the desk. "It's rather surprising. He wrote to tell me he saw Lady Mayfield again, this time in London."

"Lady Mayfield? How . . . interesting."

"I thought so."

"When was this — a long time ago, I assume?"

"No. Last week."

Hannah's heart banged against her ribs. "Obviously your friend was mistaken."

"Then he is not alone in his mistake, for he sent along a clipping from a London society column." He handed her a rectangle of newsprint and Hannah read,

Sir Francis Delaval hosted a masquerade ball at his home last night. Attendance was sadly low, as so many have returned to their estates, leaving town parties in favor of country house parties. However, the evening was saved by the appearance of a very beautiful Diana, which caused great speculation among the company. Several in attendance noted a striking resemblance to Lady M. M—, lately of Bath, who graced us with her charming presence in the past. But this time Lady M. was unaccompanied by either husband or preferred companion, the charming though insolvent Mr. F—.

No . . . Hannah thought. *It can't be.* She gripped the clipping and insisted, "It's just a rumor."

"I'm not so sure. My friend had met Marianna Mayfield before, you remember, back when my father was still Sir John's solicitor. So he recognized her and even spoke with her. Blanchard wrote with much

404

enthusiasm of her great beauty, snapping brown eyes, and flawless complexion."

It certainly sounded like Marianna. Even so, Hannah didn't believe it. There were many beautiful brunettes in London. "He must have seen someone else."

"Possibly, though he seems quite certain."

"But . . . she drowned," Hannah reminded him. "Edgar and Dr. Parrish saw her. Your friend must be mistaken." Hannah said it with bravado. But inwardly knew it was she herself who had made the mistake. Too many mistakes to count.

Was Marianna still alive? Carrying on life in London, with Mr. Fontaine? Hannah shuddered at the thought. How long until others learned of the rumor, whether it was true or not? Until everyone in Lynton knew *she* was not who they thought she was?

She asked, "Was . . . the lady in question wearing a mask? It was, after all, a masquerade ball." *Don't panic,* she told herself. The sighting could have been no more than residual rumor — Lady Mayfield once again seen flirting with another man.

"He saw her face," James replied. "For just a moment, she removed her mask."

The last candle of hope snuffed out. "And so you will remove mine," she whispered, guessing the solicitor meant to tell everyone of the discovery. She wondered what Sir John would do.

James said gently, "Do you see now why you mustn't let the deception continue, or think of marrying him?"

Hannah squeezed her eyes shut. "Even if it's true, she'll never come back to him." The threatening letter Anthony Fontaine had written flitted through her mind.

"That's not the point, Hannah. If his wife is still alive, he is still a married man." James pressed her hand. "You must get out now — while you can."

James took the letter upstairs with him and braced himself to face Sir John with the news. He hoped his client would not accuse him of manufacturing the tale for his own purposes.

The man sat in the armchair near the window as he often did, reading a trade publication or shipping manifest, his cane nearby. He looked up when James entered, his expression instantly wary. James regretted that such tension existed between them, but it could not be helped.

"Sir, I have something to tell you."

"Will I enjoy it?" Sir John asked dryly.

"I don't think so, I'm afraid." James unfolded the single page. "I've had a letter from a friend of mine."

"Oh?"

"He wrote to tell me he saw Lady Mayfield in London last week. At a masquerade ball."

"A masquerade?" Sir John asked. "Then how did he know it was her?"

The man did not seem as shocked as James would have guessed. Or liked.

"He said she removed her mask briefly. Long enough for him to see her face."

"This friend of yours was acquainted with Marianna?"

"Yes. Apparently he met Lady Mayfield when you lived in Bath."

"And I suppose your friend saw her with her lover," Sir John said. It was not a question.

"Actually, she was alone. My friend spoke to her. Told her he was surprised to see her, since he knew from me that I had spent time in Devonshire with Sir John and his . . . lady."

"And how did she respond to that?"

"He did not say."

James noticed that Sir John did not insist this friend must be mistaken, as Hannah had done. Had Sir John believed all along his wife might be alive?

The man asked, "Have you shown Miss

Rogers this letter?"

"I did mention it to her, yes."

"Of course you did."

Several moments passed, but Sir John said nothing more. James wondered what he should say. He had clearly displeased his employer, yet even had he no vested interest in the matter, he would have been obligated to inform his client of such important news.

Tentatively, James asked, "Shall I . . . leave you, sir?"

Sir John did not answer right away. Then he inhaled deeply and said, "Yes. You shall leave. I want you to go to London. Then return to Bristol, even Bath if you have to. I want you to find proof that Marianna is alive. And while you're at it, I want you to gather evidence against her and Mr. Fontaine. Evidence we would need to bring a civil case against him."

A civil case. The first step in long and tedious divorce proceedings, James knew.

He stood there, feeling queasy. He was relieved Lady Mayfield had reappeared and would gladly work to verify that she was alive. For if Sir John still had a living, breathing wife, he could not very well marry another — the woman James wanted for himself. But to help the man gather evidence against her lover to begin divorce proceedings? The whole process could take years and be ruinously expensive. Worst yet, it might offer Sir John, and perhaps even Hannah, hope that the two might one day be joined together lawfully. That possibility made him feel sicker yet. Even so, Sir John was his most important client and he could not very well refuse.

James swallowed back bile and asked, "When would you like me to start?"

Sir John met his gaze with a look of steely determination. "Immediately."

Wearing an apron over her day dress, Hannah bathed Danny in a small tub. She had excused Becky, who cheerfully left the nursery in favor of Mrs. Turrill's warm kitchen. Hannah wanted to do the sweet chore herself. Wanted to be alone with her dearest treasure and her troubled thoughts. In her pocket, she carried the threatening letter from Anthony Fontaine. Now that she knew Marianna might be alive and the two perhaps more determined than ever to be together, the letter seemed important — and the threat more real. She wondered if she should show the letter to Sir John, or to his solicitor.

The warm water felt good on her skin,

and on her son's, given the evidence of his sparkling eyes and drooling, gummy smile. She tenderly rubbed the damp cloth over his glistening cheeks, his rounded tummy, his pudgy, kicking legs. The gentle motions, the sight of her son, the peaceful maternal task soothed her nerves.

But unbidden, the water lapping in the tub and her wet, wrinkled fingers transported her back to the scene of the accident, until she saw not Danny's face nor heard his happy gurgles, but other sights and sounds less lovely. . . .

The frigid water sloshing inside the overturned carriage and lapping against its cracked walls, a cry of a distant seagull. The heavy weight pressing against her. Her hands, wet and cold. Another hand, the ring . . .

For a moment Hannah squeezed her eyes shut and tried for the hundredth time to remember. Had she seen Marianna? Grasped her hand? She could almost feel Marianna's hand in hers, feel the bite of metal in her palm — the large sharp ring. Had Marianna been alive, awake, alert, even then? Or had she been pulled from Hannah's grip and floated away, only to be revived later, perhaps by the water or a passerby, if the report of her sighting was true. If she was, indeed, alive. But how . . . how had it happened?

Danny's happy coos became mild fussing, and Hannah realized the water had cooled.

"Sorry, sweetheart," she murmured and carefully lifted him from the tub, wrapped him in a cozy towel, and dried his face and hair as best she could with her hindered hand. Then she dressed him in a clean nappy and nightdress, and swaddled him in a small blanket.

Holding his warm body close, Hannah sat in the rocking chair and looked down into his face. Her heart surged with love for him. Such a small person. Such a large part of her heart.

One of his little fists escaped his swaddling and she took it in hers. Tears pricked her eyes and she whispered, "What are we going to do, my love?"

James went in search of Hannah and found her alone in the nursery, rocking Daniel. As he crossed the threshold, she looked up at him with damp eyes. Then her gaze lowered to the valise in his hand and the coat over his arm, and her face clouded.

"You're leaving?" she asked.

"Yes. Sir John wishes me to verify the sighting of Lady Mayfield."

Her lips parted in surprise. "What did he say when you told him? Was he shocked?"

"Not that I could tell. One wonders if he had an inkling all along."

Hannah drew in a breath. "Perhaps he did. And that is why he hesitated to . . . report her death."

James nodded. "And that's not all. In case she is alive, he wants me to gather evidence against her and her lover. Evidence for a civil trial."

She stared at him.

"Do you know what that means?"

Hannah shook her head.

"If Mr. Fontaine is judged guilty of alienation of affection, then Sir John can pursue the matter in the ecclesiastical court, charge Marianna with adultery, and request a divorce."

Hannah stared at him, but said nothing.

"It will take a long time and cost a great deal of money. Even if he is successful, he would not be able to remarry unless Parliament passes a bill that allows him to do so. Meanwhile, Marianna would become a social outcast and Sir John's reputation would suffer as well, which would hurt him — and me — professionally and personally."

"Then why would he go through all that?"

James shot her an irritated look. "Why do

you think, Hannah?"

Hurt crossed her face, and he immediately regretted his sharp tone. He sat on the bed near the rocking chair and lowered his voice. "Look, I know you felt compelled to stay here with Sir John, since he was willing to acknowledge Daniel, and allowed you to carry on as Lady Mayfield. But if Marianna is alive — ! Tell me you understand that everything has changed? Please don't do anything rash until I return. Don't forget — he has forgiven her before and he'll do so again. Don't think he won't."

She ducked her head and whispered, "I know. . . ." She looked down at the child in her lap, and caressed one of his small fists.

James laid his hand over hers, holding them both in his determined grip. "Better we found out now than months from now, before this had gone on too long. We might yet hush it up. But if you had returned to Bristol with him, or some other city, and more people discovered the deception . . . ?" He shook his head, nostrils flaring at the thought. Then he looked into her eyes again. "We should be grateful. I am grateful. Promise me you'll wait, Hannah. Don't give in to him while I'm gone — and don't give up on me."

For a moment, Hannah said nothing.

Then, instead of answering, she pulled a letter from her pocket. "Before you go, I think you should have this."

James's heart froze. Had she written him a letter of farewell? "No, Hannah. Not like this —"

She shook her head, interrupting, "It's not from me. It's a threatening letter Mr. Fontaine sent to Sir John." With a meaningful look, she pressed it into his hand. "Just in case."

After Mr. Lowden left, Hannah carried Danny down to Becky and then took herself to Sir John's room.

She stopped in the doorway, arms folded. "Did you know she might be alive?"

Sir John stood at the window, leaning on his cane. He glanced over, saw her taut expression, and returned his gaze to the scene outside. "It crossed my mind."

"Is that why you didn't want to report her death?" She added to herself, *Or ask me to marry you?*

"One of the reasons, yes. Though it was only a suspicion. Still is."

She jutted out her chin. "Mr. Lowden told me what you asked him to do."

Sir John said dryly, "That man seems to tell you everything."

"We have . . . become friends, James and I."

"James, is it? Friends, or more?"

"Friends. For now."

Sir John nodded thoughtfully. "Still, one wonders why my solicitor feels it necessary to divulge my personal business."

She crossed the room to him. "It is not your personal business. He knew it would affect me if she is alive. You know it as well. But don't do it, Sir John. Do not try to divorce Marianna — especially on my account. I have enough strikes against me already."

"If I do pursue this course," he replied. "It would not be your fault, Hannah. Not everything is your fault. And surely not Marianna faking her death so she might live in peace with her paramour."

"We don't even know yet that it is true. And perhaps if she is alive, she has been unable to return, or at least to get word to you. . . ."

He shot her a withering look. "Oh please, Hannah. You cannot be so naïve. You know her too well to believe that."

No, she did not fully believe it. "But . . . divorce? So much time and expense and scandal, with no guarantee of success. And for what? To compound our sins?"

His eyes roamed her face, then held her troubled gaze. "For our freedom."

"If your wife is alive, then I cannot in good conscience remain any longer." She turned. "We shall leave on the morrow."

He reached out and grasped her arm. "Hannah, please. Stay with me. You know Marianna has never been a real a wife to me. Should I be condemned to live married yet alone all my days? Is that what I deserve?"

"No, Sir John. This is not your punishment. Perhaps it is mine, but not yours. You deserve better. And I will hope and pray that Marianna will see the error of her ways and come back to you. Be the wife you deserve."

"You know that will never happen." His hand on her arm trembled. "Look, I know I cannot marry you here, not now. But this needn't be the end of us. We can go to another of my properties. Live together as man and wife." His eyes blazed. "Why do you shake your head?"

Hannah took a shuddering breath, and said as resolutely as she could, "Sir John. I cannot be your mistress. I cannot! I know I have made mistakes. But that doesn't mean I have no sense of right and wrong, no self-respect."

"I know that, Hannah. And I do respect you."

She mustered a small smile. "I am afraid I have been spoiled by my time here. I'm no longer satisfied with pretending to be your wife. I want a husband of my own. I want my son to grow up in a real family."

He nodded and his voice grew hoarse. "That's what I want, too."

Tears brightened his eyes, but he stoically blinked them away. It was nearly her undoing.

Before her resolve weakened, she turned to the door, but he snagged her hand once more.

"Hannah, I won't press you. But don't leave. Not yet. You are right that we don't yet know if these rumors are true. It's only that I can so easily believe it of her. But did not Edgar and Dr. Parrish witness her drowning? We, neither of us, ought to make decisions based on one sighting. At a masquerade, no less. Stay. Please. At least until we hear from Mr. Lowden."

She hesitated. "Very well. Though I'm not promising to stay after that regardless. And if he finds evidence that she is alive, I will have no choice but to leave immediately."

They spent the days that followed in a tenuous truce — living as polite acquaintances but no more. Only with Danny did Sir John demonstrate care and affection, as though he knew or feared that every day with his son might be his last.

A week later, a letter arrived for Sir John. With lurching heart, Hannah recognized the handwriting and carried it up to Sir John herself. Seated at his desk, he looked from it, up to her, perhaps tempted to ask her to leave, to read it in private and then decide whether or not to share its contents. Hannah stood before the desk and folded her arms, daring him to protest.

Instead, he uttered a *humph* and pried open the seal.

He read the brief letter, then exhaled deeply. "He has not found her. Nor discovered solid evidence of her presence in either Bath or London. He is returning to Bristol and will continue his inquiries there."

He handed her the letter, and she read the words herself. Was it so wrong of her to be relieved? Then the last paragraph caught her attention:

Mr. Fontaine has been seen in London, but rumor has it that he has recently become engaged to marry a Miss Fox-

Garwood, an heiress. I will write again when I have more to report.

Hannah recalled how grieved Anthony Fontaine had been when he'd come there and learned Marianna had drowned. Apparently his grief had not lasted long. Surely if Marianna were still alive, he would not become engaged to another woman. But then again, Lady Mayfield's marriage had not hindered their affair. . . .

"Now will you stay?" Sir John asked.

She squeezed her eyes shut. Took a deep breath. "No. I've stayed far too long as it is. Until all this is settled, I think it best we part ways."

He laid a hand on her arm. She was tempted to lay hers atop his, but resisted.

"Then you stay — I'll leave," he said briskly, releasing her, and rising with effort. "I've been thinking about returning to Bristol anyway."

"Have you — why?" Hannah asked in surprise. Was he returning to help Mr. Lowden in his search, she wondered. Or to keep her from going off with his solicitor?

"Dr. Parrish recommends a great deal of physical exercise to increase my strength. I have a friend in Bristol who owns a gymnasium and fencing academy. . . ."

419

Yes, Hannah vividly recalled.

"He has replied to my letter and promises to put me through my paces," Sir John went on. "If I am to face Marianna and Fontaine again — I want to be whole and strong when I do so."

"I see." She hesitated. "But even so, I cannot remain here. I have no right. We shall make other arrangements. I'm sure Mrs. Turrill will help us."

"You have every right, in my view. But if you must leave, keep us informed of your direction. I have instructed Mr. Lowden to send money —"

"Sir John, I already told you I don't want any."

"Hear me out. You needn't use it for yourself if you prefer not to accept anything from me. But you cannot deny me the right to provide for my son. Please . . . don't deny me that."

She hesitated, stilled by his earnest appeal. "Very well."

"And take my copy of *Sir Charles Grandison,* since yours was lost. I insist."

"Thank you, I should like that. When will you depart?"

"On the morrow. But no need to hurry. Take your time packing your things and making arrangements. Even stay on if you change your mind. Just promise me you'll let Mr. Lowden know of any changes in your residence so he will know where to send the monthly stipend for Daniel's up-keep."

She said, "I don't know that I will be seeing Mr. Lowden."

"Oh . . ." He drew out the syllable, eyes glinting. "Somehow I think you will."

CHAPTER 23

Sir John, with Ben's eager help, made quick work of packing a valise of clothing and another of his books and papers. Hannah took a respite from her own packing and went down to bid him farewell. She stood near the door, Danny in her arms, as he descended the stairs, his cane in one hand, holding carefully to the handrail with the other. Seeing them, Sir John hesitated, grimacing, as though the sight of them disappointed or embarrassed him, and she regretted her decision to see him off.

He slowly crossed the vestibule, disguising his limp as best he could, his eyes trained on her face all the while. She held her breath. What did he intend to do? His stiff mouth and intense gaze revealed little — did he mean to deliver some sharp warning, or a passionate kiss? He stepped closer, then nearer yet, too close for formality or to offer a polite bow. She felt torn between backing up a step or leaning in. He looked into her eyes, then leaned down, farther and farther. Past her lips, her neck, her chest. Only then, did she realize his intention. He pressed a kiss not to her face, but to Danny's. Then, with a gentle finger, he wiped it away.

He turned and left the house without a word. Throat tight, she turned to the window, and watched him walk toward the hired chaise, leaning heavily on his cane.

Hannah returned to her packing, and found herself surprisingly ill at ease to be in the house now that Sir John had left it. She took her few belongings and only those things of Marianna's she had altered to fit her or couldn't do without. She finished with her own room an hour or so later, and then went downstairs to collect the book and her needlework from the drawing room. When a knock sounded at the front door, she started, a heavy sense of foreboding falling over her. A triple knock — *rap, rap, rap* — at a leisurely pace. Hannah's heart knocked against her ribs in reply.

"I'll answer it, Mrs. Turrill," Hannah called, setting aside her things and going to the door.

Hand on the latch, Hannah shut her eyes and silently prayed, *Dear God in heaven. I deserve whatever happens to me, but please protect my son.* She opened the door.

There she stood. Marianna Spencer Mayfield. In the flesh, and very much alive. At first glance, she looked as bright and beautiful as ever, gaily dressed in a purple cape and glimmering golden-yellow gown beneath.

Marianna smiled archly. "Surprise."

Hannah felt as though she faced a firing squad. Her throat was impossibly dry. "Hel-lo."

"Come now, Hannah. You're not going to pretend you don't recognize me?" One penciled brow rose in part amusement, part challenge.

"Won't you come in?" Hannah asked woodenly, and stepped back from the door.

Marianna hesitated, her smile fading. "Is he here?"

Hannah shook her head. "He just left."

She sighed. "Good. I'll need a drink before I face him."

For some reason Hannah didn't correct her misapprehension that Sir John had merely stepped out and would return soon.

Marianna strode into the drawing room and flopped down on the sofa. Hannah sat on the edge of a chair nearby. At closer inspection, she saw that Marianna had applied cosmetics with a heavy hand, her skin beneath lacking its former brilliancy and the fine lines at the corners of her eyes appeared deeper than she recalled. Her teeth were duller, stained from perhaps tea or tobacco. Her dress where the cape gapped was creased and showed signs of wear. The shoes peeping out from beneath were scuffed. The last two months had clearly been hard on her.

Marianna asked, "Are you surprised to see me?"

Hannah swallowed her panic and murmured, "Uh . . . yes."

"And not happy about it apparently. No joyful reunion for your old friend, back from the dead?"

Hannah faltered, "But your body . . . your cloak. Dr. Parrish and his son saw you. . . ."

"No. They saw my red cape tied around a piece of wooden wreckage and shoved out to sea. It worked quite well I thought. I hid behind the rocks and then made my way north after nightfall. Very clever of me, was it not?"

Hannah slowly shook her head. "We heard a rumor you'd been seen in London. But we didn't think you'd return here."

Again, one brow arched. "Hoped I would not, I think you mean." Marianna leaned back. "Might I have that drink now?"

"Oh. Of course." Hannah rose and stepped to the decanter on the side table, removing the stopper and pouring a glass of Madeira with unsteady hands.

While her back was turned, Hannah said, "Mr. Fontaine came here looking for you, soon after the accident. He was distraught."

"Yes. We had quite a passionate reunion, I can tell you. For a few days, a week. But not a fortnight had passed before things changed between us."

Hannah turned and carried the glass to her. "And where is he now?"

Marianna waved a dismissive hand, then accepted the glass. "You know how it is with men. Once they can have a woman anytime they want, all the mystery is gone. The thrill of the chase disappears and then, so does he."

"I am sorry to hear it."

"Are you? Yes, I imagine you are." Marianna took a long drink. "After Anthony joined me, he and I hid away in Wales for a time. Expecting any moment for Sir John or a constable to come knocking, looking for us. But no one ever came. I think Anthony liked the excitement and adventure of living on the run. But that feeling didn't last."

She looked down at her ragged fingernails.

"He liked being with me when it was forbidden. Stolen moments. Secrets. Not a nagging wife, day after day, with a child on the way. It turns out he had little interest in becoming a father." She drained her glass.

Hannah glanced at Marianna's flat abdomen and concluded she had lost the child, but was afraid to ask.

Marianna glanced up, eyes flinty. "I assumed I had been declared dead. That my plot had worked and that was why no one came looking for me. Anthony was angry with me. He thought I should have stayed in case Sir John did not recover. He derided me for giving up my widow's jointure. Money we could have lived on quite well. I told him no matter. If Sir John died, I would simply declare I had been lost at sea, lost my memory, and only recently realized who I was and return the grieving widow to reclaim what was rightfully mine. Though I reminded Anthony that Sir John had threatened to change his will and cut me off with only my jointure. But Anthony assured me it was all bluster. Another maneuver meant to force me into submission. In the end it did not matter, for Sir John did recover. Lived to spite me, no doubt."

She lifted her glass, and Hannah rose to refill it.

"Anthony and I got bored in the rustics and decided to try life in London — big anonymous London. Of course by the time we arrived, the season was all but over. Thankfully, some not enamored with country life remained in town and we were able to find some amusement. We stayed away from the finest places I had frequented in the past. We found lodgings in an unfashionable area to be safe. But that soon lost its appeal as well.

"Finally we became brazen and decided to attend a masquerade being held by a casual acquaintance. Where we might enjoy all the fine food, wine, and company we were missing, without fear of exposure. It took me ages to get ready with no proper lady's maid to assist me. Anthony lost patience and said he was going to his club and would find me at the ball later. We would meet like two masked strangers and flirt and seduce one another as though for the first time. So I arrived at the ball alone. I did enjoy myself for a while. Such august company. Such charming costumes and happy music. I began to look for Anthony, expecting any moment for him to appear at my elbow, declare me the most intriguing creature in the room and beg to dance with me, or to take my hand and lead me into some shadowy corner to steal a kiss. . . . But he did not find me. I began to fear he did not recognize me, for he had left before I had donned my mask. So, in desperation or boredom, I became more brazen yet and lifted my mask, hoping he would glimpse my face and rush to my side. Someone did come to greet me, but it was not Anthony. It was a blond officer I vaguely recognized though I could not have said from where or what his name might be. I slipped my mask back into place, fearing I had been caught. Fearing everyone would now know Mari-anna Mayfield was alive after all.

"Instead he said, quite merrily, 'Why, Lady Mayfield, I believe. I am surprised to see you here.'

"I panicked for a moment, then reminded myself it was a masquerade ball. He could not prove who I was by one glimpse of my face. So I decided to brush him off. Still I was surprised that he did not seem shocked I was alive, only that I was in attendance. Anthony had told me there had been no an-nouncement of my *death* in the papers, but until that moment I hadn't believed him.

"I said to the man, 'I don't know whom you are referring to, my good sir.'

"But he surprised me. He did not make a scene or go on about my being alive and did I not know everyone thought I was dead? Instead he smiled and said, 'Never fear, my lady. I shall not let on you are here. I imagine life in Devonshire must be tiresome. An acquaintance of mine, Mr. Lowden, has spent time there with Sir John and says it's a remote place. Very rustic. Nothing as civilized as this.'

"Mr. Lowden — that name I *did* recall. My husband's solicitor. An older gentleman who thought the world of me, I can tell you. Probably summoned to revise John's will."

Marianna swirled the golden liquid in her glass. "My mind was quite in a whirl, as you can imagine. Had he not heard about the crash? That I was missing if not assumed dead? I wondered if someone had seen me leaving the scene of the accident. I said casually, 'Oh? Does Mr. Lowden not care for Devonshire?'

"The man replied, 'I don't say that. He was loath to go in the first place. And leave his practice. But I think he was impressed. I know he was impressed with *you,* Lady Mayfield.'

"What was this? Mr. Lowden had seen me in Devonshire? I was not believed missing or dead, but was rather alive and living in the West Country? I felt quite shocked, I can tell you. I tried to laugh it off and figure out how such a misunderstanding had happened. I said, 'Come, you must tell me what Mr. Lowden said about me. I'm afraid I was . . . not very . . . kind to him?'

"The officer chuckled and replied, 'Lowden admitted you were not what he was expecting. But he said nothing critical, I assure you. In fact, he said you were secretive, but charming, and had the most darling little boy.' "

Marianna widened her eyes. "Imagine my surprise. Not only was I not dead or even missing, but I was charming and had a darling boy in Devonshire."

She ran her gaze over Hannah. "I did not think of you — not at first. For surely my most loyal companion would not be party to such a hoax. Even so, I asked him how my companion fared. He looked at me strangely and said, 'Do you jest? Or did I hear it wrong? I am sure Lowden mentioned that your lady's companion drowned in the accident.' "

Marianna held up her pointer finger. "Ah . . . then I realized. I was not missing and assumed dead. You were." She clicked her tongue. "I must say, Hannah, I am impressed. Quite a little plot you've pulled off here in my absence. I guess your years with me taught you something after all."

Hannah frowned. "I didn't plan this. The local doctor who found us assumed I was Sir John's wife, since he was expecting only the two of you."

"And you allowed that misapprehension to continue. My, my. Quite a promotion. From lowly companion to lady in a single day. What a climbing schemer you are. I would never have guessed."

"Me, a schemer? When you pretended to drown? To leave Sir John for good, or so we thought?"

"So you thought. Sorry to disappoint you, my dear, *loyal* friend."

Hannah flinched at Marianna's cutting tone. "I did nothing to you. We thought you were dead."

"Oh, please." Marianna flopped a dismissive hand. "Don't play innocent. You saw me. You opened your eyes and saw me."

"What?"

"Don't pretend you don't remember. Before I slipped away from the carriage, I put my finger to your lips to shush you, then pressed my ring into your hand."

Hannah stared at her. She began, "No. That's not what I remember. . . ." But a flitting, recurring dream danced on the edges of her mind. Lady Mayfield smiling coyly amid the horrid wreckage. Placing her own ring in her hand . . .

Hannah sputtered. "I thought it was a dream . . . my trying to keep the tide from drawing you from the carriage. I grabbed your hand — that is how your ring came to be in mine."

"Is it?" Marianna shook her head, eyeing her cynically. "I don't think so."

"But why would you give it to me?"

"I didn't want to wear any such identifying jewelry. And yes, I thought it would reward you for keeping quiet if you lived. I didn't know if you would — you looked a fright — your head bleeding profusely. And if you died, your body might be identified as mine. Which would buy me some time before anyone came looking for me. Of course nobody came, which I found somehow insulting. Now I know why."

She took a long drink. "Later Anthony was angry when he learned I'd left the ring behind. He put a notice in the paper to establish its loss or theft, hoping to claim insurance money for it. I could make no such claim, of course. But the insurance company took one look at Anthony's debts and dismissed his claim. And who can blame them?"

Hannah willed herself to remain calm. "I don't understand. You were free of your husband and your marriage, as you had long told me you wanted. Why come back now? What is it you want?"

Marianna smirked. "Why, to see my dear husband of course."

Hannah's stomach clenched. "I am sorry to disappoint you, but —"

Marianna leaned forward conspiratorially and wrinkled her nose. "I'd rather not, actually. He's more likely to strangle me than to welcome me back with open arms, I imagine."

If she didn't want to see Sir John, what did she want? Money? Hannah would have to tread carefully.

The truth was on her tongue. She said it even as she second-guessed the wisdom and the consequences of doing so. "Sir John would have taken you back. He would have forgiven you, raised your child as his own."

Marianna's mouth twisted. "I miscarried the child. Are you saying that was my fault? Had I stayed, I would not have lost her?"

Hannah was taken aback. "No. I'm not saying that. I'm sorry. I am only saying that Sir John would have stood by you either way."

Marianna regarded her through narrowed eyes. "How highly you esteem him. Almost as if you had fallen in love with him."

Hannah made no answer.

Lady Mayfield looked about the room. She asked, "Where is this supposed child of mine? Yours, I assume. You left us to bear a child in secret, is that it? I thought you were gaining weight but was too polite to mention it. I hope the father was not Mr. Ward." She shuddered. "I saw the way the odious man looked at you. Oh, I know! That young man I saw pursuing you the day we left Bath." She shook her head, tsking her tongue. "And here I thought you so innocent. Sitting in judgment of me and Mr. Fontaine."

"I never said a word about the two of you. Never . . ."

"Oh, but your face did. Like a wan Madonna in a dreary oil painting — such long-suffering disappointment. What a hypocrite you are."

Marianna leaned back in the chair, putting a hand on each of its arms as though a queen on her throne. "And so here you are," she said, "trying to pass off your base born child as Sir John's son and rightful heir? That's incredible. Is John out of his mind? Still insensible that you've got away with it this long?"

Hannah's ire rose. "Why should you care? Do you mean to return, to be his wife?"

"In name, at least."

Hannah stood. "If you are in earnest, then you have come to the wrong place. Sir John has returned to Bristol. And I plan to leave this house this very day."

Marianna slowly shook her head, brown eyes glinting. "Oh no, my dear Hannah. You shall not get off so easily. I want to see you explain all of this to your neighbors and to the servants and to Mr. Lowden. I want to see you squirm, and then I want to see you pay. They do have magistrates in this godforsaken place, I take it?"

Mrs. Turrill breezed in, wiping her hand on her apron. "Here I am. Pardon my delay." She eyed their visitor warily before returning her gaze to Hannah. "May I bring the two of you some refreshment, my lady?"

Hannah felt the words pierce her like two arrows. And fleetingly wondered how Marianna must feel to hear the woman address her with the title.

She hesitated to reply, but Marianna showed no such reluctance. A feline smile curved her features, as she looked from Hannah to the housekeeper. "Yes, I think refreshments would be lovely, thank you. Mrs. . . . ?"

The housekeeper stared at Marianna. "Turrill."

"Mrs. Turrill."

"Hannah, my dear friend," Marianna said, "won't you introduce me?"

Hannah felt sick, but complied, lifting a limp hand toward Marianna. "Mrs. Turrill, this is Lady Mayfield. Sir John's wife."

Hannah risked a glance at Mrs. Turrill. The woman stared at Marianna, eyes wide, mouth slack. She shifted an uncertain glance toward Hannah, and Hannah nodded, her mouth downturned in apology.

For a moment, no one moved or spoke. The long-case clock punctuated the silence, tick, tick, tick.

Finally Marianna prompted, "The refreshments, Mrs. Turrill?"

"Oh. Right."

The housekeeper turned, but at the moment another knock sounded at the side door. The familiar double knock of Dr. Parrish. Hannah's heart fell. Dear Dr. Parrish! How she hated to hurt him. But it was inevitable now. Perhaps it always had been.

"Shall I let him in?" The housekeeper directed the question to Hannah.

"Yes," she sighed, resigned. It was all over now.

Marianna turned to her, brows high. "Who?"

"Our neighbor, Dr. Parrish."

Marianna's face became more animated yet. "Yes, by all means, invite him in. The party is just beginning."

Or the funeral, Hannah grimly thought.

She sat stiffly and listened as Mrs. Turrill's half boots clicked over the polished floor. She heard the door latch open and then, horror of horrors, Mrs. Parrish's voice as well as the doctor's. *Oh no. . . . Not her. Not now.*

An anxious Mrs. Turrill led Dr. Parrish and his wife into the drawing room. The couple looked uncertain, and Hannah wondered what, if anything, the housekeeper had whispered to them. But they looked only curious at this point. The worst was yet to come. She would have to deliver the news herself.

The next hour passed in a painful blur: disillusioned people, once compassionate faces turning flinty, eyes freezing over, frowns of shock and disappointment replacing the smiling faces of her memories. Mrs. Parrish was, of course, the first to denounce her. Hadn't she said all along there was something fishy about this supposed "lady"? She sent Ben to fetch Edgar, took great satisfaction in telling him the news when he arrived, then sent the shocked and disapproving young man to alert the magistrate to the imposter in their midst.

But the worst was Dr. Parrish. Stunned speechless and bent over in pain as though he had been dealt a mortal blow by a bosom friend. Presented with such a clear picture of her betrayal, Hannah did not even attempt to defend herself.

Edgar returned and announced that the justice of the peace, Lord Shirwell, was occupied with houseguests at present, but would hear their case in his office two days hence.

If only Sir John had not left, Hannah thought. Or even Mr. Lowden. But she must face this alone. Well, not completely alone — Mrs. Turrill had not left her. Had God?

Mrs. Parrish took charge, toadying up to Marianna with fawning manners, inviting her to stay at the Grange with them, asking if they ought not lock Miss Rogers in her room so she would not be tempted to flee.

Marianna declined the offer with pretty gratitude, insisting she should like to stay in her "own home" at last. And, would not a manservant posted as watch outside the house be sufficient? After all, she and Mrs. Turrill would remain on hand to be sure Miss Rogers didn't stray.

Hannah sat disbelieving through it all. It

felt like another murky dream from which she couldn't awaken — the cold weight of it pressed down on her. This time she would sink for sure.

Eventually, the arrangements were agreed to, watch posted, plans made for an early departure to the magistrate's in two days' time, and Mrs. Parrish led a silent and befuddled Dr. Parrish home.

Hannah walked numbly upstairs to the nursery. Becky, who had evidently overheard some of the conversation below, sat huddled in the corner near the cradle.

Daniel lay in the cradle, awake and cooing over a drooled fist in his mouth. Hannah took him in her arms and held him close, stroking his little downy head, and feeling the tears she'd held at bay fill her eyes and roll down her cheeks at last.

She felt Mrs. Turrill's warm hand on her arm. "What will you do, my dear? What will you say?"

"I don't know. What can I say? Perhaps I should take Danny and leave. Tonight."

"If you run, everyone will assume you are guilty."

"I am guilty."

"Not of everything she accuses you of. Not half."

Alarmed, Becky asked, "What is it, Miss

Han— uh, my lady. What's wrong?"

"It's all right, Becky. You can call me Hannah now. Everyone knows. Our secret is over."

"Are we in trouble?"

"You are not in trouble. But I am, yes." At least she hoped Becky was in no trouble. She would have to find a way to make sure of that.

Becky asked, "And what about Danny?"

Hannah squeezed her eyes shut. What *would* become of Danny? She wasn't sure which frightened her more: that she would be separated from her son, or that Marianna might try to take him as her own.

"Shall I hide him?" Becky asked, eyes wild. "I saw Ben out front, but he wouldn't stop me. He's fond of me, I know. I could raise Danny as my own, if they take you away."

"Becky!" Mrs. Turrill chided. "Don't say such a thing." She softened her tone. "I know you meant it kindly, my dear, but Miss Hannah is Danny's mother and always shall be."

Hannah turned to Mrs. Turrill. "But what if they send me to prison. Or . . . worse?"

"Surely it won't come to that." Mrs. Turrill laid a tender hand on her arm. "If worse comes to worse, I will care for Danny

441

myself. And no doubt Becky will help me. You needn't fear for his future."

Hannah nodded, suddenly remembering the trust Sir John had offered. "Whatever happens to me, promise me you will let Sir John know where Danny is, will you? He will help you."

"Of course I will."

A short while later, Marianna summoned Hannah down to the bedchamber she had occupied these many weeks. Inside, Hannah's valise and a second case lay open, nearly packed. While Hannah stood in the doorway, Marianna insisted the maid dump it all out again. She wanted to make sure Hannah took nothing that didn't belong to her.

Hannah cringed. She hadn't packed many of Marianna's things, and none of her finest, but she had taken spare undergarments, a nightdress, spencer, and a few simple gowns.

Marianna plucked out one of her gowns and the pink-ribboned nightdress from the pile. "These are definitely mine."

The maid gaped at her. "Is she to have no nightdress, ma'am, or even one spare gown?"

Hannah was impressed with the girl's

courage, though she feared she might lose her place because of it.

"My things were lost," Hannah said, hoping to defend the maid, and her own actions as well.

Marianna hesitated, then tossed the gown and nightdress back into the valise. "Oh very well," she snapped. "If she has worn them I don't want them." Her eyes glinted. "Unlike some people, I have no interest in wearing another woman's clothes. Or her name."

Marianna held out her hand. "But I will have my ring back."

"I wasn't going to take it." Hannah gestured across the room. "It's there on the dressing table, along with your lover's eye."

Marianna turned and plucked up the small brooch, quickly pinning it to her frock. "The painting isn't John's eye you know. It's Anthony's. Fickle though he is, he belongs to me, and I to him. He'll remember that soon enough and come back for me. He always does."

She tried to slide the ring onto her finger, but it caught on her knuckle. It no longer fit her as it once had. Nothing else did, either, in Hannah's view.

Marianna forced the ring into place at last. Her quick look of triumph fell to a frown. "Now I shall never get it off again. . . ."

Hannah turned and quit the room, leaving Marianna tugging at the band. Carrying the hastily repacked valise in one hand and the case of Danny's things under her arm, Hannah trudged upstairs to a small room beside the nursery, leaving Marianna to claim the large, fine bedchamber for herself.

The next morning, Mrs. Turrill carried breakfast up to Hannah in the spare room and helped her dress. Then she hurried away to attend Marianna while Kitty and Ben hauled cans of hot water for the woman's bath.

Hannah tidied the counterpane on the narrow bed and was about to walk over to the nursery, when Dr. Parrish knocked on the doorjamb, head down.

"I've only come to remove your bandages."

"Oh. Thank you."

Tentatively, he stepped inside and set down his bag on the dressing chest without looking at her face.

As he snipped away the stiff bandages, he kept his distance, coming only close enough to perform the task quickly, refusing to meet her gaze. Gone were his friendly openness, his warm eyes, his eager, lengthy chats.

Hannah's heart ached to see it. She whispered, "I am sorry, Dr. Parrish. Truly."

His hands hesitated only a moment, then he gathered up the spent bandages and his bag and turned away without a word.

At the threshold he paused, his back to her, and murmured, "So am I."

Hannah spent most of that day in the nursery with Becky and Danny, hoping to avoid Marianna. Mrs. Turrill kindly brought up their dinner on trays as well.

That night — the night before they were due to see the magistrate — Hannah knelt beside the little bed, hands clasped, eyes closed in prayer. Behind her the door creaked open. Startled, she swung her head around.

Marianna stood there in the threshold, smirking. "See the contrite sinner on the eve of her destruction. Beseeching God for deliverance. You have a lot to atone for, haven't you? A child out of wedlock, impersonating another man's wife, lying, stealing, and fraud — trying to foist off your child as Sir John's heir. And those are only the things I know about. Did you also sleep with Mr. Lowden? Or Dr. Parrish? To win them to your cause?"

"No!" Hannah stared at her, feeling a

noose begin to tighten around her neck and the hearing had not even begun.

Marianna crossed her arms. "I see what you are thinking. You think it hypocritical of me to point a finger at anyone else. But I am not guilty of half of what you have done."

Hannah blinked, stunned to realize Marianna was right. How had she allowed it to happen? That she, Hannah Rogers, should be guilty of more wrongdoing than the infamous Marianna Mayfield?

Marianna shook her head, eyes alight in apparent amusement. "Do you really think God will forgive you, after all you've done?"

Hannah faltered. "I . . . hope so. I don't expect the Parrishes to forgive me, but yes, I hope that God will. Did He not, after all, forgive a man who not only committed adultery, but who also schemed to have the woman's husband killed so he might marry her?"

Marianna's eyes narrowed. "Who told you that? Mr. Fontaine did not try to kill Sir John."

Hannah gaped at her. "Why do you assume I was speaking of Mr. Fontaine?"

Marianna looked away, disquieted at last.

Hannah thought again of the rash letter Fontaine had written. Had his threats been genuine? "I was speaking of King David," Hannah said. "Not Mr. Fontaine."

"Of course you were, I knew that." Marianna turned to go, then looked over her shoulder, eyes glinting. "Go back to your prayers, Hannah. Futile as they are."

Hannah tried to hold Marianna's gaze, but shame and guilt forced her eyes to the floor. Head bowed, she could only kneel where she was, listening to the retreating footsteps of her accuser.

A few moments later, Hannah felt a hand on her shoulder. She stiffened, then relaxed as she heard Mrs. Turrill's earnest voice.

"Up with you, my girl."

Hannah's legs were numb from kneeling so long, but Mrs. Turrill helped her rise and turned her toward the bed.

"Sit."

Hannah complied. Head still bowed, she saw only the housekeeper's skirts and the toes of her boots as Mrs. Turrill stood before her.

"Now look at me." Gentle fingers lifted Hannah's chin.

"I heard what that woman said to you, but she is wrong," Mrs. Turrill began. "God will forgive you. True, some people may not. And knowing you, my girl, you will struggle to forgive yourself. But God will. He already has, if you've asked Him for Jesus' sake. We have all of us erred one way or another. Your wrongs are some swinging great bouncers, I own. But nothing is too big for God. No pit we dig for ourselves too deep. He is already reachin' a hand down to you, ready to pull you up."

Hannah looked at the woman through tear-blurred eyes. "How can you be so sure?"

"Because He told us so. In the Scriptures. You yourself mentioned King David, did you not? And look at the many blunders he made. Bigger than yours even, I'd say. But God calls him a man after His own heart."

Hannah nodded, then whispered, "But He also allowed David's son to die, as a consequence."

Mrs. Turrill nodded soberly. "Yes, my dear. God does not promise to remove the consequences of our sins, at least not in this life."

Fear prickled through Hannah at the thought. She squeezed Mrs. Turrill's hand and went to find her son.

Chapter 24

James Lowden was disappointed he'd been unable to find irrefutable proof that Marianna Spencer Mayfield still lived. But with the newspaper clipping, his friend's report, and continuing rumors hanging over his client's head, he could not dismiss the possibility — or the gut feeling — that she was alive. Nor could he dismiss the second part of his mission. But to begin gathering evidence toward divorce? He hated everything about that assignment.

James went to London to begin his undertaking. There, he heard the rumor that Fontaine had become engaged to an heiress, but little evidence about him and Marianna. He went to Fontaine's last known London lodgings, and there learned from the landlord that Mr. Fontaine had given up his rooms and returned to his home in Bristol. So James sent a brief report to Sir John and then returned to Bristol to continue his enquiries there.

He began by calling on their friends and neighbors. But while gossip and tittle-tattle abounded, he found little solid evidence and no one, beyond his friend, willing to testify that he or she had seen Marianna alive, or seen her and Fontaine together in a compromising situation.

James felt both frustrated and relieved.

He received a note at his office from Sir John, urging him to continue the search and letting him know he had returned to Bristol alone. James was more relieved yet.

The village magistrate, Lord Shirwell, had agreed to give them a hearing after his guests departed, though the date of the next assize court session was several weeks off. On the appointed day, Mrs. Turrill took Danny and Becky home with her to the cottage she shared with her sister. Mrs. Turrill had thought Hannah should take Daniel along, to show the precious lad that had motivated the deception in the first place. What better justification could there be?

"The baby will rouse sympathy for your cause, my dear," she'd said.

But Hannah feared Danny might somehow be taken from her, seized right there during the hearing and sent to a foundling home, never to be seen again, and refused to risk it.

Hannah rode in the back of the doctor's cart, driven by Edgar Parrish. Dr. and Mrs. Parrish and Lady Mayfield rode in a gig behind. Likely to guarantee she didn't jump off the cart and run away. As if she would go anywhere without her son. She shivered from more than the damp morning air biting through her shawl. *God, please protect Danny.*

A short while later, the vehicles passed through the gate of Lord Shirwell's estate and around to the back of the manor where grooms and stable boys hurried out to help with the horses. Hannah was conveyed into an impressive library, which the J.P. used as an office to conduct parish business and for his magistrate duties.

There, Lord Shirwell sat behind a wide mahogany desk. A thin bespectacled clerk occupied a smaller desk nearby. Two chairs had been set before the desk in a prominent position. In one sat Hannah, the accused. In the other, Lady Mayfield, her primary accuser. Additional chairs lined the side wall for those waiting to be heard. Seated beside Marianna, Hannah was again reminded of the two women they had seen sitting side-by-side in the village stocks. A tremor of premonition passed over her.

Lord Shirwell was a stout, balding man in his mid-fifties. Good-looking in his day, Hannah guessed, though showing signs of dissipation. His gaze roved the room. "And where is Sir John Mayfield? He ought to be present to witness this hearing and to give evidence."

Lady Mayfield spoke up. "Word has been sent, your worship. But we don't know how long it will be until my husband can respond. He is an invalid, you see, and cannot easily travel such a distance."

Had word been sent? Hannah wondered. By whom? Would the post have even reached him by now? Hannah doubted it.

Lord Shirwell frowned. "Then what is the hurry in holding this hearing?"

"Why, my worship." Marianna blinked innocently, pressing a hand to her mounded bosom. She was wearing one of the gowns formerly in Hannah's possession, but had taken it back out to fit her. "We only want to see justice done. We fear if there is a delay, the guilty party might very well abscond before the hearing."

"The *accused,* my lady, she has yet to be proven guilty."

"Of course, your worship. Forgive me, I misspoke." Marianna favored him with one of her winning smiles and the man's eyes gleamed appreciatively. Hannah knew it did not bode well for her.

The man cleared his throat. "So that all in attendance are clear, let me summarize what will happen here today. This is not a trial per se. I will hear and make an assessment of the evidence against this person. If I am satisfied that there is a case to answer, I will then determine if there is sufficient evidence to commit the accused to prison to await trial and prosecution at the next court session."

Prison . . . Hannah shuddered at the word.

He turned toward Marianna. "Perhaps, Lady Mayfield, as the bringer of these charges, you might begin."

Marianna dipped her pretty head in acknowledgement. "Very well, your worship." She took a deep breath, causing her bosoms to blossom from the neckline of her gown.

Hannah guessed the act had been intentional.

"As you know, your worship, my husband and I, Sir John Mayfield, made it our intention to move to this lovely county a few months ago. He owns a house near the best neighbors anyone could ask for in the Parrishes." She smiled at Dr. and Mrs. Parrish. Mrs. Parrish smiled in return, but Dr. Parrish stared blindly at her.

Marianna continued, "Arrangements made, Sir John returned to Bath to collect me. Our servants had no wish to relocate and we relished the notion of hiring knowledgeable local people when we arrived."

Lies, Hannah thought. Marianna had been vexed indeed not to be able to bring her own servants. But Hannah knew pointing it out would not help her case.

"But just as we were preparing to leave Bath, this person, Miss Hannah Rogers, reappeared at our door. She had left our employ some five or six months before, without notice or explanation. Of course now we know she left as her condition began to show — left to have a child in secret." Marianna lowered her voice and managed to look properly shocked. "And her not married."

"But I am getting ahead of myself." Marianna pulled a handkerchief from her reticule before continuing. "She made no mention of a child. When Miss Rogers came to me and said she was in need of a post, I consulted my husband and we agreed. Although not our preference, we could not in Christian charity turn our back on a former member of our staff in need."

Hannah squeezed the arm of her chair.

More lies . . .

"So, Miss Rogers traveled with us in our chariot from Somerset to Devon, leaving her infant behind. Though had we known she was abandoning her child, we never should have agreed to take her with us."

Indignation shot through Hannah. "I was *not* abandoning him —"

"Silence, Miss Rogers," Lord Shirwell commanded. "You will have your chance to speak soon enough." He returned his gaze to Marianna. "Go on, my lady."

"Thank you, your worship." She smiled wanly. "Now, you have likely heard of the terrible accident that befell us, when our carriage slipped from the road and went tumbling over the cliff and partway into the sea. And the unfortunate loss of the young driver. A loss I did not hear about until recently and which grieves me still to think of it . . ." Here she dabbed dry eyes with her lace handkerchief.

Hannah was surprised Marianna had not tried to blame her for the accident and the poor man's death as well.

Marianna continued, "I don't know exactly what happened immediately after the crash, for I believe I lost sensibility. I seem to remember Miss Rogers pulling my ring from my finger, but she says she grabbed my hand as the tide pulled me through a hole in the carriage and somehow the ring came off in her hand. Of course she also claims to have lost all sensibility after the accident, so who can say how my valuable ring ended up in her possession? I believe I floated on a bit of wreckage, a piece of the broken carriage perhaps. By the time I awoke, I was a great distance away and quite disoriented. I must have sustained a near-fatal blow to my head, for I could no more remember my name than how I came to be floating in the Bristol Channel. Thankfully, God sent his angels in the form of fisher-men. The men hauled me into their boat, and revived me. They delivered me to the next port, in Wales, and left me with a kindly innkeeper there. I stayed with her for some time, having no inkling of who I was. Eventually the good woman realized that with my gown, tattered as it was, and my speech and bearing, that I was a person of education and breeding. She suggested I travel to London and see if anyone there might recognize me and help me learn my true identity. It was very frightening, travel-ing by stage, all alone, not knowing where I was going and what I might find awaiting me. . . ."

Everyone hung on her words, Hannah

saw. What a gothic storyteller she was. Had she rehearsed this, or was she making it up as she went along?

"In London, I began to have flashes of memory," Marianna went on. "Then I happened into a man, a friend of Sir John's solicitor, as it turns out, who recognized me. You cannot know what a relief it was to hear my own name and have it all come back. To remember my dear husband and the life we had planned together here in Devonshire. As soon as I was able, I made plans to return to him."

She even managed to explain the sighting of her in London, Hannah realized with mounting dread.

"Imagine my devastation, when I arrived at Clifton House, hoping to be reunited with my dear husband. But instead, the housekeeper informs me Sir John had left for Bristol, but I might see 'Lady Mayfield' if I liked. In came Hannah into my drawing room, as snug and smug as any duchess or Drury Lane actress — even wearing one of my gowns, made over to fit her. My former companion, posing as me, mistress of the place and Sir John's wife. Imagine my shock."

Lord Shirwell grimly shook his head, not taking his eyes from Lady Mayfield.

She continued, "I understand that initially Dr. Parrish simply assumed Hannah was Lady Mayfield, when he discovered her and Sir John alone in the ruined carriage. How could he know I had been taken out to sea? A natural mistake. But later, when Hannah regained her senses, did she correct him? Admit she was only poor Miss Rogers, lady's companion? No. Instead she allowed them to go on believing her Sir John's wife."

Again, she dabbed her dry eyes. "Poor Sir John was still insensible and unable to correct their misapprehension. I don't know how she planned to get away with it. Perhaps she thought if Sir John died and I was dead as assumed, then she might inherit a great deal of money, or at least my widow's jointure. Not only did she allow the staff and good-hearted, trusting neighbors to believe she was me, but to compound her fraud, she returned to Bath, collected her illegitimate son, and brought him back with her, along with his nurse. She allowed everyone to believe he was Sir John and Lady Mayfield's son — and heir, mind you. What audacity. What cunning. I don't know why Sir John did not call her out when he awoke. I can only surmise that his head injury had rendered his memory or mental capacities impaired. She must have preyed on his weak mind."

Hannah, remembering the magistrate's warning, barely held her tongue.

Marianna continued, "When I confronted Miss Rogers, she said she would simply leave. Hoping to avoid charges, no doubt, and who knew how much of my husband's money or possessions she planned to take with her? Again, this is why I felt it my duty to pursue this matter immediately, even in my husband's absence."

"Very understandable, my lady. Very wise," Lord Shirwell said. "Now, if you have said all you like, I would like to hear from Dr. Parrish."

She smiled coyly. "Thank you, your worship. I have." She made to rise, but the magistrate gestured for her to remain where she was. "No need. Dr. Parrish can answer from where he sits."

He turned to the physician. "Dr. Parrish. Please tell us how you came to meet this woman." He lifted a lazy hand toward Hannah.

"Yes, my l— your worship." In halting fashion, quite unlike his usual loquacious style, Dr. Parrish told of the leasing of Clifton House, which his son managed. He then went on to describe the runaway horses, which led him and Edgar to search for a stranded coach. He described the tracks in the mud, looking over the cliff at the horrid sight of a carriage broken wide like a raw egg on the rocks, and the tangle of bodies within. His amazement at finding the two occupants alive, though Sir John but barely. He never gave a second thought that the woman must be Lady Mayfield, cradling Sir John's head in her lap. She certainly looked and dressed a lady, though injured and insensible.

At this point Mrs. Parrish snorted loudly enough for them all to hear, "I told you she was no lady."

Lord Shirwell ignored this aside, while Dr. Parrish colored and continued as though he had not heard his vulgar spouse.

"My son Edgar spotted a figure floating out to sea. At least what he said looked like a person wearing red. I own my long-distance vision isn't what it should be. We asked Lady — that is, Miss Rogers, if she had brought a servant with her. She could not speak, but laid a hand on her heart and nodded. I thought she meant the servant was her own personal maid, or dear to her heart, something like that. Not that she herself was the servant, or companion, herself.

"After we managed to remove them to the house, she was insensible for some time. And quite muddled even after she awoke. Muttering and fretting about someone named Danny, which I learned later was her child. I, of course, addressed her as 'my lady,' as did Mrs. Turrill, the housekeeper we'd engaged on behalf of the Mayfields. Looking back, I recall how this distressed her, how she knit her brow and seemed confused by it. I assumed it was the shock of the accident and her injuries. You see how determined I was to see her as I thought she should be. In all honesty, my lord, I blame myself for the misunderstanding. For she never tried to tell me or convince me that she was Lady Mayfield. I did that all by myself."

Lord Shirwell pursed his lip. "Come, doctor. Even if she was confused for a few days, surely she could have corrected the 'misunderstanding,' as you call it, as soon as she came to her senses. Did she?"

He reddened again. "No, my lord. Um . . . your worship. Not directly. Though she did try more than once to tell me. I see that now."

"What a memory you have, Dr. Parrish." Marianna smiled at the man. "It speaks so highly of your character that you assume

461

the best of everyone."

"It is one thing for her to allow the misapprehension to go on briefly while she got her bearings," Lord Shirwell said. "But to press you into aiding her cause — to return to Bath for her child? Surely you don't excuse that as well? Did she not ask you to hire a carriage for her, and even steal money from Sir John's purse to pay for the trip?"

Heaven help me, Hannah thought. Who told him that, in those terms? She would hang for sure. Or at least be sent to prison. What would become of Danny then?

Dr. Parrish shot a glare at his wife, then continued, "No, my lord. I offered to hire the carriage. She never asked for it. She intended to go on her own, by stage. But I insisted. I knew — or thought — Sir John would want it that way."

"But surely Sir John did not *offer* Miss Rogers his money, considering he was insensible?"

"No, my lord. Again that was my idea. I knew she would need money for the inns and tolls, and when I asked her if she had enough, she said she hadn't. I had removed Sir John's purse from his pocket myself and knew right where it was, and that it was heavy indeed. I took from it the amount I thought she would need and gave it to her.

She has never asked for more, nor was a farthing more missing from Sir John's purse when he came to at last and had opportunity to look within."

"How you defend her, Dr. Parrish," Marianna said sweetly. "It seems as if you are quite fond of her."

The physician blushed furiously, but whether from embarrassment or anger or both Hannah wasn't sure. He had never treated her with anything but the most proper consideration. Marianna had clearly recognized the strain between the good doctor and his cantankerous wife and decided to use it to her advantage. How brazen she was to interrupt the proceedings as though a conversation in her own drawing room. Yet the magistrate did not object, but only gazed at her benignly.

"My . . . Your ladyship," Dr. Parrish faltered. "You misunderstand me. But I do believe Miss Rogers is a good woman who acted out of concern for her child's well-being. I cannot stand by and see her so maligned."

Lord Shirwell straightened. "Did she or did she not impersonate Lady Mayfield?"

"Yes, but —"

"Did she or did she not pass off her son as master Mayfield?"

"Well, I suppose, though —"

"Did she or did she not take advantage of her situation to help herself to Sir John's money, his house, his food, his wife's very clothing?" Lord Shirwell's eyes blazed.

Dr. Parrish ducked his head, not meeting anyone's eyes. "Yes, my lord."

"And what possible excuse did she give for not bringing the child with them to Lynton in the first place?"

"Actually" — he darted a look at his wife — "Mrs. Parrish supplied that reason. She said they must have left the child with its nurse, until they could prepare a proper nursery at Clifton."

"I never said any such thing, Dr. Parrish," Mrs. Parrish huffed.

"Yes, you did my dear. Perhaps you forget. And we both decided it was a godsend, for had the little boy been in that carriage . . ."

"But of course he wouldn't have been, for he wasn't any child of ours was he?" Marianna interrupted. "He was only an illegitimate whelp Hannah decided to pass off as a Mayfield. For the inheritance."

Dr. Parrish shook his head. "I can't believe she ever thought of that. I think she only wanted to be reunited with her son and to provide for him."

Marianna's mouth twisted bitterly. "And

what better way than to make him a rich man's heir?"

Lord Shirwell spoke up. "Em . . . thank you, my lady, but perhaps it is best if I conduct the hearing, hm?"

"Oh. Yes, your worship. I do beg your pardon. It just rouses my passion most fiercely to hear of her greedy deception."

"Here, here," Mrs. Parrish seconded.

Dr. Parrish spoke up. "But one more thing, my lord, if I may. When Sir John did regain his senses, and was presented with, um, Miss Rogers here as Lady Mayfield, he did not object. Nor did he correct me. In fact he addressed her as his wife and, well, acted toward her as a husband would."

The magistrate's brows rose. "Are you suggesting they had marital relations?"

Again the physician blushed. "No, my lord. I suggest no such thing. I only meant that he spoke to her and teased her as a husband might. He gave me no reason to suspect Miss Rogers was not Lady Mayfield. Even invited us to dinner, him at the head of the table and her at its foot. Why would he do that?"

Lord Shirwell entwined his stubby fingers on the desk. "You said he suffered a serious head injury in the accident and nearly died. Is it not possible his senses were still befuddled as Lady Mayfield suggests? That he has yet to, may never in fact, return to his right mind?"

"Pardon me for saying so, my lord, but that seems an awful presumption to make based on one woman's accusations. When he isn't even here to defend his actions."

"Dr. Parrish." The magistrate's eyes grew cold, his voice harsh. "Do I tell you how to dress wounds and lance goiters? You will do well to leave my responsibilities to me. Do I make myself clear?"

"Yes, my lord. But, I must add that in my professional opinion, Sir John did regain his senses, not immediately, but eventually."

Lord Shirwell's lips tightened. "Thank you, Dr. Parrish. For your opinion. Well . . ." The magistrate set down his quill and folded his hands, as though he'd heard enough to pronounce her fate.

"I'd like to say my piece, if I may, your worship," said Mrs. Parrish.

Oh, Lord, have mercy. Not her, Hannah thought.

Before the magistrate could respond, Marianna beamed encouragement in her direction. "Oh yes, Mrs. Parrish, I am certain you have a great deal to say on the matter, having witnessed so many of the happenings personally." Marianna widened her eyes imploringly toward Lord Shirwell. "But of course, the decision is up to you, your worship."

"Very well. But do endeavor to be brief, Mrs. Parrish, if you please."

"I will, my lord. I only wanted to say a few words. My husband you see, is a good-hearted soul, but blind to the ways of people. Women especially. I may have been taken in for a day or two, while she was still insensible. But as soon as she started babbling about a child and not responding to the title 'my lady,' I began to suspect. She acted too common, too humble to be a real lady of quality. And then later I took one look at that scrawny troubled mite of a wet nurse she returned with and knew something was amiss. No self-respecting lady would engage such a low girl for the care of her prized son, not if she could help it."

Mrs. Parrish went on. "And then Sir John's solicitor arrived. A younger man and quite good-looking. He'd come to make some changes to the will I overheard. Perhaps to add her son to the will, I don't know. But I wonder if he was in league with her all along."

"That's not true," Hannah sputtered, but the magistrate silenced her with a glare.

"So you say, but can you deny that I saw

the two of you all alone in the garden one morning, very cozy and private like? And him not the first man I saw her with, either."

Hannah shook her head. "No, but we were only talking. It had nothing to do with the will."

"Sure, sure. You weren't behaving like any lady then, I can tell you. I don't know why Sir John didn't call you out like the Judas you are. Maybe he wasn't in his right mind, or maybe you promised him some . . . reward . . . if he let the deception go on."

Hannah sucked in a shocked breath. "I did no such thing."

"Silence, Miss Rogers," Lord Shirwell commanded. "You will have your chance to try to defend yourself in a minute."

Hannah pressed her lips together and clasped trembling hands in her lap.

Mrs. Parrish smirked. "I noticed the solicitor did not like her at first. Was quite cold to her in fact. But she soon had him eating from her hand. Likely used the same wiles on both men."

Lord Shirwell made a note in his logbook. Then looked up, quill poised. "Did Sir John not deny the child was his?"

"I couldn't say, my lord. Though Dr. Parrish mentioned to me that Sir John said that he saw no resemblance between himself and

468

the boy."

Dr. Parrish hung his head.

"Of course not," Lord Shirwell said. "Thank you, Mrs. Parrish."

The magistrate stood and called for a short recess, and departed the room. The clerk rose to stretch his legs and quietly thanked Dr. Parrish for the safe delivery of a niece. Marianna complimented Mrs. Parrish on her testimony and the two women chatted as though at a cheerful charity tea, and not the worst day of Hannah's life.

After a few more days of fruitless enquiry, James had landed upon an idea. Out of curiosity, he looked in the files to find Marianna's address before her marriage — the former home of Mr. Sydney Spencer, her father, who had died a year or two before. The street wasn't far, so James decided to walk there, though the day was grey and wet.

Reaching the place, he had to leap out of the way of a coach-and-four pulling into the curved drive. He watched as a footman scurried out with an umbrella, let down the step, and escorted a gentleman inside — the new owner of the place, James assumed. When the passenger had alighted, the coachman drove the horses around back toward the carriage house. It was probably futile, but James followed the coach. If society people were unwilling to speak against one of their own, perhaps a servant would have no such scruples.

James followed as far as the large double doors and from the threshold hailed the coachman. "Hello there. Nasty weather to be out driving in."

The coachman eyed him warily. "I'm used to it."

A groom and stable boy came and took charge of the horses.

James squinted through the drizzle at the dark manor. "Is this the old Spencer house?"

"Aye. Though it's gone to a distant relation. Kirby-Horner's 'is name."

"I see. Did you know Mr. Spencer?"

"That I did. I was his coachman for five years afore he died. Mr. Kirby-Horner was kind enough to keep me on." The coachman battened down the carriage for the night.

"And how was Mr. Spencer to work for?"

The man wrinkled up his face. "Don't get me started. It ain't polite to speak ill of the dead."

"Very well. And did you know his daughter, Marianna?"

Again his face puckered. "Look — who's

askin'? What's it to you?"

"My name is James Lowden. I am a solicitor." He handed over his card.

The man glanced at the card but made no move to take it. "So?"

"I represent my client, Sir John Mayfield."

The man's eyebrows rose. "Sir John, is it? Well, why didn't you say so. Sir John I know. I was groom to him years ago. It was him what got me this post here. Knew I wanted to be a coachman, but he already had a capable man, didn't he? Right decent of him it was, too. Though he was the better master ten times over, I don't mind tellin' ya."

The coachman belatedly stuck out his hand. "Tim Banks."

James shook the man's hand and said, "Then perhaps, Mr. Banks, you might help Sir John by helping me. I am looking into a rather delicate matter related to Lady Mayfield."

"What's she gone and done now?"

James hesitated. "You know then, that Sir John married Marianna Spencer?"

"Course I do. Dashed sorry I was to hear it, too."

"And why is that?"

He glanced about to make sure the groom and stable hand were otherwise occupied. "Come now, man. You can't have your offices here in Bristol and not have heard the old rumors about her and Anthony Fontaine."

"I have heard. Sir John is also painfully aware. But all I have are tidbits of gossip and innuendo and no real evidence. Sir John's coachman won't say where he took her or whom she met. And I have yet to find an innkeeper who can prove the two stayed together in his establishment. I need evidence. Something I can show in a trial. Now I don't say Sir John will accuse Mr. Fontaine in court, so please don't mention it. But he is considering it, that I will say." James shrugged. "But without evidence . . ."

The coachman frowned. "So she's still involved with Fontaine? After all this time?"

"She has been, yes. At least we believe so."

"Thunder and turf. What a couple of scapegraces."

"Yes."

Banks pursed his mouth, looking up as he considered, then he took a long breath. "I can do you one better than an innkeeper, friend."

"Oh?"

"Aye. I'm off duty in half an hour. Meet me at the Red Lion and I'll tell you everything I know."

"Very well. But I hope it is more than

mere hearsay."

"Hearsay?" Banks shook his head. "I was there, wasn't I? A gen-u-ine eyewitness. Buy me a pint and I'll tell you a tale to make your ears burn."

Chapter 25

Lord Shirwell returned ten minutes later and took his seat. He faced Hannah and began soberly, "Miss Rogers. You may tell us your version of the events. I remind you that this is not a trial. I am examining evidence to decide if there is a sufficient case against you to commit you to the house of corrections in Exeter until trial in the county courts there. Still, let me warn you that if I find you are dishonest, I will make it my personal vow to see you prosecuted to the full extent of the law. Do I make myself clear?"

"Yes, your worship." Hannah's nerves quaked. Most of what had been said against her was true, though not the motivations and exaggerated maneuvering behind her actions. Even if she revealed the truth of her child's father, they wouldn't believe her, and would twist it to use against her. Perhaps accusing her of threatening Sir John to go along with her scheme or she would publically accuse him and cause a scandal. Only Sir John himself could authoritatively acknowledge Daniel as a Mayfield. And he was not here. *If only he were here!*

What could she say in her defense? How tawdry and unbelievable it all sounded now.

Lord Shirwell consulted his notes, then looked up. "Miss Rogers, before you begin." He gestured toward Lady Mayfield. "Look at this lady and tell me honestly, is she or is she not Lady Marianna Mayfield?"

Hannah glanced over. "She is."

"And your name is?"

"Hannah Rogers."

"And did you or did you not impersonate this woman?"

Had she? She had never wanted to be Marianna, no. But Lady Mayfield . . . ?

"They thought I was Lady Mayfield."

"But you did not correct them?"

"I tried. . . ."

"Tried? Is it so hard to tell the truth. To say, 'Excuse me Dr. Parrish, but you have it wrong. I am not Lady Mayfield, I am only her companion.' Are you telling us that was impossible to do?"

Hannah ducked her head. "No, your worship."

Lord Shirwell entwined his fingers on the

desk. "Was it your intention to position yourself and your son as Sir John's heirs should he die?"

"No, your worship."

"Then why did you do it?"

"I had no other way to return to Bath and rescue my son."

"But you chose to leave him behind."

"Only temporarily. He was being held by the matron of a corrupt maternity home. Though I didn't know the true nature of the establishment when I left Danny under her care. I needed to find a situation not long after I delivered him. And one cannot do so with a child in arms."

He frowned. "Has this any bearing on the current situation?"

"Yes. The matron said I could not have Danny until I paid her exorbitant fees. Fees she'd raised over and over again after I'd agreed to her initial terms. I could not pay them. That's why I returned to the Mayfields in Bath and asked for the allowance I'd previously earned there as lady's companion, but had never collected. When Lady Mayfield asked me to travel to Devonshire with her as her companion, I thought I would stay with her just until I earned enough money, and then return for Danny."

"That is not the way Lady Mayfield recounts the events. She said you came begging for a place. Are you calling her a liar?"

It was a trap, and how tempting a trap it was. If she began speaking ill of her former mistress, the magistrate would of course defend the lady of his own class. It never went well for anyone who spoke against her master or mistress.

Hannah said carefully, "I sit in judgment of no one, your worship. Perhaps she and I saw the arrangement differently."

His eye glinted. "Lady Mayfield is right, you are cunning."

She shook her head. "No, your worship. I am only a mother, who did what she had to do to rescue her son. Did I do wrong? Yes. But did I intend to take more money from Sir John, for either myself or my son? No. I did not."

"I will decide who did wrong, Miss Rogers. That is why we are here, after all." He returned his gaze to his notes, then said, "If this sorry tale is true, why did you not end the ruse when you were reunited with your child? Why return to Lynton at all?"

Hannah nodded. It was a logical question. "I thought about it, your worship. But Edgar Parrish was so concerned about me, it felt rude . . . wrong . . . to refuse to return with him. How they all would have worried.

Besides that, my arm had been broken in the crash. I could not very well find another post until it mended. How was I to provide for Danny on my own? So I returned to Clifton, thinking I would stay until I had the full use of both arms and then I would try to find a post somewhere in Devonshire." She self-consciously cradled her arm. "Dr. Parrish only removed the bandages yesterday."

"So, you do not even deny that you allowed these good people to believe you were Lady Mayfield."

"I cannot deny it. Though my reasons —"

"Reasons? What care I for your reasons? Can reasons excuse deceit? Theft? Fraud?"

Hannah tried to hold his burning gaze, but she could not succeed for long. He was vehemently set against her. Thanks to Marianna. Thanks to the truth. And he was right. She had done wrong. Knowingly committed fraud. God may look at the heart, but the law cared little.

He gestured toward his clerk for some document. "I have heard enough. There is clearly enough evidence to have Miss Rogers committed to the house of corrections until a trial date may be set in the county courts." He dipped a quill and signed the paper with a flourish.

Dr. Parrish sputtered. "But Miss Rogers has a child! Surely there is no cause to separate mother and child for such a period."

"There is *more than* sufficient cause, Dr. Parrish." He fixed the doctor with an icy glare. "And I am the only judge of that here today."

Hannah thought she would be sick. Everything she had done to try to protect Danny . . . and now she would sit in jail and he would be taken from her. Would the court even allow Mrs. Turrill to keep him? And even if Mrs. Turrill were willing, could she care for Danny and support herself? Not to mention Becky?

Hannah was back to where they had started. Her hands tied. Danny out of reach. What if Becky ran off with him again? She recalled the image of Becky huddled over him in a Bath alleyway and shivered. *Oh, God in heaven, have mercy! I deserve this, but he does not. Please help him, watch over him. . . .* Tears streamed down Hannah's face.

The magistrate spoke quietly with his clerk, giving him some instructions. The clerk, in turn, wrote something in his register.

While they were occupied, Hannah looked

at Marianna, hoping to see a crack in her cold facade. "Why?" she whispered. "Is it not enough to simply send me away in shame? Why are you determined to destroy me?"

Marianna lifted her chin. "You were my companion. You were supposed to stand by me, remain loyal, no matter what. That you of all people should betray me . . . ?" Her dark eyes sparked with ire.

Hannah shook her head. "I did nothing to you. I took nothing from you — nothing you wanted. But you will take everything from me?"

The magistrate gathered up his papers and pushed back his chair. "The justices will want Sir John's testimony of course. That is, assuming he is in his right mind."

"I am."

Hannah snapped her head around at the sound of his voice, as did everyone in the room.

Her heart soared to see Sir John standing there, leaning on his cane, greatcoat splattered, tall boots mucked, face wind-chapped, hat askew. Had he ridden the final stretch on horseback?

He tossed his hat down on a side table. "And if you dare harm one hair of this woman's head, or even think of separating her from her child, you will be guilty of a gross injustice, and I for one shall not stand for it." He slowly ran a smoldering gaze from Lord Shirwell to the Parrishes, to her, to Marianna. He lifted a hand in is wife's direction. "What pretty tales has the missing Lady Mayfield been telling you?"

Marianna lifted her chin. "The truth."

The magistrate said, "Only that this person, Hannah Rogers, has impersonated her, and defrauded you." While the magistrate summarized the charges against her, Sir John's nostrils flared, and his jaw clenched.

"Stuff and nonsense," he said. "She told you just enough to poison your minds to the real story. And how quickly you have sipped at her honeyed hemlock. And swallowed it whole, no doubt."

"Can you deny that Hannah Rogers impersonated your wife?"

Sir John threw up his hand. "It's about time someone impersonated my wife! Marianna never felt the need to act the part. She was too busy meeting with her lover on a nearly daily — or should I say nightly — basis."

The magistrate sent Marianna an uncertain look. "Lady Mayfield is not on trial here."

"Then perhaps she should be."

Sir John limped a few steps forward. Dr. Parrish rose and offered him his chair, which Sir John sank into gratefully.

He began, "When the good doctor here came upon the wrecked Mayfield carriage and found only myself and the woman in question, what other conclusion was he to draw? By the time Miss Rogers returned to her senses after suffering a head wound, everyone at Clifton believed her to be Lady Mayfield. And there is only one reason she did not correct them — because she had no other way to return to Bath and collect her infant son. Doctor Parrish gave her ten pounds from my purse, which, yes, she accepted, to finance the journey and to pay the extorter holding her child. That woman, by the way, has since been jailed for illegal and harmful practices. But that is another story. . . ."

While Sir John spoke, Hannah noticed James Lowden slip into the back of the room. He looked unkempt and windblown as well. Apparently, both men had traveled on horseback, although not together.

The magistrate addressed Sir John. "Yes, yes. We have heard much of this already. But is it not true Miss Rogers coerced you into naming her illegitimate son as your heir?"

"Absolutely not. I had already planned to change my will before the accident, to disinherit Marianna Mayfield, my unfaithful wife. Which my solicitor, who is here now, I see, can confirm. But no, since the trip to Bath, Miss Rogers has not asked for, nor accepted, any money for herself, though I offered her a large sum."

Marianna's eyes flashed. "But she fraudulently passed off her base born child as your son!"

Sir John coolly met her gaze. "No, she did not. For I am the boy's father."

Gasps rose around the room. Lady Mayfield gaped at Sir John as though he were a stranger to her. Mrs. Parrish pressed a hand to her mouth, and Dr. Parrish slowly nodded in understanding.

Sir John continued. "If anyone should be on trial today, it should be me, or perhaps Marianna, but not Miss Rogers. For I took advantage of her while she was in my employ back when we lived in Bristol. She made no demands on me then. Requested no support for herself or her infant. In fact, she did not even tell me she was with child. Before her condition became evident, she simply left, planning to raise the baby on her own. Only when she believed my wife was dead and I a widower, did she acknowledge that I was the boy's father, though it was quite obvious to look at him that the lad is a Mayfield."

Again, Dr. Parrish nodded sagely. And Hannah noticed that everyone attended Sir John's account as they had hung on Marianna's words before.

"When I told Miss Rogers I wished to support my son financially," Sir John went on, "she was reluctant to accept. And she refused to allow me to include her in my new will."

He flicked a hard glance at his wife. "And no matter what Marianna may have told you, I was in my right mind and knew very well Hannah Rogers was not in reality my wife. In fact, Miss Rogers confessed all to me as soon as I regained my senses — even before I regained the power of speech. She would have confessed all to Dr. Parrish as well, but I forestalled her."

"Why on earth would you do so?" Lord Shirwell asked, brows low, papers forgotten.

Sir John shrugged. "At first I only wanted to test her. To see how far she was willing to take the charade. I wrongly suspected she and Marianna had plotted the switch to allow Marianna to flee with her lover. I wasn't fully convinced Marianna had drowned, you see. But even though others assumed we were married, Miss Rogers and I were not . . . intimate. Not since the conception of our child, though some gossips" — he eyed Mrs. Parrish — "may have spread that lie."

He glanced at Hannah's burning face, then looked back at the magistrate. "I convinced her to keep up the pretense, since Marianna was believed dead, and had no close family left to mourn her. Because if Hannah was thought to be my wife, then her son could legally inherit my entailed property, as well as my other holdings. Every day I was sure Miss Rogers would cry off and leave. And I know she was tempted to more than once. But she stayed — not for personal gain, but only for her son's sake. And for mine, since I asked it of her."

Sir John gestured toward his wife. "What has Marianna told you? That she had been swept out to sea, lost her memory, and only recently remembered who she was, and came scurrying back?"

Dr. Parrish alone nodded his head.

"Rubbish, the lot of it," Sir John continued. "She saw her opportunity to leave me after the accident and she took it, sneaking

485

away, faking her drowning, leaving her companion bleeding and disoriented. Her husband broken and near death. And I would have died, too, had Dr. Parrish not found us so quickly. Meanwhile Marianna hid for a time, then sought out her lover, as she had done before. It was the reason I decided to move here to Devonshire in the first place — a desperate, futile attempt to separate my wife from her lover. How dismally that plan failed."

He shook his head. "Marianna has been in London, attending balls. While Miss Rogers helped nurse me back to health, hour by tedious hour."

For a moment Sir John's eyes met hers, and Hannah's heart beat hard.

He dragged his gaze from her face and continued, "And now here she is — traipsing back from the dead." He looked at his wife. "What happened, Marianna? Did your money run out? Did your lover tire of you and abandon you? So the gossips claim."

Marianna lifted her chin but did not deny it.

"So only now does she resurface. With a mouthful of deceit. And tricks you all with her beauty and artful lies." Sir John's gaze swept over the assembled company before returning to the magistrate.

"Would you like to hear from my solicitor? He has been gathering evidence to prove Marianna has been living in secret with her lover, not as one lost trying to find her true identity, but as one fearing to be discovered."

Was that true, Hannah wondered. Or was he bluffing? She looked at James but his flinty expression gave nothing away.

Lord Shirwell grimaced. "That will not be necessary. Again, your wife is not on trial here. Nor do these accusations against her bear on the present case — the wrongdoing committed by Hannah Rogers."

"Of course they do," Sir John insisted. "For there sits Marianna, pretending to be the injured wife, when nothing could be further from the truth."

"Even if that is true, it does not change the fact that Hannah Rogers perpetrated a fraud. She doesn't even deny it."

Sir John rose, cane forgotten, and stood tall and straight. "If you insist on pursuing this farce, if you try to punish Miss Rogers in the slightest degree, I shall avenge her if I have to go to Parliament itself and argue my case. For all the wrong I have done, I could never forgive myself, nor any of you, if any harm befalls this fine woman or her son, because of my stupid, prideful posturing."

He speared the magistrate with a fierce gaze. "Do you hear me, your worship? Let this woman go."

The magistrate sputtered, "But . . . there has been wrongdoing. Laws have been broken. . . ."

"Yes, there has been wrongdoing, but not by Hannah Rogers. She has helped me, succored me, aided me. Not harmed me. Do you understand? What sort of a travesty of a trial is this, when the man supposedly defrauded is not even pressing charges, but is defending the falsely accused?"

"She has done something to Lady Mayfield. She has tried to take her rightful place. She —"

"Her rightful place?" Fire sparked in Sir John's eyes. "This woman has done everything in her power to dishonor me and our marriage vows ever since our wedding trip. She has committed adultery with her lover again and again without discretion or thought to my feelings or reputation. There is no shortage of people who know of this affair. She has detested her rightful place and has lost any claim to it in my eyes, no matter what the law says. Now will you release Miss Rogers or must I remove her by force and charge you with lynch law and intention to riot?"

For several moments Sir John and the magistrate locked gazes. Hannah feared Sir John had pushed too hard against the man so keen on demonstrating his superior power. But at last Lord Shirwell tore the paper in two and handed the pieces back to his clerk. "Very well. Miss Rogers, I hereby dismiss all charges against you based on Sir John's evidence. You are free to go."

Dr. Parrish murmured, "Thank God."

Marianna sat stone-faced, while Mrs. Parrish looked at her like a child regarding a cheap toy, quickly broken.

Hannah rose on shaking legs.

Sir John turned to Marianna, jaw ticking. "So. Shall we go home, *wife*?"

Lady Mayfield formed a sour smile. "For now."

Hannah walked out of the magistrate's office before any of the others. Alone. She trembled all over and felt physically ill. Relief at her freedom washed through her but along with it came nausea from all the seedy tales and lies she had heard this day. Marianna's lies. Her own past lies. Even Sir John's lies, in omission if nothing else. She felt coated with tar as foul as sin. All she wanted to do was take Danny and go away somewhere clean and sunny, peaceful and true. And maybe have a long bath.

She stopped short at the sight of Mrs. Turrill rising from a bench in the hall just outside the door. She barely resisted the urge to throw herself into the woman's arms.

Hannah breathed, "I thought you weren't coming."

"I had to come. Don't worry, Danny is safe at home with my sister. I wanted to be here, whatever the outcome. You're not vexed with me, I hope?"

Hannah shook her head. "I'm glad."

Mrs. Turrill smiled. "I heard the last of it, my girl, sitting here as I was. And I can't tell you how relieved I am."

"Me, too." Hannah's chin trembled.

Mrs. Turrill put an arm around her and together they walked outside. "Well, thank God, that's over. What will you do now, my dear?"

"I don't know." She looked at the kind woman. "Mrs. Turrill, why are you so good to me, after all I've done? After I've deceived you and everyone else?"

"Oh, not everybody. Sir John knew. He was no victim, no matter what *she* said. And I had my suspicions. But I saw your heart.

Even if you took it too far, I knew you were thinking only of your son." Her dark eyes sparkled. "And perhaps a certain gentleman."

Hannah shook her head. "At this point, I want nothing to do with either of them."

"Don't forget how they rushed in and saved you today."

Hannah lowered her head, cheeks flushing anew. "I won't forget."

Mrs. Turrill patted her hand. "Now, come home with me and have some tea. We'll talk and sort things out, all right? Becky got awful scared when you were taken away. Thought she was next, poor creature. She'll be over the moon to see you again, and that's the truth."

Hannah hesitated.

"Come, my dear," Mrs. Turrill insisted. "You heard the justice. You're free to go. It's all in the past."

"Is it?"

"Well, that's for you to decide, isn't it?"

Behind them, the door opened. Nervous, Hannah glanced back, and saw James Lowden step outside. James met her gaze, his mouth drawn tight, eyes intense. Hannah was uncertain what else she saw in his expression, but it wasn't good. He looked away first.

He did not approach her. Instead he crossed the drive, signaling a groom to bring the carriages back around.

The others came out, Sir John and Marianna, followed by a trio of sheepish Parrishes.

Sir John saw her with Mrs. Turrill and broke away from the others with the help of his cane. "Miss Rogers. Where are you going?"

Hannah was aware of the others ceasing their own conversations and turning to watch them. "To Mrs. Turrill's. For now."

He opened his mouth, thought the better of what he'd been about to say, and pressed his lips together, making do with a terse nod. He clasped his hands, cane and all, behind his back as though they were tied. And indeed, they were.

Hannah swallowed. "And are you and . . . Lady Mayfield . . . going home?"

He winced. "Yes. To Clifton for now and then back to Bristol. I shall endeavor to forgive her. To do my duty by her, but I don't pretend it shall be easy. Especially after today."

Tears pricked Hannah's eyes. She whispered, "You are doing the right thing."

He grimaced. "I hope so. But if you need anything —"

Hannah interrupted him gently, "I appreciate you defending me so gallantly. I do. But that's the end of it. It's time I was out on my own."

She half expected him to ask, *"On your own, or with James?"* But he did not. His gaze flickered to the solicitor, who watched them from a distance.

Mrs. Turrill spoke up. "She'll be in good hands, Sir John. Her and Danny both. Never you worry."

Again, that pained terse nod. "Thank you, Mrs. Turrill."

A few minutes later, Hannah walked side by side with her former housekeeper to the yellow cottage at the bottom of the Lynmouth hill. It had been their parents' home, she explained, which she and her sister had inherited together — and now shared when not employed elsewhere.

Inside, Hannah warmly greeted Martha Parrish, a spinster, and thanked her for her hospitality. The woman was gracious, though a bit more reserved than her sister.

In the small sitting room, they drank weak tea together, took turns cuddling Danny, and assuring Becky that all was well.

Was it? Hannah silently asked herself. Inwardly, she was not as confident as she tried to appear.

CHAPTER 26

James Lowden watched Hannah walk away with the housekeeper. Seeing them together reminded him of Hannah's change in status. At one time, she had seemed far above him as "Lady Mayfield." Then she'd descended closer to his social equal as a clergyman's daughter. And now? Side by side with a housekeeper. Was she even lower than that? Fallen woman that she was, and nearly a criminal? Perhaps he should feel relieved to be parted from her and take advantage of the jarring turn of events to make a clean break. A part of him thought it would be wisest to do just that.

Another part of him longed to run after her, regardless of who was looking. Beg her to marry him, to allow him to provide for her, take care of her. Remorse filled him. He felt embarrassed, weak — when he thought of how he'd sat there, silent, while Sir John spoke up so nobly and effectively on her behalf, and gained her release. James was the solicitor, after all. Should it not have been him? But he had not said a word.

Even now, James was hesitant to speak. To make known the information he had learned while in Bristol. He had set out to uncover evidence of Marianna Mayfield's fate and affair — but he had found so much more. Was he obligated to make it known? He had planned to. After all, he had even brought along a witness to his astounding claim. Otherwise he doubted anyone would believe him.

But seeing the passionate plea Sir John had made on Hannah's behalf, and her obvious gratitude afterward, almost made him wish he had not been so hasty in bringing the fellow along.

It was too late now. He hoped he wouldn't live to regret what he was about to do.

James waited until the Mayfields and Parrishes departed in cart and gig — a silent, somber party — before making his way to Lord Shirwell's stable yard to reclaim the horses. And his guest.

Arriving at Clifton House a short while later, James left the horses in the stables, and asked his guest to wait outside for a few minutes.

Then James trudged with leaden legs

toward the house.

In the drawing room, he found Sir John standing at the cold hearth, hand propped atop the mantel, staring at the ashes within.

Lady Mayfield walked to the decanter on the sideboard and lifted the stopper. She paused when she saw him in the threshold. "Mr. Lowden, I believe? Nice of you to join us. Yes, I do see a resemblance to your late father, now I see you more closely." She poured herself a tall drink. "May I pour you one as well?"

"No, thank you."

"You will join us for dinner, I hope?" She formed a vague smile. "That is, if we still have a cook?"

James wondered what the Mayfields would do now — rebuke and rage at one other? Attempt some civil, stilted domestic scene? James found he could not stand the prospect of either. As tempted as he was to keep silent, it was time to put an end to this sham once and for all.

"Sir John," James began. "Do you honestly plan to live with this woman?" He flicked a glance at Marianna, who was staring down into her drink as though for answers.

"You are the one who counseled me against divorce," Sir John said dully. "Unless — have you found the evidence we'd need?"

"Not exactly. But I have discovered something that bears on your situation."

Sir John's eyes narrowed. "What is it?"

"As you and I have discussed before, divorce is nearly impossible to achieve, scandalous, and typically unconscionable. But there is little typical about your case. Because you were never legally married to Marianna Spencer in the first place."

Marianna's head snapped up.

Sir John frowned thunderously. "What?"

James continued, "You are only too aware of Marianna's longtime lover. But Anthony Fontaine is not only her lover — he is her husband."

"Ha!" Marianna blurted. "I wish!"

Sir John scowled. "What are you talking about?"

James glanced at the woman — saw her dark look — but addressed his client as though she were not present. "Marianna Spencer eloped with Anthony Fontaine before her marriage to you. Her father found the wayward couple in Scotland a few days later and, knowing any attempt he made to publically annul the marriage would end in scandal and ruination for his daughter, he instead bribed Fontaine to hide the elopement and not object to Marianna's marriage to you. A marriage that would bring his daughter not only the advantages of title and situation, but wealth as well. Wealth that would benefit all three of them."

Marianna scoffed. "That is preposterous!"

Sir John ignored her. "After everything else we've been through today . . . You have got to be joking."

"No. I am perfectly serious."

"But that's impossible," Sir John said. "I heard nothing of any elopement. And why would Fontaine go along with such a scheme?"

"I imagine Marianna assured him that her marriage to you would be a marriage in name only and would not hinder them from being together."

Sir John ran a hand through his hair. "Can you prove any of this?"

Marianna's lip curled. "Of course he can't."

"I can actually," James said. "All of it. I have the testimony of the coachman who drove them to Gretna Green, a certificate attesting to the marriage, and —"

Marianna protested, "No such evidence exists!"

James looked at her. "You mean, because

the coachman burned it? He only pretended to — burnt a stage bill or some such in its stead."

Marianna stiffened in her chair, white-faced, but met his gaze straight on. "Any certificate you have is a forgery, no doubt."

"Oh, I think you will find it all too real," James said. "As would a judge and jury." He then again focused on his employer.

Sir John's eyes pierced his. "How long have you known?"

James took a deep breath. "I learned of it just before I received your urgent letter summoning me here."

"But you didn't think it worth mentioning at the hearing?"

"Not really, no. If your marriage is to be annulled, that is for an ecclesiastical court to decide. Besides, I was not sure you would wish it aired in public. And . . ."

The taller man's eyes glinted. "And you didn't wish to reveal it for personal reasons."

"I cannot deny it hindered me for a time, yes."

Sir John crossed his arms. "Then why tell me now?"

"Because it's the right thing to do. And I wouldn't want Miss Rogers to . . . regret any decision she might make, without knowing all the facts." Sir John met and held his gaze. Eyes keen with understanding.

Marianna lifted her chin. "I have done nothing illegal. It was all my father's doing."

James shook his head. "I disagree. I think you are guilty of the very charges you tried to lay at Miss Rogers's door. And worse. For you entered a second marriage contract, knowing you were already legally bound to another man. That is bigamy as well as fraud." James's ears picked up the sound of stealthy footsteps entering the room.

"Do you not concur, Mr. Fontaine?"

Anthony Fontaine stepped into the room and leaned against the doorjamb. "Indeed, I do."

Sir John rose to his feet. "How dare you enter my house?"

Fontaine's eyes flashed. "How dare you marry my wife?"

Sir John threw up his hands. "Can this day get any worse?" He shot Marianna a thunderous look before turning back to Fontaine. "I had no idea she was married to you, if that is indeed true. While apparently you have known all along and have never bothered to protest before — our engagement or wedding. Why start now?"

"Revenge, I suppose." Fontaine casually crossed his arms. "I thought to myself, what is good for the goose must be good for the gander. But when Marianna heard that I was wooing an heiress, she quickly squashed that relationship by sending an anonymous letter to the girl, letting her know I was already married. The girl cried off, taking her money with her." He shook his head and tsked. "And after I'd been so under-standing about Marianna and her knight."

"Understanding?" Marianna sneered. "You were the first to agree when Papa proposed the scheme. I would never have gone along with it, had you not persuaded me to do so. How I longed for you to throw Papa's plan back in his face and tell him no one would have me, save you. I would have defied him, had you stood by me. But you never could say no to money."

Fontaine shrugged and gave them a self-satisfied smile. "I can't deny it. It's part of my charm apparently."

James shook his head in disgust. Anthony Fontaine had initially been reluctant to ac-company him to Devonshire, but finding the threatening letter he'd sent to Sir John in the solicitor's possession had convinced him. Now, James Lowden looked from the smirking dandy to the vain adulteress and thought they made a well-matched pair. For the first time, he felt true sympathy for his client. And he was glad he'd uncovered the truth at last. . . .

James had waited in the dim parlor of the Red Lion, with its smoky fire and men in low conversation all around him. Right on schedule, the coachman, Tim Banks, appeared. James bought the man a pint and the two found a quiet corner.

Banks took a long drink, then began. "I was there, see, the night Mr. Spencer realized his daughter had up and left his house. He guessed straight away which way the wind blew, and lost no time in calling for his traveling coach and fastest horses. It was me at the reins, and the groom, Joe, alongside. We heard the old man swearing and shouting orders and had little doubt what had happened — his daughter, the spoiled Marianna — had gone off and eloped with her young man, against her father's express orders to stop seeing him and marry the man he had chosen for her."

"Sir John."

"Right. So with Mr. Spencer and his spinster aunt in tow, we went charging out of the city on a direct course for Scotland. We drove day and night, only stopping to change horses. Joe and I took turns driving while the other tried to get a bit of sleep without being tossed to the ground."

"When we finally crossed the border and reached Gretna Green, we stopped at the blacksmith's shop. Mr. Spencer, his aunt beside him, asked where they might find a man who performed marriages. I was supposed to wait with the coach, but I left Joe with the horses and went to listen at the blacksmith's door. I was curious. After all, had I not just ridden head over tails and barely slept for days to do whatever it was Mr. Spencer was determined to see done?"

The coachman took another drink of his ale. "The parson was called for and soon arrived. At least he called himself a parson, but didn't look like no parson I'd ever seen. You know in Scotland, any adult can set 'imself up as a minister of weddings. No bans required, no license. Only two witnesses. Had himself a tidy little business from the looks of things. Even kept a room in a nearby inn they called 'the nuptial chamber' where couples might consummate their marriage quick afterward, to deter an angry father who might otherwise try to undo the marriage. Mr. Spencer asked the man if he kept any record of the marriages he performed, or sent any notice to the registrar. The man said he kept a book for his own records, but did not feel bound to notify the parish, since so many of the couples he wed lived elsewhere. He did say he provided any couple who wanted one — and had a shilling to pay — with a certificate of their marriage."

The coachman slowly shook his head.

"Then I heard Mr. Spencer tell the supposed parson a tale of woe as I've never heard! Why I barely recognized my master's voice, so grieved was he. Would the man not spare the reputation, nay the life, of his one and only daughter? She and the young man had realized the folly of their ways, he declared. And, filled with remorse, the repentant children had not even consummated the marriage after they'd said their vows. Could the good man not see his way clear to rubbing out that entry in his records . . . a spill of ink would do the trick and no one would be the wiser. Might a donation to his 'ministry' be unwelcome?

"I was nearly sick to hear him. Especially since we had not yet even found Marianna yet. And even if Mr. Spencer succeeded in having the record blotted out, there was no erasing the fact that the couple had been alone together — first in a post-chaise, then at an inn — for two or three days. And nights." Again Banks shook his head. "The parson agreed out of the *vast* goodness of his heart — and Mr. Spencer's purse.

"Afterward we went to the inn. When we arrived, Mr. Spencer bade me come in with him, with a blunderbuss in hand, in case Mr. Fontaine raised a violent objection. We found the happy couple, there, lodging under an assumed name. The picture of connubial bliss, I might add. How Mr. Spencer shouted. Marianna shouted back, waving the marriage certificate in her father's face. He grabbed it from her, crumpled it, and flung it out the window. But then he thought the better of it and sent me to collect it so he could dispose of it more permanent-like. I ran down and collected the crumpled thing. When I returned, Mr. Spencer told me to toss it into the fire. Then he told me to wait outside. I left, hearing his voice change from shouting to cajoling to wheedling, though I did not hear the details of what he said."

Banks paused, looking up at the hop-strewn beams above them as he reviewed the memory in his mind. "An hour later Marianna emerged from the inn, dressed and pale, and stepped inside the carriage with her aunt and father. Mr. Fontaine watched her leave from the inn doorway, oddly calm about the whole affair. Which made me suppose Mr. Spencer had promised him a great deal of money to forget the thing had ever happened. Later I heard that he'd paid his aunt a handsome sum to begin spreading the tale that she had escorted Marianna on some sightseeing trip, to cover for her absence."

The coachman cringed. "He gave Joe and me money, too. Bonuses for the long trip and for our discretion in keeping to ourselves the 'unfortunate events' of the previous few days 'til the grave. Joe, I know, has done so. For he has a wife and five children to support and couldn't afford to lose his place."

"And you?"

"I'm ashamed to say I've kept quiet, too. Had I known Mr. Spencer still planned to marry her off to Sir John, and so quickly, I might have gone to him and told him what I knew. But I only learned of the wedding after the fact, by special license, I understand. And then I figured, well, Sir John won't welcome such news now. Not when he's gone and married her. It would ruin his reputation as well as hers. But I should have. Now that Mr. Spencer has passed on, I don't feel the need to keep quiet anymore. Not if I can help Sir John."

"Can you give me the name and direction of this Scottish 'parson'?"

The coachman looked at him and shook his head. "I can do you one better. I can give you the marriage certificate." The coachman pulled a folded paper from his pocket, slight wrinkles remaining from its long-ago crumpling, but otherwise intact.

"I've kept it all these years. I only pretended to toss it on the fire, but pocketed it instead. I don't know why. I had no specific plan, it just seemed a clever thing to do at the time." He shrugged. "Talking to you now. Maybe it was."

James could not believe his good fortune. Yet he felt no sense of victory. Only regret and distaste. He nearly wished he had never gone to the old Spencer house.

He roused himself from his misery and reached into his pocket. "Allow me to give you something for your help. . . ."

The coachman raised a hand, palm forward. "No, thank you, sir. I never felt right about accepting Mr. Spencer's money to keep quiet. So I won't take a farthing this time."

Afterward, James had gone in search of Anthony Fontaine to confirm the story. Then he called at Sir John's Bristol house. The butler had met him with a frown and the news that Sir John had left in haste for Devonshire. He'd handed him a letter, unsealed and clearly read by the old, trusted retainer. Sir John's hasty scrawl explained the urgency.

Special messenger arrived from Dr. Parrish. Miss R. in dire trouble. Accused of fraud by M.S.M. Called before Shirwell, J.P. Hearing on the twelfth. Come as soon as possible. She will need a good lawyer. And our prayers.

James had left Bristol without delay. But feared it might already be too late. For him.

Standing in the Clifton drawing room now, James saw no victory on Sir John's face, either. He wondered what his client would ask him to do next and hoped it did not involve bigamy charges. Whatever the case, James was ready to shake the Devonshire dust from his boots forever. If only Hannah would be willing to leave it all behind as well.

The night of the hearing, after Danny and Becky were asleep, and Martha had excused herself to prepare for bed, Hannah and Mrs. Turrill sat up late talking.

"You are very kind, Mrs. Turrill, but I can't stay here for long. Not when everyone here knows what I've done and suspects me guilty of even more, at least where Sir John and Mr. Lowden are concerned. For myself I wouldn't care so much, but I don't want Danny growing up under a cloud of scandal. I need to go somewhere new and start fresh."

Mrs. Turrill said gently, "But think what running from the truth has wrought, my girl. How guilty you've felt. Why not stay and face your past. Shine the light of truth on all them dark days?"

Hannah expelled a weary sigh. "How far back in the past would I have to go? Back to my father — tell him I'm alive, that I've had a child, and by whom?"

"Oh, my dear." Mrs. Turrill said, dark eyes wide and sad. "Wouldn't he want to know?"

"It would break his heart."

"More than thinking you dead and lost to him forever?"

Hannah nodded bleakly.

"Are you certain? Remember, 'whoever conceals their sins shall not prosper,' " she paraphrased the Proverb, " 'but whoever confesses and forsakes them finds mercy.' "

Mercy . . . Oh, how Hannah longed for it — from God and her father. "I'm afraid to face him," she said. "I don't know how merciful he'll be. And I don't want to hurt

509

him more than I already have."

Mrs. Turrill squeezed her hand. "Think of how you feel about Danny. Imagine him grown. Would you love him any less if he made some big mistake? Would you wish him dead? Or, even if you were hurt and disappointed by his wrongdoing, wouldn't you want to know he was all right? That he had made his way back to the straight path? That he still loved you?"

Hannah nodded again, tears filling her eyes. "Yes." Her throat tightened. "But my father is a clergyman."

Mrs. Turrill brought her face near, and looked solemnly into her eyes. "Yes," she agreed. "But the clergyman is also a father."

CHAPTER 27

Hannah left Devonshire without speaking to James Lowden or seeing Sir John again. She decided Mrs. Turrill was right. It was time to go home and make peace with the past — and with her father. To confess all, and hope for mercy.

Hannah traveled with Becky and Danny by stagecoach to Bristol. A city she'd once doubted she would ever return to. Mrs. Turrill had insisted Hannah not travel alone. But she promised Becky she could return to her and her sister's house whenever she wished, and had even pressed coach fare into the girl's palm to seal the promise.

Upon arrival in Bristol, Hannah first secured a room in a respectable lodging house and, there, left their luggage. After changing and feeding Danny, they walked to the carter's stall where Fred Bonner worked with his father. Hannah carried Danny while Becky trailed behind, gaping and craning her neck to take in the tall buildings of the unfamiliar city.

"Hannah!" Fred called when he saw her. He jumped down from his cart, reins and horses forgotten and bounded over to her like the overgrown boy he was. She was relieved to find him there on her first attempt, and not en route to Bath.

He beamed at her. "How good to see you again."

"You, too, Freddie." Fred seemed to have forgotten that they'd parted on bad terms when he came to Clifton. He always had been a forgiving sort.

He stooped down, hands on knees, to regard the child in her arms. "Is this little Daniel? My goodness, he's grown."

Hannah turned and gestured. "And this is Becky Brown, his nurse. And . . . my friend. Becky, this is my dear old friend, Fred Bonner."

Fred tipped his cap. "Hello, miss."

Becky bobbed a shy curtsy. "Sir."

He found a chair for Becky and Danny several feet away and then returned to Hannah's side, dark eyes penetrating deep. "How are you, Han — ? It is Hannah now, I hope?"

"Yes." She hesitated. *How was she?* It was a complicated question, considering Marianna was back in Sir John's life, while Mr. Lowden was apparently out of hers. But the lengthy truth could wait for another day.

Instead she smiled and said, "I am . . . well. And how are you? Your cart looks dashing. New paint?" She walked over to it, away from his too direct gaze.

He gathered the reins and set the hand brake. "It is, yes."

"And how goes your route? Business good?"

"Very well. Or, well enough. Han —"

"Oh. I wasn't hinting or anything like that," Hannah hurried to say. "Truly. I just wondered . . . hoped it was going well for you."

His hound-dog eyes turned downward. "Hannah. I know better than to hope. Though the offer still stands. So tell me, what it is you want? Why did you come to see me?"

"Dear Freddie." She swallowed. "I wanted to let you know I was back. And to ask about my father. How he fares . . . ?" To herself she added, *What he knows.*

"He seems all right. Sad of course, but he's in good health, if that's what you mean. He told me Mayfield's solicitor came to see him as he did me."

"May I ask what you told my father?"

513

Fred shrugged. "I've told him nothing since I saw you in Devon. You asked me to let it lie."

"I know I did. Though now I think it's time I faced the truth. Confessed everything. But I'm scared, Freddie."

"As well you should be."

"Freddie!"

"I'm sorry, Han. But it's true. It's a deep pit you've dug for yourself."

She bit her lip and asked tentatively, "I don't suppose you'd help me out of it?"

"You don't want my help."

"I just meant, ease the way for me. Let him know that the newspaper had it wrong, and I'm still alive. And . . . have a child. And I am here in Bristol if he wants to see me. I'm staying in Mrs. Hurst's lodging house, in Little King Street."

"I don't know, Han."

She recalled Mrs. Turrill's words, "But nothing is too big for God. No pit we dig for ourselves too deep. He is already reachin' a hand down to you, ready to pull you up. . . ."

Silently, Hannah prayed, *God, will you help me?*

She looked at Fred and suddenly straightened with resolve. "You know what — you're right. I will go and see him myself."

His brows rose. "Now?"

Fear flooded Hannah at the thought. "Oh. Um. Not this moment, but very soon." *After I find the courage,* she thought. If only she had thought to pack some.

Hannah pressed her friend's arm. "Thank you, Freddie."

"I did nothing."

"That's not true. You gave me just what I needed."

On Sunday, Hannah stood outside the Bristol church where her father served as underpaid curate. He had not the connections to bring him a good living as rector or vicar. The humble life suited him, he had always insisted. Though it had meant his sons had to be sent to sea quite young, and his daughter had needed to seek a paid position to support herself.

From outside the ancient grey stone building, she heard the low drone of her father's voice, delivering his sermon. Followed by the reedy voices of the elderly congregation, singing a solemn hymn.

She did not intend to enter. Nor interrupt. She would wait until she could greet him alone, in private. But knowing he was occupied inside, Hannah felt at her ease to meander through the churchyard and gain her bearings. Oh, the hours she'd spent there as a girl.

Seeing the gnarled yew tree in the corner, Hannah walked toward it to visit her mother's grave. As she neared, she suddenly stopped and stared, craning her head forward even as her feet felt rooted to the mossy ground. There was a new grave beside her mother's. And the name on the headstone . . .

It was her name.

She stepped forward and melted to her knees before the modest headstone.

IN MEMORY
HANNAH ROGERS
BELOVED DAUGHTER
1796–1819

Tears flooded her eyes. Had he really? Had her father, with his threadbare stockings, worn-out shoes, and watered-down soups, actually spent such a sum? To memorialize her life and death, when there had not even been a body to bury? She would never have thought it. Not in a hundred years. The man would burn only a single tallow candle to read by or compose his sermons by, only when the window stubbornly refused to provide sufficient light for his ever-weakening eyes. He had spent such a sum on her?

Seeing the headstone made her sick with regret. She felt she would lose her meager breakfast then and there. It stole her courage, even as "beloved daughter" ought to have bolstered it. How doubly sorry he would be to have spent his modest savings on such a stone, when she had been alive all along. Alive and living a lie in the bargain. How sorry he would be to have memorialized her as beloved daughter, once he had learned of her many sins.

She ran gloved fingers over the carved letters of her name.

That Hannah Rogers — cherished, blameless daughter — had died. Had died more than a year before. And there would be no resurrecting her now.

Hannah returned to the lodging house without seeing her father. She could not face him after that. She would write a letter and invite him to call on her if he wished.

Thoughts of a letter reminded her of Sir John's admonition to keep Mr. Lowden apprised of her whereabouts. So, Hannah sent a note to his offices with the direction of the lodging house.

Then, she waited. Several days came and

went. And with each passing hour her nerves and fears escalated. She had written to him and told him they had been apart too long. She wanted to see him again and proposed a meeting. But did he want to see her, after the way she had left him? She didn't know.

Mrs. Turrill had advised her to meet him on neutral ground. Away from his usual territory. So, she waited in the lodging house's private sitting room, which she had let for an extra half-crown for the occasion. The proposed meeting time came and went. Tea waited and grew strong then cold. Cool cucumber sandwiches wilted and Hannah began to lose heart. And courage.

She paced the room again, wringing her hands. Practicing what she would say. Becky and Danny napped in their room above. Hannah wanted to see him alone first — wanted their reunion to be a private one. But would he even come?

Another half an hour passed. Tears threatened and she blinked them back, refusing to give in to them. She and Danny were managing on their own. She reminded herself that they had each other. They had friends in Mrs. Turrill, Becky, and Fred. They didn't need —

A knock sounded and Hannah froze. Her

heartbeat seemed louder than the distant knock. Footsteps followed — thump, thump, thump. The owner of the lodging house going to the front door in her heavy-heeled shoes. Muffled voices and then two pairs of shoes crossing the entry hall. Hannah's pulse accelerated with each approaching step. A single knock on the sitting room door, the hinge creaking open, footsteps entering. Hannah took a deep breath, wiped her damp palms on her handkerchief, and turned.

There he was.

Mrs. Hurst nodded solemnly and shut the door behind her visitor. Hannah's heart squeezed to see him again. He stood stiffly, wearing neither coat nor hat. Mrs. Hurst must have polished her manners and taken them. Could she not have taken his grim expression as well?

She reminded herself to breathe. To hold herself erect. To pray . . .

"Hello. Thank you for coming. Please, won't you be seated?"

Her father stared at her a moment, but remained where he was.

Nerves quaking, she gestured toward the tray. "Tea?"

He shook his head. "No, thank you."

Her father's voice. Ah, what memories it

evoked. He looked older, even thinner than she recalled.

She was strangely relieved to allow the tea she had paid for to go to waste. She was sure her hands would tremble if she tried to pour.

She decided she would not presume to call him "Papa" as she used to do. She cleared her throat and began. "Father, I have asked you here to seek your advice."

"Oh?" Wary reserve steeled his expression. "You did not see fit to seek it before."

"No, I did not. That was just one of my many mistakes. But I am asking now."

He crossed his arms over his thin chest. "I am listening."

"I have many decisions before me. Decisions that affect my future and that of my son. Yes, I have a son now."

He nodded. "Fred told me a few days ago — even before I received your letter. He came to let me know you were alive. Why did you not tell me yourself?"

So dear Fred had broken the news after all. She said, "Because I knew my fall from grace would cast a shadow on your reputation, perhaps even cost you the curacy. Don't worry. I have not come to ask for money or help. Only for advice and . . . perhaps, forgiveness. I have no wish to be a financial burden, nor a burden of any kind. But I do long for your forgiveness."

He had been staring down at his hands during this, her practiced speech, but now he looked up at her. "You assume I care more for my reputation than my daughter's well-being?"

"Well, you cannot help but be concerned about it, and I don't blame you."

"You thought I wouldn't forgive you?"

"Will you? I am so sorry, Papa. For everything." There. It slipped out.

He looked down at his hands once more. "Do you know how I worried? How devastated I was when I heard that you had died? I would have given up a hundred curacies to have you back."

Hannah's chest ached. Tears filled her eyes. "And when you learned I was alive?"

"I was relieved, and yet angry. Why did you not come to me yourself? Tell me what was going on? I might have helped you."

"Forgive me, Papa, but I know you well. You would not have easily forgiven my being with child, nor bringing shame upon you. In all honesty, I thought it would be better for you if I had died."

He gaped at her. "Are you so new at being a parent? Yes, you're right — I would have been greatly disappointed, shocked, embarrassed, everything. I might have even asked you to go away somewhere and have the child in secret. But I would never, ever, wish you dead."

"I'm sorry," she whispered.

"So am I," he said, voice low and gravelly. The voice she had often heard when he prayed over a dying child or a favorite old parishioner. He stepped closer, and she noticed tears in his eyes, too. "And, yes, I forgive you."

He reached out and took her hand, and she squeezed his in reply. For a moment they stood that way, in thick silence, eyes damp.

Then he tucked his chin and looked up at her. "Now. Do I get to meet this grandchild of mine or not?"

CHAPTER 28

The next day, her father surprised her by sending over a few of her finer gowns from those she'd left behind when setting off as lady's companion. What a pleasure to wear something of her own.

Becky helped her into a lovely walking dress of jaconet muslin trimmed in white lace. Over this, she wore a wine-colored velvet spencer and a matching bonnet — its upturned brim lined in pleated white satin. She tied the ribbons beneath her chin, thanked Becky, kissed Danny, and left the room. Reticule dangling from her wrist, she started down the stairs, intent on a few errands.

Below, the lodging house door opened and James Lowden stepped inside. Hannah halted on the half landing, a storm of conflicting emotions flooding her. She glanced nervously about, relieved not to see Mrs. Hurst, who had strict rules about gentlemen callers. Had her landlady mentioned this was her afternoon to play whist at a friend's house? Hannah hoped so.

"Mr. Lowden."

His head snapped up and he spotted her there on the landing. His gaze swept her person, head to toe, and back again. "You look . . . well," he breathed. But his eyes said "beautiful."

"Thank you." She was relieved to be dressed in a becoming gown, her freckles lightly powdered for good measure. James looked handsome as well, and cut a dashing figure in frock coat, snowy cravat, and patterned waistcoat. He removed his hat, and continued to watch her.

She self-consciously descended the remaining stairs.

"Perhaps you would step into the sitting room, Mr. Lowden?" she suggested, errands forgotten. "We may talk there."

He gestured for her to precede him, set his hat on the sideboard inside, and with a meaningful look at her, slowly closed the door behind them.

Hannah removed her bonnet, pulse racing. His compliment and warm look were a relief after their cool parting. After she had turned him down. Followed by that mortifying hearing. She was pleased James still could — would — speak kindly to her. For a moment she felt a flicker of disloyalty. Then she reminded herself that despite her long-held affection for Sir John, her chance with him was lost now that Marianna had returned. Like it or not, he was a married man, and she herself had urged him not to pursue divorce.

James slowly crossed the room to her, his eager gaze locking on hers. Her breath hitched. Might there be a future for them yet? Could James help heal her heart?

The blacks of his eyes dilated, nearly eclipsing the green irises. His nostrils flared. "Hannah . . ." He drew out the syllables in breathy longing.

"I'm . . . here," she faltered, and waited for him to kiss her.

He raised his hand, gently stroking her cheek. "Darling Hannah," he murmured, yet remained where he was.

Why did he hesitate? she wondered.

James dropped his hand and cleared his throat. "Before we say or . . . do . . . anything else, I need to tell you something."

But inhaling the smell of his cologne, and focused on the grooves carved alongside his mouth, Hannah barely heard his demur, his words, whatever they were. She didn't want to talk. She wanted to forget. All her fear and humiliation of the last weeks. All her conflicted feelings for a man who would never be hers.

"Hush," she whispered, running a finger over his lips and then along one of those appealing grooves.

Instantly, James bridged the gap between them and pressed his mouth to hers. He gathered her in his arms and held her close. Angling his head, he deepened the kiss. Warm, passionate, intense. His hands bracketed her waist, pulling her more tightly against him.

He broke their kiss and trailed his lips over her cheek, her neck, her ear. "Marry me," he whispered.

A shiver passed over her, and she drew in a shaky breath. But then she thought again of Sir John and her chest tightened.

"James, wait —"

Hannah pushed away. "I'm sorry. I thought, perhaps, but . . ." She shook her head. "I can't. Not now. Too much has happened."

He grimaced as though in pain, and pressed his forehead to hers. "I know." He panted, catching his breath. "Forgive me. I got carried away."

James released her, took a step back, and blew out a ragged exhale. "I came here determined to keep my distance. At least until I had told what I need to tell you."

She looked up at him in concern. "What is it?"

He looked at her warily. Pursed his lips, then began. "I have learned that Sir John was never legally married to Marianna Spencer."

"What?" Hannah frowned in confusion. She must have heard wrong.

"You remember Sir John sent me to find evidence against Mr. Fontaine — about the affair?"

She nodded.

"Instead, when I returned to Bristol, I discovered that she had eloped with Anthony Fontaine before she wed Sir John."

Hannah gaped. "You can't be serious."

"I am — unfortunately. Her father wanted her to marry Sir John. He was outraged and refused to acknowledge the elopement as legal. So he covered it up. Paid the parson, the coachman, etc. to keep it quiet. To pretend it never happened."

"And Mr. Fontaine?"

"Quite willing to go along with the scheme, for a price of course. Apparently he and Marianna never had any intention of ending their relationship."

"I can't believe it. What a risk!"

"Yes. A gamble that could cost her dearly in the end. Bigamy can be a hanging offense, you know."

"Surely it won't come to that."

"I doubt it, but it is possible."

Hannah felt as though someone had let the air from her lungs like a punctured balloon. She weakly lowered herself onto a chair. The warmth of desire evaporated into a chill.

She closed her eyes and murmured a mournful, "Oh, Sir John . . ."

James rubbed the back of his neck. "Yes. Even I feel sorry for him."

"What does he plan to do?"

"He is seeking a decree of nullity on the grounds of fraud."

"Will he succeed?"

Mouth tight, James turned away. "With both Fontaine and the coachman willing to testify, I think it a foregone conclusion."

She looked at his tense profile, his averted eyes, and said quietly, "No wonder you didn't wish to tell me. . . ."

"I did try —"

She held up a placating palm. "I know you did. I don't blame you for . . . anything." She forced a feeble chuckle. "I am rather surprised you told me at all."

"I admit I was tempted to wait. Perhaps

even to suggest an elopement of our own, before you heard the news from someone else. But I —"

"You are too honorable for that," she finished for him.

"Am I?" He took her hand. "In any case, I am still tempted to press my suit. But I will give you time to absorb the news first. May I call again?"

"Yes, of course."

But long after James left the house, Hannah remained in that chair. Revisiting scenes from the past through the lens of this new revelation.

She recalled little things Lady Mayfield had said, things Hannah had attributed to Marianna's general disappointment with Sir John, like, "I wish Anthony would do something — end this farce of a marriage once and for all."

It had never crossed Hannah's mind that Marianna's marriage to Sir John really was a farce — and worse — a fraud. No wonder Fontaine had been devastated by news of Marianna's "death." She was his wife.

Other little snippets of their conversations came back to her. The teasing. The double entendres. Marianna coyly asking, "And how is Mrs. Fontaine tonight?" And his suggestive replies that always made Hannah feel left out of some private joke: "You tell me." Or, "My dear wife is at home and plans to go to bed early. . . ."

The two of them had slyly referred to Marianna as "Mrs. Fontaine" right in front of Hannah, and she had never guessed. Who *would* guess such a sordid thing possible?

Finally, Hannah rose wearily and went back upstairs to her room, her heart aching for Sir John Mayfield all over again.

The next day, Hannah paced her small bedchamber, walking a fussy Danny back and forth across its length, rocking and shushing him. Becky had already tried and given up. Mrs. Hurst did not approve of crying babies. Perhaps Hannah ought to have accepted her father's offer to move home, but she wasn't ready. Not yet. Nor did she wish to flaunt her illegitimate child before his congregation.

A knock sounded on her bedchamber door and Hannah stiffened. She crossed the room to answer it, anticipating a reprimand.

"Hello, Mrs. Hurst. I am sorry. But Danny —"

The woman interrupted her. "There's a gentleman to see you."

Hannah's heart skipped a beat. Was it Sir John? But she told herself to stop being foolish. Danny, she noticed, popped a fist in his mouth and silently stared at Mrs. Hurst, tears still clinging to his long lashes. He didn't like the woman, either.

"Here's his card," Mrs. Hurst said, extending it toward her. "A solicitor. You're not in any trouble, I trust?"

"Oh." She glanced at James's card. "No."

Suspicion lit the woman's eyes.

"Mr. Lowden is the solicitor of Sir John Mayfield," Hannah explained, trying to ignore the disappointment flooding her. "My . . . former employer."

The woman's head tilted to the side and her face puckered in thought. "Mayfield . . . Isn't that the name of the woman in the newspapers this morning?"

"I . . . don't know," Hannah murmured, distracted. She had been too busy with fussy Daniel to read the news. She inhaled. "Well, I shall go down and speak to Mr. Lowden in the sitting room if you don't mind, Mrs. Hurst."

"Well, you'll not see him here in your bed-chamber, that's for certain. I run a respectable house, I do."

"Yes, I know." Hannah gave her a brittle smile. "For which I am duly grateful."

She handed Danny to Becky and passed by the woman. Gripping the handrail tightly,

531

she made her way downstairs and into the sitting room.

James turned at her entrance. "Miss Rogers."

She dipped her head. "Mr. Lowden." She smiled at him, but he did not return the gesture.

"Was that Daniel I heard? He doesn't sound very happy."

"I am afraid it's the colic again."

"Ah," James murmured vaguely, clearly distracted.

Hannah closed the sitting room door and turned toward him, but he held up a hand to forestall her. "I am afraid this is not a social call."

She hesitated, feeling both confused and strangely relieved. "Oh?"

"I am here in my official capacity as Sir John's solicitor. I've had a letter from him. In it, he enclosed a letter to you, and asked me to forward it on, as he does not have your direction."

He withdrew a folded rectangle from his pocket and handed it to her.

She accepted it, glancing at the seal and finding it still in tact.

"No, I did not read it," he said dryly, noticing the direction of her gaze.

She looked up at him from beneath her

lashes. "But you want me to tell you what it says?"

He held her gaze a moment. "I didn't say that."

"You didn't have to. If you weren't curious, you might have sent it by messenger."

"That's not why I came in person."

She expected to see a grin on his face or flirtatious light in his eyes. Instead he remained somberly officious.

He looked down, clearing his throat. "Pardon me. I have one more duty to discharge."

He extracted a small leather purse from another pocket and kept his gaze averted. "The stipend for Daniel. Sir John insists he be allowed to support him, at least as long as you remain unmarried, and beyond that if your . . ." He swallowed. ". . . husband . . . is agreeable. He bids me to state that accepting the money on Daniel's behalf in no way obligates you to him."

Looking at James, Hannah was reminded of palace guards with their raised chins and stiff lips, staring straight ahead while carrying out their solemn duties.

"Oh, James . . ."

Again he held up his hand to forestall her. "Miss Rogers. I am compelled to ask. Are there any questions or requests you would

533

like to make of my employer? Any news of Daniel's health or needs you would like me to pass on?"

Tears bit Hannah's eyes. "Only one request, Mr. Lowden."

His soldier eyes flickered to hers uncertainly. "Yes?"

Her voice trembled. "Tell me what to do."

His Adam's apple convulsed up and down the long column of his throat. "That I cannot do."

He bid her farewell and left her to read the letter in private.

Dear Miss Rogers,
No doubt you have heard by now the sorry tale of the elopement of Marianna Spencer and Anthony Fontaine before our own marriage. I wanted to let you know, before you saw it in the newspaper, that I am seeking a decree of nullity on the grounds of fraud. I know you have strong feelings against divorce, but I hope that in this, you will absolve me. My solicitor assures me my case will succeed. I dread the proceedings and scandal and vile gossip, but feel it must be done, as quickly and quietly as possible. I have no wish to expose Marianna publically nor to punish her, and if anything,

a formal release from me will be welcomed by her.

I want to give you every assurance that I pursue this course for my own sake without expectation or hope that there will be, or ever can be, a future between us. I wish you to do nothing out of guilt or a false sense of obligation. You are free. And hopefully, I will soon be free as well.

I am sorry to involve Mr. Lowden in this particular duty, but as I had not your direction, I have asked him to forward the letter to you in the manner he sees fit. Hopefully by post or messenger to avoid any awkwardness between the two of you.

I also wish to reiterate my determination to support Daniel, at least until such time as you marry, and beyond that only if you and your future husband are agreeable. Again, the stipend is not to be construed as a bribe and rest assured that accepting the money on his behalf in no way obligates you. I simply wish to guarantee neither you nor Danny suffer want while you are considering your options for the future.

I hope and daily pray that you have been able to reconcile with your father.

If there is anything I can do to help in that regard, please don't hesitate to let me know. I don't wish to presume or interfere, but if he rebukes you in any way, I would be happy to speak to him on your behalf — accept responsibility for your situation even as I cannot regret Danny's existence. I will gladly accept any blame, while giving you all of the credit for the healthy and delightful child he is, and the kind and honorable man he will no doubt become, thanks to your influence and upbringing.

May God bless you with a long and happy life.

Sincerely,
Sir John Mayfield, KCB

Hannah sank onto the sofa and read the letter again. It was almost as if he *wanted* her to choose James — a younger man not tainted by a sordid past. But she had her own sordid past to consider. Although she believed God had forgiven her, that didn't mean she was free of the consequences — the disgrace, the gossip, the end of her acceptance into respectable society.

If she were truly selfless she would release both men.

But she was not.

CHAPTER 29

Hannah's father invited her and Danny to dinner, which afforded Becky a well-deserved evening off. Hannah offered her extra money in case she wished to go out somewhere, but Becky said all she wanted was to nestle in bed with a book and a tin of sweets. Hannah happily supplied both.

How strange it felt to enter her former home as a guest. Her father smiled in self-conscious welcome and took Danny into his study, suggesting Hannah see if there was anything else in her bedchamber she wanted.

Walking slowly around her old room felt like visiting a museum of her youth, everything much as it had been when she had moved to the Mayfields' a few years before. She flipped through a long-forgotten diary and found a faded love letter from Fred. She had lost that Fred, the young suitor, but was so thankful to have kept him as a friend. Next she sorted through the baby clothes her parents had saved, a few of which she would wash and reclaim for Danny — a nightshirt, woolen coat and cap, and soft knitted blanket. She also found a brooch of her mother's — tiny bluebells painted on ivory — and thought it might make a nice gift for Mrs. Turrill, who had mentioned bluebells were her favorite. Finally, she selected a few books to give to Becky, and for herself, a lovely leather-bound edition of the Proverbs, containing a Psalter and the Sermon on the Mount.

Returning to her father's study, she paused in its threshold. Her heart warmed to see her father pray over Danny in his arms, and then contort his usually solemn face into comical expressions his congregation would be stunned to see from the pulpit.

The maid of all work prepared a simple meal of chicken and leek soup, which Hannah ladled out at table like the woman of the house, her mother's memory very near. The maid admired Danny, calling him a handsome lad, but Hannah did not miss her surreptitious glance at her bare ring finger.

Back in the lodging house the next day, Mrs. Hurst knocked to announce that Hannah had another caller.

"That solicitor has returned," she said with a concerned frown. "Are you sure you're in no trouble?"

"No trouble, Mrs. Hurst." *Not any longer,* she thought. *Thank you, God.*

Leaving a content Danny in Becky's care, Hannah went down to speak to James. She wondered what errand brought him this time — and if this would be a business or personal call.

In the sitting room, James stood fidgeting, twirling his hat brim in his hands. As soon as he saw her, he blurted, "Have you heard the news?"

She blinked. "Which news?"

"About Marianna?"

Hannah held up a "wait" finger. Knowing Mrs. Hurst would eavesdrop if she could, Hannah closed the door firmly behind her. "Go on."

"She has been charged with bigamy."

Hannah stared at him, incredulous. "No . . . I can't believe Sir John would expose her so publically." Hannah felt queasy disappointment at the thought. "In his letter, he said he would not do so."

"Sir John did not. Mr. Fontaine himself was the complainant, the 'injured party,' whose wife married another man."

"Unbelievable . . ." Hannah slowly shook

her head. "Marianna must be livid. Did Sir John testify?"

James nodded. "He was summoned, so yes, he did. But reluctantly."

Sir John was there in Bristol, Hannah realized, and yet he had not called on her or visited Danny. . . . Feeling suddenly weary, she lowered herself into a chair.

Mr. Lowden continued, "Marianna got off lightly, considering the charge. She managed to lay most of the blame at her father's door — her father who is conveniently dead. She isn't to be hung or even imprisoned —"

"Thank God," Hannah interjected.

"Only to sit in the Redcliff Hill stocks for three hours."

Shock washed over Hannah. "The stocks? Marianna?"

"Yes. I thought you'd be glad."

Hannah shook her head. She felt no such vindication. Did he know her so little? "Glad? Never. Poor Marianna."

"Poor Marianna? After what she tried to do to you?"

"I know, but . . ." Her words trailed away as the image of pampered, beautiful Marianna formed in her mind — sitting in the stocks in one of her fine gowns. Alone. The object of scorn and humiliation.

James unfurled his pocket watch. "In fact, she should be placed in the stocks about now." He clicked his watch shut and asked warily, "You do realize what this means?"

Hannah rose suddenly to her feet. "It means I must go to her."

"What? No. I meant, what it means for Sir John."

But Hannah's mind was not on Sir John. It was on Marianna. "Please let Becky know I'll return when I can."

She rushed from the house. Vaguely she heard James calling for her to stop, or at least to wait for the carriage, but paid him no heed. She ran past Queen's Square, crossed the bridge, and then made haste up Redcliff Hill. By then her sides ached and she panted with exertion.

She passed St. Mary's, its churchyard fenced by thickest hedge, and there, just outside its gate, the stocks. Double stocks, but only one occupant. Hannah's heart twisted at the sight. Lady Mayfield — or was it, Mrs. Fontaine? — sat on the muddy ground, ankles pinned in the low stocks, scuffed slippers listing on her small feet. She stared blindly ahead as passersby gawked or hurried their children away.

A small crowd began to gather, jeer, and taunt, and Marianna scowled, snapping at them with words Hannah was too far away to hear and likely better off spared.

As she walked closer, a boy of nine or ten reeled back with a rotten apple and took aim. Noticing, Marianna covered her face with her hands.

Hannah lunged forward and grabbed the boy's arm. "No! Remember, let him who is without sin cast the first stone."

"Ain't no stone, miss. It's an apple."

"Don't." Hannah held his gaze, then released him. She lifted her skirts and tiptoed through the mire left by last night's rains. Marianna had yet to see her, but Hannah was close enough now to hear her quiet sobbing.

Hannah rounded the stocks, accidentally kicking one end as she stepped behind them. The reverberation startled Marianna and her eyes darted open. Her arms shot up to ward off a projectile or a blow.

For a moment she gaped at Hannah, a frown line between her brows. Hannah tensed, imagining Marianna would rebuff her.

"Come to gloat?" she asked.

"No."

"Why *are* you here then?"

Hannah swept her skirts to one side and sat on the ground beside Marianna, aligned with the second set of holes.

"I am here to stay by you. To be your companion through this."

"Ha." Marianna's scoff lacked malice. In fact her chin quivered.

Ignoring the damp seeping through her gown, Hannah looked out at the uncertain, shuffling crowd, silently daring any of them to throw something. Praying no one would.

She glanced over and saw Marianna's lips twist bitterly. Even as they trembled.

"I ought to tell you to go away," she said. "That I don't need you." Tears filled her eyes. "But I am too weak. I can't bear this on my own."

Hannah held her gaze, and slowly shook her head. "You don't have to."

Jogging onto the scene, James glimpsed Anthony Fontaine leaning against a tree some distance from the stocks. As James passed by him, Fontaine laid a staying hand on his arm. "Leave them."

James scowled. "I am surprised at you, Fontaine. This is beneath even you."

"She might have been hung or sent to prison. This is nothing."

"To a woman like Marianna Spencer?"

Fontaine shrugged. "It will be good for her to be knocked down a peg or two. She

543

holds an altogether too high opinion of herself."

For a moment James stood where he was, torn between wanting to rush over and help Hannah up, and not wanting to be seen interfering. It would not help his professional reputation. He eyed Fontaine again. "What will you do now?"

"I leave for America in three days' time."

James reared his head back. "America?"

"Yes. I'm ready for a fresh start."

"You'll leave Marianna then?"

"Heavens, no. She goes with me."

James felt his brows rise. "Does she indeed? After this?"

"Yes. She is my wife after all."

"And she has agreed to go?"

"Not yet. But I know her well. She thinks she has lost me. Suddenly I have very great appeal." He nodded with confidence. "She will go with me."

James studied the man's implacable profile and asked quietly, "Do you regret it? Going along with the scheme in the first place?"

Keeping his focus on the stocks, Fontaine considered. "I wanted the money, and knew she didn't love Sir John. I didn't think I would mind." He inhaled deeply. "But I was wrong."

James turned and looked again at the stocks.

Across the distance, Hannah met and held his gaze. Solemnly, she nodded once, and then looked back at Marianna.

James waited one minute longer, then turned and walked home alone.

Later, after Marianna's release, Hannah returned to the lodging house, cleaned herself up and changed. She made sure Becky and Danny had all they needed, and then went back out. James had mentioned that Sir John had been called on to testify. She assumed — or at least hoped — he was still in Bristol. She wore her lovely walking dress for confidence. Would he receive her? If so, eagerly or reluctantly?

She walked to the house on Great George Street — Sir John's Bristol residence. A place she had lived as Marianna's companion before they'd moved to Bath. The place Danny had been conceived.

She swallowed at the thought and hoped she would not be met by a sneering, lascivious Mr. Ward. She was thankful anew to have avoided that man's clutches in the past.

As she walked up the steps to the front door, she felt her palms perspiring within her gloves and prayed silently, *Thy will be done . . .*

She rang the bell and was relieved when Hopkins, the elderly butler, opened the door.

"Hello, Hopkins."

His snowy brows rose. "Miss Rogers. What a surprise."

"No doubt. I . . . was hoping to have a brief word with Sir John. Is he at home to callers?"

"No, miss. I'm afraid not. Men from the newspapers have been hounding him since his return. He left as soon as he could after the trial."

"May I ask where he went?"

He hesitated. "I'm not to say, miss."

Hannah felt the sting of rejection. "He told you not to tell me?"

"No, miss. Not you specifically. He didn't want me telling any of those newspaper men."

"Oh. I see. Can you tell me if he has returned to Devonshire? I promise not to tell anyone else."

He looked left then right, a twinkle in his old eyes. "Well, you didn't hear it from me. But it's a southwest wind that blows, aye."

Hannah walked back to the lodging house. There, she found Mrs. Hurst and paid up in full, and then returned to her room to pack the last of their things. She left the door open and cracked a window to "air the place after all them nappies," as Mrs. Hurst had instructed.

Becky, eager for the journey, hummed as she dressed Danny in the little wool coat and cap to protect him from the damp wind. They would go and briefly bid farewell to her father, and from there, it was only a short walk to a nearby coaching inn.

As she tucked a pair of gloves into her valise, Hannah felt the back of her neck prickle. She started and turned.

There stood James Lowden in the threshold. She'd forgotten she'd left the door open behind her.

She put a hand to her heart. "James, you startled me. You're not to be up here. My landlady has strict rules about gentlemen callers."

She managed a wobbly grin, but his expression remained bleak.

"You're packing."

"Yes."

His lips tightened. Turning to Becky, he said, "Would you mind taking Danny down to the sitting room for a few minutes, while I talk to Miss Rogers?"

"Very well, sir." Becky bobbed a curtsy

and carried Daniel from the room. Hannah no longer worried about Becky running off. The girl was far too eager to return to Devonshire and dear Mrs. Turrill.

When Becky's footsteps faded down the stairs, he asked, "Are you moving to your father's house?"

"No."

He flinched. Hands fisted, he inhaled through flared nostrils, eyes squeezed tight. "You are returning to Clifton."

"Not to the house, but to Lynton, yes."

"To see Sir John."

"To see Mrs. Turrill," she clarified, distractedly adding a handkerchief to her reticule. "She's offered Becky a home with her and I promised Becky I'd escort her back as soon as I finished here."

"And are you . . . finished here?"

She stilled from her nervous motions of packing and faced him. She took a deep breath and said quietly, "I think I am."

His mouth twisted. "You would have left without telling me? I don't know why I'm surprised. You chose him before and I should have known you'd choose him again."

Hannah wistfully shook her head. "He probably wants nothing to do with me. Now that he's free and clear of me and Marianna and the whole rotten scandal. I will likely deliver Becky and return empty-handed."

"I doubt that."

"I don't know. But if there is any chance with Sir John, I have to try."

"No, you don't."

"James, please . . ." She reached for him, but then thought the better of touching him. Of playing with fire. The embers were still there, just beneath the ashes.

She said, "I saw you at the stocks. Your expression. Your distance. And I understood. You must avoid scandal, and that's what I am. A child born out of wedlock. Impersonation. Bigamy."

"You had nothing to do with that —"

"I know. But I am a link to all of it. You want to build your practice. Of course you do. And I cannot help you in that. I can only hurt you. If you married me, I would live to see your admiration fade into resentment and regret."

His face contorted in frustration, and perhaps grief. But not, she knew, denial.

"But, Hannah," he protested. "I want to be with you. I could not bear to never touch you again. . . ." He ran his hands up her arms, lowered his head and kissed her exposed shoulder, prickling her skin into gooseflesh. "Don't go yet. Stay and give me a chance. Give us a chance."

For one moment, she considered it. But then Marianna's duplicitous face appeared in her mind's eye and her stomach soured.

Drawing a deep breath, she stepped away from him. "No, James. I will not."

He shook his head, anger flashing in his eyes. "Tell the truth, Hannah. Your concern for my practice, or even for Daniel, is not the real reason you refuse me, is it? You prefer Sir John."

She allowed her silence to answer for her. She was attracted to James, it was true. But she loved Sir John and had for a long time.

James ran an agitated hand through his hair. "Then what am I to do? Soldier on, and try to pretend there is nothing between us? Carry on as Sir John's solicitor as though I am not aching to take you in my arms every moment?"

She looked into his eyes, and exhaled a deep breath. "Then perhaps it is time Sir John engaged a new solicitor."

CHAPTER 30

From the road, Clifton looked like a landscape painting — a turreted stone house nestled between whitebeam trees, its flower garden framed by privet hedges and an arched trellis. Or perhaps it was more like a still life — too still. Too quiet. No Mrs. Turrill waving from an open doorway. No Dr. Parrish calling out cheerful greetings from the neighboring Grange. No Sir John sitting in his chair at an upstairs window.

She walked closer, but saw no one about the place. Where was he?

Mrs. Turrill could not tell her for certain if Sir John was once again living in Clifton House, because she no longer worked there. She had declined to return after Hannah's trial, and then the Mayfields had left for Bristol. She'd heard that Sir John had recently returned to the area, but didn't know if or how long he planned to stay.

Hannah hoped Sir John had not suffered

a relapse. Is that why he had not visited her when he'd been in Bristol? Or worse, had he changed his mind about her? After all, he no longer had to settle for a woman willing to assume Marianna's place. He was free to marry any fine lady he wished. Far finer than she could ever hope to be.

Even so, it was good to see the place again — and see it peaceful. When she was last at Clifton, she had been under guard and then led away like a criminal. This was a better, more pleasant memory to tuck away for some lonely someday to come.

Hannah stood at the edge of the garden a moment longer, silently bidding the house and its former inhabitant farewell. In a few minutes, she would walk back to Mrs. Turrill's. Becky and Danny were there now, catching up on all they'd missed in each other's lives since they had last been together. But for now, one more minute to remember . . .

She closed her eyes and there he was. Sir John holding her hand. Pulling her onto his lap and kissing her. Taking his first steps. Saying, *"You are beautiful, Hannah. Just as you are."* Cradling Danny in his arms. Coming to her rescue. Letting her go . . .

The sound of galloping hooves interrupted her reverie. Startled, she stepped behind a privet hedge, afraid to be found like a trespasser should it be Edgar Parrish or perhaps a prospective new tenant.

She watched in surprise as Sir John Mayfield came cantering over the rise on a muscled bay. He sat tall and straight, the tails of his greatcoat flapping behind him, hat brim pulled low. He held the reins easily in his gloved hand. Knee-high cuffed boots in the stirrups, thighs melded to the horse's sides. He looked strong and confident. The Sir John Mayfield of old.

Hannah's breath caught at the sight.

As he neared the stables, she expected Ben or some new groom to come out to help him dismount and hand him his cane. No one came. She thought about running forward to help, but doubted he would welcome any witness to his weakness. Especially her.

When he reined in, he did not wait for anyone to assist him, but swung his leg over and dismounted with apparent ease. He gathered the reins and patted the horse's sleek neck. Only then did Ben jog out with a ready smile and take the horse from Sir John.

Hannah decided she would wait where she was, and greet him there in the relative privacy of the garden on his way inside. She smoothed back her hair and took a deep breath to steady her nerves. But Sir John did not walk toward the house. Instead he snatched up a walking stick propped against the stable wall, and set off at a brisk pace away from the garden. For a moment, Hannah feared he was avoiding her, but she didn't think he had even noticed her there. Would he be glad to see her? She wished she knew.

Hannah followed after him. Sir John walked with a swift, sure stride toward the Cliff Road. *My goodness,* Hannah thought. He was not weak any longer.

Unable to keep up with his long legs and rapid pace, she finally called out, "Sir John!"

He looked back, and hesitated upon seeing her. Her heart sank. No welcoming smile broke across his face. Nor did he use his newfound strength to run to her. In fact, he stood there regarding her almost warily. Did he think her presumptuous for coming uninvited?

Her confidence left her. She hesitated as well, unsure how to proceed.

She pushed herself slowly forward, trying to catch her breath and calm herself. "Hello," she managed.

He nodded. "Miss Rogers."

So formal. After all they'd been through

together.

He laid both hands over the head of his walking stick, propped in the ground before him. "I didn't expect to see you here," he said, eyes narrowed. "Visiting Mrs. Turrill, I assume?"

"Yes. I've returned Becky to her. The dear woman has invited her to share their cottage."

He nodded his understanding. "How is Danny? He fares well, I trust?"

"Yes. He is napping at Mrs. Turrill's as we speak."

"Ah. Good."

She glanced back toward the stable. "I saw you ride in." She shook her head in wonder. "How recovered you are. It's amazing how you've regained your strength."

"I've been working at it," he allowed. "And if you will excuse me, I will continue my walk. . . ."

His dismissal stung, but she persisted. "You look quite fit," she blurted, before he could turn. "I am pleased to see it." She felt herself flush at the words.

One brow rose. "Flattery, Miss Rogers? It isn't like you."

She recognized it then. The shell of cold indifference he'd adopted when he first suspected her of helping Marianna plot her escape. A way to protect himself.

He touched his hat brim. "And now I shall bid you good day." He turned smartly and continued on, determined either to take exercise or to keep his distance from her.

Hurrying to keep up with him, Hannah said, "I wonder, Sir John, if you even know what I am really like. You've only known me as a hired companion and an imposter."

"On the contrary," he retorted. "I once thought I knew you very well."

This was certainly not the romantic reunion she had hoped for or imagined. She needed to do something to divert the course of this conversation and quickly.

"Will you please slow down, so I may talk with you?"

"You're young. Keep up."

Sir John had reached the Cliff Road before she managed to overtake him. Or perhaps he had taken pity on her and slowed down.

Hannah crossed the road and looked out at the channel, struck by the sight. She looked west toward Lynton and east toward the Countisbury church tower to gain her bearings. The wind buffeted her, threatening to yank the bonnet from her head.

She walked several yards east, waving Sir John over. "Look." She pointed. "That's where the carriage crashed."

He followed and peered down reluctantly, as though expecting a gruesome sight or perhaps a ghost. But only one carriage wheel and a moldering velvet bench remained to mark the spot.

His expression grew thoughtful. "That's where my former life ended — and my new life began."

"Mine, too," she whispered, the words swallowed by the wind.

Keeping his face toward the channel, Sir John said, "Mr. Lowden is not here, if you are looking for him. He is working from his offices in Bristol." He kept his gaze averted, as though not wishing to see her disappointment.

"I know," she said. "I am not looking for him."

He gave her a sidelong glance. "But you have seen him."

"Yes," she replied. She took a deep breath and added, "I am afraid I dismissed him."

He turned to stare at her, both brows high. "Dismissed him?"

"Yes. Will it be a terrible inconvenience to engage a new solicitor?"

He blinked, clearly taken aback. "No . . . But, may I ask why you felt it necessary to dismiss him?"

With relief she noticed he did not demand

to know what gave her the right to do so.

She said, "Do you need to ask why?"

His grey-blue eyes glinted. "You thought it would be awkward to marry him were he still my solicitor?"

She shook her head. "I do not plan to marry your solicitor."

"No?"

"No. But I do think it would be awkward to be married to *you* were he still your solicitor." How forward, she realized, neck heating. Would he rebuff her then and there?

His mouth quirked. "Afraid you'll be tempted to go astray?"

"Not at all," she said in her stride. "But it would be painful for him to see the two of us happy together."

He stilled, as though holding his breath. "And will we be happy together?"

"I dearly hope so."

He studied her closely. "I already told you I will support Danny. You needn't marry me. James Lowden is younger, good-looking, and clearly in love with you."

She held his gaze and took a small step closer. "Yes, Sir John, all those things are true." She looked down and then back up. "But he is not the one I want. . . ."

The sentence was barely out of her mouth before he hooked his arm around her waist and pulled her close.

"What are you trying to do to me?" he asked, voice hoarse, his breath warm at her temple.

"I'm trying to . . . convince you."

He eased back just far enough to look her full in the face. With his free hand, he smoothed a lock of hair from her cheek and tucked it behind her ear. "Convince me of what, Miss Rogers?"

His eyes sparked with challenge, as if daring her to say the words he longed to hear.

"That I love you," she whispered, softly but firmly, placing her hand over his heart.

"And if I were not recovered? If I were still confined to an invalid chair?"

She traced gentle fingers along the side of his face. "I was ready to be your wife then, before Marianna returned. Before you could even walk. I admire you, Sir John, whether sitting or standing."

For several moments he simply stood there, gazing down at her. Then one corner of his mouth quirked. "Miss being Lady Mayfield, do you?"

She shrugged. "Maybe."

He chuckled. "Lady Maybe, that's what I shall call you."

She bit her lip and looked up from beneath her lashes. "I can think of several other endearments I would prefer."

"Can you?" His arm around her waist tightened. With his other hand he cupped her face, stroking her cheek in feathery caresses. He murmured, "Shall I call you . . . dear friend, desired lover, or . . . cherished wife?"

Her heart beat hard, a bubble of hope and joy filling her chest. She smiled and whispered, "Yes, please. All of the above."

"My sentiments exactly." He leaned down, his hand gently tilting her face toward his. His lips touched hers softly, sweetly, then more firmly. Her lips parted of their own accord, and he deepened the kiss, melding his mouth to hers, her body to his, until her legs felt wobbly, her mind languid.

How had she ever doubted her feelings for this man? How foolish she had been. How blind. Sir John was handsome and passionate. Honorable and generous. He loved her and he loved her son — their son.

So, this is what love feels like, she thought. She found she liked it very much indeed.

He broke their kiss and dragged warm lips over her cheek, her temple, her ear. In a husky voice, he asked, "Shall we go and see the parson, my love?"

"Yes," she breathed. "As soon as possible."

AUTHOR'S NOTE

I wrote the first draft of this novel before I ever visited Lynton & Lynmouth, twin villages in North Devon, England. I picked the area for its coastal setting within Exmoor National Park, and its steep cliffs along the Bristol Channel. In 2014, my old friend Sara Ring and I had the privilege of traveling there, and found the landscape, the villages, and the local people even more lovely than I'd imagined.

Sara and I hiked along the Lyn River, out to the scenic Valley of the Rocks, and along a carriage road hundreds of years old and dangerously close to the cliff's edge near Woody Bay. Together we searched for the perfect spot to send a carriage careening down into the channel. Wind whipped hair in our faces, pulled hoods from our heads, and made it almost impossible to hear our voices in the video Sara shot. She also took many beautiful photos of the area (as well as one of me in ankle stocks as described in the book). Thanks, Sara! Visit www.julie klassen.com to see a sampling.

My thanks to Dick Croft and the other helpful volunteer guides at the Arlington Court and the National Trust Carriage Museum, also in Devon. There I learned the difference between a landau, barouche, traveling chariot, town coach, governess cart, dogcart, gig, cabriolet, and more. How fascinating to see so many historic carriages up close and personal, to peer into the rich interiors and imagine my characters heading off on their life-changing journey.

Keen readers may recognize a certain "Jane and Mr. Rochester" flavor to a few lines in Chapter 22. I humbly acknowledge the influence of Charlotte Brontë's *Jane Eyre,* which I have adored since the sixth grade.

Warm gratitude to the two Wendys in my publishing life: Wendy McCurdy of Berkley Publishing Group/Penguin Random House and Wendy Lawton of Books & Such Literary, my agent, for their enthusiasm about this book. And also to my friends at Bethany House Publishers, who graciously gave me their blessing to test the waters of writing for two publishers. I appreciate your trust and support.

A grateful shout-out to talented reviewer and author Michelle Griep for providing such helpful feedback — again!

As always, thanks and love to my cherished friend and first reader, Cari Weber, who gave input on two drafts along the way, and who blesses me in so many ways. And to my beloved husband and sons. I'd be lost without you.

And finally, heartfelt thanks to you, my readers. I appreciate each and every one of you!

■ ■ ■ ■ ■

READERS GUIDE:
LADY MAYBE

BY JULIE KLASSEN

■ ■ ■ ■

DISCUSSION QUESTIONS

1. What did you think of the story's protagonist? Did you admire her? Were you at times frustrated by her actions? Cite examples.

2. At the beginning of the novel, Sir John goes to great lengths to keep Marianna and Mr. Fontaine apart, even relocating his wife against her will. Ultimately, it is during one of these sudden moves that the accident occurs. Do you think Sir John was at all to blame for this calamity?

3. Marianna is the first character the reader meets and yet, for a significant portion of the novel, her personality is described to the reader secondhand. Did your perception of Marianna change throughout the novel. How so?

4. Hannah attracts the interest of several men in *Lady Maybe.* Which suitor, if any, did you hope she would choose and why? Did your choice change as the story progressed?

5. When considering what was at stake, do you think Hannah's ruse was necessary, or was it entirely unethical? If you were in Hannah's situation, what would you have done?

6. Did the identity of Danny's father surprise you? Did it change your opinion of Hannah's deceit?

7. Hannah's relationships with both Mr. Lowden and Sir John significantly evolve throughout the novel. What were some turning points in her connection with each?

8. In the Regency-era world of *Lady Maybe,* divorce was viewed with much disdain. As Mr. Lowden states: "Divorce is nearly impossible to achieve, scandalous, and typically unconscionable." Do you think divorce is seen in the same light today? If not, how have opinions changed?

9. In the time period of *Lady Maybe,* marriages were often more like business arrangements than affairs of the heart. What do you think of this custom? Would you marry for anything other than love?

10. When it's a question of Marianna's word versus Hannah's in court, Marianna's is held in higher regard — until Sir John gives his account and his testimony takes precedence. How do the power struggles of class and gender come into play in *Lady Maybe*?

11. The magistrate, Lord Shirwell, asks in court: "Can reasons excuse deceit? Theft? Fraud?" How would you answer this question? Is it ever acceptable to commit crimes under certain circumstances? When considering the transgressions committed in *Lady Maybe,* should any character be excused of his or her misdeeds?

12. At one point, Hannah thinks, *How had she allowed it to happen? That she, Hannah Rogers, should be guilty of more wrongdoing than the infamous Marianna Mayfield?* Do you believe that this is true? While both women commit the same wrongdoings of

adultery and lying, why do their crimes seem different?

13. At the novel's end, Hannah goes to support Marianna at the stocks despite all Marianna had done and said against her. Did you pity Marianna in that moment or do you think she got what she deserved?

14. Eventually, Mrs. Turrill becomes much more than a nurse and lady's maid. She becomes a source of guidance and comfort for Hannah. What do you think was the driving force behind this change?

15. Hannah's father is the last to know the truth about her secrets. Furthermore, he is told via letter and by a third party (Fred), rather than by Hannah herself. Did you disagree with Hannah's timing and method, or did you find it understandable?

The employees of Thorndike Press hope you have enjoyed this Large Print book. All our Thorndike, Wheeler, and Kennebec Large Print titles are designed for easy reading, and all our books are made to last. Other Thorndike Press Large Print books are available at your library, through selected bookstores, or directly from us.

For information about titles, please call:
 (800) 223-1244

or visit our Web site at:
 http://gale.cengage.com/thorndike

To share your comments, please write:
 Publisher
 Thorndike Press
 10 Water St., Suite 310
 Waterville, ME 04901